Praise for the runaway *New York Times* bestseller

REAL

"I have a new book crush and his name is Remington Tate."
—*Martini Times*

"Unlike anything I've ever read before. Remy and Brooke's love story is one that has to be experienced because until you do, you just won't get it . . . one rollercoaster ride that you'll never forget!"
—*Books over Boys*

"Sweet, scary, unfulfilling, fulfilling, smexy, heartbreaking, crazy, intense, beautiful, oh did I mention hot?! Kudos are in order for Ms. Evans for taking writing to a whole new level. She makes you FEEL every single word you read."
—*Reality Bites*

"I loved this book. As in, I couldn't stop talking about it."
—*Dear Author*

"Wow—Katy Evans is one to watch."
—*Wicked Little Pixie*

MINE

a **REAL** love story

by katy evans

Gallery Books

New York   London   Toronto   Sydney   New Delhi

Gallery Books
A Division of Simon & Schuster, Inc.
1230 Avenue of the Americas
New York, NY 10020

First Gallery Books trade paperback edition November 2013

GALLERY BOOKS and colophon are registered trademarks of Simon & Schuster, Inc.

For information about special discounts for bulk purchase, please contact Simon & Schuster Special Sales at 1-866-506-1949 or business@simonandschuster.com.

The Simon & Schuster Speakers Bureau can bring authors to your live event. For more information or to book an event contact the Simon & Schuster Speakers Bureau at 1-866-248-3049 or visit our website at www.simonspeakers.com.

Manufactured in the United States of America

10 9 8 7 6 5 4 3 2 1

Interior design by Davina Mock-Maniscalco

Library of Congress Cataloging-in-Publication Data is available.

ISBN 978-1-4767-5560-1
ISBN 978-1-4767-5563-2 (e-book)

This book is dedicated to everyone
who felt the same way I did,
and wanted just a little more.

MINE PLAYLIST

These are some of the songs I listened to while writing *MINE*. I hope you enjoy them when Remington and Brooke do! ☺

"**IRIS**" by Goo Goo Dolls

"**DARK SIDE**" by Kelly Clarkson

"**I CHOOSE YOU**" by Sara Bareilles

"**BENEATH YOUR BEAUTIFUL**" by Labrinth featuring Emeli Sandé

"**FIRST TIME**" by Lifehouse

"**STAY WITH YOU**" by Goo Goo Dolls

"**BETWEEN THE RAINDROPS**" by Lifehouse

"**BREATHLESS**" by the Corrs

"**ACCORDING TO YOU**" by Orianthi

"**HERE WITHOUT YOU**" by 3 Doors Down

"**WHEN YOU'RE GONE**" by Avril Lavigne

"**FAR AWAY**" by Nickelback

"HOLD ME NOW" by Red

"UPRISING" by Muse

"DEMONS" by Imagine Dragons

"KISS ME" by Ed Sheeran

"FROM THIS MOMENT ON" by Shania Twain and Bryan White

MINE

❤ ❤ ❤

The heart is a hollow muscle, and it will beat billions of times during our lives. About the size of a fist, it has four chambers: two atria and two ventricles. How this muscle can house something as encompassing as love is beyond me. Is this heart the one that loves? Or do you love with your soul, which is infinite? I don't know. All I know is that I feel this love in every molecule in my body, every breath I take, all the infinity in my soul. I learned that you can't run if you tear a ligament, but your heart can be broken into a million pieces, and you can still love with your whole being.

I've been broken and put together again.

I've been loved, and I have loved.

I'm in love, and I will be forever changed by this love, by this man. I used to dream of medals and championships, but now I dream solely of a blue-eyed fighter who one day changed my life, when he put his lips on mine. . . .

❤ ❤ ❤

ONE

WELCOME BACK, RIPTIDE!

Brooke

IT'S BEEN TWO months, exactly sixty-two days, since I returned to him. A thousand four hundred eighty-eight hours of wanting, longing, and needing him. It has been even longer than that since thousands of women, men, and fans across the world watched him fall.

He's back.

This is it. The first fight of the new Underground season.

He's been training like mad. He's put on more muscle. He's more ripped than ever, and I know this season he's ready to take what's his.

The audience in the Washington, D.C., fighting arena consists of about a thousand people, and when the winner of the current match is announced, the crowd grows restless.

We all know it's *his* time to be called. His assistant, Pete, sits tense and alert to my right. He'd told me he's the "draw"—that most everyone in the arena is here for him.

I know *I* certainly am.

The air is charged with excitement and scented with perfume, beer, and sweat. The two previous fighters are exiting the ring now, one of them assisted by his team, and my heart pounds as I sit motionless in my seat, in the first row, at the very center, just where my man wants me. So here I am, waiting, my body hyperaware and my heart pounding his name. *Remington, Remington, Remington . . .*

The speakers crackle as the announcer turns on the microphone, and I almost jump out of my skin.

"Ladies and gentlemen, we all remember our crushed souls—our crushed spirits!—when the crowd favorite lost the championship final last year."

The crowd boos in memory, and my throat clogs thinking about how Remy's broken body had been carried out of the ring.

"Have no fear, people. Have no fear!"

"REMY!!!!!!!!!" someone screams.

"Bring him out already!" another yells.

"Oh, we will. Have no doubt about it; we will," the announcer somberly says, painfully drawing it out for the crowd. "After much speculation and many rumors, it's completely official. The man is fighting this season, and he's taking *no* prisoners, people! Here he is, ladies and gentlemen. Here. He. Is! You all know who I'm talking about?"

The crowd roars, "RIP-TIIIIIIIDE!"

"Who?"

"RIP-TIIIIIIDE!"

"One more time, 'cause *I can't hear you*!"

"RIPTIIIIIDE!"

"That's right, ladies and gentlemen! Here's our favorite bad boy with that infamous smile and those deadly fists, ready to carve R.I.P. into anyone who stands in his way this year. The one, the only, Remingtoooon Tate, your RIPTIIIIIIIIIDE!!"

Wild excitement rushes through me as the crowd stands and roars like never before.

"My god, the fans are thirsty for him," Pete breathes.

And so am I. My god. *So am I.*

Across the ring from me, women are waving panties in the air. Panties! Another lifts a sign that reads PULL ME UNDER, RIPTIDE!

My mouth is dry, and a thousand and one winged things flutter in my stomach when I see a flash of red.

And then, he's closer.

Trotting out of the walkway and to the ring.

To *his* ring.

My body enlivens with sensations as he breaks through the crowd.

Some fans have escaped their seats and make a grab for him, but he easily shoves his way through the throng, his face shadowed by the hood of his red satin robe. Remy. My Remy. The man I love with every ounce of me.

"Riptide, you put the sex in SEXY!"

"Remy, I want you to fucking impregnate me!"

He climbs into the ring with a fluid jump, and then he removes his RIPTIDE robe, slowly, without hurrying. Hundreds of female screams ring in my ears as he goes to his corner to hand the robe to Riley, his coach's second.

Riley pats his muscled back with a smile and tells him something. Remington throws his head back as if he's laughing and then takes the center of the ring, spreads his long, ripped arms out, and starts doing his slow and cocky I-know-you-all-want-to-fuck-me turn.

I'm dying.

I will never, ever, get used to the sight of him in that ring. My heart whams excitedly into my rib cage while all my insides pulse with need, and my chest feels like a balloon about to burst in excitement. Hard, lean, and perfect, he is all dangerous, all beautiful, and *all* mine.

My eyes absorb every inch of what every other woman here is drooling for, and I helplessly let my gaze run up and down his perfect athletic form. My eyes lovingly caress his tan and kiss the inky Celtic bands over his biceps. I admire his torso and his long, strong legs, his sculptured arms, his narrow waist and broad shoulders. Every muscle in his perfect body is so defined that you would know exactly where one structure ends and the next begins if you trailed your fingers along his magnificent form.

And as he turns even more, I see the washboard abs with eight squares—eight! Yes, it is impossible, but he's got them . . . and his face.

Oh god, I can't even take it.

The scruffy jaw. The brilliant blue eyes. The sexy smirk. The *dimples*. He's got a smile on his face; his expression, one that tells you he's got a whole lot of trouble planned for the evening and you don't want to miss it, is playful and boyish.

A collective gasp spreads out in the rows behind me as he moves to face us.

The butterflies in my stomach burst awake when those dancing blue eyes start scanning the crowd, silently laughing at all of us. He's clearly amused by our obsession over everything Remington Tate!

Beside me, a middle-aged blonde with too much Botox jumps up and down and screams like a lunatic, *"Remy! Give me a taste of that Riptide!"*

The impulse to drag the woman down by her hair seizes me, but at the same time, I know you can't look at him without dissolving into a pool of lust.

He is a stud. He was made to mate. To *procreate*.

And I want him like my next breath.

I want him more than any one of these screaming women wants him.

I want every fragmented part of him. I want his body. His mind. His heart. His beautiful soul.

He says he's mine, but I know that there's a part of Remington Tate nobody will ever have.

I am his, but he is untamable and unconquerable.

The only one who can defeat Remington Tate is himself.

He's up there, ever elusive and mysterious, a black box of mystery without end. And I want to get lost in him, even if I never come out the same.

Pete elbows my ribs and whispers in my ear, "My god, it's unfair he gets all the attention and this"—he signals at his skinny self—"gets nothing."

I smile. With his curly hair and brown eyes, Pete's always dressed in a black suit and tie. He's not only Remy's personal assistant, he's also like his older brother and one of my closest friends.

"Nora likes you just as you are," I taunt him about my younger sister.

He smiles at that and wiggles his eyebrows as he nods pointedly back toward the ring, where Remington finishes his turn and almost completely faces me.

My nerve endings stir and tingle in excitement as his twinkling blue eyes glide down the length of my row, where he knows I will be. I swear every part of me quivers in anticipation, waiting for those eyes to find me.

They do.

He electrifies me. Invisible currents leap between us. His smile blazes through me, and suddenly, the inside of my chest, where my heart beats, feels like a burning torch he's just lit.

His eyes hold me clasped in the loving heat of his, and I can see his quiet joy tonight, his possessiveness, the territorial stare that tells everyone in this room that I. Am. His.

Then he points at me.

My heart stops.

It seems that everyone's eyes follow the finger pointing in my direction, aimed straight at my chest, where my heart races for him, his red-hot blue gaze clearly saying, "This one's for her."

A delighted roar from the crowd explodes around me. It hits me like adrenaline, like a shot of tequila that flies straight to your head, the way his fans love him. The way he loves them back. The way he loves *me*.

I'm amazed by the way the public reacts to him and by the way he stands there, with his dimples flashing, sucking in all the energy in the room and channeling it into "Riptide."

God, I *love* him, and I never want him to forget it!

Overcome with the impulse, I blow him a kiss.

He catches it and smashes it to his mouth.

The crowd grows even louder. Remy points at me, laughing, and I'm laughing too. My eyes burn a little because I'm so happy that I just can't fit inside my skin. I'm happy that *he's* happy, and he's where he belongs.

This is his season. This year, nothing will stop Remington Tate from being the Underground League champion. *Nothing.*

He will do whatever it takes, because he's a driven, powerful, passionate man, and whether I am afraid, worried, excited, or all of the above, I will support him.

"And now, ladies and gentlemen, may we have a round of applause to welcome a newbie to the Underground, from the Fighter's Club, the famed, feared, and deadly Grant Gonzalez, "Goooodzilllaaaa!"

As his opponent is announced, Remington circles the ring restlessly like a panther until a huge lump of silver comes out from a second walkway. Remy flexes his fingers at his sides as he watches the man take the ring. Tonight, they all wear their hands taped with bare knuckles exposed, much like men used to fight in older times.

The new fighter is barely out of his robe when the public starts shunning him. *"Booooooo! Booooo!"*

"That guy has killed a couple people fighting," Pete tells me under his breath. "He's a dirty and mean motherfucker."

"Don't tell me people have died in *these* events?" I ask in horror, feeling a disturbing quake inside my stomach. Pete rolls his eyes.

"Brooke, these are uncensored fights. Of course shit happens."

The thought of Remy fighting with killers catapults my usual pre-fight fears to a whole new level. Fears I had repressed as my man drank up the audience's adoration. Fears that now grip me by the tummy and squeeze me like a fist.

"Pete, *death* is more than 'shit' happening."

Remington taps his fists to his opponent's and the crowd falls quiet. My insides go utterly still. I'm wildly, almost anxiously, measuring the new guy, as if I can get any knowledge from his looks alone. The young man's white skin is slicked with something that looks like grease. Are they allowed to be slippery when fighting? He has long hair tied in a ponytail and beefy muscles like most every other fighter I've seen. Nobody is as lean and beautiful as Remy. I'll bet no one takes care of their body and trains with the same dedication that he does.

When the bell rings, I don't think I'm breathing.

They approach each other. Remington waits for the other man to move, his guard perfectly up, every one of his powerful muscles relaxed so they can quickly engage. Finally, Godzilla swings. Remy ducks and rams the side of his body and—unbelievably—knocks that enormous monster down with a crashing noise.

I gasp in complete disbelief when the referee's counting begins.

A private smile curves Remy's lips as he looks down at the motionless figure and practically dares him to move.

He doesn't.

A roar rips through the crowd.

Pete jumps to his feet and pumps his fist in the air. *"Yeah! That's right! Who's the man! Who. Is. The MAN!"*

"ONE PUNCH, ladies and gentlemen!" the voice yells through the speakers. "One fucking punch! He's back! HE'S BACK!!! Men and women, girls and fucking boys, I give you tonight, your one and only Riiiptide!!! RIPtiiiiide!!"

The ringmaster yanks up Remy's arm in victory.

And although the entire arena screams his name, his dancing blue eyes immediately come to me, and my whole body starts to ache in every single place.

God.

He's a fucking sex god. And he freaking turns me *on*.

"Riptide, please, oh, *please* let me touch you!" A screaming woman runs to the edge of the ring, stretching her hand through the ring ropes toward him.

Remington seems to take pity on her and seizes her hand. He buzzes his lips across her knuckles, and she begins to scream hysterically. I laugh, but then a snake of jealousy curls around my gut. He looks up at me as he releases her, and then, in that lithe way he moves that reminds me of large deadly cats, he swings down from the ring.

Complete stillness settles over the arena until all I can hear is my heartbeat.

Remington . . . Remington . . . Remington . . .

He walks up to me, the smile on his face telling me he thinks he's all that.

"You're jealous," he says in that deep, toe-curling voice of his.

"A little," I say, laughing at myself.

He doesn't laugh, but he smiles a smile that sparkles in his blue eyes as he slides his fingers up the side of my throat, then I feel the pad of his thumb gently stroke across the flesh of my bottom lip. The butterflies in my tummy awaken. His eyes are at half-mast as he surveys my mouth. He does it slowly, from corner to corner, and then, because he seems to think he owns this mouth, he swoops down and takes it.

His lips fire me up. My stomach spins as he forces my lips apart, and when his tongue flashes, hot, damp, and powerful, to take a quick and heady taste of me, I trap back my moan.

"Don't be," he roughly tells me as he looks down at my kissed mouth and appreciates his handiwork for a moment. He presses his lips to my forehead for a fraction of a second, and then he heads back to the ring in that graceful way he walks, relaxed and almost ambling.

Behind me, I hear breathless voices.

"Holy shit, I want to do that ten ways till Sunday."

"Ohmifucking god he was right here!"

I lick my lips, and I can still taste the sexy fucker, which only makes my nipples bead and my sex swell with complete possessiveness of him.

As his next opponent is called up to fight, Remington flexes the muscles of his arms, down to the tips of his fingers. His smile flashes at me from the ring, and very clearly, his two dimples tell me how much he enjoys leaving me in a puddle of love and longing. The devil.

A fighter I remember from last year, Parker Drake, "the Terror," gets up in the ring to face him. And the bell rings.

Ting.

The crowd quiets as the fight begins, and both men start swinging and hitting. Remy's punches are powerful, and you can hear the sound of his fists landing, deep, strong, and fast as lightning. *Poom poom poom!* Squirming in my seat, I watch and listen, alternating between thrill and worry, when Parker crashes to the ground. I shoot to my feet and scream *"Riptide!"* in chorus with all the other people, knowing that this is the first of many times I will be here watching Remington reclaim everything, every single thing, that he gave up for me.

TWO

HAPPINESS = HIM

I've only spent the night with one man in my entire life. I love bumping into his muscles while we sleep. I love how the sheets smell of him, of *us*, and how his shoulders have become my favorite pillow, even though they're hard as hell and I can't understand why I like sleeping on them, but I do. They come with his arm around my waist and his scent, and his heat, and I love it all, every bit of it. Especially when he ducks his head to tuck his nose into my neck, and I bury mine into his.

The problem is that *his* side of the bed seems to eject him exactly at ten in the morning, and *my* side seems to have no eject button.

Today I feel like a deadweight, while I can tell he's not even in the room.

The air is different when he's not near. He charges it when he's nearby, like a slow, powerful vibration around me that makes me hyperalert and feel both safe and excited.

I've really fallen for him.

Six months ago, I wanted a one-night stand—to have a little fun after dedicating my years to my career. Instead . . . I get *him*.

Unpredictable, infuriating, sexy him . . . the man everyone lusts after and I didn't want to. I ended up not only lusting after him, but falling face-first in love with him. And now, loving him is the most exhilarating roller coaster I've ever ridden in my life.

Sitting up on the bed, I rub my eyes to shield them from the streaming sunlight and wish I had Red Bull and Monster running through my veins like Remy does. We hardly slept doing our favorite sexy stuff, and he's already raring to go. I even see his suitcase by the door, ready for us to leave for the next tour location, while *I* still need to pack.

Squinting again as I slide out of bed, I go to the small closet to find something to wear when I spot the letter on his nightstand next to his iPhone—which he rarely even powers on except for music-listening purposes. The sight of my letter brings a rush of awful memories to me, I have to quell the urge to grab it, tear it, and flush the pieces down the toilet.

But Remington would be so mad. He treasures that stupid letter I'd left him when I left.

Because in it, I tell him what nobody had ever told him before.

I love you, Remy.

My legs start shaking, and I close my eyes and tell myself I'm not perfect. I've never been taught to do this. I never dreamed of love, a partner . . . I dreamed of sports and the latest running shoes. Not of spiky black hair and blue eyes. I'm trying to learn. To be the woman a man like him deserves. And I want to spend the rest of my life showing Remy that I deserve him, and the rest of my days making sure he takes back what he lost because of me. If anyone in this world deserves to be a champion—it's him.

"He's a pussy, just relax," I hear his gruff, manly voice outside the master bedroom.

I laugh at my own body's response to hearing Remington say "pussy"—my womb clenches and I feel instantly a little warm. *Whore.*

Grinning, I search through his stuff in the closet, then have to go to his suitcase. I know that he likes it when I wear his things. I think it makes him feel like I'm his property, and it's insane how much I like to pick on his alpha tendencies. When he's blue-eyed, he's possessive, but when he's black, he's downright territorial.

It delights me when he gets all growly you're-mine and it delights him when I wear his stuff.

So this morning, why not have the both of us be delighted? I take his RIPTIDE boxing robe and slip it on, then I hurry into the bathroom, brush my teeth and wash my face, wrap my hair in a ponytail, and pad outside.

I hear his laughter in the living area, more like a soft chuckle over something Pete murmured, and my insides do all the stuff he makes them do as I round the corner.

My god.

I can't believe what he does to me. I can't even explain this shivering-shuddering-twittering combination inside me, but it's ridiculous.

"He's checking up on you, dude, I don't see the amusement here," Pete says, in alarm. "His scouts have been asking all around the hotels to know where we'll be staying *next*."

"Just relax and keep watch, Pete," Remington says, and I just stare for a moment, hearing a catch in my breath.

My blue-eyed lion.

His black hair stands up devilishly. The inky Celtic bands across his muscled arms flex as he slowly sips on an electrolyte drink. I see his glorious tanned torso. Those sweatpants riding low on his narrow hips and revealing just the tip of his star tattoo. His bare feet. He looks hot, strong, and cuddlable, and the pulsing energy that seems to radiate from his very being feels like a magnet to me.

"Brooke, good morning!" Diane Werner, his chef and nutritionist, says from the kitchen.

Almost lazily, Remington turns and slowly, ever so slowly,

stands, his muscles rippling with the move. Brilliant blue eyes rake over my body, taking me in in his red robe, which drapes all the way down to my ankles, and a territorial gleam sparks in his gaze in a way that makes every single womanly part of me tighten with wanting.

"Well, hello there, Miss Riptide," Pete jumps in, his brown eyes glowing in amusement.

I smile. Because I not only want to wear my Riptide's clothes, I wish he'd ask me to wear his *name* even when I'd once told my best friend I would never, ever, marry because my career would always come first. *Snort!*

"Hey, Pete and Diane," I say in a sleepy voice, but my eyes are on Remington, and my heart won't stand still.

Will it ever stand still when I'm around him? As I stare at him this morning just like every morning for the past few months, I tell myself I am not dreaming, he's not a fantasy, he is real. *My* REAL.

He saved my sister from the claws of a man I can't even name. Remington threw last season's championship fight in exchange for her freedom—without even hesitating. Without even *telling* me. He lost his title, a huge amount of money, and could have lost *his life,* all to rescue my sister, Nora.

But I didn't *know* it was for me.

All I knew was that suddenly he was at the last season's fight. Losing. Being beaten. Battered. Falling down. Getting up. Spitting at Scorpion.

I wanted to *die.*

My fighter, always so driven, persistent, passionate, and determined, refused to *fight.*

God, I was so, so wrong.

He wasn't punishing me—he was saving my sister for me.

If he hadn't come back to my hometown of Seattle, with Nora delivered back safely, I'd have made the biggest mistake of my life, and I'd have paid for it for the rest of my life.

I'd have lived the rest of my days loveless, smileless, and, worst of all, Remyless. Like I would have deserved.

As I struggle with the thousand pounds of remorse this memory gives me, his dimples flash, and if I thought I was happy moments ago, nothing compares to this avalanche.

"Hey," I whisper.

"So my little firecracker lives," he says with a devilish glint in his eye.

"Only barely after you."

He bursts out laughing, and Pete coughs. "Guys, I'm kind of still here, and so is Diane."

My smile fades, but although Remington's doesn't, his smile softens, and so does the look in his eyes. Suddenly, he makes me feel shy. Virginal. Like he stripped me naked last night and this morning I am without all my bravado, without any stitch of protection, wearing only something that belongs to him.

Still using those dimples like lethal weapons against me, he comes over.

My body is all over the place as I force myself to walk and meet him halfway, and I bite back a squeak when he reaches out one muscled arm, hooks one finger into the sash of my robe, and pulls me the last distance to him. "Get over here," he rumbles.

He bends his head and sets a kiss on the back of my ear as he spreads his hand open on the small of my back, stroking up to the RIPTIDE letters on the back, as if to remind me they are there. I'm breathless when he ducks his head to my neck and drags in a long, deep inhale of me. Shit, he kills me when he does that, and between my legs, I feel a painful little clench of need.

"Remington, are you listening to me?" Pete asks.

Remington growls my name softly, low and deep, in the way he does when he fucks. "*Good morning, Brooke Dumas.*" My tummy clenches in response to that, and with the soft kiss he sets on my ear, my knees going buttery, because he always does this to me, and as Pete's voice repeats what he just said, I start stepping away, but Remington won't let me.

He kicks the chair farther out and drops down, hauling me with him. Then he shifts me to one of his thighs so he can grab his sports drink from the table and finally looks at Pete, his voice low but firm. "Double our scouts and follow theirs."

His fingers trace down my back as he downs the bottle, and Pete is left scratching and shaking his head in complete confusion.

"Rem . . . *dude* . . . the fucking bastard cheated to win, and he knows he's going to *lose* as long as you're fighting this season. He's spying on us now, and he's going to do his best to sabotage you this year. He's going to try to screw with your head. Provoke the shit out of you!"

I'm barely wrapping my head around the topic, but whatever it is, "provoking" Remington is not a good idea. He's got a temper, usually. He's hardheaded and insistent and stubborn, but especially, he is Bipolar 1, and you don't want to rouse his black side unless you're prepared to deal with more than two hundred pounds of reckless that doesn't sleep.

I like my more than two hundred pounds of reckless, but his reckless still worries me even if he doesn't seem in the slightest perturbed by Pete's warnings.

Instead of answering his PA, he turns to me and threads his fingers at the hair on my nape. "Do you want breakfast?" he asks me.

Biting the inside of my cheek, I lean over and drop my voice to spare Pete. "You mean aside from the one that walked out of my bed?" He pinches my nose and now leans to me. "Business called your breakfast out of bed today."

"I actually feel strangely hungover this morning, I'm not hungry at all."

"Hungover from what? My mouth?" he asks, his eyes dancing.

I look at his mouth and it is so full and perfect. The way he uses it is perfect. Every measured word he speaks is perfect. Sexy bastard. Of course he gives me hangovers, the kind I'd never *met* until him.

"You know," Pete interjects, "I'd feel less concerned about him and what he plans to do if he didn't know your Kryptonite now." He nods at me.

"He's not even getting near my Kryptonite. I'll break him first." The quiet conviction with which he says this makes gooseflesh jump on my arms, and I think I'm a little nauseous.

Last season's final match is my worst nightmare.

"Yet I can totally envision him finding ways to reach out to your Kryptonite already," Pete says. "Finding ways to push your red button, get you all bothered and reckless."

Remington turns to me, then he shoves my hair aside and tips my head back to study me, like he knows I can barely hear that man's name—much less hear them talk about it.

The Black Scorpion is my own personal Voldemort. That asshole hurt my sister, then me. And worst of all, he hurt Remington. At that season final. He hurt him because of *me*. God, I fantasize killing the bastard.

"He's gonna tease you, torment you . . ." Pete continues in an ominous tone.

Remy watches me in silence, his chest bare, his neck tanned and strong, and when he turns his attention back to Pete, his voice is more somber.

"Pete, he hasn't even made a play, and you're losing your shit," he tells him.

"'Cause I'm the one left to fix things when *you* lose it." Pete smoothes a hand down his black tie. "This season could get downright nasty. We want you strong and prepared, dude. We need to head to the airport in a half hour, tops, but I warn you, Phoenix might not be as calm as we anticipated."

"I'll keep it together. Just double our scouts," Remington says, serious now, then he takes one last swig of his sports drink and sets the empty bottle aside.

"All right, let me call in some more. . . . " I watch Pete head over to the kitchen and punch his cell phone pad.

Now Remington's voice deepens as he gives me his undivided attention. "You overslept," he murmurs, cupping my face as he smiles down at me. "Wore you out last night?"

His voice oozes all kinds of sex and tenderness. As I nod, I feel myself go warm inside. "I hear sex gods do that," I tease.

He laughs softly and strokes my lips with his thumb. "That's right. You ready to go?"

I nip his thumb and smile as I nod.

"I missed you in bed this morning," I whisper.

"God, me too. I need to be the first thing those pretty eyes see every morning."

He presses me to him and buries his face in my hair, and all the tension from hearing the word "Scorpion" and the nausea leaves me when I smell him. I tuck my nose into his chest and inhale him as he inhales me, and the room falls, and the world falls, and in this moment nothing matters. Nothing matters but him, his arms around me and my arms around him. I think a part of him still can't believe I'm in his arms again, because he's squeezing me so tight I can hardly breathe, but I don't want to breathe. I'm so affected by his scent, the feel of his powerful arms around me, when just two months ago I'd stupidly given up on him, I can barely take it.

"I love you," I whisper, and when he doesn't respond, I open my eyes and shiver when I see his fierce gaze trained on me. He rubs my bottom lip with his thumb again, then tucks me back into his chest as if I'm precious. He lowers his head, his lips to my ear: "You're mine now."

THREE
FLYING TO ARIZONA

The private jet is Remington's biggest toy.

The team always takes the first section of seats at the front of the plane, while Remington and I like the bench in the back, which is closest to the enormous wood-paneled bar and flat-screen TV, even though we rarely use either.

There's excitement in the air today as we board. The season is officially *on*—and after a taste of Remington's fight last night, the team is pumped. Pete and Riley even bumped fists with the pilots as soon as we jumped out of the Escalade.

"Things are so much better with you here," Diane tells me as she settles in her plush, better-than-first-class seat. "I get so excited seeing you two together again."

"I have to say," Coach Lupe jumps in, and honestly, since the man is a grumpy-fest all week round, it's almost odd to see that smile on his bald head, "you motivate my guy more than anything I've ever seen. I'm not only glad you're back, but I secretly prayed for it, and I'm a goddamned atheist."

I laugh and shake my head as I keep heading down the aisle, and before I can reach the back, Pete seems to have boarded and calls to me, "Brooke, did you see our new Boss suits?" he asks.

Frowning, I swing around to look at Pete, and see that Riley is also already on board. Pete grins at me and smoothes a hand down his black tie as I scrutinize his appearance, and Riley grins and spreads out his arms as though to let me have a good look. I had no idea their suits were new.

They are basically all these guys wear, and today, like every day, they are both ready to be cast in *Men in Black XII*—or whichever it's up to by this point.

Pete, with his curly hair and brown eyes, would be some sort of intelligence geek. Riley, with his blond hair and that surfer look, would be the one who accidentally kills demons while slowly opening a car door or something.

"What do you say?" he prods.

I make sure I'm wearing a *wow* look on my face when I answer. "You guys look sexy!" And squeak when I get a squeeze on my ass, and Remington hauls me by the waist down the rest of the plane's aisle to our seats.

He settles me down and plops down next to me, his eyebrows drawn low over his eyes. "Say that again about another guy."

"Why?"

"Just try me."

"Pete and Riley look sooooooo—"

His hands fly out and he tickles me under my armpits. "Try that again now?" he prods.

"Ohmigod, your men in black are so fricking—"

He tickles me harder.

"You won't even let me say the word 'sexy'!" I squeak, as he stops.

Blue eyes gleaming, Remy's lips form the most tantalizing smile I've ever seen, and coupled with that scruff on his jaw and the dimples, my toes are definitely curling. "Would you like to try that again, Brooke Dumas?" he huskily prods.

"Yes, I would! Because I think Pete and Riley look amazingly—"

He tickles me so hard I kick and flail in the air, and then I gasp for breath and somehow finish up half-sitting, half-sprawled on my seat, my breasts pushing into his hard pecs with every harsh breath. Our smiles fade as a delicious sexual awareness starts crackling between us as we stare deep into each other's eyes.

Suddenly, he reaches out, and uses his thumb to tuck a loose tendril of hair behind my ear, his voice thickening as one dimple disappears before the other does. "Say it when you say my name," he says, and a shiver goes through me as he runs the back of a finger down my jaw.

"Your ego not big enough?" I whisper breathlessly as I memorize his face. The square jaw, the spiky hair, the sleek dark eyebrows over those piercing blue eyes, that watch me with a little mischief and just enough jealousy to make my pussy clench.

"You could say it shrunk sizably when my girlfriend ogled those two dipshits." He eases back to let me sit up, and as I do, he leans back comfortably in the way sexy guys sit, with his legs spread out and his long, corded arms outstretched on the back of the seat as he watches me with a half frown.

"What was I supposed to say?" I taunt with a smile. "That they *don't* look good in the new suits? They're like my brothers."

"No, they're like *my* brothers."

"See? And I'm yours, so it's the same thing." I shrug and pull my skirt down to my knees. "Now you know how I feel when a thousand women scream at you," I add smugly as I strap on my seat belt.

He takes my chin and turns me to look at him. "Who cares what they scream when I'm crazy about you?"

Thud. My heart did that. "Same with me then. You don't have to growl when guys look at me."

His eyes darken, and he drops his hand at his side and clamps his jaw into a firm line. "Be grateful I have some control in me and I don't pin them to the nearest lamppost. I fucking know what they're doing to you in their heads."

"Just because *you* do that doesn't mean that others do."

"Of course they do. It's impossible not to."

I smile, because I know he fucks me in his head tons of times when he can't do it physically. And I do the same, of course. I bet even a nun who saw him would do the same.

Feeling mischievous, I slide my fingers under his T-shirt and feel the bumps of his eight-pack, savoring the feel of his skin under my fingertips. I worship everything about the human body. Not only because I'm a sports rehab specialist, but because I used to be an athlete and I absolutely marvel what our bodies can do, how they endure when pushed, how they kick into gear with innate mechanisms for mating and survival. . . . But I can fiercely love the human body, and yet Remy's body is my ultimate church. I can't even explain in words what it does to my own.

"All the girls undress you when you fight," I tell him, and my smile fades as a little jealousy seeps in. "It makes me insecure you picked me out of the crowd."

"Because I knew you were for me. Solely, exclusively, for me."

My body instantly tightens at the words, so sexy when combined with that confident smile he wears. "I am," I agree, looking into those dancing blue eyes. "And now I don't know what I want to kiss most, you or your dimples?"

The dimples fade, and so do the lights in his eyes as he reaches out to rub my lower lip. "Me. Always me first. Then the rest of me."

My lower lip feels warm and deliciously massaged by his thumb as the attendants finish loading the luggage and shut the plane door, and I'm vaguely aware that the team is talking in their seats, for I hear my own eager whisper, "Let me power down my phone for takeoff. . . . But you definitely owe me a morning kiss. Even if it's noon." I nod at him in warning.

His chuckle is low, and I feel it roll all over my skin. "I owe you more than that, but I'll start with your lips."

God. Remington? He kills me. He speaks casually, almost boredly saying—*Yeah, I'm going to kiss you now.* And my systems jack up. My blood bubbles as I start thinking about it, and I quickly pull my cell phone out of my bag to power it off when I spot a text from Melanie.

> MELANIE: My best friend! It's been ages and I really miss you. When are you coming home?

Mel! I straighten to use both hands to text back: I miss you too! So very much, Mel! But I'm so happy! I'm so fucking happy it's not funny! Or maybe it is! See? I sound drunk! Hahaha

> MELANIE: I want a Remy.

> MELANIE: And a Brooke! Waaah!

> BROOKE: Now that the season's started I'll plan a good place for you to come visit! It's on me! Nora can come too.

> MELANIE: But will you still be keeping your place in Seattle?

For a moment, I frown at the question, because when I dropped my life and decided to follow my sex god to the ends of the earth while he kicked up his training regimen and got ready for this season, my rent hadn't really crossed my mind.

I text Melanie back: I'm really committed to him, Mel, so I will probably not renew my lease when it expires. My home is here now. I'm taking off, but I will text you later. I love you, Melly!!!!!

> MELANIE: DITTO!

I turn off my phone and tuck it into my bag. And when I lift my head, my sex clenches when I see Remy holding his sleek silver iPod. Thud. This man seriously knows how to seduce me with music. I watch as his thumb scrolls through the selections, and the slow, sensual manner in which it circles causes a flood of moisture between my thighs.

He looks up at me with a devilish smile, then he reaches out and sets his headphones over my head, and I'm terribly excited when he clicks PLAY. The song starts, and penetrating, curious blue eyes stay on me, watching my reaction.

Which is melting in my seat.

And feeling my soul shudder inside me.

Because the song he chose has completely made me stop breathing.

He presses his forehead to mine as he watches me listen, and I'm so moved by this song, my hands tremble as I exchange his headphones for my earbuds and place one in my ear, and one in his, so that we both listen together.

Pressing our foreheads back together, I watch his expression as intently as he watches mine . . . and we both listen to this amazing song. Not just any song. *His* song.

Iris . . .

By the Goo Goo Dolls.

His gaze darkens with the same emotions burning inside me, and then he cups one side of my face in his hand. My body tightens in anticipation as he moves closer. I feel his breath bathe my face as he slowly eliminates the distance between our mouths. By the time he brushes my lips with his, I've already parted them and let my eyes drift shut. He brushes once, twice. Softly. Lazily. A sound escapes me, like a moan demanding he kiss me harder, but instead of hearing that, I hear this:

> *When everything's meant to be broken*
> *I just want you to know who I am*

God, I can't listen to this song without feeling eaten on the inside. I need to get as close as possible to him. As close as I can get. Head to toe, I crave him, every bit of me craves every bit of him. I tip my face up and press my lips lightly to his, eagerly sliding my fingers into his hair. *Remy, oh god, kiss me harder.*

He makes me wait a little more as he uses his hand to turn my head at an angle, and then, then, his lips finally lock over mine, his tongue tracing through the seam of my mouth until I open wider and gasp, electrified, when our tongues brush. I don't hear his groan, but I feel it vibrate through his chest against my breasts, and I shudder as I touch my tongue to his and relax my mouth under the command of his. Because there's no one I trust more, no one I drop all my walls with in the way they came tumbling down with this man. Stroking one hand up the side of my body, he sucks gently on my lower lip, and I feel the swelling heat between my legs. The hitching of my breath. The hardening of my nipples. The pulling sensation along my skin.

I didn't even know how much I needed this kiss until right now, when all my body buzzes under his mouth, and I move my lips and use my tongue to coax his tongue back in me.

I don't even know if Pete or Riley or anyone is watching; *Iris* is playing in our ears and our mouths are wet and hungry. He eases his fingers under my top as he sucks, suckles, probes, tastes. It seems impossible, but every quaking inch of my body feels pleasure merely from what his mouth does to mine.

I moan in need and bite him, and he loses a little control.

He unsnaps my seat belt and leans me over until I'm spread all over the backseat.

The music stops and another song starts, but he makes a frustrated noise when the cords get tangled between us, and he jerks our earbuds off and tosses them aside. Then he runs his eyes over my body. Suddenly, I'm no longer listening to anything except the pounding of my heart as he lowers his head again.

"Fuck, I want you," he says, then I hear the slick sound of his mouth meeting mine once more. Heat blazes through my bloodstream as he takes over my mouth again. Tongues rubbing. Hands fondling. Breaths mixing.

Between my thighs, I'm getting so swollen, I squirm restlessly under his weight and move my mouth faster and more anxiously under his. I feel the bumps of his eight-pack under his T-shirt, and my nerves ignite as he slides the tips of his long, strong fingers under my top again.

He's killing me. I wanted this kiss —but now I want *more*. Every pore, atom, and cell heats up to supernova. Our mouths move so right together, I feel alive, expanded, loved. I love, I want, I need . . . him. So freaking much. I don't think he will ever truly know . . . how ashamed I feel for leaving . . . how I ache for the way he hurt for me . . . how determined I am to stay with him . . . how much I really love him. . . .

His thumbs find my nipples through my bra and they feel so sensitive, the merest stroke arrows a bolt of pleasure to my toes.

"Remy, we have to stop," I gasp, panting, while I still have a couple of neurons working in my brain. But even as I say one thing, I'm clutching his muscles and the crazy-as-hell aroused part of me doesn't even care if we do it right here, right now.

But I'm guessing he'll go ballistic if anyone here listens to me come.

He edges back a little and drags in a long, audible breath. Then, he looks at me, his eyes on fire, and kisses me again, a little rougher. He groans softly and stops, leaning his head on mine, his breath harsh in my ear. "Play me a song," he says in a rough murmur, pulling me up to sit.

Very aware of my swollen mouth, I grab my iPod and start browsing my playlists while trying to ignore the throbbing between my thighs. "Just give me back my brain first."

He laughs and tweaks my nose. "Play me one of your sassy anti-love songs."

"There're so many, I don't even know where to start." I begin searching when he puts his thumb over mine and swiftly, he starts guiding me.

"I got one for you. The kind you like."

His voice close to my ear causes pleasant little chills to rush through me. He clicks PLAY on a saucy song like the ones I like, but it's not a girl power song at all.

It's Kelly Clarkson's "Dark Side."

My insides melt when I hear the music. I love Kelly, but oh, this song. The words. Remy wants to know . . . that I will stay, that I will promise not to run away . . . ?

He looks at me again, with that cocky little smile. But his eyes are not so cocky. His eyes are questioning. He *wants* to *know.*

And when he takes my hand and laces his fingers between mine in a very boyfriend gesture that never fails to get me, I go to the ear without the earbud and tell him, "I promise. I promise, you have my heart, and you have me. You will always have me."

There's just no song on this earth, and no playlist big enough, to tell him that I truly love him. I love him when his eyes are black, and when his eyes are blue, and although I know—deep down—that he doesn't believe I'm here to stay—one day, I swear *one day* I will make him believe me. We smile as we keep listening to this song, and when he squeezes my hand, I squeeze back, telling myself no matter what happens, I will never, ever, let go of this hand.

❤ ❤ ❤

OUR PHOENIX HOTEL looks like something out of a drawing. The long, twenty-story adobe building spreads out prettily over a desert land-scape, surrounded by blossoming cacti with flowers so ginormous and bright, I have the urge to go and touch—just to make sure they're not plastic.

Inside the marble lobby, two teenage girls whisper and point at Remy as he passes—because *of course* they noticed him. You notice him like you'd notice a bull walking past you in a hotel lobby. Their gazes quickly seem to scan us—the group that came in with him—and they start checking me out next.

I lift one of my eyebrows with an amused smile, and they seem to determine that I am probably his girlfriend, but I can't help that my stomach does crazy twisting motions of proprietorship as they give him one last up-and-down with their starved little gazes.

"Look at those two infatuated girls! He's always drawing eyes," Diane tells me. "It doesn't make you jealous?"

"Extremely," I say, wrinkling my nose in disgust at my own jealousy.

Remy glances my way and winks as he and Pete wait for the keys, and Diane elbows me with a laugh.

"Goodness, that man knows his own appeal!" she says. "But I wouldn't be jealous, Brooke, the entire team feels the love between you two. We've never seen him like this over anyone. No matter how many women paraded through here, he still went back for *you*."

"What do you mean?" I frown at her. "Women paraded through where?"

"Our hotel."

"You mean *recently*?"

My stomach drops, and I mean, drops, when Diane's eyes widen, and her face loses all color.

She starts shaking her head, and then . . . then she starts glancing around as if she wants to hide in a fucking flowerpot! "Brooke," she whispers, her tone apologetic as she backs up a step. Why?

Does she think I'm going to hit her?

Do I look like I'm going to hit someone?

I don't want to hit someone, I can barely even stand.

Everything blurs as I turn to stare at Remy's back. Across the lobby. I think of the way he moves, like a predator taking me, when we make love. In my mind, I see his eyes, the way he watches me come for him. I imagine him thrown across a hotel bed while dozens of women pleasure him, his blue eyes—*my* blue eyes—watching them come apart for him too.

And then, then I think that he might not have been blue. He could have been black. Remy in his rawest form, intense and manic, as reckless as he will ever be.

Because he's not normal. Not even close to normal. He's not only fucking Remington "Riptide" Tate—he's bipolar and he swings from one mood spectrum to the next. When he goes manic, he does not remember, sometimes, what he does. And the month I left, he was very, very manic. His eyes, black and mysterious, looking at me desperately from a hospital bed . . .

My insides twist until my lungs feel jammed in my throat as I remember how he tried to pull his respirator off and stop me.

Heart pounding fight or flight, I locate Riley across the lobby, and he's scanning his phone while I vividly remember him leading a bunch of glittery, beautiful women into Remington's suite not so long ago—to "cheer" him up when he had a black episode.

Before I can stop myself, I charge over to him like a bullet, my fists trembling at my sides. "How many whores did you bring to Remington's bed, Riley?"

"Excuse me?" He lowers his phone in complete puzzlement.

"I asked how many . . . whores . . . you brought to his *bed*. Was he even aware of what he was doing to them?"

He glances at Remington's broad back, then he grabs me by the elbow and pulls me aside to the elevator bank. "You don't get to have an opinion, Brooke. Remember? You left! You left when he was broken in a fucking hospital bed, Pete was babysitting your sister—in *drug rehab*—and I could barely pick up all the pieces of

what your letter . . . your fucking letter . . . did to him! Something
that you will never, ever even so much as comprehend! In case you
have forgotten, Rem has a *mood disorder*. He needed to be pulled
out of the fucking dark—"

"Hey." Remington yanks him back by the collar and makes a fist
as if he's about to lift him. "What the fuck are you doing?"

Riley jerks free and glares as he retucks his tie into his stupid
new Boss jacket. "I was trying to explain to Brooke, here, that
things weren't as happy as they are now when she was away."

Remy shoves a finger into Riley's chest. "It's done with. You got
that?"

Riley clamps his jaw, and Remington rams his finger into his
chest so hard, he forces him back a step. "You *got* that?" he demands.

Riley nods tightly. "Yeah, I got that."

Without another word, Remington curls his hand around the
back of my neck and steers me into the elevator.

But the entire elevator ride, my insides squeeze with hurt even
though I try to reason with myself that I have no right to feel this way.

Without really seeing anything ahead, I stare at our penthouse as
we walk in. It's our new home. Our hotel rooms have always been
like home, but they're not my home. My home is far away. My home
is now this man. And I need to accept the fact that loving him might
break me. Over and over, loving Remington is going to break me.
When he's fighting and takes more punches than I can bear, I will
break. When he's tender with me and gives me all the love I don't feel
I deserve, I will break. When he has an episode, where his eyes go
black and he doesn't remember things he said or did . . . I will break.

"You like the room, little firecracker?" His body heat envelops
me as he comes up from behind and tucks me into his body with
his arms. I feel warm. Protected. "Want to hit the running trail
when it gets dark?"

His lips graze the curve between my neck and collarbone, and the feather-touch sends a painful little ripple to my heart. I feel as if I've swallowed the entire garden full of searing-hot cacti as I pull up the collar of my shirt and turn.

"Did you fuck other women?"

Our eyes meet, and a familiar shiver of awareness runs through me as I stare into his face. For the life of me, I can't figure out what he's thinking.

"I realize I have no right to ask you." I search deep into his blue eyes, and they search me back with equal intensity. "We broke up, right? It was the end of it. But . . . *did you?*"

I wait, and his eyes begin to twinkle.

He. Is. Actually. Grinning!

"It matters to you?" he asks cockily, one eyebrow high. "If I slept with anyone?"

The rage and jealousy bubble up inside me so fast, I grab a couch pillow and slam it into his chest as I explode. "What do you think, you fucking jerk?"

He grabs the pillow and easily discards it. "Tell me how much it matters." The sparkle of mischief in his eyes only makes me grit my teeth harder, and I shoot another pillow his way.

"Tell me!"

"Why?" He deflects the pillow and comes after me as I start backing off, his smile full of amusement. "You left me, little fire-cracker. You left me with a sweet letter telling me, very nicely, to go fuck myself and to have a nice life."

"No! I left you with a letter that told you *I loved you*! Something you hadn't told me until I came back to you and *begged you* to tell me."

"You're so fucking cute like this. Come here." He grabs the back of my head and pulls me into his arms, and it takes all my force to yank free.

"Remington. You're laughing at me!" I cry wretchedly.

"I said come here." He gathers me back into his arms, and I twist my head and shudder as I try to squirm free.

"Remy, tell me! Please tell me, what did you do?" I beg.

He pins me to the wall and sets his forehead on mine, his gaze completely territorial. "I like that you're jealous. Is it because you love me? Do you feel proprietary of me?"

"Let go," I breathe angrily.

He lifts one large, tan hand and cups my face so, so gently, I could be glass. "I do. I feel completely proprietary of you. You're mine. I'm not letting you go."

"You said *no* to me," I breathe, blazing with hurt inside. "For months and months. I was dying for you. I was going crazy. I . . . came . . . like a fucking idiot! On your fucking leg! You withheld yourself from me until I was . . . dying a little inside with wanting you. You've got more willpower than Zeus! But the first women they bring to your door . . . the moment I'm gone, the first whores they happened to bring you . . ."

His smile remains on his face, but the light in his eyes has dimmed, and now there's a fierce intensity in his stare. "What would you have done if you were here? Stopped it?"

"Yes!"

"But where were you?"

My breath comes in jerks.

He lowers his head and looks deep into my eyes, now curious. "Where were you, Brooke?" One big, warm hand curls around my throat, and he strokes his thumb across my pulse point.

"I was broken," I cry in a mix of anger and pain. "You broke me."

"No. You. Your letter. Broke me." The laughter has faded from his gaze as he runs the pad of his thumb up my throat then runs it, lovingly, along the curve of my jaw then finally trails it, like a feather, softly across my lips. "What does it matter if I had to kiss a thousand lips to forget these?"

There's a knock on the door, but our warring energies are locked like missiles on their targets. He's too busy caging me in with his arms, and I'm too busy having my heart broken inside me, loathing that *I'm* the actual wielder of the axe, because we'd broken up. I know he needs sex when he's manic. I know I left. I had no right to Remington or anything he did or said.

So I broke my own heart when I left, and now the reality of what happened when I left is coming back and continuing to break it. And here I am, with a huge lump in my throat and exhaling as hard as a fire-breathing dragon.

He eases back to open the door and pull inside one of the suitcases a bellman is standing there with. As I try to pass, he grabs the back of my shirt and says, "Come here, settle down now."

I push his hand away and don't know if I want to let him settle me down or not. I'm being irrational. I broke up. I left. The one I'm angry with right now, the one I want to hit right now, is *me*. My insides wrench with pain as we hold each other's gaze. I wipe a tear as I head to the open door, where Remington continues pulling the rest of our things inside.

I *know* I caused all this. Because I thought I was strong and had tried to protect myself, and so I hurt me, and I hurt him and a whole shitload of people, because I was *strong* and thought I could protect him and my sister—and I fucked everyone instead. But I'm so wounded inside, I just want to lock myself up somewhere and have a good, long cry. I imagine the glittery whores coming into this hotel room when he wasn't even in his full senses, and I know I'm going to vomit.

I tell the bellman, "Thank you. Would you send this duffel with that other suitcase to the other room?"

The guy pushes the cart back toward the elevator bank and nods.

"Where are you going?" Remington asks as I step into the hall-way.

I drag in a breath and turn. "I want to sleep with Diane tonight.

I don't feel so well and I'd rather we talk about it when I . . . when I . . . am *settled down*," I say with a closed throat.

He laughs. "You can't be serious."

When I go over to the elevator and press the CALL button, his laughter quickly fades.

When I board with the bellman, I'm holding it in, my vomit and my tears. The young guy smiles at me and asks, "First time at this hotel?"

I nod and swallow.

As soon as I arrive at Diane's room, I burst out crying. She brings the suitcases inside and shuts the door. "Brooke, I didn't mean to cause trouble! I thought you knew. The groupies and women—it's always been like this except when you're around. I'm so sorry."

"Diane, I broke up with him! Yes! I understand it's all *my* fault. Everything is all *my* fault. Even him losing the championship."

"Brooke," Diane tries to console as she sits me on the bed. "They came and went. It wasn't . . ."

I wipe my tears and sniffle, but my misery feels like a steel weight. "He lived like that before I came into the picture. I don't know what I expected when I left. I thought it would take him a little time to get back on the horse, you know? But I know that being helpless and moping around isn't Remington. He would've been . . ."

Reckless. Manic. Or causing trouble. Or breaking things. But what if he was low and feeling down? I left him to bear it alone, and for Pete and Riley to handle it the way they always have. Fresh tears stream out of me.

"Go on," Diane encourages me. I wince when I hear the room phone. "Yes, Remington," she whispers into the receiver and then hangs up.

"He's on his way here. He wants me to open the door, or he's crashing it."

"I don't want to see him like this," I cry, sniffling and grabbing a tissue as if I can hide the fact I'm crying like a baby here.

I feel him approaching like a tornado as Diane swings the door open.

"Diane," he says in a low murmur, then he cuts across the room straight to where I'm curled in a ball on the bed.

His eyes are dark blue with emotion. "You," he says, opening his hand. "Come with me."

"I don't want to," I say, wiping a stray tear.

His nostrils flare and I can see he's having trouble controlling himself. "You're mine and you need me, and I want you to please come the fuck upstairs with me."

I duck my head and wipe a tear.

I sniffle.

"All right, come here." He swings me up in his arms. "Good night, Diane."

I kick, and he grabs me to him and squeezes me as he speaks in my ear, "Kick and claw all you like. Scream. Hit me. Curse the fuck out of me. You won't sleep anywhere but with me tonight."

He carries me into the elevator and then into our room. He kicks the door shut, drops me on the bed, and jerks off his T-shirt. His muscles bulge with the powerful movement, and I see every glorious inch of that beautiful skin—skin that some other women touched and kissed and licked, and a rush of new jealousy and insecurity knifes through me. I scream like crazy and kick when he reaches out and starts stripping me. "You asshole, don't touch me!"

"Hey, hey, listen to me." He traps me with his arms and his gaze. "I am insane about you. I've been in hell without you. In hell. Stop being ridiculous," he says, squeezing my face. "I love you. I love *you*. Come here."

He gathers me onto his lap. I didn't expect his gentleness, I expected a fight so I could vent, but he disarms me, and instead I bawl in his arms as he holds me, his lips open on the back of my ear, his voice soft but firm and regretful. "How well did you think I'd cope when you left? Did you think it would be easy on me? That I wouldn't feel alone? Betrayed? Fucking lied to? Used? Discarded? Worthless? Dead? Did you think there wouldn't be days where I loathed you more than I loved you for tearing me apart? Did you?"

"I've left everything for you," I cry, so hurt I have my own arms curled around myself as I physically struggle to hold myself together. "Since I met you, *all I wanted* was to be yours. You said you were mine. That you were my . . . my . . . *Real.*"

He groans softly and squeezes me hard against him. "I'm the realest fucking thing you're ever going to have."

My tears keep streaming as I look into his eyes, and they are so beautiful, Remington's eyes. They are blue and tender, the eyes that see straight through me, the eyes that know everything about me, and they are no longer laughing and instead reflect a little bit of the pain I feel. I can't look at them anymore and I cover my face as new sobs overtake me.

"It should've been me all those times," I say. "It should've been just me, only me."

"Then don't fucking tell me you love me and leave me. Don't fucking beg me to make you mine and then run the first chance I'm not fucking looking. I couldn't even come catch you. Is that fair to me? Is it? I couldn't even get up on my own fucking legs and come stop you."

I sob harder.

"I woke up to read your letter instead of getting to see you. You were all I wanted to see. All. I wanted. To see."

His words are so painful to hear, I can't even talk through my tears.

I think I cry myself to sleep on his lap, and when I wake up in the middle of the night, my eyes and head hurt from crying. I'm naked. I realize he's stripped me like he always does, and his skin is hot against mine, and his nose is in the crook of my neck and shoulder, and I feel his arms around me and I curl closer even when it hurts. We're the object of each other's hurt and each other's solace. He pulls me closer, and I hear him scent me as if it's the last whiff of me he'll ever take, and before I know it, I scent him back just as fiercely.

FOUR

PHOENIX RISING

I feel like shit the next day, but then I hear Remington murmur, as we quietly have breakfast, "Run with me to the gym?"

I nod.

He seems to be watching me like he can't figure out what to do with a detonated grenade. I'm trying to figure out what to do with myself too. I have never felt so consumed with jealousy and hurt, anger and self-loathing in my life. I'm so nauseous I don't even eat, just sip an orange juice, and then I slip into my running pants and tennis shoes, and try not to barf when I brush my teeth.

Arizona today is an inferno of heat, and on the trail outside our hotel, I pull on my cap and quietly stretch my quads, trying to concentrate on the second thing I love most in the world after Remington: running. I know it's going to make me feel good—if not good, then at least better.

We haven't talked about it.

We haven't kissed.

We haven't touched.

Since I bawled like an idiot in his arms last night. When I woke he was looking out the window, his profile unreadable, and when he turned, as if sensing me, I had to close my eyes because I'm just afraid that if he's gentle with me I'll break again.

Now he bounces in place as I stretch. He's wearing his gray hoodie and sweatpants, every inch of him a running boxer you would die for. Kill for. Leave your entire life in Seattle behind for.

"Okay," I whisper to him, nodding.

"Let's hit it." He smacks my butt gently and we start running, but the sleepless night means I don't really have the speed that I want. Remington looks just a little tired today, quietly running beside me, pumping his fists in the air.

I keep waiting for my endorphins to kick in, but my body isn't my friend today, and neither are my emotions. I want to sink into a quiet corner and cry again, until I cry it all out and it doesn't hurt anymore, until I'm not angry at myself anymore, or at him, for saying yes to everything, anything, he could get his hands on while for months he refused to put his hands on *me*.

I've stopped running and put my hands on my knees, sucking in a breath to calm down. Remington slows down and pumps his fists in the air as he comes back. I want to groan in protest over how shitty I feel when he looks more than decent. He stops close to me, and I use my cap to shield my stupid face.

"If we're running to the gym, we need to get there today," he whispers in amusement, reaching out and tipping my hat back. I bite down hard on my lip as he surveys me, forcing myself to hold his gaze.

He smiles down at me, his dimples popping as he stands there. A little arrogant, a lot hot, Remington Tate, the man of my dreams. In that gray hoodie. Those blue eyes peering at me. He's so aerodynamic as he runs; even when tired, he defies gravity. His shoulders, rock hard, stretch the material of his sweatshirt as his feet tap the sidewalk.

Just please somebody kill me now.

"I think I'll walk there," I tell him, kneeling down to add another impulsive knot to the laces of my tennis shoe, so I can look at my Nikes instead of him. "Go on without me and I'll be there."

I've never refused to run with him. This is our time, this is special, but I feel weak and faint and miserable.

Dropping to his haunches to level with me, he pries my cap off and surveys me, no more dimples on his face. "I'll walk with you," he tells me easily, putting my cap back on as he straightens.

"You don't have to. Coach Lupe is waiting."

He seizes my chin and pins me down with tormented blue eyes. "I. Will walk. With you. Brooke. Now give me your hand and let me help you up."

He spreads out his hand and I see it, and I want it, and it's there. I get up on my own and start walking.

He laughs softly as he steps to my side. "I don't fucking believe this," he mutters.

He shoves hands into his sweatshirt, dark head bent as he glares down at the sidewalk and ambles next to me. His hoodie fell when he bent to offer his hand, and his black hair is an adorable mess, and god, I want to rumple it and kiss it and pretend I'm strong like I used to be, but instead I'm nauseous and feel as strong as a little stick.

"How many were there? Do you know?" I hear myself ask.

He makes a low, growling sound and pulls two fistfuls of hair before dropping his hands. "Just tell me what you want me to do. What do you want me to say? You won't stop crying, you won't fucking eat, you circle around my touch. Why *the fuck* are you letting it matter?"

"Because you don't even remember; you don't even know what you did to them, who they are. One could be pregnant with your fucking baby as we speak! They could take pictures of you. They could . . . take advantage of you!"

He bursts out laughing and looks at me in tender amusement, as though nobody could ever hurt him, but they can. Fucking smug asshole—they can!

Even when he is the strongest, most powerful human being I've ever known, when he's black, he's both reckless and *vulnerable,* and he could hurt himself and he could definitely get hurt. The thought that anyone, especially some tarts, had access to him when he was like that, makes me feel like going nuclear. I wipe an angry tear and keep walking, then he crowds me with his body and purposely brushes the back of his hand to my own. He rubs his thumb over mine. "Just take my hand, little firecracker," he softly prods.

Dragging in a breath, I force my pinky finger to move, and he hooks our little fingers around each other. I feel the warmth of his touch race up my arm, and I think he notices I can't suppress a little shudder. He teases me, in a low voice that melts everything in me, "I give you my hand, and you give me your pinky?"

"Remington, I can't do this right now!"

I start running ahead, and he just joins me at the gym, unzipping his hoodie and slapping his gloves on. He starts pounding his bags without a single glance in my direction and with very, very hard slams. I stand by the sidelines, tense by the way the air crackles between us, like a suddenly haywire electrical circuit about to combust. Coach looks at him, and looks at me, and Riley comes up, equally concerned as he surveys us both.

Nobody talks to him and nobody talks to me.

I go to the bathroom and start throwing up.

❤ ❤ ❤

THE HEAT IN the Phoenix Underground arena is oppressive.

The costly seats are crammed together, one after the other, and about five hundred people are now wildly screaming as

Butcher and Hammer have a go up in the ring. Then *wham!* *Smack!* And Hammer ends up bloody and motionless on the floor.

"Wow, that was unfortunate for Hammer," Pete says.

Kirk "the Hammer" Dirkwood hasn't even twitched since he dropped *splat* on the canvas.

Butcher, though, is an enormous fighter. So meaty he's double or triple the size of any other fighter, his fists look like iron balls, and his knuckles look like spikes. He's just been announced the victor, and now he yells out a string of curses to the crowd, tells them he's the "greatest motherfucker this ring has ever seen!" and suddenly, the canvas shudders under his feet as he angrily starts marching in the ring, yelling even louder, "BRING ME RIPTIDE! *Let me have a fucking go at Riptide!!!!*"

They're dragging an unconscious Hammer out of the ring, and my stomach is knotting up by the second as Butcher bangs his chest like a gorilla and keeps yelling in a voice that is frighteningly craggy and monster-like. "RIPTIDE!! You hear me? Come out, pussy! Come face me like you did Benny!"

"He's chums with you-know-who," Pete tells me with a roll of his eyes. "And now, thanks to last year's final, he thinks he can beat Rip too."

The crowd gets restless. I notice that the Butcher's hunger has only aroused the public. They heard the name, and it spreads like wildfire across the stands, starting with murmurs and rising to a crescendo: *Riptide! Riptide! RIPTIDE!*

Immediately I know, with every fiber in me, that they're going to bring him out. He's wanted, not only by Butcher, but by the entire screaming arena.

"*Riptide! Riptide! RIPTIDE!*" they chant.

I feel like a ginormous fist is squeezing the contents out of my stomach as I wait for a glimpse of him. He's angry at me. He's angry at me because I'm being ridiculous and I hate that I can't stop being ridiculous and then I'm angry at myself.

"*Riptide, Riptide!!*" the crowd continues screaming for him.

There's a commotion as the organizers seem to scramble to comply as the crowd's demands get even louder.

"*RIPTIDE! RIPTIDE!*"

"*Give us fucking RIPTIDE!*"

The speakers flare to life, and the announcer sounds breathless. "You asked for him, ladies and gentlemen! You asked for him! Now, let's bring out tonight the one you are all here to see! The one, the *only*, RRRRRRRiiiiiiipppppppppppptiiiiiiiiiiiiiiiiiiide!"

The crowd roars in delight and my body screams in silence as all my systems kick into overdrive. My heart pumps, my lungs expand, and my eyes hurt as I pin them fixedly on the walkway. All the vessels and capillaries in my body dilate to accommodate blood flow, and my leg muscles feel ready to run, even though all I can do is squirm uneasily in my chair. I can't ever seem to make my body realize that Remy is not in danger. Nor am I. My brain cannot comprehend that the man I love does this for sport, for a living. For his mental well-being. So I sit here while my body unleashes all the same hormones it would if I were being cornered by three raving bears ready to eat me.

And then I see him enter the arena—strong, magnificent, in control.

He takes the stage quickly and removes his robe while Butcher keeps pounding his chest as the crowd receives Remington with all their love and devotion. Like they always do.

I hold my breath and my hands fist in my lap as I wait for him to look at me.

It kills me. First, I watch in anticipation, then in dread, then in disbelief, as he makes his turn, unsmiling, then drops his arms at his sides and gets into place. The bell rings.

The men charge. I wince when Remy's head flies to the side from the impact.

"Oh, no!" My stomach drops, my eyes blurring when I see blood.

The awful sounds of bone cracking against flesh follow, one after the other, as Butcher delivers three more consecutive blows, all to Remy's face.

"Oh, god, Pete," I gasp, covering my face.

"Shit," Pete tells me. "Why didn't he fucking look at you?"

"He hates me."

"Brooke, come on."

"We . . . he's . . . I'm having trouble coping with the women, all right?"

Pete looks at me with a conflicted expression, and his stare bores into my profile, as if he wants to say something but can't.

Remington growls angrily and lifts his guard as he shakes his head, easing back. His face is bloodied from the nose, the lips, the little scar on his eyebrow, and I don't even know where else.

Butcher swings again, but Remy blocks, and they exchange jabs for about a minute until the round break is called and they go to their corners. Riley puts something on the wounds, and Coach is yelling stuff to him. He nods, shakes his arms out, flexes his fingers, and comes back, angry now, as he goes toe-to-toe with that burly awful beast and his spiked knuckles.

They go at it again. Swinging and slamming.

Remington feints to the side and Butcher throws his fist into the space where Remy used to be. Remington comes back with an uppercut to the face that connects so hard Butcher rocks sideways.

It takes a few moments for Butcher to recover his footing. He swings out his arm, but Remy ducks and comes back with a punch to the ribs, the gut, and the face, all landing with perfect speed and precision. *Pow, pow, pow!*

Butcher throws a fist out once again, aiming for Remy's face, but Remy blocks the punch and once again returns with a hit of his own—slamming his knuckles straight into Butcher's ugly fat face. Butcher falls to his knees.

At my side, Pete's excitement keeps building, and I hear him mumble, "Come on, Rem. Why are you letting him get in? You've got this." He turns to me and whispers, "You can teach speed and agility, but you can't *ever* teach a man to be a heavy puncher like Rem is. Soon as he starts hitting like he wants to, it's over." I see he's grinning, but I am not.

Remy is still bleeding, and as the fight progresses, he keeps catching a couple of punches with his body.

I loathe, loathe, loathe when he gets injured, even though it's my job to help him recover. He laughs and spits, almost like he's enjoying it.

Last season's nightmare of a fight did something to me, and watching this—this—kills me all over again.

My fear has grown and festered, and tonight, it is overwhelming. For a moment, my head spins faintly—but at the same time, I'm sure my adrenaline is keeping me awake, keeping my body fed and ready to defend him.

Butcher stands up again and whacks out another punch to the face, and Remington's head swings, but his body stays firmly planted. My tree is always so firmly planted. He swings, and hits back even harder. The two men clinch, then shove away from each other, and Remington charges again, the blood on his face pouring in streams now as, once again, he goes *pow pow pow*!

His rapid, consecutive punches cause Butcher to start backing off. The fat man bounces on the ropes behind him but refuses to fall. Remy corners him, his chest glistening with sweat and his muscles rippling as he smashes Butcher's gut and then his face.

My breath has left me. Fear chafes my insides along with other, colliding, sensations, like this incredible arousal that always seizes me as I watch him battle. He's so spectacular. The power in his body, the ripple of his muscles, the perfect flex when each muscle hardens and lets go. Remington uses both intellect and gut instinct to fight. He seems to plan, plot, then just roll with it, but more than anything, he seems to live in the moment. To *love* it.

His face is concentrated now as he pummels Butcher until the man has crashed down in a red pool at his feet. Literally, at his feet. His face *splat* on Remy's boots.

Remy's lips curl in pleasure by the sight, and he steps aside, turning his body in my direction.

"RIPTIDE!" the announcer yells, and as his arm is yanked up high in the air, his gaze finally targets me.

My pulse stops inside me. The noise is gone. Even my heartbeat feels nonexistent. It's stupid how much I need this, but when he finally lifts his arm and swings his head to me and his desperate, angry, blue eyes land on me, I shudder in my seat.

His gaze is vividly possessive and furious, a drop of blood sliding to his eyelid from his cut eyebrow, blood dripping from his nose and lips.

And when the ringmaster asks him something, he nods, and they call up another fighter for him.

"Yeah, now he's gonna need to work off that rage," Pete mumbles to himself.

A new tornado of nerves sweeps through me when I hear this. I swear, if I didn't know better, I'd think he was doing this just to torture and punish me. The endorphins will keep him from feeling any pain. In fact, he's so proud and driven that he's relentlessly taught his body to embrace it. He constantly pushes it to the limits, and I think his threshold for pain might be higher than that of any other athlete I've ever met, but my own limits have been way beyond met for the evening.

Remington scores several hits on the new guy, using great combinations of punches, but although Riley tried curing him at his corner, blood continues pouring down his face.

Both fighters exchange hard jabs and suddenly the ring is a swirling maelstrom of flesh moving and muscles hardening. I keep track of Remy through the ink bracelets on his biceps as he throws what I've heard Riley call "punches in bunches." He scores one in the ribs, one in the jaw, and then he throws in a right hook, his most powerful punch.

His opponent rocks, stumbles, and falls, flattened out.

The crowd screams.

"RRRRRRRIPTIIIIIDE! Ladies and gentlemen, your victor, once again! Riiiiptiiiiiiide!"

I'm so worn out. I've turned to jelly, Jell-O, everything soft and stupid.

"RIPTIIIIDE!"

It feels like an eon passes, but in fact, it takes only about twenty minutes to get out of the Underground riding a stretch limo to the hotel, and my legs shake as we shuffle into the car. All my senses scream for me to tend to my man as he plops down on the seat across from mine, while the feisty part of me still wants to hit him because . . . what the fuck went on out there?

"Dude, what the fuck were you doing?" Riley starts up, sounding as puzzled as I feel.

"Here you go, Rem." Pete passes him a gel pack for his jaw. "I think the eyebrow cut might need a stitch."

"How do you feel, boy? Did getting the fuck pounded out of you feel good?" Coach demands in complete indignation from where he sits up front. "Where in the fuck was your game?"

Remington takes the gel pack, sets it aside, and looks directly at me, where I sit motionless on the seat across from his.

He wears his gray sweatpants and a comfortable red hoodie, the hood drawn over his head in order to keep his body temperature leveled. He's sprawled, big and quiet, in the seat, but his nose is bleeding, his lips are bleeding, the slash above his eyebrow is bleeding. His face is such a mess, I feel like there's a bomb inside my stomach just looking at it. And yet he looks back at me with clear, observant blue eyes.

I guess I should get used to the fact that my boyfriend gets punched for a living, but I can't. I can't sit here and see his face, bleeding and swelling, without wanting to hurt whoever did this. I want to punch something really badly, and I'm shaking with the need to reach out and hug and draw him to me while I mentally count the minutes it will take to reach our hotel.

I hear Riley tell me, "Here, Brooke, let's exchange so you can tend to him." Jolting from my seat, I settle down on Remington's right, and quickly delve into his open duffel bag, extracting my alcohol swab packets, some salve, and strips.

"Let me try to fix you," I whisper to him, and my voice, oh god, it sounds so intimate even when the entire car is watching. It's just that I don't seem to have any other tone except the one that came out: low and sandpapery with emotion.

He turns fully in my direction to let me disinfect the wounds, and his gaze . . . I can feel it, a roaming, curious, palpable thing on my face as I apply the salve to the part of his lips that always gets cut—the fleshy part of his bottom lip. My teeth instinctively bite down on my own as I press some salve into his. God, I loathe when he gets hurt.

"Do the eyebrow one too; it looks a little deep," Pete instructs.

"Yes, I got it," I reply, still in that voice I don't want to use right now but can't seem to modify. I'm trying to be efficient with my hands, but they're shaking more than I want them to, and the heat of Remington's body, which is extra hot after the fight, surrounds me as completely as his arms sometimes do. His fast breath bathes my temple, and it takes everything in me to quell the impulse to lean closer and breathe it inside me just to appease myself with the knowledge that he's all right. And at least breathing. Still pumped up with adrenaline, I head to the gash above his eye and press the wound closed between two fingers. God. I almost can't take being this close to him. A hundred little prickles run from my fingers, to my arms, straight to my throbbing little heart.

Dragging in a breath, I add gentle pressure to the cut while I inspect the rest of his face . . . to find the blue of his eyes completely zeroed in on me. Things grip inside me.

He's sprawled in the seat, angled in my direction, but his stillness makes me hyperaware, for I can feel all the coiled energy in his body as if he's ready to spring. On me.

My heart kicks up a little more in speed, and I hold my breath as I lean closer, grab another tissue, and whisper in the most level voice I can manage, "Close this eye."

Keeping the slash above his eyebrow pinched together, I start cleaning the blood that's dripped to his eyelid. Obeying me, he squints one eye closed and remains watching me with the other as if there's something in my expression that he craves to see.

His voice suddenly rasps through the dark. "I'm all fucked up." The unexpected, guttural whisper prickles across my skin and almost makes me jump. "My right bicep's fucked and my shoulder, my left oblique and trap."

"Dude, that's insane. How can you fuck all that up in a night?" Riley asks in bewilderment.

"Brooke, you know what to do," Coach commands from up front.

Quickly nodding, I look into Remington's blue, blue eyes, the way they shine in male contentment, and I clamp my jaw when it finally dawns on me what's going on here.

❤ ❤ ❤

WHEN WE REACH our hotel suite, I am fuming.

"You let him punch you on purpose."

He plops down on the bench at the foot of the bed and looks at me, tossing an empty Gatorade bottle aside. "I'm all fucked up, come fix me."

"You *are* fucked up, all right, but it's not the bicep that needs some tender loving care!"

"You're right—it's not." His eyes shimmer in the soft lamplight as he watches me. "Are you going to come fix me?"

"Only because you *pay* me to." Huffing angrily, I grab my massage oils, specifically my arnica oil and my mustard oil for inflammation, then I go and turn on the shower. "We're getting you in a cold shower."

His lips curl as he stands and waves me over, and when I come over in puzzlement, he wraps his big arm around my shoulders. "What? You need help to walk? You were bouncing a few minutes ago," I tell him.

"Endorphins killed the pain," he murmurs into my ear as I curl my arm around his waist and lead him to the bathroom. "I told you I was all fucked up."

I prop him against the wall and open the shower door, and as I check that the water is ice cold, he sweeps me up in his arms, turns the knob to medium, and carries us inside, clothes and all.

The water rushes over us, and I gasp in surprise and kick in the air while all my clothes get plastered to my skin. "What are you doing?"

He pulls off my shoes and tosses them over the glass partition above the tub, then he sets me on my bare feet and tugs my skirt down my legs. All those pheromones he puts out after fighting suddenly wage a war on my senses, and I start feeling so hot, the only thing keeping me from turning to ashes is the water pounding on my skin. "What are you *doing*?" I breathlessly demand.

He yanks off my top and it splats to the marble floor with a wet sound. He strips, and I'm so overwhelmed with anger over the way he let himself get punched, and so stimulated by the sight of his muscles flexing as he strips down to his golden, wet skin, I want to hit him and kiss him at the same infuriating time. When his boxing shorts hit—*splat!*—and he kicks them aside, ohmigod, my eyes hurt.

I have to bite down on my lower lip, trying to quell the instinct to fling myself at him and give him anything he needs. Keeping his eyes leveled on mine, he steps back into the spray, his broad shoulders shielding me from the water, then when I feel the slow scrape of his thumb sliding up my chin and gently tugging my lower lip free of my teeth, I hear his voice thick as he whispers, "That's mine to bite."

I'm not breathing. He has this overpowering effect on me. I could fight my reactions to him, but I'd lose. My eyes hold his, and the possessive glimmer in his gaze bullets through me. Rivulets of water slide down his jaw as he grabs my ass and presses me close, his erection biting into my tummy as he stares down at me with relentless intensity.

"You," he says, his voice terse and commanding as he drags his wet thumb across my lips, "are going to love me until I die. I'm going to make you love me even if it hurts, and when it hurts, I'm going to make it better, Brooke." He eases his thumb into my mouth and rubs it purposely against the tip of my tongue, the move quietly demanding that I lick it. When I do, my breasts ache and I watch him extract his thumb to brush the wet pad across my bottom lip. "You're going to fucking love me if it kills us."

My lungs ache for breath and the rest of me aches for his hands on me. And when my gaze flicks upward to find those blue eyes pinned on mine, his face hurt and sweaty, all the testosterone in the world courses through him, pulling and enveloping me, so I can barely take living right now I want him so much. He makes me feel this all-consuming, soul-searing, heart-wrenching, painful need for him that's more than physical, more than emotional.

My sex grips so tight, it takes all my effort not to whimper. My senses are heightened by his nearness. I can't help but notice how the drop of blood on his lip is the color of his RIPTIDE robe, bright and perfectly oxygenated. How his steady, hot breath bathes my wet face. How, slowly, his fingers spread wider on my ass, and one of his thumbs grazes the skin of my jaw. He destroys me.

"Stop hurting yourself," I say miserably, trying to ease out of his arms only to hit the cold marble behind me.

"It doesn't hurt," he rasps, then pulls me close by the ass and nuzzles me. "You. Crying in my fucking arms. Because I fucking hurt you. That hurts. You . . . not touching me. Not looking up at me like you do, with those sweet little happy eyes. Hurts. I'm hurting like a motherfucker and not one piece of me hurts on the outside like it does where *you* make it hurt."

Fighting to hold my raw emotions in check, I drop my gaze and furiously blink back the moisture in my eyes.

"I hurt here too." He guides my hand over to his massive erection. "I hurt all night, watching you come apart for me. This morning. And at the gym." He presses me close, and I moan softly and drop my forehead to his pecs as I struggle not to fall apart again.

He takes pity on me and lets my hand go, but my fingers burn at my sides, and I don't know what to do with my hands. My head spins with his nearness. I want to take my fingers up every inch of his muscles and erase the touch of every other hand that has ever been there. I want to—

I don't even know. I can't think of anything now except the growing, painful throb inside my body. Inside my heart. My sex. He's grabbed the soap and starts soaping up my naked flesh. As if doing it for the first time, he watches his hands work between my legs, his fingers curl and lather up my breasts, his thumbs rubbing soap over my nipples.

"Did you like the fight?" he asks in his quiet, deep voice as his powerful hands glide smoothly down the outside of my legs, up the inside of my thighs, rubbing my pussy. He goes around then, soaping and massaging the flesh of my ass cheeks and in between.

The pleasure of his sure, familiar touch is so complete, I bite back a moan as I watch him wash me.

One of his eyes is a little swollen, and the gash above his eyebrow still looks bright red. His plump bottom lip is still cut at the center. He's hurt, but getting hurt is nothing to him. He wanted my attention and would do anything to get it, and even if I want to hit him for being so reckless, the urge to kiss every cut and gash is stronger than anything.

Remington has been abandoned his whole life. Parents. Teachers. Friends. Even me. Nobody has ever stuck with him long enough to show him he's worth it. What he did, just to get me to touch him and give him some love, makes me burn to drown him with my love until he never, ever, has to ask for it.

"I refuse," I whisper in a fervent voice, "to sit there and watch you getting hurt on purpose."

"I refuse to let you push me away," he says with equal fervor, filling one large, soapy hand with the weight of my breast.

Shaking my head with a frown, I let my eyes drift shut when he tilts the showerhead to my face. The spritz washes away my shampoo, and when he slides his hands down my hair to help the soap trickle down my body, I can barely keep it together.

Taking action before I lose it, I seize the soap and make lots of bubbles, then I reach out to the slick muscles of his chest and rub my soapy fingers over his hard, smooth flesh. His chest jerks at my unexpected touch, and when my eyes flick up to his, my knees almost give. All of my body clenches as I hold those starved blue eyes, my fingers rubbing wetly up his thick arm, down his chest, across his eight-pack. My voice, thick with emotion, is barely heard above the trickling water. "Is this what you wanted? When you were out there, recklessly letting yourself be hit?"

Gently, he grips my face in one hand, his voice stern and passionate as he enunciates every word. "I want you. I want you to touch me, to put your lips on mine—like before. I want you to love me. Stop fucking punishing me, Brooke. I love *you*."

He presses his lips to mine, testing me with a fast, rough kiss, withdrawing to look at me with panting breaths.

His grip tightens on my face. "Is my girl going to let this break her? Is she? She's stronger than that. . . . I know she is, and I need her to live. I need her to fight for me and I need her to fight with me. As far as I'm concerned, that never happened. Only you happened, Brooke. And you're still happening, aren't you, firecracker?"

Our gazes hold, and I don't know who is hungrier, needier, or more desperate. His gaze claws into me, he looks so starved, and I feel rabid. My chest starts heaving, my heart hammering, and before I know it, my fingers push into his hair and I pull him to my lips at the same time he slams me back against the shower wall and crushes his mouth with mine.

I gasp as his taste zings through me as he forces my lips apart, sliding one of his hands up to frame my face, locking me in place as he opens me up with the force of his mouth, making me groan and claw at his scalp as I anxiously seek out his tongue with mine.

But he finds me first. No. He does not find me. He plunders me, his tongue rubbing and fucking mine. A low, pleased growl runs through his chest as he lifts me up in the air to align our mouths better. His closeness, the touch of our flesh, exhilarates me. My skin prickles where we touch as the need builds between us. I feel roped to him in a way that makes me certain that nothing can ever pull me back.

I suck hungrily on his tongue as he turns off the shower and carries us outside. He drapes a towel over me while I continue clinging, sucking his tongue, nibbling his lips, my blood rushing fast through me like an awakened river as he walks us to the bed.

He lowers me over the comforter, and he drapes the towel over my body, lightly rubbing it over my skin while he ducks his head and whispers, "Let me go get dry."

I moan in protest when he leaves me. I'm so hot, but so wet and cold, my teeth chatter as I watch his muscled buttocks flex in the sexiest way a man's buttocks can flex as he disappears into the bathroom. Even as every inch of my body pulses, I shakily tuck my towel tighter around me and absently dry myself, my eyes fixed on the bathroom door.

Ohmigod, I hurt like a motherfucker, too.

When he finally fills the threshold with those magnificently broad shoulders and that beautiful eight-pack, rivulets of water still slide from his hair, down his throat, to his chest and down to the towel draped around those narrow hips. My breath goes. I can see he's run a towel over his head and his dark hair is standing up and spiked, those blue eyes shining greedily as he makes sure I'm on the bed as he left me. Suddenly all the love and painful jealousy I feel rushes through my bloodstream like lightning.

He steps in without removing his gaze from me, and I pull open my towel to watch his face harden and his eyes flash as he takes me in, completely naked.

He reaches for his towel and strips it away, and my airway constricts when I see his large erection bobbing heavily as he comes to bed and uses another towel to gently dry my wet hair.

"I'm rubbing you down with oils first," I warn in a breathless whisper as he finishes.

Smiling devilishly, he tosses the towel aside, grabs the arnica oil I was reaching for, and tosses it onto the carpet to join it; then he brushes my wet hair back, his eyes weighted as he cups the back of my head and lowers his head to mine. "Rub my tongue with yours."

He parts his mouth on mine, and our breaths mingle, and a delicious shiver runs through me as his lips pull me apart and our tongues flick out.

"Your lip," I breathe, so he's careful.

He playfully nips me and brushes my tongue with his again, rubbing a little harder and driving me insane. "Your lip," I moan, squirming needily beneath him.

He draws back. Then, torturously slow, he caresses the backs of my legs, awakening a thousand and one tingles.

"Remington, your lip . . ." I protest when I see the cut bleeding again, and I reach out to catch a drop of blood with my finger.

"Shh . . ." His tongue flashes out, and he licks and sucks my finger; then he lets go and watches me with those violently tender blue eyes as he trails his fingers up the backs of my legs to stroke my buttocks.

My breasts rise and fall as he runs his fingers up my legs, then possessively cups my ass. "Are you turned on by this?" he asks.

"Yes."

He slides his hands to the backs of my knees, down my calves, then slowly back up until I'm dissolving into my bones and dying.

"How turned on are you?" he asks softly, settling a kiss on my stomach.

"I have to put something on that lip again," I breathe. A thousand flames lick my body as I sit up and reach with trembling hands for my salve and manage to press some to his cut.

He presses a kiss to my fingertip, and I close my eyes as a bolt of pleasure arrows through me. "Remy . . ." I say, melting.

"Lie back down," he tells me. Dizzy with anticipation, I do as I'm told.

"Don't kiss me, Remington," I warn.

He whispers roughly, "Fix me up later."

A shudder courses through me as he caresses my sex, briefly opening my lips with his thumb while, at the same time, he ducks to slide his tongue across the tip of one nipple.

I buck a little, mewing, and he laughs softly as he licks my other nipple, tonguing it, playing with it, before covering it with his hot, wet mouth and sucking.

He runs his hands up my body, growling, "God, Brooke. You knot me up and tear me open. You're getting me in you now."

"Okay," I gasp eagerly as he spreads me wide, his erection pulsing and hard as he flattens me on my back and covers me with the heat of his body. His mouth sears my own, and I disintegrate on the mattress. We're both wound up. I need him like I need air. The way our skins touch. The way his calluses rasp over me. The way my hands slide over his slick chest. I claw his back as he buries his face in my neck and his mouth works hungrily over me like he doesn't know whether to kiss, bite, or lick, so he does all three.

"Who do you belong to," he rasps urgently.

"You," I pant.

He grabs my legs and pulls them around his hips, then pins my arms above my head, looking down at me, his eyes devouring my face, my mouth, raking me with a look that is dark, and tormented, and starving.

He curls his fingers into mine and crushes my mouth with his. This closeness to him—the tangle of our limbs, our tongues, our breaths—activates all the pleasure centers in my brain and all the mating instincts inside me. Fire streaks through my veins as our tongues rush to meet. I moan, he groans, my body tingles on every point of contact with his as he rocks his hips against me. His chest against my nipples. His cock against my sex entry. His thick, powerful leg muscles almost crushing my thighs. Our palms against each other.

My every cell knows this is my mate and prepares me for him. Just him. He lets go of me and palms my ass as we intensify the kiss, his fingers proprietary and firm, bringing me closer until we are perfectly aligned, and I tip my head back so that his tongue reaches every corner in my mouth. "*Yes . . .*" I gasp.

He draws back, and our eyes meet in the shadows. The need I see in his eyes takes my breath away. He is the most male and mesmerizing thing I've ever seen. He ducks once more to set his hot lips on mine. Wet. So, so, hot. I gasp as he slides a hand between my legs. He turns to suckle my earlobe, and I run my tongue over his skin and the stubble of his jaw, anywhere I can taste as he passes his thumb over my sex.

"Oh, that feels so right . . ." A burning rush spreads through my body when his fingers slide between my legs to caress me. My blood starts boiling, and my folds grow damper.

He murmurs my name in that thickened voice that drives me crazy and lowers his lips to my breasts, laving the tips. They feel extra sensitive today, shooting ripples of pleasure to my sex. I gasp and bite his earlobe, saying his name. I can't say it enough. "Remy . . ."

"Go off for me," he pleads, plunging his longest finger inside me. I thrash and clutch his shoulders as his fingers burrow into my cleft. I'm soaked, my whimpers of pleasure echoing in the room.

"Shh, baby, loosen up for me." He slides down my body and bends to lick my belly button. He drags his tongue down my navel and then I feel him trailing it lower. I scream when he traces my clitoris. He pulls me open with his thumbs and licks into me. Pleasure rushes through me as my body tightens for release. Then I come.

I gasp as he licks me all up and am still thrashing in residual waves when he goes up to his knees between my legs, takes his cock in his hand, and feeds it into me. I see his muscles clench, his body working as he pushes himself deep. I moan when he presses my clit down with his thumb and fucks me even deeper with his big, thick cock.

Thrashing as a sound of pleasure escapes me, I tilt my hips up for more. He mutters my name and leans over to brush kisses along my face, cooing down at me, *"You're so fucking tight, baby. . . . You drive me so crazy."*

When he's buried in me, we stop.

I hear our breaths, my own rapid heartbeat, in this stillness.

The urgency is there, pulsing and shimmering in our bodies. But he's in me. I have him. I fucking grip him and don't want to let go.

He doesn't want to come out of me—he's in me. Hard and pulsing. Completely possessing me.

We start kissing as he sinks a little farther in, his mouth primal and raw, loving but deliciously rough. I feel that familiar stretch of him inside me and bite his neck, whimpering as I adjust. He stays in place, waiting for me to start moving.

I wait, though, and pant, my eyes close as I relish him, wide and long and alive, inside me. I love his nipples, his skin, him. I rub the tips of my fingers over the dark points. I hear him exhale in pleasure as I raise my head to suck one softly. I love his rumble. He takes my head in his palm and tips it back, kissing me lovingly. I tear free and run my tongue over his other nipple. "Remy . . . I can't wait. . . ."

He growls and starts moving, whispering as he nuzzles the top of my head and tangles his fingers in my hair. *Tight . . . beautiful . . . my Brooke Dumas . . .*

His words caress me.

Nobody every taught him how to love.

He does it instinctively.

Pulling me closer, he suckles, nips, bites, and licks me, drawing out the pleasure until my eyes burn. My body clutches him. I can't

breathe, and all I hear in the room are our combined sexy sounds—
and the ones he makes drive me half-crazy.

He thrusts, slamming hard. He's wound me up by now, and I
scream. He fists his fingers in my hair, kissing me as our hips pump
fast and violently, with hardly any rhythm now.

I come a second time, and he penetrates completely and holds
me tight as he goes utterly still. I feel his warmth and a hot growl
followed by a kiss in my ear as he comes in me. Then we ease in
relaxation, our breaths calming.

He grabs me and pulls me to his chest as he rolls, our bodies
slick with sweat. He wants me naked, and I want him to hold me
naked. He eases out as I start relaxing, then he tests my entry and
pushes his semen back in, surprising me.

Our instincts suddenly take over. My hips rock to his fingers.
The warmth of his breath bathes my throat as he presses his mouth
to my skin. I can hear us, the noises we make—my whimpers and
his growls of male satisfaction of pleasuring his mate. A bubbling
sound tears out of me as I begin shuddering.

He's not touching my clitoris. It is not receiving any stimulus,
but the way he pets my body with his hand, shoves his semen back
into my body like he never wants to leave, and licks my skin with
slow drags of his tongue, makes my sex grip around him and my
nipples bead so that even the air is a stroke that he means to give to
me. When he bites the back of my neck, I buck and cry out, "Oh
god!"

He pushes me down on the mattress on my stomach and keeps
gently biting my neck, marking me as he fucks me doggy style.

By the time we sag onto the bed, it's a task for me to summon
my energy to move. I'm a boneless heap beneath him, still trying to
make my lungs work.

Slick with sweat, he rolls to his back and uses one arm to bring me
with him, our skins glistening from our workout. My chest is so full

of love and my body so well fucked, I feel both dead from exhaustion and as alive as the sun. I spread out over him and cup his hard jaw.

"Do these hurt?" I lightly graze the cuts and the slight purple area on his temple. Before he can answer, I buzz a kiss over each one, and I wonder if he's ever been kissed where he's been hurt. So I kiss him there, on every mark, and then I kiss the one on his lips, briefly buzzing it.

I ease back and smile at him, stroking his hard jaw. "Did you think about me before you had me? Did you wonder if I existed? How I would be?"

He tucks a strand behind my ear and studies my face. "No."

"I didn't think I'd ever fall in love. Did you?"

"Never," he says again, those sexy dimples out in full force.

I drag my fingernails up to his temple, teasing them into his hair. "What did you think about when you grew up there?"

"I just took what I had and was satisfied with it." He brushes my hair back and strokes my earlobe. "But if I'd known you existed, I'd have hunted you, I'd have caught you, and I'd have taken you."

"But isn't that what you did?" I ask, smiling.

"Exactly"—he bumps my nose with his, his blue eyes laughing—"what I did."

Sighing, I rest my head on his shoulder and rub my fingers over his nipples.

He's the best bed. He's lying on his back, one arm behind the pillow, the other trailing over my spine, and I'm spread all over him, my tummy to his abs, my breasts on his lower pectorals, my head on his shoulder and perfectly aligned to tuck into his neck. He smells of different soap every time, with so many hotels we go to, and at the same time, he always smells like him.

Quietly, I run my fingers up his bicep and lightly massage it. "That better?" I prod, working deeply into the muscle and realizing it *is* fucked up. Damn him.

But he says, "Yeah," like it's nothing and rolls me to my side. My insides immediately go hyperaware as he starts maneuvering me. He tucks me closer, and I moan softly deep in my throat and my sex swells because I realize what he's going to do. He rolls me around to my side and adjusts me to spoon me, his big body warm and hard behind mine. He brushes my hair back and licks me, and I shudder as he slowly starts petting one heavy hand down my curves.

He licks me, pets me, drags his hand down my body while he flicks his tongue along the back of my ear, at my nape, the curve of my shoulder, lapping and tasting me.

Remy has thrived without love, even paternal love. He has thrived even when he fights a mood disorder every day of his life. He has thrived and gotten up every time he has fallen. The only times I have truly fallen, in my Olympic tryouts and when he lost last year's fight, I've been permanently marked and have hobbled to get back walking. Yet *he* instantaneously stands to run.

He is so complicated and unpredictable, I fear that even when I've given everything of myself to this man, he will always have me, but *he* will never really be mine.

"I'm hungry," he tells me in my ear, then eases out of bed and jumps into his drawstring pajama bottoms.

"Oh, no, I want to sleep . . ." I groan, and clutch my pillow as he grabs my ankles and hauls me down the length of the bed.

"Come eat with me, little firecracker."

"Noooooo . . ." I clutch the pillow to me as he drags me down the bed and, in my last attempt to remain in bed, I kick into the air. "I'm getting fat because of you!" I laughingly squeak.

With a low, sexy chuckle, he lifts me up as if I were just the pillow, then tosses the pillow aside, only keeping me to kiss. "You're beautiful."

"Every beautiful woman in the world is beautiful because she *sleeps*," I protest weakly, at the same time nuzzling his throat.

He grabs one of his T-shirts from his suitcase and hands it to me. I wiggle into it as he carries us out to the living area of the penthouse suite, then he drops me down on a chair and fishes out his food. He brings two plates, one heaping, and the other containing more normal portions. Then he plops down across from me and pats his lap with a meaningful stare.

I lean back in my chair and start eating an asparagus spear from the tip. "We have very bad eating habits. If you take me to a restaurant, I can't eat perched on your lap like some sort of canary. People will think we have problems."

He sticks a roasted cauliflower floret into his mouth and munches. "Who cares?"

"Excellent point." Eating the stalk of asparagus down to the end, I observe him across me, with those tattoo bracelets on his arms, his hair a delicious mess, and his blue eyes twinkling. God. He is all. I want. In this world. Right on that chair. "And this is actually not as comfortable as you, I admit." I squirm in the chair for emphasis.

He lifts a brow, his eyes sparkling devilishly. "Stop playing hard-to-get, Brooke. I already got you." He tosses a paper napkin at me. I grab another, wad it, and toss it. He sets the fork down and reaches one long arm out to grab the end of my chair. He hauls it across the floor, and the moment he can wrap his arm around my waist, I squeak as he transfers me over.

"Settle down now. We both want you here." He cups my face and turns me, his lips curling in a tender smile as he surveys my features with new intensity. "We okay now?"

Linking my fingers at the back of his neck, I meet his gaze. "Mostly I'm just angry at *me*. I'm hurt and jealous. . . . It makes no sense in my head, but the rest of me doesn't listen. I just didn't expect to have so much trouble figuring out how to cope with this."

"You cope knowing I love you, that's how you cope. I fucking love *you*," he hisses.

My heart squeezes when I look at him. I take a roasted cauliflower floret between two fingers as a peace offering and lift it to his
lips, feeding it to him.

Eyes glinting, he takes it all in his mouth, including part of
my fingers, licking them. He's still feasting on my fingers when he
follows suit and grabs a piece of cauliflower and feeds it to me, and
as all the herb flavors and olive oil melt in my mouth, I suck on his
fingers too. I love the way his eyes flash when I do that.

"I love you, but don't ever let them punch you on purpose like
you did tonight," I tell him in a raw, emotional voice, rubbing my
wet fingertips over his lips, feeling them move under my touch at
his gruff whispered, "I won't until you make me."

FIVE

A PRESENT

Sunlight steals through the window. Remington isn't in bed. I twist to scan our cute little cottage but can't see him anywhere. I force myself to slide out of bed and hop into my track pants, then my sports bra and top.

After freshening up, I grab my sneakers and pad out barefoot to find Diane in the kitchen. "Good morning, Brooke," she says merrily. I love how she travels with her aprons and gives every one of our hotel rooms such a cozy ambience.

She even travels with her green ceramic pans—ones that don't shed aluminum, so Remington's food is completely pure.

"Hmm, it smells divine," I say as I wander around in search of breakfast.

"Dive in. The big man asked me to set a ton aside for you."

I lift a bowl of sweet potato hash and munch. "What time did he leave?"

"Pete came and got him a couple of minutes ago."

"Pete? Not Riley? What gym did he go to?" There's a knock on the door, and I lick the coconut oil Diane used to cook the hash from my fingers as I go to open it.

"Brooke Dumas?"

A woman stands holding a medium-size box wrapped in red paper but without a bow. "Yes?"

Her smile widens. "Mr. Tate ordered this for you." She hands me the huge box, and I stare in disbelief.

"Remington sent me this?" I ask stupidly.

"Yes, miss. Enjoy." I kick the door shut as she leaves, my hands full of the big box of surprise Remington sent me.

Ohmigod. He's completely unexpected. He not only seduces me with music, with his blue devil eyes, with his spiky hair, with his dimples and his delicious fucking smell, he gets me presents?

I immediately tear the box open and discard the top, and I see lots of white packing peanuts inside. I stick my hand among the bubblelike shapes and feel a bunch of tickles running up my finger. Frowning, I take my hand out, and three enormous scorpions come out attached to it.

For a moment, everything is in slow motion.

Everything.

I can see the insects perfectly moving up my arm. I can see the long, segmented tails. The claw on the tail's tip, the two claws up front, and the eight legs moving on my forearm. I also dazedly register three black dots on each of their heads, as if they have three eyes. Do scorpions have three eyes?

Everything, I register.

In half a second.

And then, in the very next second, I register something else. That this is one of the most WHAT-THE-FUCK MOMENTS *OF MY LIFE.*

I fall back and kick the box. A dozen or more scorpions come crawling out as I try shaking off the ones already on me. My heart has flown up to my throat and now it's constricting my airway as it flutters and pounds in my pure building hysteria.

"HOLY SHIT! HOLY SHIT! DIANE!"

I have scorpions. Scorpions. Crawling. Up my fucking arm! They are huge, half the size of my palm, each with eight legs. Seriously? Only eight legs? I feel *a thousand* legs on me. I feel legs on every inch and centimeter of my skin. I start convulsing and shaking like crazy on the floor, screaming when I feel my first sting on my forearm. "OH MY GOD, DIANE!!"

Suddenly I feel a fourth one crawling up my ankle and I notice that all this time, Diane has been screaming hysterically. "*Brooke! Oh my god! Somebody do something!*"

"GET THEM OFF ME, DIANE!! GET THEM OFF!"

I don't know why I am yelling frantically as if that will scare them away. Afraid to touch them with my hand, I'm instead twisting and squirming on the floor when a bucket of water crashes upon me. I suck in my breath as I watch Diane rush back to the kitchen, fill another pan full of water, and throw it at me. But the scorpions are hanging on.

I reach for one and try to push it off me, and its tail snaps at me. The stinger hits my thumb. Instant pain shoots into me as the others keep crawling. Crawling. On me. I don't know if these animals have been drugged or starved or given something to alter them. They are almost crawling on me like spiders, fast and frantic over me. One swings its tail and sticks its stinger into the skin of my forearm. Then it sticks a second stinger into me. Pain shoots through me. I feel another sting up on my arm, and then I stop squirming and freeze. Fight or flight is full force in me. But I can't run, and I can't fight, and now I freeze, my body paralyzed in fear while all my organs go wild at the threat these things pose to me. All my fear rushes to the forefront, and I start crying helplessly.

I'm on the floor, sobbing, the only thing moving on me is the awful legs belonging to these awful creatures, when I hear Diane screaming tremulously into the phone, "Get back here! Get back here *please*!" She keeps repeating the same thing, over and over, when she suddenly swings the door open and screams out into the hall, "REMINGTON!"

Everything's hazy as almost immediately, or maybe a few minutes later, I don't know, the door slams open wider with a crashing noise. Through my tears, I see *him*, and I can picture what he sees. Scorpions all over me and *me*, doing nothing, crying like a baby, as afraid as I've ever been in my life. My vision blurs completely from something other than tears, and I wonder if it's the venom. I feel shocks all over me. I feel the scorpions being yanked from me with bare hands, one after the other, as I sob.

Then he grabs me, and I'm in his huge arms, steady arms that hold a body that is mine—is it mine? Is this body that is falling apart mine?—and I am shaking and in an agony of pain.

I try climbing up him higher, like a tree, and cling to his neck as I sob and try to breathe, sucking in his scent like it's the only way my body can remember to breathe again. He's breathing hard. His hands are fists in my back, and they are shaking. Then they start rubbing up and down. His hands reach my face and he furiously wipes my tears.

"I got you," he hisses passionately in my ear, squeezing me none too gently. "I got you. *I got you*."

"A woman just came and knocked!" Diane's frantic words tremble with tears. "She said Remy had ordered the box for her!"

"*Jesus*," Pete says in disgust. "Let's not throw them away, Diane; we need to see what kind they are. Call an EMT and let's just crush the motherfuckers—give me a pan."

Remington's voice is hard as granite in my ear. "I'm going to kill him," he promises me. "I swear to god, I'm going to kill him so slowly."

"Just save it for the ring, Rem. Sabotaging your championship is exactly what he wants," Pete says between whacking noises.

Remy's voice is a hiss as I feel him rub his hands over me. "Where did they bite you? Tell me exactly where, and I'll suck all the poison out."

I'm gasping for breath as if my air ducts were suddenly swelling. "I . . . e-everywhere . . ."

"You shouldn't suck on these—let me have a look at her," Pete says.

I cling to Remington, and he tightens his arms around me and slowly rocks me, his entire body shaking almost like my own as he speaks into my ear. "I got you, little firecracker, I got you right here in my arms," he whispers, and I can hear the barely unleashed fury in his voice.

"Rem, let me see her," Pete begs him.

"No," I moan, and I clutch Remy harder because I know that if I die, this is the way I want to go. Oh my god, am I going to die? Who's going to take care of him? "Don't let go, don't let go," I moan.

"Never," he promises in my ear.

"According to Google, they're Arizona bark scorpions. Venomous but not deadly."

"Hang on to me," Remy whispers, and then we're in motion. My vision blurs even more. My tongue is thick. Saliva in my mouth. Can't breathe. I'm shaking as he lifts me, and the sensation of being electrocuted from the inside increases to an alarming level.

"Where the heck are you going with her, Tate?"

Remington's growl rumbles against my chest and somehow comforts me in my shaky, altered state. "To the fucking hospital, dipshit."

I hear the crash of the door as he opens it with all his might, and then a creak as if he unhinged it. Then we're in motion, going somewhere . . . his breathing hard and fast. . . .

Pete calls behinds us, "Dude, Diane just called the EMT. Let's just take a fucking chill pill and give her some Benadryl."

"*You.* Take a chill pill. Pete."

We're walking rapidly somewhere, and I can hear in his voice that he's hanging on by threads. The thought that this could greatly affect him and make him speedy makes me panic.

"I'm awright," I tell him; then I hear my own voice. I sound stupid. Maybe some brain cells are dying from the venom. I can't form the letter *l*. I say it again, "I'm awright, Wemy. . . ." Ohmigod.

Remington freezes, and I can feel him look at me but my eyes are blurry; then I hear him say, "FUUUUUCK ME!"

The elevator arrives. When the rolling doors open, Riley's voice reaches me. "All right, what's going on? Coach is waiting at the gym, Rem. . . ." He trails off.

"Live scorpions," Pete tells Riley. "Venomous, but fortunately not deadly."

"I can't bweathe," I say out loud. I am freaking. The hell out. For the first time in my life I don't understand what the hell is going on in my body.

"The poison spreads through the nervous system, but it doesn't enter the bloodstream. Try to stay calm, Brooke. These bark scorpions are nasty suckers. Can you feel your legs?"

I shake my head. My tongue feels leaden, every spot where I was stung hurts so bad that my face is stuck in a permanent grimace, and I'm breathing in pants.

Pete reaches out. "Let me see that. . . ." I feel Remy wrap his hand around my arm and stretch it out and whisper, "I'm going to kill him," while Pete studies me.

"It'll be all right, B," Pete says. "I've had the experience once. Awful, but you really don't die from a North American scorpion."

I nod and am clinging to that reassurance when Diane calls from the door, "There's a note! I turned the box over and there's a note!"

"What does it say?" Pete asks. Then I hear a crumpling sound as he reads, "'You've kissed me. Now you've been kissed back by the Scorpion. How does it feel to have my venom in you?'"

Remington's body engages. I can feel it suddenly, a complete change in the way he holds me. He was protective and proprietary, and suddenly . . . he wants to fight.

An image blooms inside my head: I'm standing before that embodiment of gross and kissing his disgusting tattoo of a scorpion so I could see my sister. I moan as a fresh wave of nausea roils up my throat.

"Pete, I saw his goons downstairs in the lobby. I think he's here at the hotel," Riley says.

"The motherfucker is probably downstairs waiting for Remington."

"Oh, he has it coming!" Remington thunders. "He's *already dead!*" he explodes.

I close my eyes tight as his tumultuous energy surrounds me, and I know, no matter how he might have struggled to stay blue . . .

Remy has gone black.

His lips are suddenly in my ear, and he whispers as he cups the back of my head, "I need to do something right now. I love you. I fucking love you to pieces, and I'm going to come back and put you back together again, all right?"

I nod, even though I feel like shit. Little jolts run through me. I bite my lip hard to focus on that pain instead, but it cannot compete with the stings on my body. I'm trying to be brave, but I remember the scorpions on me . . . on my body . . . the ugly bodies, the pincers . . . the three black dots on the head. . . . I shudder in his arms and feel like vomiting.

"Why is she shaking like this, goddammit?" Remington demands as we start moving again.

"It's the nervous system being affected. She sustained several stings, so it'll be painful. While the EMT is on his way, let's give her some Tylenol."

We're walking back into the room, as far as I can tell, and Remy sets me down on something soft. From the blue blur I see, I think it's the couch. He brushes my hair back, and I can feel his eyes on my face.

"I'm going to go crush him now."

Then he's gone, like some sort of hurricane out to destroy anything in its path, and my brain is so stunned by how fast he made this decision—by how calm and cold he sounded when he made that last statement—that for a moment I convince myself he really just went to get me some Tylenol.

"Damn it, he's full speed ahead, Ri, go after him before he sees Scorpion or *any* of his goons—Diane! Get some cold compresses and wait for the EMT. We need to go get that man!"

The last time I saw Remington have an episode and go fully manic, Pete jammed a syringe containing a sedative into his jugular, and as I hear the men's footsteps on the carpet, I immediately yell, "Pete, don't fucking shoot anywny up his thwoat!" then I groan, turn my head down, and start vomiting.

❤   ❤   ❤

THE EMT HAS come and gone, and we're still waiting, over half an hour later, with the remains of the scorpions in an awful Tupperware container glaring at me from the kitchen.

I was told to take Tylenol and Benadryl, use cold compresses, and to call if it got worse, in which case they would procure an antidote for me.

Now the Tylenol and Benadryl have kicked in and I'm a bit better. I have a trash can next to the living room couch in case I puke again.

I have thrown up half my body weight, it feels like. Diane is now putting ice on me so the stings don't swell, but still I feel shocks. I'm now groggy thanks to the Benadryl, but at least the swelling in my tongue is down some.

"I told you that man has the reddest self-destruct button I've ever seen," Diane says gently as she presses a cold compress to my arm. She reminds me of my mother, and for the briefest second, I am so homesick I want to cry. But the home I really want to cry for is the man downstairs ready to beat to death the sicko who did this to me.

"Please don't let him even set eyes on Scorpion," I say miserably. "If I screw things up for him again—"

"You don't screw it up for him, Brooke," Diane assures me. "You love him. You're the only woman he's ever loved and the only person who's loved him and accepted him as is. He wasn't given love growing up. He was rejected and cast aside. How hard do you think he will *defend* you?"

My eyes blur, and my voice breaks.

"I want to defend him too and can't even stand right," I say, feeling suddenly pitiful and weak.

By the time the guys come back, it's been almost an hour, and all my nerve endings have been corroded by my anxiety.

I'm lying on my side on the couch with my eyes closed, drunk on the Benadryl, when I hear muffled voices outside the door.

". . . hold the door . . ."

My heart dies. I swear it dies. Because there's just no other reason to hold the door except if your arms are busy holding something.

Something big and reckless and beautiful.

I hold my breath as Diane goes over to help with the door, and then I see them. Not them—him. Remy.

Pete and Riley are grunting and huffing as they lug him inside, his feet dragging in the ground, his head facing the floor. His dark hair is all I can see, and the anger and protectiveness I suddenly feel is so overpowering that the only reason I don't charge over to hit those two is because I still can't feel one of my feet.

"You assholes!" I cry.

They look at each other and say nothing when suddenly, unexpectedly, I hear his voice, slurred and still somehow determined. "Need to see Brooke."

"Hang on, buddy," Pete breathlessly says as they head to the master bedroom.

"Need her," Remy repeats in a low, garbled voice.

Diane hastens to help me to my feet and follow them. I swear, my heart feels like a Kleenex in my chest, one that has been used to a tiny pathetic wad. I hate when they shoot that freaking sedative into his throat!

Keeping her arm around me, Diane helps me limp my way into the master bedroom, and we find the guys jerking Remington's clothes off until he's in his gray boxers. Then they struggle to get him onto the bed.

"Get the other side," Pete says, and Riley hauls him up from the bed's far edge.

"Rem, what the hell are we to do with you? Huh, dude?" Pete chidingly says as he puts him into bed and cleans him up.

"Brooke," Remington growls angrily.

"She's coming, dude!" Pete says with a laugh.

They struggle to adjust him on the bed so that he faces me. They plop a pillow behind his head, and I see his eyes are halfway open. They fix on me as Diane helps me to bed, and they're fully black and almost frantic when he sees me. I still marvel at how fast they can change, those beautiful eyes of his. How his body can completely make this transformation within minutes. His large, tanned hands are idle at his sides, but his finger twitches like he wants to touch me, and suddenly *all* the fingers of my hands ache with the same urge to touch and comfort *him*.

"Okay?" he rasps to me, his gaze stormy and dark and vivid with frustration.

I can also *feel* his frustration. He wanted to go defend me, and they stopped him. I can feel his angry turmoil whirling around us as I clamber into bed with him and cover us to the waist.

"More than okay," I say gently as I put my arms around his hard shoulders and stroke the top of his head.

I can feel the tension ease from his body as he closes his eyes and suddenly sags. Sinking my face into his hair, I desperately haul his scent into my lungs and hold him tightly as his weight settles against my side, shifting so that his head is pillowed by my breasts. "I love you so much," I hiss into his ear. "Wake up soon, okay? I've got you now."

"This is going to be a difficult season," I hear Pete say.

I nod in understanding, but I can't take my eyes off *him*, his beautiful lashes resting on his cheekbones, his lips slightly parted. I stroke my fingers over his boyish face with that sexy scruffy jaw.

Riley says, "Let me go pick up Lupe from the gym and tell him our guy's not coming."

Pete watches me as I slowly start rubbing Remy's scalp, then he brings me some water and another ice pack and sets them on the nightstand while Diane tells me she'll clean up outside.

"How you doing?" Pete asks me.

I nod. "Better with the pill combo," I whisper. Then I add, "I'm sorry I called you guys assholes."

"I'm sorry we had to . . . but he was there. The motherfucker." He flattens his lips into an angry line, then keeps staring at me oddly.

"You're the one thing that calms him, Brooke, but you're also the one that completely triggers him." Pete sighs and stares out the window at the little desertlike garden outside our room. "And Scorpion knows there's something about you that makes Remington lose it. He's going to keep provoking him. He's going to try to fuck with his head and lure out every inch of Remington's beast."

"We can't, Pete, we can't let anybody fuck with his head." I kiss Remy's forehead, sending all my love to his beautiful brain and quietly promising, *I won't let anyone fuck with you.*

"Remington is as strong as he's ever been right now," Pete says. "But you're a big weakness of his. He'd lose for you, quit for you. Kill for you. Medicate his ass off for you."

I wipe my tears and pull Remy's head deeper between my breasts. "Pete, please don't sedate him anymore. We have to find another way."

"Dude, he's as strong as half a dozen men combined. How do you suggest anyone stop him? Let me tell you, if the Underground organizers decide to make that final match one of full submission . . ." He shakes his head and stands.

"What do you mean? What is that—submission?"

He looks at me drearily, then sighs. "Nothing. But Remington's got a hankering for Scorpion. He's a noble man, but he won't have mercy on that asshole—and if he gets a chance to kill him up in the ring, let me tell you right now, he will." He walks to the door. "Now let me go and find us another hotel."

Nodding at him and whispering, "Thank you," I turn back to my big lion.

"Let's get comfortable," I say to Remy. I pull off my clothes with shaky, clumsy hands, then peel off his underwear because I know he's always naked in bed. Then I come back to take his head and press it against my breasts, caressing his hair. I kiss his temple. "I got you now." His breathing is slow and even. His finger twitches at his side, and I grab his hand and wrap it around my waist. "Do you like holding me like this?" I ask softly, not really expecting an answer. I snuggle and coil my arms around his shoulders, picturing him the day I left him in the hospital.

Black and confused, manic, and desperate to say something to me. And I was too afraid to stay . . .

My eyes well up again, and suddenly, not only the stings hurt, but all my body aches on the inside.

Swallowing back the lump in my throat, I tighten my hold and bury my face in his hair, kissing him fiercely several times, anywhere I can. His breathing is slow and even, but mine is still hitched over what happened. All I know is that it stops hurting when I look at him, when I smell him, and when I touch him.

So I run my hands around the hard muscles of his bare shoulders and then lean over and kiss the shell of his ear, then his smooth, warm temple. He smells like him, seducing me, and I duck to smell his neck as I run my fingers down his back, the hard squares of his abs, then buzz my lips across his jaw.

He murmurs something unintelligible, and his finger twitches. I frame his jaw within my hands and place a soft kiss on his lips. "Thank you for defending me, but I won't let you ruin your dreams for me anymore," I tell him.

I run my fingers over his muscled chest, his neck, his corded arms, up his thick neck, where I bend to kiss his low, steady pulse point. He makes another noise, and I wonder what he thinks. Does he hear me? I think he does.

I grab his iPod and my earbuds so that we can share, and I look for a song that I've wanted to play to him. I place one earbud in his ear and one in mine and play him the Goo Goo Dolls' "Stay with You." I take his hand in one of mine and kiss his knuckles, stroking his hair as we listen, the song making me forget that every part where I was stung hurts as if I still have the stingers inside me. I hold him as we listen. My fighter. He fights everything, even himself, but I love that he's never fought loving me.

HE'S COMPLETELY SPEEDY.

Two days after the Gift—as we now call it—it was all over the news that the Underground fighter known as Scorpion and his team had been apprehended and charged with damages to a motel room due to the explosion of firecrackers inside.

Yes. *Firecrackers.*

When I asked Pete and Riley what happened, they just said Remington never leaves a message unanswered. "He could've tried for something that would've gotten Scorpion kicked off the tour, but he clearly wants to end this *in the ring.*"

Now Pete is getting some sort of device to protect me during the next fight, and I very much hope that I will be carrying one of those devices in case I need to beat the shit out of anything Scorpion related.

The rhythmic sound of Remy punching his speed bag echoes in the large gymnasium, and today, we can *all* feel the magic.

I can always tell when he's having a good training day, because his energy takes over the room. He inspires me, he inspires anyone nearby. His fire lights our fires. It's palpable, like a rope swishing in the air. Remington's energy is so powerful, I can smell it, taste it.

Coach has been pacing around the area Remington is training in, clearly buzzed with all that energy. Riley has been watching nearby while swinging in the air in shadowboxing style, and I spent two hours running on a treadmill, facing in Remy's direction and getting all my inspiration from the way he takes on his every athletic task.

Now I stretch on the sidelines, my body, which is still peppered with scorpion marks, spread out on the floor mats as I do some yoga.

I still remember stirring awake the night of the stings, the small garden outside our room completely dark by then. Little pinpricks of pain ran all over my body when suddenly I felt Remington haul me to his hard body and start swiping all my stings with my own salve. God. And his voice, so lazy, a little drunk with the sedative, but oh so tender and concerned as he said, "Look at you."

I said, completely disbelieving, "Look at me? Look at you!"

And we laughed miserably. Mine was really just a bluff, because, frankly, he looked lazy and relaxed, his speediness not really apparent because of the downer quality of the drug. He didn't look pitiful in any way, shape, or form, as I felt. Remington oozes strength. Even when he's asleep. Or down. A lion sleeping is still a *fucking lion.*

Now he's killing it at the gym, and I'm up on down-dog pose when suddenly, I hear him stop punching. Unaccustomed to the silence, I lift my head from where it hangs between my arms to the floor, and peer up at him. He's looking at my ass—up in the air. My insides do something weird, and I straighten and give him a little smile. His dimples peek out at me in return, then he lifts his powerful arms and starts swinging again, hitting his speed bag again and again.

I love the way he trains. Each powerful hit lands hard and dead center, and his beautiful face has that quiet look of concentration I find so sexy. His biceps bulge as he slams the bag repeatedly, and he's so focused on what he's doing, I hear him growl at the bag sometimes, low and deep in his throat.

Thwack! Thwack! Thwack!

Coach is having one of his loud afternoons, and I hear him start up again: "We won't take shit this year! We won't give anything away. We take what's ours!"

Remington has no reply except to hit harder.

"We're going to need a heavier punching bag if we're going to be champs, Riley," Coach says from the side of the bag opposite from where Riley is now taking notes.

I love how Coach Lupe uses the word "we" as if he's up in the ring himself, fighting alongside Remy. *Pfft!* Like that man really needs any coaching.

"What do you mean?" Riley yells back, signaling at the large, heavy bag Remington is crushing with his fists. "It's the 270-pound bag—there's no heavier one here."

"Sways too much!" Coach yells, shaking his bald head.

Riley laughs and jabs a finger toward Remington. " Let's switch him over to speed."

Coach whistles and signals him to the speedball, and Remington pulls off a glove so he can hydrate.

His gray T-shirt is plastered to his chest, and sweat trickles down his throat, his torso, and his toned, muscled arms. A Celtic tattoo peeks out from under his sleeve as he lifts the bottle to his mouth, his bicep bulging like a mountain at the move, and he looks so fuckable, my nipples bead. He's been at it for so many hours, I can almost feel the heat of his body all the way across the gym. My fingers itch to work on him, and I'm not even getting started on the rest of me. Let's just say that when he's black, I'm particularly aware of his "needs." And I can't wait to tend to them in a very good, girlfriendly way.

I'm already tingling in anticipation when a soft vibration nearby jerks my eyes to my cell phone, which I cast aside along with a water bottle. I pick up and read.

MELANIE: I'm having nightmares of that he-beast on your behalf! You recovered from those insects yet?

BROOKE: No. ☹ I can sometimes still feel the legs crawling on me! UGH! But I don't want Remington to know Scorpion fucked me up like this—I don't want him to fuck with our heads any more than he already has. But I feel shitty. Like, malaise. I go to the second bathroom as discreetly as possible at night and puke!

MELANIE: But why don't you want to tell Remy that HE-BEAST MUST DIE!

BROOKE: Mel! Because he WOULD do it!

MELANIE: GO RIPTIDE! KILL THE HE-BEAST!

BROOKE: No, Mel, I have to tell him I'm FINE. I'm trying to appease his caveman.

MELANIE: I know of no other way to appease cavemen but through food and sex, and I just felt bats in my stomach thinking of you getting to "appease" an agitated Riptide!

BROOKE: I know, it's such a HARD task! ☺♥ ?

MELANIE: OMG, where's my athlete friend, you whore? I miss you, fly me up soon!

MELANIE: Let him show you how much he loves you again by bringing up the BFF—I mean, what's the matter with him? He's got you and now he forgets about impressing you by flying the BFF in?

"Stop looking around and focus! She's not going anywhere, Tate," Coach barks as I text Melanie a farewell; then I hear the sounds he makes on the speed bag.

Thadumpthadumpthadump . . .

Today, we aren't alone in the gym.

Two gymnasts are training at the far end, and my stomach has not been too happy as they blatantly ogle him. They watched him when he was jumping rope. Then, they watched, their eyes almost popping out of their heads, when he was doing his pull overs, mountain climbers, and his upside-down ab work. My beast looks so sexy when he trains, those two have been gaping *all* morning and afternoon. One even fell on her butt for all the staring she was doing.

And I guess the problem with me now is that with every pretty woman I catch admiring him, I remember the groupies or whores and feel sick to my stomach again.

Exhaling as I lean forward into a downward dog yoga position, I hold it for a moment, then pass on to a cobra stretch—where I'm spread facedown on the mat with my back and neck arched backward—and I get a glimpse of him at the speed bag. There he is, punching and punching, a walking advertisement for sports and sex, his every muscle hot and engaged, powerfully striking. He swings his fists so fast, the ball never stops flapping.

He's sans T-shirt, and I can see all his muscles as they contract and relax. The sweatpants ride low on his hips, gifting me with a peek at his sexy star tattoo—god, it just drives me crazy. I start thinking about the way his erection somehow rises to tease it, his cock so tall it covers the ink when it's fully standing, and the memory pierces through me and heats me up in more ways than I'd like to be heated up right now. Aware that my nipples are beading with want, I squeeze my eyes shut for a moment.

Exhaling, I force myself to slide and stretch my legs out on the mat, first one and then the other, and once again.

Coach snarls, "You training or ogling today, Tate?"

Snapping my head back, I see Remy turn back to his bag, take position, lift his gloves, and slam so viciously hard that's it's the only thing I can hear in the gym. His punches.

"That's what I'm talking about! Who's that motherfucker you're killing?" Coach demands.

My skin tingles when Remington's voice explodes across the room as he yells back, "You know damn well who it is!"

"Who's that fucker you're going to send into a fucking coma?" Coach continues.

"He's fucking DEAD!"

"That's right! He took what belongs to you! Messed with you! Messed with your girl . . ."

Remington roars hard and he hits the bag, sending it crashing to the ground. He kicks it, and it launches into the air before it collides with the wall with a *boom*!

Riley chuckles as he comes over. "Would you say he's a tad pissed, B?" he teases me.

My stomach tangles when Remington looks up and straight at me. His chest jerks on each breath, his eyes bore into me, and I feel a little bit naked under that stare. I'd bet my life on the fact that, right now, Remington is fucking me in his head.

"In two more weeks Scorpion fights the same evenings we do. We could bump into him. You nervous?" Riley asks, briefly surveying the gymnasts as he talks to me.

Just the name Scorpion spikes my adrenaline and makes me want to run to the hills. I drop my face and do a pigeon yoga pose to open up my hips, then I switch legs and repeat the exercise. "Yeah, I'm nervous. I should say extra nervous, since I'm nervous every fight, but with that asshole around, let's make it ten times my normal nervous." I roll my eyes at myself, and Riley chuckles.

We've seemed to "make peace" by strategically avoiding talking about "it," even though I am actually dying to ask him and Pete what *exactly* went on. But do I want to know any more?

No.

We were broken up. I have no right. He doesn't even remember, with his bipolar disorder, and it's gone. It's *over*. I am his and he is mine.

"Heck, even I'm nervous, B. Scorpion's message was pretty clear," Riley tells me with a smirk. "It's *on*—out of the ring, and in it. And Rem's message only told the bastard his days are numbered. Nobody messes with his firecracker."

I straighten up at that; then I look at those sad surfer eyes, and I swear there's some enjoyment in there. I laugh. I just laugh. Because, honestly, these are full-grown men here. Men. But they are still . . . boys. And when I look across the impressive gymnasium at Remy, he's the biggest, sexiest, and strongest boy of all.

"Riley, you need to help me make sure that whatever happens, Scorpion does not mess with Remington's head. Both you and Pete need to watch out for that too. Do you hear me?"

"Yes, ma'am," he says, saluting like an army cadet. "Now go earn your keep."

"Ha-ha. I work just as hard as you do," I say.

"Yeah, but I don't get the royal treatment *you* do."

"Because you suck, and I rule."

"I'm not even going to answer that. I value my face too much." He smiles at something past my shoulder.

A tower of brawn right behind me, pulling the tapes off his hands. "I'd be happy to break it for you," he murmurs.

"I'll take a rain check on that, if you don't mind."

As Riley goes to help Coach clean up, Remington trains his black eyes on me, and I notice his nostrils flare as if he can scent me without even ducking his head, just looking at me.

"Ready?" He speaks in his I've-worked-out-for-hours-and-am-sexy-as-hell dehydrated voice as he strokes his fingers up the small of my back, and I'm not immune to any of it.

"Born ready," I say, a little breathlessly. I don't know what it is about the times he's manic, but I'm extra aware of the energy crackling around him when he's black. He's a powerhouse, but when he's black he feels like two. We both head to the small rehab room at the back of the gym. And when he puts his hand on my ass, I say nothing, but feel everything. Then, when he squeezes, it takes every effort in me not to turn around and grab his hard ass and squeeze that massive rock-hard flesh back.

"Up on the table, Riptide," I command. I just like ordering him around because he gives me this *whatever* look of amusement. Like he does now, like he's supremely entertained by me. He lies down on the table, which is much like a massage table, at the center of the small room. Nearby there's also a refrigerator, for meds and cold items which I'll raid later for his ice massage.

He spreads facedown first, and his body temp is so high after his workout, I can feel his heat before I even touch him.

"You feel okay?" I ask, my gaze caressing up the line of his spine. "Anything knot up? Bothering you?"

"I'd like to have my hands on you as soon as possible," he whisper-growls at me, and I bite the inside of my cheek.

"All right, but like they say, ladies first."

He groans. "Don't torture me, baby, I want to fuck you already."

I bend over and set a kiss on his ear. "It's not torture, try to relax," I whisper, and I really want him to relax, to focus on his body, so I curl my fingers around his shoulders. The breath hisses out through his teeth, and I also quietly hold my own—but our contact does that to me. Exhaling softly, I acclimate to him and start massaging with my fingers. He also acclimates to me and I know he's starting to relax when he groans softly.

We're so connected, I can't touch his skin without feeling delicious little ripples radiate through me. It sometimes feels as if I am tapping into that powerful source that makes Remington Tate *Remington Tate*. Every centimeter of my body becomes cognizant of his muscles and skin under my fingers—and of everything else about him. The way he smells right this second, of ocean and soap, and just him. The way his chest expands with his exertion. The way his hair is spiky and rumpled and wet.

I love working on him with my hands.

This is my job, but this is also my love.

I can't think of anything better than this.

I feel each muscle, one at a time, seeking their heat, digging deep into the belly of the muscle so that there is perfect blood flow into every part of his body. I massage and separate the fascia, kneading the muscle tissue with my fingers to provide good nourishment to the area. When the muscle is loosened, his blood, ripe with every nutrient of his healthy way of living, enters to help repair and grow that muscle.

Once I've rubbed him down on both sides, I go to the fridge so I can give him an ice massage. Ice massages are perfect for any knot or injury, but Remington loves them, and I sometimes give him one to speed general recovery.

There's a Styrofoam cup already in the freezer. It contains a frozen block of water inside, and I rub my palm over it several times, to smooth out the ice and make sure it won't nick his skin. Then I run it all over his muscles while I hold the back of the cup, almost like I'm sliding roll-on deodorant over his skin.

He lays there and lets me tend him, his sexy male pheromones clinging to his skin like sweat, his body so hot, the ice immediately begins melting. I watch the rivulets of water zigzag playfully along his broad back, and when he flips over, those rivulets do the same down the front of his hard chest.

My eyes follow them while my brain swims with thoughts of licking each of them up with my tongue, especially the ones that slide into his belly button, the ones that curl around his nipples. While I watch and mentally lick every beautiful inch of him, he watches me work on him, his gaze hot and tender and, somehow, grateful.

"I love the way you work out," I whisper.

"I love the way you work me."

❤ ❤ ❤

BY THE TIME we ride up in our hotel elevator, we're both tired—and I'm especially so. I just haven't recovered from the fucking Gift and I'm tired enough to skip dinner and head straight to bed.

After eight hours of working out, Remy has punched most of his speedy energy off for now. He leans back against the elevator wall with an arm loosely draped around my hips, while I half stand, half sag against his side, resting part of my head against the side of his throat.

"Cold shower, eat a cow, see you tomorrow," Coach says as he exits on his floor.

"I'm on it," Remington answers in his low and powerful voice.

"Good night, Coach," I say.

And as soon as we're alone in the elevator, Remington ducks his head to scent me.

The press of his frame against my back is all hard, hot muscle. He exhales warmly against my skin, then licks the back of my ear, and an electrical jolt surges through me. He then nuzzles his way across the back of my head, to the back of my other ear, and he scents me there too. My nipples bead painfully against my top, and at the first lick of his tongue across the back of my ear, need rips through me. He holds me snug against his big body, and whispers into my ear in a thick, appreciative tone, "I watched you stretching. Were you doing it for your muscles' sake or for mine?"

As his words run through me like a sexual caress, he slides one open hand down the front of my body, and I shudder as he cups me over my Lycra pants. "Brooke? Was it for your sake or mine?" He licks and sucks a bare spot of skin on the back of my neck, igniting a painful thrumming inside me.

"Yours," I moan.

He chuckles softly as he slides that hand upward. "Did you enjoy watching me work out?" His husky question presses every sexy button inside me as he fills his palm with one breast over my tank top.

"Me and the rest of the gym," I say breathlessly.

Here comes his chuckle again. Sexy. Deep.

His fingers coast up and down my bare arm, wreaking all sorts of havoc in me. Lava percolates inside me when he adds teeth to my earlobe and gently tugs. Suddenly, I can't bear it; I turn in his arms and, god, he smells so good I feel light-headed.

He's in a clean T-shirt, his body emanating heat like a roiling volcano, and I fist my hands in the soft material to brace myself as I kiss his neck, licking him hungrily and desperately. His taste sends dull pangs of want to places I didn't even know I had.

He growls softly in satisfaction and lowers his head to buzz my mouth with his. Then he cups my ass in his big hand and squeezes me as the elevator climbs the rest of the way. I rub my hands up his chest, over his T-shirt, and keep recklessly tasting him.

"Remy," I moan. I press my nipples into his chest and undulate coaxingly, and he chuckles softly in my ear as he clutches my ass harder in his hands.

"Do you want me?" he prods, his breath hot and cajoling against my lips as he presses his mouth to mine.

"Yes . . ."

He slides his hand between my ass cheeks and, from behind, suddenly strokes his thumb over my clit through my Lycra pants. My knees nearly fail.

"Are you wet?" he entices.

"Remy . . ." I can only say, my sex aching painfully between my legs.

"Are you wet in your pussy?" he asks in my ear, sinuously dipping his tongue into the crevice.

"Yes. God, yes."

"Let me see." He flips me around so that we're both facing the doors, then eases his fingers into both my pants and panties and caresses me for a brief second, verifying my wetness, slipping his finger into my swollen entry, making me gasp, rock my hips, and moan, until he says, in a husky and satisfied whisper, "Hmmm."

Ping.

Hmmm . . .

It's a sound between us, and when he says it, it means he wants to eat me.

All of me.

About a million cells in my body quiver with need, and my heart rate kicks up as the doors roll open. He swoops me up on his shoulder and grabs my butt on our way to our suite, and I laugh in surprise at the caveman move and kick in the air.

"Diane's going to be in our room already!" I squeak, but he squeezes my butt like it doesn't matter and carries me inside, dipping his thumb, once again from behind, between my legs, so it's swiping over my clit.

My pussy swells with need, and I fall utterly still, letting him rub me.

My eyes roll to the back of my head as he rubs and rubs, his shoulders hard and strong under my stomach as he carries me.

"Hey guys," Diane says as he carries me into the suite, and before I can answer, he heads directly to the master bedroom, saying over his shoulder, "We're not hungry yet—we'll be out in an hour."

And he slams the door shut behind us.

SIX

FLYING TO BOSTON

On our way to Boston, I have the opportunity to get better ac-quainted with the jet's toilet. Half the flight I spend puking in it.

When I come out after my first round, Remington's scowl greets me, while Diane ushers me to her seat up at the front where she has a plate of melon, papaya, nuts, and cottage cheese waiting. I love papaya. It's got fiber and loads of vitamin A, and is great for the digestive system. There's a lemon wedge on the side, which I usually love squeezing onto the papaya too. My body has a different idea, though, and the scent of papaya . . .

About to barf in my mouth, I shove the plate aside and run to the bathroom, lift the toilet lid, and heave again. Diane imme-diately appears at the door, and I hear her speak to someone just outside. Of course I have a general idea of who that someone is.

"Don't let him come in here," I plead to her between heaves.

Remy has been speedy for over two weeks now.

He called himself the "king of the world" a couple of days ago, followed by "king of the jungle" and then "king of the punching bags" and then, that evening, he asked me to be his queen, and I laughed. But at the same time, he looked so charming and adorable with his dimples that it almost felt like he was proposing.

He's so energetic. He's been wearing us all down, but at least Pete—circles under his eyes and all—is happy that he hasn't switched to depression. Manic Remington fights like a gladiator, and lately, he seems in a very good mood as long as he gets to kick the shit out of people and have a lot of sex—which I am more than happy to provide, since I've been about as hot and lusty for him as I always am or—strangely—maybe a little more.

As I flush the toilet and try to breathe again, Diane shoots me a smile that tells me she thinks Remy is adorable for worrying, but her smile vanishes when she takes a good look at my complexion.

I really feel like shit, so I *must* look like shit. Funny that no matter how old I get, when I feel this sick, I'm flashed back to my soup days and I miss my mom. She would never let us eat in bed, except when we were sick, and then we got a tray with warm soup.

"Could it be a stomach bug?" Diane feels my forehead. "No fever. Would you like some mineral water? Or Alka-Seltzer?" she asks.

"Maybe some sparkling water," I admit, flushing in embarrassment when I think that the entire team will now know about me and my regurgitating. "Do you have any gum?"

She nods and watches me as I quickly try to rearrange my ponytail. "You should stay in this afternoon," she suggests.

"Miss his training? Never!" I gasp.

"You look so pale, Brooke."

I pinch both my cheeks and add a bright smile. "There."

Chiding me with a shake of her head, she leaves and then returns with a packet of gum, and a small hotel travel bag containing a plastic toothbrush and tube of Colgate. "I collect these from everywhere we go. Shampoos too," she tells me proudly.

"Oh, you're a lifesaver, Diane."

As I brush my teeth at the small faucet, I start to seriously wonder what's wrong with me, and when I come out, he's on the edge of his seat, elbows on his knees, his black eyes fixed on the plane restroom door.

Added to his, three other pairs of worried stares follow me as I make a straight line for my seat. I feel so weak and dehydrated, I fall into the cushions and sit right on top of my travel bag. Remington pulls it out from under me and sends it flying to the end of the bench, then he firmly cups the back of my head and tips my head up to his. "What's wrong with you?"

"I don't know. I haven't been myself since the stings."

I sense, more than see, Diane's presence nearby, and she seems to be studying us, though that's neither here nor there; I just want to be coddled. I want to crawl into Remington's lap and stay there, with my arms around his neck, and my nose in his throat, sniffing the hell out of him, but I'm too tired to move from my seat, so I just tuck my face into one of his hands and close my eyes for a moment and smell his soap.

"Brooke, are you certain it began with the stings?"

Both he and I turn to Diane at the same time, and she wears this devious smile I have never seen before. Her merry brown eyes fix on Remington, rather than me, and when she speaks again, her voice trembles with something that sounds like excitement. "Have you asked Brooke whether you're going to be a dad?"

Excuse me? I think I just choked on, and then swallowed, a bowling ball. By the time I feel a certain pair of familiar black eyes staring at *me*, my lungs feel like they're expanded to the limit.

He waits until I slide my gaze over to his, his voice hardly audible through the plane's engines. "Am I?"

Holy shit . . . *am I?*

Pregnant?

The mere word makes the bowling ball in my stomach double in weight. Is he worried that I am? I stare into his face and . . .

nothing. Pure handsomeness, and that's all. I can't read him with those dark eyes.

"*No,*" I stress. All my inner walls shoot up in defense mode as the utter fear of what something like this would do to us takes hold. "I have birth control. I've had it for years. It's been making my period fade so I don't really know when it's my time anymore. . . ." I pause when Diane wiggles her eyebrows at me. "I'm *not*," I assure her grinning face, glowering now.

She brings over a bottle of sparkling water, and Remington takes it from her outstretched hand.

"I can't be. I couldn't be," I say, addressing only him now.

"I want someone to look at you." He opens the bottle for me, then passes it over as he turns his head to the front of the plane. "Pete, I want someone to look at Brooke right fucking now!"

"Right on, sir," Pete answers. "I'll make some calls as soon as we land."

"Make it a female, with a perfect record and experience, not some newbie!" he adds.

"I don't want anybody to look at me," I protest.

He seems to be getting extra speedy, so I drive my hands through his silky black hair to appease him. He exhales noisily through his nose, and when I sense him start to calm, I bury my nose in his throat. Not sure why, but this is the only place where I don't feel sick or nauseous, with my lungs filled with pure Remy.

"You're getting looked at," he says gruffly into my hair, then he snakes his arms around me and pulls me onto his lap. I almost moan in gratitude, I feel so ridiculously safe in his arms.

He lowers his head to smell my neck as if to calm himself with my scent as well, then his roaming lips trail to my ear, where he speaks softly and gently to me, gaining momentum with each word, "If those scorpions caused any permanent damage, I swear I'm going to kill that motherfucker and nail his head *to a goddamned pike!*"

"Why don't I at least run out to get her a pregnancy test?" Diane asks.

Remington assesses her with shuttered black eyes. And I can't help but notice, with a little bit of panic, that they're not glinting at all, and they're certainly not laughing.

"I'm not pregnant. I can't be," I insist. My arm thingy birth control can't fail me! Could it?!

Extra slowly, he rakes his gaze over my body, running it from the top of my head to my ponytail, the swell of my breasts under my comfortable sky-blue tank top, my tight pink jeans, and slowly back up, his expression unreadable.

"What? Do you think I am?" I ask in disbelief, and before he can answer, I add, "Remy, a baby would be very scary right now."

He scoffs. "Who's scared of a baby?"

"I am. You adorable man. Me."

He chucks my chin and smirks. "Maybe I'll take it if it looks like you."

"You won't take shit because there's nothing to take!" He observes me for a couple of heartbeats, and I vow he looks kind of . . .

"You look smug, don't you," I accuse, hardly believing what I'm seeing.

He lifts one sleek black eyebrow.

"You *do*. You look smug thinking you got me pregnant when my birth control says it's near impossible."

He laughs in that deep, throaty way of his that makes my skin come alive and all the little hairs on my arms rise, then he kisses my lips in that boyfriend way of his where the kiss isn't meant to arouse us—but just to express some sort of connection—then he surveys me with those adorable black eyes that are now shining very, very much in entertainment.

"I'd rather you have a baby of mine in you than be sick with his poison," he half whispers, half growls.

"Neither is the case," I assure. And yet, why am I holding a two-week puke-fest?

Shit.

Fuck.

Shitfuck!

He flattens me lightly to the hardness of his chest and rubs my back, quickly, up and down, then tells me quietly, his soft words packed with warning, "I'm going to tuck you in bed when we get to the hotel, and you're not moving from it. I don't care what's wrong. You're not moving from that bed until somebody looks at you and tells me you're going to be all right."

"Ha! There's no way I'm staying in bed all day, not even if I feel bad. I've never missed a day of work in my life."

He kisses my ear again in that boyfriend way I'm starting to like so much. "Then you haven't lived properly."

❤ ❤ ❤

SO I'M NOT only missing work and living on the edge now, but I just peed on a stick.

Pete got us an appointment with an experienced male gynecologist for tomorrow, and Remington is growing impatient; he even forgave Pete the male-doctor part, but he won't wait that long to know. Of course, Mr. Speedy wouldn't wait. I've told him a thousand times I am *not* pregnant, and the more I say I am not, the more smug he looks. Now, he seems more excited about me peeing on a stick than I am.

When I come out of the bathroom wearing his black T-shirt, I find him shadowboxing in the room.

I watch from the threshold, admiring his swings. He knows exactly where his fist goes, and even when he gives the impression of relaxation, I know the power behind each swing is equal to a bulldozer.

Leaning on the doorframe, the athlete in me can't help but admire the athlete in him. I've known thousands of sportsmen in my life. But I have never, ever met anyone like him. His speed. Agility. How he ducks. Swings. The way he fights seems to be instinctive, and yet at the same time, I can also see in both his training regimen and fights that his head is always in the game.

I think about my parents for a moment. They know I'm on tour working, though they have no idea how deeply I've involved myself with the man who hired me. The day I left Seattle, my main concern was whether or not Remington would take me back. I didn't even consider telling my parents that I was in love. That I met *the* guy—the one I never thought I'd find. The one that made me fall harder than I ever thought I could fall. I know that they trust me to be levelheaded. Throughout the years, I've proven to be the most responsible of their offspring, but if this test is positive . . . Ohmigod, if it's positive, it will scream "reckless!" all over the place.

My god, what if I am pregnant? And a little baby Tate comes into my life like Remington did, taking it over, telling me, "You know what? You might not know you need me, want me, and will damn well love me, but here I am."

"You check yet?"

His voice jerks me back to awareness. My stomach tangles from the nerves as I stare at him. He's been running his fingers through his hair, and every time he does that, he seems to dishevel it even more. His eyes are dark, but the light coming in from the sunset illuminates the tiny blue flecks in his dark eyes. He looks warm and sporty in his sweatpants and hoodie—boyish—and the thought of carrying his baby makes me feel hot and restless and very, very unprepared.

"Brooke?" he softly insists.

My stomach turns once more. A part of me is curious, and another part doesn't want to know and all it wants is to keep the status quo. Just us. Remy and Brooke.

"Did you or did you not pee on a stick, baby?" he prods when I continue to hesitate.

"I did! I told you I did!" I groan as I go get the test, then I bring it back to the nightstand and read the instructions a third time. Then I gather my courage and put on my imaginary big-girl pants as I peel off the cover and peer into the screen.

The butterflies go off inside me.

My parents flash before my mind. Mom and Dad. Another generation. Maybe Nora told them that I'm seeing the man I work for, but if they don't even know I'm with him, a baby on the way will leave them in need of therapy for a month. I shake off the thought, because honestly, what's important now is what he thinks. *He. Remington Tate.* Your one and only *Riptide.* Possibly, my baby-daddy soon?

Shit.

This can't be happening.

But it is.

I turn around to see him, and a whole truckful of love slams into my heart.

He's jumping in the room, swinging his fists in the air, up and down. He hooks, jabs, frowns, and slams into his imaginary boxing partner—who seems to be a fast one, by the way Remington is jabbing and hitting back.

He is mesmerizing.

Ripped, raw, and so real. He is all mine—or at least, that's all I want in the world. For him to be mine.

Calmly, as if sensing me, he stops swinging and lifts one of his sleek black brows that always seem permanently slanted. "What's it say?"

"It says . . ." I stare at the small screen, and no, I'm not seeing double. I mean, I am, but it's not a hallucination.

I think rocks have replaced my lungs, for I can't breathe as I set the test down at the foot of the bed and walk over to him. Step by step, I stare into those black-gray eyes with the blue flecks that watch me approach in growing curiosity. Lifting my hands, I hold his scruffy jaw and really look up at him as he looks down at me, except I'm perfectly sober, and he's perfectly amused.

"Remington, don't forget this," I anxiously whisper, my chest swelling with need of his support. "You're black right now, and I don't want you to forget what I'm going to tell you. I need all of you here *with me*."

"Hey." His dimple vanishes as he frames my face in his huge, callused hands. "I got you."

"God, please do."

"Yeah, I do. I got you. Now what's wrong here? Hmm? If you aren't, then we figure out what's wrong with you. If you are . . ."

Jerking away before he can finish, I run over, grab the test, and bring it to him, my heart picking up a wild rhythm. I want his strength. I want his confidence. Even when he's volatile, he is always so. Damned. Strong! I need that now.

Never taking his eyes off me, he takes the little stick I extend out.

But god, he might not be smiling for long.

My voice is calm and surprisingly steady. "Two lines means, supposedly, that I am."

His eyes stay locked on mine for a moment longer, and then his lashes sweep downward as he turns the test screen slightly into the sunlight.

My own anxiety eats me on the inside as I wait for a reaction. We were joking on the plane, but he's serious now. As serious as I am. His profile is completely unreadable as I take in the perfect form of his nose, how elegant it is. His mouth, relaxed and full, so freaking beautiful. His eyebrows, drawing slightly together in puzzlement as he deciphers the lines. Impossible for me to make out any emotion whatsoever.

When he sets the stick aside, my breath stops in my lungs, and when he lifts his dark head, nothing else exists in the world but this moment. He raises his eyes to mine, and my stomach wrings as hard as my heart does in my chest.

What if he doesn't want me like this?

What if this is too much for us?

What if we're strong enough to love each other, but not strong enough to love someone else—together?

What if we are not *ready*?

Our eyes meet. He studies my reaction while I study his even more desperately. And out of the thousand things I could have imagined to see in his face, I never imagined I would see what I see. He's . . . pleased. No. He's more than pleased. His eyes glow as if he were sexually hungry, but what he's hungry for is something else. Then his dimples flash, and he laughs, and his perfect happiness explodes like a rainbow in me.

"Come here." He picks me up and lifts me so that my abdomen is on his face, and he smacks a noisy kiss on me. I squeal when he flings me down on the bed and hovers over me.

The sight of those two dimples on his scruffy jaw delights me so much, I start laughing. "You're a crazy man! You're the only man I know who throws his pregnant girlfriend onto a bed!"

"I'm the *only* man," he says, "as far as I know. There's only one man in your world, and it's me."

"All right, but don't tell my dad I agreed so easily . . ." I rub his shoulders, and he frames my face and settles down over me. If I thought he looked smug before, he gives a new meaning to the word now.

"Brooke Dumas pregnant with my baby," he says slyly. His hair is standing up so much, I shove my hand in and watch my fingers play with it. A ripple of joy rushes over me. "My head is reeling. Kiss me."

He lowers his head and tenderly mates his tongue with mine, tracing the flesh of my lips first, and then stroking my tongue with his so deliciously, all my taste buds awaken. He eases back to caress the back of one curled finger down the side of my face. "Make it look like you."

"You're the one who gave this to me."

"No, *you're* giving this to me."

"All right, we're both such giving souls."

His laugh is so marvelous, it's catching as he rolls to his side and gathers me in his arms and starts raining a bunch of slow kisses on me. "You're mine now, from the top of your pretty dark head to the soles of your little feet." He caresses my face with his callused thumb as he kisses the tops of my eyelids. "Don't even think about leaving me again or I'll come after you and so help me god, I'm going to tie you to where I am, and where I sleep, and where I eat. Do you hear me, Brooke Dumas?"

My already sensitive breasts bead under my bra, and I nod breathlessly. Shit, I love how possessive he is—and he's doubly so whenever he's black. I feel myself grow wet between my legs. "There isn't a single part of me that doesn't know I'm yours," I assure him, and I take his hand and set it on my heart.

He clamps his jaw, and a spark of primitive awareness flashes in his eyes as he clenches his fingers around my breast. We start kissing. We start hard, and then go softer. We both slide closer at the same time, needing the contact like oxygen. He whispers in my ear, "*I'm so crazy about you,*" and as he nuzzles the top of my head, I clutch him close and gasp, "*I love you so much.*"

Looking extremely satisfied, almost like he does when he's given me several multiple orgasms in a row, he turns me over and adjusts me, holding my stomach as he starts nuzzling the back of my neck while my mind continues reeling, and I imagine a little Remy running the way little boys run, clumsy and stumbling, and I touch my stomach as I let my lion pet me.

SEVEN

SIN CITY

We're in Sin City now, and his eyes are back to his usual electric, piercing blue.

He woke up fully blue after he found out we're expecting. We. Are. *Expecting*. We didn't sleep that night. Remy was hard, and having his way with me, all night. He fucked me, sucked me, made me suck him, fondled me with his fingers, put his hand over mine so that I fondled him while he fingered me.

The next day, we were both well-fucked and sleepless when we ended up with the doctor who removed my contraceptive capsule. The kind man reminded me that after five years, any "arm thingy" needs to be changed. Mine was going on five and a half years, embarrassingly, and I admit I felt completely stupid for having completely forgotten to count, especially when I'd assured Remy I was on birth control.

But then I catch a glimpse of his twinkling, and *smug*, blue eyes as they silently tease me that I did it on purpose.

"Well, *you* could've used a condom," I whispered with a scowl.

"With you?" he scoffed. Then he poked my ribs. "You're mine."

"Your birth control hasn't been working for some time now, and it takes time for the body to increase its own hormonal production, although you seem to be doing just fine," the doctor had said, and then he told us my due date. Which was thankfully almost two months after the season was to end.

I swear Remy looked so adorable at the doctor's office, strong and athletic in his sports attire, sitting in a chair by mine, listening attentively to what the doctor said. A lot of the terms could have been Chinese to both of us. But he looked curious and concerned about me being able to run. And about how much should I eat? How many grams of protein? How many carbs? The doctor seemed confused at his need for specific gram counts, and I wanted to kiss my guy just for going to the appointment with me.

Lie. I didn't want to just kiss him. I wanted to press my breasts against his chest until my nipples stopped aching and I wanted to blend my mouth to his, impale me down on his cock, and ride him to Australia and back.

If Remy is crazy aroused with my pregnancy, I won't even begin to describe what the combination of his carnal blue eyes and my rioting hormones do to me. Now he's determined that I go sniff food that doesn't make me vomit so I can start eating for two. I'm worried that he'll fatten me up to elephant size, so if he wants me eating, I'd rather eat fresh and filling foods than empty junk. And here we are, Diane and I, wandering through the Whole Foods on Las Vegas Boulevard.

Outside the store, there are billboards of gaming, women, and booze. This is Las Vegas, baby! But none of us are doing anything that needs to "stay here" at all. Remington is kicking ass at the gym, and Coach has actually upped his training hours.

He's packing on more muscle and getting more ripped, and the entire team agrees that Scorpion deserves nothing but Riptide's finest at this season's final. So my beast has been training nine hours while I indulge in a bit of extra sleep in the mornings and then join him at the gym before he's done. He's eating protein like mad, and Coach has put him on L-glutamine shakes to preserve muscle mass, so now I'm also helping Diane choose the best foods for his body and mind.

Pete says if Scorpion wants to fuck with his mind again, we must make sure Remy sleeps right, exercises right, and eats right—so that he's as stable as possible. Most especially he needs lots of omega-3 fats.

Today, we get so many fresh goods for my T. rex, that Diane and I need two carts. We stay all along the edges of the store buying fruits, vegetables, the best cheeses, dark chocolate, sprouted grains, and nuts. Then we head to the protein part and order fresh Alaskan king salmon, king among fish and as toxin free as fish hopefully get.

While we wait for several pounds of fish to be packaged, I inspect one of the lovely heads of broccoli we've got in one of our carts. I used to call them "little trees" and Melanie called them "green things," which was what she called anything green—the only reason she ate veggies was because of the color. Mel loves color.

"My grandmother taught me all I know about food. She cured my grandfather's depression with diet," Diane tells me.

We order some wild-caught shrimp as well, and anything else that is wild caught and fresh, and the counter guy packs it all up.

"I had depression once," I suddenly tell her, my eye on one dead fish eye. "It's not a fun thing to have."

"You? Brooke, I could never tell looking at you. Did something happen to bring it on?"

"I guess my life changed before I was ready for it to."

I shrug and smile sadly at her. "I couldn't believe the things that went through my head in those days," I admit. "It all seemed so pointless. So dreary. It's hard to think anyone can get out of that alone."

"How did you?" she presses.

"I don't know, I think a small part of me realized I was not my brain. It's just another organ, like our kidneys or our livers."

She's perfectly sober, nodding in understanding, so I add, even though it sounds crazy, "My brain wanted me to die, but in some surreal way, I could feel my soul fighting it."

Sometimes I can't stop thinking and comparing: While I was depressed once in my life, for about two months, Remington goes through it continually, cycling again and again, rising and falling. Anyone who goes through this is a warrior. So are their loved ones, who fight with them. I swear, Remington's soul is so strong . . . I know that when he sinks into the dark vortex, it's his soul that conquers it. All that simmering energy inside him is too powerful not to rise back up. Like a . . . riptide.

"How did that feel?" Diane whispers as the man finally packs us several bags of ice.

"You know how you get any visual or audible stimulus, or when you touch something, your brain dictates a response to this sensual stimuli," I tell her. "I see you, and my brain immediately sends out a response at the sight of you, which in me is comfort and happiness. But in my depression, I saw things, normal things, and the responses my brain would fling out would not match. It was crazy."

"It sounds crazy!" she agrees.

I smile and we take the ice the man offers, say thank you, and push our carts down the lane to the deli meat and cheeses. I add, "The way I see it is as if our brains were the doctors, and the adrenals are the pharmacies that fill up the prescriptions. You could see a commercial with laughing children, and an unbalanced mind will quickly prescribe anxiety and tears over laughing children. Even if it logically makes no sense—it doesn't matter. That's the prescription your body was given."

"I'm really sorry, Brooke. I'd never really thought about what all that must be like."

We add some organic goat cheese to our carts, some coconut milk, almond milk, and whole milk. "They put me on pills, but it worsened pretty bad. The only thing that got me out of it was my family and Melanie, exercise and sun."

"I know our guy gets it several times a year," Diane whispers as she inspects the label on a container of organic Greek yogurt. "I knew there was something about him; I just hadn't known the diagnosis until the guys told me the last time he was hospitalized."

Suddenly I'm transported, once again, to the hospital, to Remington trying to tell me something, and me running away . . . and then him, trying to cope, with a thousand women in his bed.

I swear I ache deep, so deep, right where my soul is.

Before I know it, I've wrapped my hand around my abdomen, as though I can feel him there. In me. In our baby.

"He's an amazing fighter," Diane tells me admiringly, her eyes glowing with praise. "All the effort he puts into being well. You've got to have noticed Remington never eats something that isn't completely right for his body. Not ever."

My stomach rumbles as I remember his healthy mountainous breakfast and compare it to the mineral water and crackers I had. But I can't seem to get anything into my stomach in the morning, not even my mouth-watering seedless organic dates. But of course I've noticed how well Remy eats. He eats the cleanest foods, and keeps his body in the most natural state possible. I *love* this. I love how he is, and how he treats his body kindly with food after demanding the most from it for hours and hours of each day.

And then I look at Diane, and I really see her, see how well she gets him, this woman almost in her forties, with her big smile and kind eyes, and all the aura of comfort she emanates, and all the warmth she instills into every one of our hotel suites, and I know how well she takes care of him, how she could very well be the closest thing to a mother Remington has ever had. Impulsively, I let go of my cart and hug her, whispering, "Thank you. For taking care of him, Diane."

"Oh, bah! How can I not, when he takes care of me so well? If you think I take good care of him, I can't say enough about all the things he's done for us, anytime he hears we need anything. He even went to my mother's funeral."

She pauses at my look of surprise, and as we start down to the cashier and start unloading, she adds, "He doesn't even have a mother, not a *real* one, but he knew I cared about mine, and he flew across three states to the funeral for me. He didn't say a word—he just hugged me in the end—but just him being there . . ."

Her voice cracks unexpectedly, and I understand so much how Remy's quiet show of affection gets to her that my throat feels tight too.

"We're so excited about the baby," she blurts out, changing the subject. "All of us. Pete. Riley. Coach. We're so excited about this little baby. We think it's the universe giving back something good and pure to Remy, we really do."

She comes around my cart as if she wants to make contact with the baby somehow, and then she hesitates before touching me. I reach for her hand and slowly spread it on my flat stomach. I whisper to her, "I never knew how much I wanted this baby until I knew he was coming."

Her brows quirk up in complete intrigue. "He?"

I just have this feeling in my gut. I don't know if it's that sixth sense females are supposed to have. If it's the way I instinctively envision a little Remy in my head when I think about this baby. I don't know why, or how I think I know, but it feels so certain to me, as certain as I am right now of his father's love, that I nod excitedly. "*He.*"

BOSTON IS COMPLETELY sucked in by Riptide.

Young college students cram the arena, and the girls? The girls are the noisiest, jumpiest group of young women I've ever encountered. They're crushing on him so bad that all my jealousy, which I've come to realize is magnified to the tenth power by my pregnancy hormones, has been fully unleashed inside me. Girls scream, and I even hear them talk about him close behind, talking about how big his hands are and what that means.

Pete also seems to hear that, and he chuckles at my side and shakes his curly head.

Across the ring and to the left, a group of friends wear red shirts with each of his letters stamped on one, and they're all practicing standing up at the same time, so that everyone can see they spell RIPTIDE!

There's even an exclamation mark for the poor friend who didn't get a letter.

By the time his fight approaches, I've already observed each and every one of these ladies with my jaw clamped, and then, suddenly, I love them because they love him too and he *deserves* the adoration.

What do I want? For them to cheer for an asshole like Scorpion? Hell no! So there. I think I've conquered my jealousy nicely for the evening.

In fact, I conquer it so nicely that I'm feeling as jumpy as the fans when they announce him. "Riiiiiptiiiiiiiiide!!" the announcer yells, with all the enthusiasm I swear every announcer I've heard reserves for him. "The one and only, people!! The ONE and ONLY!"

He appears like a beautiful red bolt of lightning and then hops up into the ring. The man is strong as an ox but aerodynamic as hell, and as he jerks off his robe and I see it flutter in the air as he passes it to Riley, I can almost feel it on my skin. The satin on me, how I love the way it hugs me, and the way it smells of him.

"And now, Joey 'the Spider' MANN! Who has terrified his opponents tonight!"

Before the Spider-Mann can take the ring, Remington looks at me, his blue eyes burning hot. Desire swells between my legs. Last night flashes through my head. I know what he's thinking of—I can feel it inside me. I don't know what connects me to him, but something does, and as the testosterone spins through his body I can tell that he's primed to fight and thinking of me watching him. And it turns him on. And he's going to fight, like he does, and then fuck me right after. Like he likes to. Oh god, I can't even wait. I can blame my pregnancy all I want, but the one who is truly to blame for setting me on fire with the merest look is *him*.

"That motherfucker gets high on you," Pete says.

"He's got this," I answer. Remy tells me that a fight is half head, half body, and maybe he's right, but when you see Remington fight, I'd bet all of myself on the fact that he fights with his whole heart. My heart whomps harder just now because of him as I watch him tap gloves with his opponent as they both get ready.

The fighting bell sounds with that familiar *ting* and the public goes quiet. It doesn't really matter how many times I've seen him fight, I'm always mesmerized by the way he moves. They both go to center, warming up. I know Remington's strategy is different with every opponent. He plays with some. He goes straight to the punch with others. Sometimes he tires them out and saves his swings for the heavy-handed opponents, but today he starts hitting fast, so fast, I hear the popping sounds go *poo poo poof!* sending Spider-Mann—the man who'd been terrifying his opponents tonight—stumbling back within the first minute.

"*We love you, Riptide!!*" the R-I-P-T-I-D-E! girls scream. "*Knock him out for us!*"

"Although every time you're here, he fights like a lunatic," Pete adds.

"Lunatic" is not even the word. He's a machine.

The fight is in full swing and my tummy's twisting motions hardly let me pull in a good breath. His muscles ripple as he hooks with his left, then covers. Spider-Mann misses, and Remy coun- terattacks. He jabs several times with both right and left, then fin- ishes off with a straight punch that slams into Spider-Mann like a fast-moving wall.

Spider-Mann rocks.

Remington bounces back and lets him breathe.

The other man charges.

Remington feints and his hapless opponent swings and swings, missing every time as Remy ducks and comes back up to punch him in the gut, the ribs, then the jaw. By the time he uses his most powerful punch and hooks with his right, Spider-Mann is sweaty, bloody, and dead tired. He stumbles.

I watch Remy wait for him to get back up, and I'm sure that all the females in the stadium are screaming and ogling the same thing I am. How drops of sweat slide down Remington's muscled torso. How the vine tattoos on his arms glisten with a thin sheen of perspiration, and they look as inky black as his hair. How those sexy dimples flash as he smiles to himself every time he rocks his victim's center.

The R-I-P-T-I-D-E! girls talk to each other in between their screaming, like Mel and I do when we see him fight. Two of them, the P and the T, are jumping together, hugging each other because I'll bet the lust is just too much.

Oh, god, it's even too much for *me*. And supposedly, he's mine. But I just can't believe it. I see him, I touch him, I kiss him, I love him, and ninety-nine point nine percent of me can't believe some- one as elusive, complex, and male as him could belong to anyone— even if he loves me.

One right hook and a noisy splat on the canvas later, Reming- ton's arm is being held up in the air by the ringmaster. Chest heav- ing, hungry blue eyes see me, eyes that singe me down to my very bones. He doesn't smile. His nostrils flare. My heart pounds and my entire body prepares for what I see coming in his eyes.

"Do you all want more?" I hear yelled through the speakers. "Are you ready for MORE?"

The public screams, the R-I-P-T-I-D-E! girls scream, and Remington keeps looking at me as he catches his breath, his eyes brilliant blue and stripping me in my seat, and I'd bet everything that I own on the fact that he's fucking me in his head. My sensitized breasts grow even heavier, and when he takes on his next opponent, my sex floods and grips as I see his muscles flex, the way he strategizes with that brain of his.

I'm dying to have him all to myself tonight, his tongue in my mouth, doing the things it does, him inside me, riding me hard and fast or slow and deep. . . . I just want to cuddle with my lion and give him all the love nobody in the world ever has given him but me.

The crowd shrieks, "Gooooo, Riptide!!!!!"

They want the excitement he always delivers, and I'm certain Remington wants to deliver. He glances at me, and I don't know what he's expecting to see in my gaze, but whatever it is, he seems to get it. He glances at his next opponent, a young fighter whom I've never seen before, and before I know it, with the speed of light, he delivers three fast blows, to the side, the center, and finishes with a hook up his jaw—and he falls splat.

"YES!" Pete hisses, pumping his arm into the air. "YESYES YESSSSS!"

The entire room is screaming, "Riptide!!!" while I sit motionless in my chair.

The pain starts like a throb, and it progresses into a cramp. I put my arms around my stomach and shift uncomfortably.

"Riiiiptiiiiiiiiiiiiiiiide, folks! Once again, I give you, Riiiiiptide!!!!!!"

His arm is yanked up in victory, and I notice the open gash in the center of his plump bottom lip. He flashes his dimples at me, his eyes twinkling, and I'm dying to lick up that drop of blood and put salve on it. Then the cramp feels like a pinch and I fold over a little, and when they bring out his next opponent, I'm not even watching. I feel more than a little sick.

My lungs constrict as I glance up and see every possible muscle in existence working as he fights, his arms corded and flexing. I see him, but I keep retreating into my head. Worried sick. Wondering what's happening to me.

"Pete, I need to go to the bathroom right now," I say in a voice I've never heard before. It sounds scared, truly scared, and it trembles. But he stands with his eyes on the ring and distractedly follows me to the filthy makeshift bathrooms.

There, I wait in line, standing there for a couple of minutes, and when it's my turn to go into the little plastic house, I pull down my panties—which feel gooey—and I see they're soaked in red, as if I'm having a bad period. "Oh, god," I say.

I drag in a thousand calming breaths, but they do nothing to actually calm me, and instead a nauseating, sinking feeling of despair takes over. For minutes, I try to settle down, then I come out and at least *try* to appear put together until after the fight. Pete grins at me. "Dude, I've never seen someone puke as much as you do. How many pounds have you lost?"

"Let's just go sit," I say. I walk slowly and slightly hunched over, because standing hurts even worse, and instinctively my body seems to want me to curl into myself. I lower myself to my seat with extreme caution, while Remington is still up there, his name being screamed. "*Remy!!*" they call.

He seems to be waiting for another opponent, his head turned in Pete's and my direction as if he'd been waiting for us to return to our seats. He winks when he sees me. Then his sleek eyebrows pull low over his eyes and he looks at me more closely.

Suddenly he grabs the ring ropes and jumps down, and the public comes alive when they realize he is up to his usual mischief, like he always is when he climbs out of the ring. *"Rem-ing-ton! Rem-ing-ton! Rem-ing-ton!"* the crowd chants, and when they realize he's headed toward me—and that all that tower of brawn and strength and testosterone is coming my way—they change their tune to *"Kiss, kiss, kiss!"*

He swings me up in his arms.

The public goes crazy and my heart does too.

But he looks down at me, alert and on edge. "What's the matter?"

"I'm bleeding," I say tearfully.

❤ ❤ ❤

THE NEXT HALF hour goes by in a blur.

"Get the car," Remington instructs Pete as he carries me out of the arena.

The word "Riptide!" still rings in the background when we go outside, into the fresh Boston air, and to the parking lot of the warehouse hosting the Underground tonight. He tucks me into the back of the Escalade, and Pete gets behind the wheel, punching at the GPS buttons to pull up the nearest hospital. I hear myself speak almost frantically, "I'm not losing it. I won't lose your baby."

Remington doesn't hear me. He's talking to Pete in a hushed voice as he holds me to his chest, telling him to "turn right—into the emergency" and I continue talking, in my most determined voice. "I won't lose it. You want this baby, *I* want this baby, I eat right, I exercise, *you* eat right, you exercise."

He carries me into the hospital and stalks over to the counter to demand attention, and when they bring a wheelchair, he speaks to the nurse behind it, "Tell me where to take her."

I can hear his heart beating under my ear, and I've never heard it pump so furiously before. *Poom poom poom.*

He carries me into a room, sets me down on the bed, and holds my hand a little too tightly while two nurses and one doctor check me and Pete waits outside the room. Thank god because my legs are spread and I'm terribly uncomfortable having Remy see me like this. But he's looking at our hands, intertwined, as if he's very uncomfortable by this too, until the doctor eases back and slips off his gloves, and tells him, "Your wife is in the early stages of a miscarriage."

While my brain tries to make sense of what I'm hearing, I roll to my side, curl my hand around my stomach in the fetal position, and shake my head, saying nothing, just shaking my head because . . . no.

Just . . . *no.*

I'm a healthy young woman. Healthy young women don't just lose babies.

The doctor ushers Remington aside and speaks to him in low tones, and I lift my head to look at his face. It is the face of my dreams, and I swear I will never forget his fierce expression as he tells the doctor, in a hushed voice, "It's impossible. "

The doctor continues speaking, and Remington shakes his head, his jaw tight. He looks suddenly younger and more vulnerable than I've ever seen him. God, he looks as disheartened as I imagine he looked the day they told him he'd been kicked out of pro boxing and he would never box professionally again.

He drags a hand down his face and drops it to his side, and the train of panic running inside my head is gaining such speed, I stretch my arm out of the bed and hear myself speak in a voice choking with fear. "What's he saying? What is he saying?"

Remington leaves the doctor in midsentence and comes over to my side, instantly taking both my hands in his big, callused ones. I can't even put into words how I feel at the contact, but a rush of calming chemicals run through me and my eyes drift shut as I desperately savor the feel of my small hand inside his bigger one. There's no cramping. Nothing. Not even fear. Just Remington's dry hands on mine, and his steady strength, seeping into me. He bends down and starts kissing my knuckles, and I sigh softly, angling my head to his with a drunken smile.

I don't find out why he doesn't smile back at me. Or why he looks so completely run-down. Until he takes me back to the hotel and calls two more doctors.

EIGHT

HOME IS WHERE THE HEART IS

There's no song for this. Or maybe there is, but we just don't feel like music.

All that is audible between us comes from the soft hum of the plane engines out the windows. Remy refused Pete or Riley to come along on this flight, and the guys were concerned he might go speedy when they're not around. But nothing could move him this morning. He wanted me alone with him. He carried me downstairs to the car. Then to the plane. God, I want him to carry me as an accessory as long as he doesn't take me back home. But he *is* taking me home. To Seattle. Where I will stay, and he will go.

All three doctors say I can't travel. All three of them say I'll miscarry for sure if I don't get rest.

Bed rest.

And a progesterone cream.

That's what they tell us I need.

They don't know that what I need is my blue-eyed devil, and the thought of being separated for two months, until I'm past the first trimester and out of the danger zone, makes me want to weep.

Now Remy is sprawled in his usual seat, his head flung back as he stares at the ceiling of the plane, absently stroking my hair.

He looks about as miserable as I feel. I can still hear him, sternly telling both the doctors he summoned to the hotel room—when they prescribed "no travel" and "bed rest" for me —"*That's impossible. I need her with me. She goes where I go.*"

And when the third doctor said that he was sorry and left, I remember begging pathetically, "*You can't seriously be thinking of sending me back? Right? Remington, I'll lie down. I won't fucking move. This is your son. He's going to hang in there! He will. I don't see how being sent away will stress me any less. I don't want to go home. I'll stay in bed all day, just don't take me back!*"

He looked so frustrated, ready to tear something in half with his bare hands as he told Pete, "Get the plane ready." And then he turned to me, and looked at me with blue eyes that lost all their sparkle. He didn't even have time to explain because I started crying.

And here we are now.

Sucking *balls*.

Forty thousand feet above the ground, flying to Seattle.

I lie across the bench with my head on his lap, my face tipped up as he strokes his fingers through the length of my ponytail, and then into my scalp. He's been staring at the ceiling for an hour, his chest expanding, slowly, as though each breath is meant to calm him but doesn't quite succeed.

My heart hurts when I think of how much effort it's going to take him not to let this fuck with his head. I want to whisper reassurances, but I can't even seem to speak, I'm so pissed at life for throwing me a curveball again.

Suddenly, he starts kissing me softly, first the top of my ear, then my earlobe, then the center nook, his hot breath sending shivers through me as he part breathes, part growls out words that seem to be wrenched from out of him. My eyes burn and I'm sure I've got a dagger sticking out of my chest as he tells me, "*I'm going to miss you . . . I'm going to need you to be good . . . take care of yourself . . . I need you . . .*"

My throat feels so swollen I can only nod as I watch him reach into his jeans and pull out a platinum credit card.

"Use it," he whispers.

I suppose Melanie would die if a man gave her a credit card, but I don't want to go on a shopping spree or something. I don't want . . . anything but my life. I want our baby to be all right. I want us to be together. I want my new life, on tour, with *him*.

"Brooke," he warns, and I feel him tuck the card into my palm. "I want to see charges. Daily," he warns. He looks down at me with half a grin, his black hair standing up more than usual, his scruff even darker this morning because he didn't shave, and how can you love someone so much that it burns through you? I love the way his sooty lashes frame his blue eyes, and the exact slant of his eyebrows. I love his hard forehead, cheekbones, and jaw, and how his mouth manages to look both plump and soft, but firm and strong.

Raising my arm, I drag the tips of my fingers along the square line of his jaw. "When I came back, I promised myself I'd never leave you."

"I promised myself I'd never let you go. What else do you expect me to do?" His eyes are dark and tortured, and I know he didn't sleep.

He paced all night, curling and uncurling his fingers as he asked me if I felt any pain. Yeah, I did. I felt little stabs in my heart, and said, *no cramping*. He returned to bed to gather me close, kissing me like he wanted to devour me. I remember every movement of his tongue on mine. The temperature of his breath on my face. And how many times he tore his lips away, kissed my forehead, and disappeared into the bathroom.

Because we're not allowed to make love either.

So our last night together, we spent kissing. And the several times he took a cold shower, I spent crying into my pillow.

Now he brushes loose strands of hair behind my forehead, his eyes holding mine. "We're going to be all right, little firecracker," he whispers to me. He runs his gaze down my body and spreads his hand open on my stomach. The proprietary gesture makes my heart burn with love. "We've got this." He rubs me softly through my cotton shirt, looking down at me with tender blue eyes. "Don't we?"

"Of course we do," I say, with a sudden surge of determination. "It's just two months, right?"

He tweaks my nose. "Right."

"And it's not like we can't communicate in other ways."

"Exactly right."

Sitting up, I rest my forehead on his shoulder, and he slides his hand around my waist as I massage his muscle. "Let your body rest. Ice yourself after your workouts. Warm up properly."

He buries his face in my neck and pulls me closer, and I hear us both scenting each other with the deepest breaths possible. His hand clenches on my hip bone, and suddenly he licks my neck, his voice guttural when he rumbles in my ear, "I can't let anything happen to you, Brooke. I can't. I had to bring you back."

"I know, Remy, I know." I run my fingers through the back of his head because he sounds so tormented. "We're going to be all right, all three of us."

"That's the point of all this."

"And like you say, we've got this. We really do."

"Damn right we do."

"You'll be back before we even have time to feel sad or miss each other too much."

"That's right. I'll be training and you'll be resting."

"Yeah."

When we fall silent, we stay close and embracing for a long time, and I can almost hear the minutes ticking by, like little bitches intent on ruining my life. Remington scents me again, as if he wants to get enough of my scent to last him two months, and almost frantically, I do the same, inhale his scent and close my eyes, feeling his shoulder muscle under my fingers, so strong and solid, as I start to massage him lightly again. "I left some arnica oils in your suitcase. If you have any muscle soreness or any pain."

"Are you still seeing blood?" he asks quietly, and when I nod, he brings me to his lap, where I cuddle closer and press my temple into his jaw.

"Every time a cramp starts, I feel like it's going to come out of me."

He strokes his hand down my back and presses his lips to my forehead. "I know it'll kill you not to run. Stay off your feet for me."

"Not as much as it would kill me to lose our baby," I whisper.

I've run my whole life. But right now, I'm scared even of walking, for dread of having the cramps return and finding red in my panties. I swear if I can't hold the man I love's baby in me, I don't know what I'll do, but I can't—I *refuse* to—lose this baby.

"Your parents know you're coming? Your sister?"

"I let them know I was coming, but they don't know about us yet. I'm saving that for face-to-face. Only Mel and my two other besties know about it." He draws my head back so he can look at me, "All right. But who are you going to call first if it gets worse? Me. Who are you going to call when you need anything? *Me*. I'll be your everything. I'll be your fucking booty call by phone. Anytime, wherever I am. Am I clear, Brooke?"

"I'm sorry. My mind froze on 'booty call.'"

"It did? What about it do you need me to clear up for you?"

The devil's lift of one dark eyebrow heats up my body like a live little volcano. The idea of phone sex with Remington makes me both laugh and feel, suddenly, incredibly tingly, and I end up shoving his chest playfully. "I won't call you for that! I know you're going to be busy."

His eyes twinkle. "Not too busy for that."

"Why that glint in your eye? Have you done it before? I'll bet Melanie has done it with Riley."

Smirking, he runs his hands down the back of my head and back, then gently kisses my earlobe, my nose, his voice a little thick. "I want to do it with you."

My sex grips and my nipples ache, and a hot flush spreads over me. I love our first times. The first time he played me "Iris." The first time he invited me to run. The first time he kissed me, made love to me. We've never had a first of this type before.

"I want it too, but I don't know if I can. If I touch there . . . with blood . . ."

His lips press into my forehead as he fingers the two top buttons of my top, his voice ten times terser than moments ago, "It's just blood."

The scent of him, the pheromones he puts out, spins me into a frenzy. My womb grips with want, and suddenly I throb so fiercely, my already sensitized breasts feel too constrained in my bra. "Remington, god, only you could make me horny right now when I'm so worried."

His hands spread on my ass, and suddenly I feel his lips sliding over my ear; then he's tonguing me gently, and a new heat builds between my thighs. "I want you so fucking much." His voice is a raspy breath as he slides a hand under the waistband of my jeans and palms one of my ass cheeks under my panties.

He cups both my breasts and presses them together as he nuzzles me, side to side, growling against my skin.

"Whenever you want to, I want to," he tells me, lifting his head and pressing his mouth to mine, his words vibrating against my tongue as

I stroke hungrily across his. "Just call me and tell me. Tell me you want me. That you're hot for me and I'll take care of you. I'll take care of my woman—whenever she wants. Whatever she wants."

"Me too. You call me and I'll take care of you." I rub my thumb along the hard square of his jaw, then we close the distance between our mouths, and during the rest of the flight, he grabs the sides of my head and kisses me, and kisses me, and kisses me raw and swollen.

❤ ❤ ❤

A CHAUFFEUR IN a fancy black Lincoln town car waits for us at the airport, and Remington tells the pilots he'll be back in two hours. We ride in the back of the car in silence and as close as possible, and I scan the familiar scenery and power on my iPhone. I realize I'm doing anything to distract myself as we approach my apartment. Just like he carried me down the steps from the plane and into the car, Remy carries me out and into my apartment.

I squeeze my arms around his neck. "Stay. Remington, *stay*. Be my male prisoner. I promise to take care of you all day, every day."

He laughs a rich male sound, looking into me with those heart-breaking blue eyes, then he scans my place with curiosity, and I feel butterflies when I see his genuine interest. He wants to see where I live. Oh, god, I love him so much it hurts me.

"I'll give you a quick tour, and then you have to get your fine ass out of here," I warn him.

He grins. "Show me my woman's lair."

With him carrying me around, I spread my hand out and show him my colorful living room. "My living room, Melanie decorated. She's really good. Eclectic. She's been mentioned in some local magazines, too, but of course she dreams about being featured in

Architectural Digest. Pandora, one of my other friends, tells her she has a better shot at *Playboy*, though. They're decorating rivals and like to pick on each other."

He winks at me, and the wink travels all the way to form a little tingling in my gut as I point to the room adjoining. "And then that's my kitchen. Small, but it's only me here. And then the door here takes us to . . . my bedroom."

We go in, and he sets me down at the foot of the bed; then he takes it all in with quiet wonder. I glance around and look at it through his eyes. It's simple, the walls in nude colors. Some black-and-white pictures of athletes hang on the walls—close-ups of muscles. There's a pinup wall with pictures of me, Melanie, Pandora, Kyle . . . some other friends. . . . I have two nutritional charts hanging, speaking of carbs, protein, healthy fats. And a framed quote Melanie gave me: A CHAMPION IS SOMEONE WHO GETS UP WHEN HE CAN'T.—JACK DEMPSEY. She got it for me when I damaged my ACL and was depressed, and I tried to be this champion.

I am looking at one now. Every day I look at one.

He walks to the pinup wall and inspects a picture of me sprinting past a finish line—number 06 on my chest—and runs his thumb over the photograph. "Look at you," he says with ill-concealed male pride, and I didn't realize I'd walked over to him until he turns and spots me.

He scoops me up and sets me back on my bed, this time in the center, brushing some escaped tendrils of hair back behind my forehead. "Stay off your feet for me," he chides.

"I will. I forgot. It's habit." I scoot back so I rest against my headboard and pull him to me.

"You should go or I won't let you leave me," I whisper in his ear.

He cuddles me for a moment, his hard, solid arms wrapped snugly around my waist as he ducks his head and kisses, licks, and scents my neck, swiftly alternating between the three. He's never scented me as much as he has in the past two hours. Now, he scents me slowly and deeply, then licks me just as slowly, and I feel his attentions, and lastly, his kiss, right in my sex. "When you tell me you're in bed, this is what I'll picture. This is what you see," he rumbles as he lifts his head.

I'm getting teary, but don't want to make this any worse, so I nod, but I know there's no way on earth he could miss the crumpled expression on my face.

His eyes clasp mine as he draws back. "I'll be back soon," he tells me, cupping my cheek in his big, callused hand, and I hate that a tear slips out. He smiles at me, but that smile doesn't reach his eyes. "I'll be here soon," he repeats.

"I know." I wipe my cheek, take his hand, and set a kiss inside his palm, then curl his fingers around it so that whether he wants my kiss or not, he holds it. "I'll be waiting for you."

"Shit, come here." He crushes me in his arms, and all my efforts to hold myself in check are shot to hell, and the waterworks begin. I start bawling.

"It's all right," he says, smoothing his hands down my back as a series of wrenching sobs take over me. *It's all right,* I hear, *it's all right, little firecracker,* but I just don't feel like it's all right. How could it be? He could need me. *I* need *him.* He could be black, and Pete could shoot more shit into his neck. Something could happen in a fight and they could not tell me because of not wanting to stress me and cause me to lose the baby. I feel weak and helpless when all I wanted in life was to be strong and independent. But I fell deeply and irrevocably in love. And now I am ruled by this love, for *this* man, who sounds like thunder when he talks in my ear, and smells like soap and him and like the ocean, and holds me in the strongest arms in the world—and when these arms are gone, my whole world will be gone with them.

"You need to go," I say, dragging in a ragged breath as I push him away. Instead he sets his forehead and his nose against mine, and we breathe each other's air.

We just don't need to say it. *I love you* crackles between us and I hear the words as if he were yelling them to me.

He takes my hand, kisses my knuckles fiercely, and then frames my face and wipes my tears with his thumbs. "You okay, baby firecracker?"

"I will be. More than okay," I promise.

My phone vibrates in my pocket and I shakily check the message.

"Melanie is five minutes away." My voice is raw. Mel knows where I keep my spare key and will burst in here any minute, and Remington will leave.

He will *leave*.

My eyes blur again. "Please go before I cry," I beg. Which is ridiculous, because I'm already crying like a baby and feel and probably look like shit. He curls his fingers around the back of my neck and closes his eyes as he leans his head on mine. "Think of me like crazy."

"You know I will."

Stormy blue eyes hold mine, his voice gruff as he leans over. "Now give me a kiss."

I do, and he groans softly as his lips connect with mine. Little fireworks explode in me, and I feel his kiss, soothing my mind and my soul and my heart too. He spreads out his hand and fondles the small of my back gently as we kiss, low, deep, savoring, memorizing; then his mouth comes back up to absorb a stray tear from my cheek.

"Brookey!! Where's the hot dad and the upcoming momma?"

He curses under his breath, and we kiss quickly once more. He nips and sucks my tongue, more roughly now, holding the back of my head in his hand, his delicious, raw kiss making my body feel sucked and bitten by a lion. My breasts hurt. My nipples throb in my bra.

And I squirm and press my thighs together as he finally edges away, our eyes briefly meeting. Clinging. His are hot and desperately hungry, like he's a moment away from tearing my clothes off.

"You're everything I never knew I wanted." He tucks back another tendril of hair behind my ear, his eyes a little too brilliant as he draws back. "And all mine, remember that tidbit." I hear Mel's heels clicking outside, and Remington stands, somehow looking bigger than ever. Large, hard, blue-eyed, and beautiful. "Completely mine," he says. "Brooke Dumas."

A shudder runs through me as he backs away, his stare pinning me down on the bed.

I feel fucked here, in my bed, with his eyes alone, as I try to recover my breath. "I'm pregnant with your baby, if there was any doubt about whose I was," I tell him.

"You're both mine," he says, pointing straight at me. "Especially you."

I swallow back my excitement, and he turns to leave.

"Hey!" I call. "You're *mine*, too."

He nods, then flings his iPod in my direction. "Don't miss me too much."

I catch it and hold it against my chest. "I won't!" I flippantly retort, all false bravado, then his low voice rumbles out in the hall, and I hear Melanie quietly reassure him, and then comes the awful sound of my front door closing.

A stillness follows, the kind of stillness I sense only when he's not around.

That's when I tuck my face into my pillow and bawl my eyes out.

NINE

A RAINBOW IN SEATTLE

Melanie is the best thing about Seattle, and anyone who thinks otherwise can just kiss her ass. Mel is like a permanent rainbow in a city that's eternally gray. From her flashy earrings to the line of bracelets up to her elbow, she clinked and clanked her way into my room in an explosion of colors, trying to cheer me up when my world had just walked out my apartment door and it took all my willpower to keep from running after him.

Mel took the merest second to assess the situation before taking action. She spotted the bawling mass on my bed, which was me, and she quickly pried my pillow free and replaced it with her big-breasted chest, and now her designer top is soaked from my tears as she waits for me to run out of them.

It's been at least a half hour, or more, and I'm still going strong. Every couple of minutes, I just seem to need to pause for air.

Now, in one of my breathing moments, she pushes me away to stare into my eyes with a saucy curve of her lips. "You weren't lying when you said Riptide Tate wanted you to be the mother of his sexy babies, were you? You two got right down to work, didn't you! Huh?" She shoulders me a little and peers down at my stomach. "So when are you going to show? I want to see a little bump somewhere!"

"I know! Me too!" A smile tips my lips as I think about this baby. Oh, baby, the things you're asking us to do to prove that we love you. "I want to show so bad, Mel."

She grins at that, then examines me with assessing green eyes. "Hmm. Pregnancy glow. You've got it in spades, even with those weepy eyes. I can't wait to be pregnant—I think it's so sexy!" she cries. "What most makes pregnant being sexy to me is the fact that the baby daddy is sexy. It's just *sexy* having a part of them inside you! How does it feel? Chicken, you have to feel like a woman now; you got the sexiest baby daddy there is!"

Oh god, I can't even talk about Remington with my best friend without feeling my bones turn liquid inside me. Even my voice takes on a different tone—the exact same tone it seems to take when I'm alone in bed with him and loving him. "It feels amazing, Mel. Like he's with me. Like we're bound. Like I was supremely, royally fucked." I groan and lie back in bed and rub my lips, and I love that I can still taste my Riptide on them.

"Brooke, let me just say . . ." Mel drops down on her back next to me and stares at my ceiling. "When I saw him just now, I felt like dying a little inside. He's so big and so hot my heels almost melted and I instantly felt four inches shorter."

I can't control my sudden burst of laughter, and Mel kicks her shoes off and rolls to her side, smiling at me in signature Melanie mischief. "His mouth was all red like he'd just French-kissed you to death. Riptide is a bit of a Neanderthal, isn't he? He's so fucking primal, ohmigod! I bet you guys do anal sex."

"We do not! He's animal but protective!" I squeal, squirming a little at the thought.

"Doggy style for sure?"

"Yes, but stop reminding me!" I cry good-humoredly. Then I close my eyes and spread my hands open on my abdomen savoring his baby inside me. "There's truly something extremely sensual about being pregnant by him," I admit. "I'm so hyperaware of my body, how it feels, how it is changing for this little baby. I feel my ribs and hips expanding to make room for it, my breasts changing, all of me . . ." I sigh, then turn my head and stare at my best friend. The only one who ever really "got" me until Remy. The only one who likes me in any form I've come. "Mel, I can't lose this baby."

The smile she had been wearing vanishes, and she squeezes my hand over my still-flat abdomen. "You won't. It's Riptide's baby."

"We didn't know there was a pity party here, but we're glad we didn't miss it!" says a male voice from the open door.

Sniffling, I lift my head to see my best male friend, Kyle, in Dockers and a polo shirt, standing right next to Pandora, her dark hair held back in a careless knot that sends spikes out of her hair everywhere. "You're *preggo*?" she demands.

"According to tons of lab work and pregnancy tests, yes. But my body still hasn't gotten the complete memo, aside from the throwing-up part."

Kyle heads to my desk and flips the chair around, and Pandora jumps on the bed with shoes and everything, her leather jacket suddenly all I can smell.

"Pan-Pan, I don't really feel like your vibe is babyish enough for Brookey, so you sit over there." Melanie pats her side so she gets me all by herself, but Pandora reaches over me and shoves her playfully.

"Shush up, let me hug her."

Pandora looks at me, with her dark eyes and dark lipstick. People don't know that goths are extremely sensitive people—at least, Pandora is. You turn goth for a reason. I think she's just naturally dramatic and angsty, and it was all after some asshole broke her heart. It's a miracle, Mel says, that Pandora didn't turn lesbian.

"You okay?" Pan asks, and before I can nod or speak, she pulls me into her leather jacket, and I feel Melanie snuggle my back too. Melanie can't ever resist a hug. She even says *hmmm*.

"It's gonna be all right, Brookey," Mel says. Then she adds in my ear, "I promised your man I'd take care of you. He asked me to make sure you were not alone, were well fed, and taken care of. Riley told me he and Pete will need a daily report from me so they can keep Remington appeased, and he also told me you've been puking and that your baby daddy wants you to fucking eat!"

I groan in protest and ease away from their hug. "I'm all right. When I get hungry, I'll eat something. If my body wants food, it will tell me. Guess what hunger was designed for?"

"We don't care if you *want* to eat or not. We're your man's minions on a mission, and we already got you something, in memory of old times," Kyle informs me as he gets up from the chair and returns with a Jack in the Box bag. That instant, I vividly remember how these three dopes teased Pete and Riley before in the drive-through, ages ago, the night Remington hired me. And I think of that fateful evening, and how he'd already changed my life without me even realizing. All my feelings crowd around my chest, and as Kyle brings over the bag, a surge of nausea overtakes me.

"Get that out of here!" I plead as I pinch my nose, which only alters my voice to the ridiculous. "I'm not doing so well with certain smells. Plus I need veggies for this baby. I need folic acid and calcium—stuff that shit doesn't have, I guarantee. What kind of friends are you?"

He laughs triumphantly. "We knew you'd say that or you wouldn't be you, so the Jack's for us. We got you something else." He leaves the room, then returns and reveals a brown bag from Whole Foods. "Likey? You wanna talk about good friends now?"

I toss him a pillow. "Bring that over!" I peer into the bag and spot a turkey wrap, the kind I like, and suddenly my friends' gestures and support enfold me like the hug they just gave me, snug and tight.

"You guys are so good to me," I say, setting the bag on my nightstand.

Melanie tugs my ponytail. "Have you noticed you're mush now?" She squeezes my arm and when my little bicep responds to her, she amends, "Uh, on the inside."

I burst out laughing, then close my eyes and see blue eyes, spiky hair. I want to squish him so hard, but he's so far away. I wrap my hands around his baby instead. Then I look at my phone. Remy isn't as dependent on phones and Internet as other people are. Neither am I, but now I'm clinging to my phone as my thread to him. He's not even the type to text, but I don't freaking care. Call me tonight if you want to?

It takes over an hour for him to answer, but I grin like a dope when he answers: Just landed. I'll call.

We watch a movie, then Melanie hops up from the bed. "Hey, Chicken! Did I tell you? Next guy I sleep with is in for a treat. I just took pole-dancing classes!" She grabs my floor lamp and proceeds to show us just what she learned, moving sinuously with her body, one jean-clad leg wrapped around the stem. "Kyle, that get your motor running?"

"Dude, it would be like incest if it did," Kyle says, from where he straddles my desk chair.

"Why? You're not my brother!" she protests. "Come on. Does it get your motor revving?" She moves her tush for him to see.

Kyle sits there, looking exactly like Justin Timberlake, and he says, hesitantly, "It's . . . sputtering."

"Pan, come here. Peter Pan, move with me so Kyle can get his rusty motor up and going. I'm going to teach you what I learned for free." Pandora goes to the iPod dock and sets her phone on the base. A rock song immediately blasts inside my bedroom.

"All right, let's get Kyle hard over there!" Discarding her leather jacket as if she's stripping for the poor man, she heads over to Mel. And then she and Melanie start bumping asses and having a blast, and I find myself listening to the song, trying to find the lyrics through all the noise, wondering if it's even something I'd ever play to *him*.

It's useless, so I grab Remy's iPod and put in my earbuds and listen to Avril Lavigne's "When You're Gone." It's so nice to listen to a song that you *get*. Or that gets you. That makes you realize what you're feeling is human, and normal, even if it may be a feeling you wished you didn't have.

I text him the YouTube link. He doesn't text back, and I assume he's in the gym, punching his bags unrecognizable.

How is he going to cope these two months apart?

I can't shake off the thought that, even though I'm the more emotional one, this will test him more than it will test me.

I'm still wondering about it when the cramps begin. I shift on the bed as my friends keep talking and all my awareness hones in on the god-awful cramps that make my fight or flight surge to life. If feels like someone is hurting my baby. My own *body* is hurting my baby. I search the iPod for songs that calm me, and the only song that succeeds is "Iris."

But the pain intensifies. I quietly remove my earbuds and slowly get up from the bed. My friends fall completely quiet when they see me walk, folded over, to the bathroom. I shut the door and when I check, I realize the blood is back. And heavy.

For a moment I just breathe roughly through my nose and lean my head against the tile, trying to calm down. I touch my stomach lovingly and try to talk to my baby in my head, telling him that nobody is going to hurt him. That he is very wanted and already very loved.

I imagine looking into the blue eyes I love while having to tell Remy that I lost his baby. A well of emotion seizes me again, and tears I thought I no longer had threaten to surface once more.

"Mel," I shout through the door. "Mel, I don't know if this baby is going to make it."

She opens the door with a forlorn expression. "Brooke, he's calling. It's been ringing several times. Do I answer?"

"No! No!"

"You look bad, but he told me to tell him the instant you needed him. Brookey, I think I should let him know—"

"No! Melanie, NO. Look, he can't do anything. He needs to fight! There's something he needs to do. Our baby and I will support him, not hinder him. Do you hear me?"

"Then at least let me take you to the hospital—you look like you're being torn in two!" she says.

"Yes—no! I shouldn't move around. I need to . . . rest. I am not . . . losing . . . this baby. . . ." I drag in a breath and shake my head; then I sniffle. "Please bring me my phone?"

She brings it over and I text him instead. My friends are still here. Maybe we should talk tomorrow?

Same time?

Yes, any time

Ok

Good night Remy

You too.

I set the phone aside and close my eyes as another tear slips free. He's a good and a quiet guy and he doesn't text, but I already feel torn apart from him. Deep breath.

"Help me pull the progesterone cream out of my suitcase?" I say out to the room.

Mel comes out to the bathroom and starts clapping like some fifth-grade teacher who's had enough already. "Guys, playtime's over, I'm tucking Brooke into bed."

Kyle and Pandora clean up their snacks, and I'm embarrassed

to look at them with my swollen face, but I can feel their concern as I come out and lie down on the bed. When they leave, I smear myself with the cream, getting it on my stomach, my thighs. Then Melanie comes out of the bathroom in an old T-shirt.

"It's been forever since we did a pj party—I mean just us." She grins and dives in under the covers with me; then she disappears and I hear her voice near my stomach. "And you? Didn't you get the memo? You're a fighter! Son of Riptide and Brooke! Show your mom and dad what you're made of!"

I smile when she comes back up, and I close my eyes, feeling hopeful that our little baby is listening.

TEN

FAMILY VISIT

I wake up and smell something that, for once, does not make me nauseous. It's sweet and fragrant and it invites me to take a good long whiff. I look around, and Melanie is going in and out of the room. Riptide red is splattered everywhere. Riptide-red *roses* are bursting open inside my room.

"Good morning, Juliet. Your Romeo sent these. They're still unloading the rest off the truck. And I'm calling in to the gym that I already put in my hour workout."

I smile and try to stand, but Melanie says, "Tut-tut! No standing. What do you need?"

"To pee! And to smell these, be still my fucking heart! Is this a note?" I pull open a note that's nestled among the roses on my nightstand and my eyes well up when I see a song name. Melanie gathers a couple more notes and brings them over, and I open one to discover another song name. I haven't heard these songs, but I'm already excited.

I give myself permission, because I'm pregnant and so fucking stressed, to have a little cry. Everyone knows if you hold it in, you get sick, and I don't want to be sick. I want to be healthy—I want to give Remy a baby and a family. Something he has never had. So I cry. Then I text him, I miss your eyes. Your hands. Your face. Your dimples!

Then I take a picture of my room, so full of roses so that I can barely see my window, and send it.

That's what I see now from my bed.

I then kiss my phone.

"You're a dope!" Mel says as she brings the rest.

"So what, who cares?" I saucily return as I set my phone aside, because I know he won't be checking it when he's training, and he'll probably train extra hard, so I go rub progesterone on myself again. I read that I can get a headache if I overdo it, but Melanie and I were on some forums last night reading that the cream stopped tons of women from miscarrying, and I want to put my name on that list.

I grab some books, set my laptop on the bed, and basically set up a mini office so that I don't have to stand. I feel like my ovaries ache, but they're not cramping, and I'm starting to wonder if this cream is really working.

I hear Mel finish with the florist and decide to skip my shower, merely because I don't want to be standing up all that time, so I just find fresh clothes and change with caution.

Nora is supposed to visit during the day so Melanie can go to work, but instead of Nora appearing after Mel brings some fruit and cottage cheese for us to breakfast on, I get to hear Melanie call me from outside my bedroom, saying, "Brookey! Your parents are here!"

Melanie goes to let them in, so I edge out of bed, very attentive to how I'm feeling. I don't feel any cramps, so I walk to the living room and immediately take a couch, and there they are, wide-eyed and shocked at me, standing and staring.

"Brooke."

The way my mother utters my name fills me with dread.

And the moment I see both my parents, coupled with the way they say my name, I *know* they know. Grief settles over me when I absorb their normally bright expressions and realize they seem to have aged an entire decade. How can news of a beautiful baby age them like this?

"We would have expected it from Nora, but from *you*?" my mother says, and ohmigod, they *do* know. How *come* they know?

She sits down across the coffee table from me, and my father drops down at her side, arms crossed, glaring the glare he uses to intimidate his PE students.

They don't speak for about three minutes. Which feels, under the circumstances, like an entire lifetime, and I'm so uncomfortable I don't even know how to sit.

I love my parents. I don't like hurting them. I'd wanted to tell them the good news, face-to-face, that I'm in love and that Remington and I are having a baby. The last thing I want is to make them feel let down, to treat this as the tragedy that they seem to be taking it as.

"Hello, Mom and Dad," I say first.

I shift and shift until I plant my elbow on the couch arm, put my head in my hand, and curl my legs under me, but even when I'm finally comfortable, the tension in the air could be cut with an axe.

"Hey, Mr. and Mrs. Dumas," Melanie says. "I'll let you have your family reunion and check in with my job." She looks at me and makes the sign of the cross to ward off vampires, then she tells me, "I'm back at seven. Nora texted that she's on her way."

I nod, and then there's an awkward silence in the room.

"Brooke! We don't even know what to say."

For a moment, I really don't know what to say either, except "I really want this baby."

They both give me that look of disappointment parents have been giving their children for eons.

But I won't let them make me feel shame.

I felt shame when I tore my ACL. My father said sprinters didn't show those kinds of tears, but I did. I fell from grace with them after that, and now I can sense that I've fallen even further.

"I'm sorry I didn't tell you. I wanted to tell you in person, but it seems somebody already did."

"Nora," my mother says. "And she's worried about you—all three of us are. She tells me she had to learn it from somebody else? How could you hide something like this from us? Let me tell you that despite you being somewhat mature, you were always too sheltered from boys. Boys . . . they just use and discard . . . especially when something inconvenient happens. Nora says this boy is known to be a troublemaker and linked to all kinds of problems?"

I am reeling from the way Nora's presented Remy to them.

If I weren't sitting down, I swear I'd have fallen on my butt.

My betrayed, stupid, foolish butt.

So it seems that Nora is home, acting the perfect princess, doing what's right after *my boyfriend* helped her out of the worst relationship in the world and *could have died* saving her ass.

Her betrayal rips through me with such force, I can't even talk for a moment. Hell, if anyone should know what kind of a man Remington is, it should be Nora!

"The father of my baby is not a boy. He is a man." I clutch my stomach when it begins to hurt under their accusing gazes. "And we, this baby and I, are not *inconveniences.*"

My father has not said one word. He just sits there, looking at me like I'm a gremlin that got wet and turned ugly and has to be contained.

I feel like there's a continent between us. Like I am going north, and they are determined that south is the best path for me and will never, ever be happy that I went the opposite way.

"But Brooke, this is so reckless and so unlike you. Look at you!" my mother says in complete agony and despair.

"What?" I ask in confusion. "What's wrong with me?"

Then I realize I probably look like shit. I haven't slept. I'm worried to death I'm losing this baby. I don't want to be here. I haven't showered and my face is swollen from all my tears.

"You look . . . depressed again, Brooke. You should stop wearing that athletic gear, now that you're no longer a sprinter and put on a dress . . . brush your hair. . . ."

"Please. *Please* don't come here and hurt me. You're saying things you don't mean to say because you're confused. Please be happy for me. If I look depressed it's because I'm dangerously close to losing this baby, and I want him, I want him so bad, you have no idea."

They stare at me like I have lost it, because I've never, ever, opened myself up like this, and I feel so misunderstood and so unloved and so hungry to be comforted because I hurt inside. My hormones are out of whack and I am feeling angry because I am here instead of where I want to be. I am here, misunderstood and judged, instead of with him, loved and accepted.

I don't even know how to tell them they're being unfair to me, but I'm trembling as I suddenly get to my feet, go get his iPod, and set it on the speakers I have in my living room. Then I just click PLAY and raise the volume high, letting a song speak for me. Orianthi's "According to You" begins, a little bit angry and rebellious, describing something of the tumult I feel, how they see me one way, as less than perfect, but he sees me another way, as beautiful and strong.

"Is this how we deal, like a teenager with loud music?" my mother yells.

"Turn the volume down now!" my father yells.

I turn it down, and for a moment, just focus on this silver iPod, which to Remy and me could be a journal, or a microphone, or any other way of expressing any other thing. "You don't understand."

"Talk to us, Brooke!" my mother says.

When I turn, they look as forlorn as I feel. "I just did, but you're not listening."

They are quiet, and I drag in a breath, trying to calm down, even with all these hormones rioting in me. I want them to know that I am no longer a young girl. That I am becoming a woman, so I tell them. "I'm seven weeks pregnant. Right now, his little limbs are forming. And I say 'his' because I think it's a boy, but it doesn't matter, because a girl would be wonderful too. While we speak, his heart is growing stronger, and he's generating about a hundred new brain cells per minute. In two more weeks, his heart will have divided into four chambers and all its organs, nerves, and muscles will be kicking into gear. He will have a nose, eyes, ears, a mouth, everything already formed, inside me. This baby is his. His and mine. And it makes me so, so happy you have no idea."

My mother looks heartbroken. "We are *worried*. Nora tells me they use drugs in those places he fights."

"Mama, he's not into that. He's an athlete, heart, body, and soul." Coming over to them, I pat her hair and grab my dad's hand in my other one. "He doesn't have a family like I do, and I want him to have mine. I want you to welcome him into our family because you love me and because I'm asking you to."

My mother visibly softens, but it is my father who speaks first. "I'll welcome him into the family when he proves to me he deserves to be the father of my grandchild!" He stands up, huffing, and walks to the door, slamming it behind him. I hang my head.

"I shouldn't even be up. I'm going to bed, Mom," I whisper.

"Brooke." Her slow, hesitant footsteps follow me to my bedroom. She stops at the door and says nothing as I climb into bed;

instead, I feel her worried gaze on my back for a moment. "Didn't you use protection, sweetie?" she asks quietly.

"God, I'm not going to even answer that," I say.

She remains at the door while a heavy silence settles between us, and I curl into a ball and stare off into my pin wall, at the picture that Remington touched. I won't cry. I swear, I'm sick of crying, and I'm trying not to hate them just because I'm lonely, misunderstood, and hormonal. I know they love me. All they know is that some guy got me pregnant and dumped me here and that this baby will be a challenge for me. They don't know anything except that my life will change, and they're afraid I can't handle it. They can be so judgmental even though they love me, I feel myself building up my walls, refusing to share Remy with them. Refusing to share the most precious, valuable, and imperfectly perfect thing in my life. "Go home, Momma," I say, and she quietly leaves as I remain in bed, staring at all the roses he sent me.

And I see those blue eyes. . . .

You're mine.

Both of you.

My throat hurts, and my eyes follow.

"Brooke, I'm here," Nora says from the hall.

I don't answer her. I'm so angry. She seems to sense danger in the air, because she lingers by the door and doesn't enter. "You okay? Did you lose the baby?" she asks. My rage roils inside me.

"Thanks for betraying me, Nora," I mumble. "And thanks for showing your complete and utter appreciation for Remington and what he did for you!"

"They had to know you were pregnant, Brooke!" she cries.

"It was my secret to tell, not yours!" I burst out, shooting up to sit on the bed. "Why are you attacking him? He did nothing but save you! What, you wanted a chance to look good to them, so you screwed me over? Who told you? I know it wasn't Melanie; she'd never do this to me."

Nora's eyes are also a shade of amber, just a fraction darker than mine, but that's where all our similarities end. How can we be so different? She was always the dreamer, and I the realist, but even so we've never felt so apart as we do today.

"Pete told me," she says.

I groan, forgetting they have something for each other.

"It slipped! He assumed I knew and I felt embarrassed I didn't know! You wouldn't be hiding it if it weren't wrong, Brooke. He's Riptide! You'll be discarded just like I was, if not worse. Those men are dangerous, Brooke. You're never free of them, never."

"Remington is not like your sick asshole of an ex-boyfriend! I am freaking *in love* with him and he *loves me* and I will have his baby if it KILLS ME, Nora!" I scream.

She blinks and I can't even go on. Maybe I'm resentful that because of her, I almost ruined my life. Because of her—and me wanting to "rescue" her—Remington got *hurt*. "I'm sorry, Nora, I just . . ." I rub my face and shake my head drearily.

"I thought he was in love with me too, you know." Her sadness creeps up on me, and I feel an awful wringing sensation inside me. "Benny, I mean. I thought he would give anything for me, and the moment it was difficult to keep me, he threw me away." She looks at me, her face tired and sad. "He told me he loved me, and then he didn't even look me in the eye to say good-bye. If I said anything to Mom and Dad, it's because I don't want that to happen to you."

"Remy is different, Nora," I say softly.

"Exactly. He has *a thousand* more women after him, Brooke. No. Not a thousand. A *million* more than Scorpion. He's the SEX GOD of the Underground. Those guys don't do wives and babies, they just don't. I was there too, you know. He just can't love you that much to go rescue me, *me,* somebody he hadn't even met! And lose a prize that was practically already his, all for *you*? Nobody in their right mind can love anyone like that!" she cries and runs out, slamming the door shut.

The door shudders afterward, and I blink at it, completely floored. What. The hell. Is my sister smoking now?

I sit there, reeling about it all. Then I get up, turn the lock, strip my clothes, and brush my hair, setting it loose because I need to feel pretty and I need my Real. Holy god, how I need him. I just want something good to happen today and I want him to think I'm all right and safe, just like he wanted me to be.

I text him telling him I'd downloaded Skype to his iPad before the flight and left his user name and password on a Post-it. I then open my laptop and log in and wait. I seem to doze off with the phone next to me, and when I wake up later, I see *Remington Tate: 11 missed calls*.

"Oh, no!" I dial, and it rings, but he doesn't pick up. I dial and dial, then I groan and shove it aside, pulling the covers up to my neck, suddenly cold.

I'm falling asleep again when I hear a little buzz. I see his name blinking, and my heart jumps and I click to answer, the sheets falling to my waist. "Are you there?" I ask.

I adjust my laptop screen while butterflies roar inside me. "Hey. I can't see you! Move your—"

"This is the stupidest thing I've ever done," he says.

"You won't think that when you see me," I dare.

I see him then. Propped back against the headboard . . . bare-chested and, I suspect, recently bathed . . . and my breath is history at the sight of his achingly boyish face. The hotel room is completely illuminated behind him, and my eyes narrow in suspicion.

"You're not sleeping, are you?" I ask him.

He surveys me, and I survey back, trailing my gaze over his tan chest, all along his muscled arm, to the half-full blue Gatorade in his hand. The sight of all those muscles, the Celtic tattoos, his pectorals, his throat—god, those thick tendons of his throat, where I tuck my nose in at night—makes all my body tingle with remembrance of what it feels and smells and looks like.

A ribbon of need unfurls painfully inside me, and it spreads throughout my being until I can think only of this need: to kiss and hold him, touch and nuzzle him, smell his neck; his hair, feel his breath on me and every little callus of his.

Then I realize he's still looking at me, the top of my body fully naked, and I'm instantly wet when I see the territorial, fuck-my-mate look in his eyes.

"Is this supposed to make me feel good?" he asks gruffly, staring at my breasts. "It's fucking torture looking at you behind a screen."

"Remy . . ." I say.

His eyebrows draw low over his eyes. "I don't want you on your own. Is somebody there with you?"

"Nora was here, and I think Mel is outside with her now." I leave it at that, because right now, I don't want to tell him anything about my parents until it has all calmed down. He was rejected by his own parents and I swear that whatever I have to do, he won't be rejected by mine. "Don't worry, I'm not alone," I assure him.

He nods, raking his fingers through his hair in frustration. Then he drops his face and rubs the screen with both hands. He lifts his head and narrows his eyes. "I want to touch you. I'm about to take a bite out of this fucking screen."

A small laugh leaves me, then I groan and cover my eyes, too. Skyping is not such a great idea. Oh god, it makes you yearn. I see him and yearn and hurt and it aches. "It hurts to see you. I want to smell you too," I say.

He lifts a camisole of mine. "I found this in my suitcase." He lifts it and smells it, and I gasp and can almost feel his nose at my neck, scenting me. Licking me.

"Shit, Brooke, I want to be there, take you in my arms, spread you open on your bed, and fuck you until tomorrow."

Desire explodes in my stomach as those rough words hit me. "Oh, god, me too."

His eyes flash as he leans forward, the muscles in his upper body rippling with the move. "I wish I were there so I could squeeze your breasts and bite the tips and tell you how much I want you."

My bones have disintegrated inside me. The place between my legs now burns and yearns. My voice is achy and needy, full of arousal. "I want you like I've never wanted anything in my life," I breathe, my bare breasts already puckered in the air and sensitive even to the brush of the air-conditioning.

"Do you want my cock in you?" he asks roughly.

Exhaling a shaky breath, I curl my fingers around my breasts merely because they're suddenly heavy and hurting. They're hurting so much for him. "Remy, you're killing me."

"No. This is killing me," he says softly, rubbing the screen in a way that lets me imagine his thumb scraping my lips, running down my jaw, circling the hard points of my nipples. "Tell me you want my cock in you and then pretend your fingers are me. Drop your hands, Brooke. Show me your nipples."

"Remy," I say, my heart squeezing in need as I close my hands around my breasts.

A low, rumbling growl rips up his throat as he leans even closer. "Brooke," he rasps, rubbing his thumb over the screen again. "When I see you I'm going to get my fucking hands all over you. I'm going to run my tongue all over your pretty body. Then I'm going to rub it for hours against your clit."

"Oh, god, Remy . . ." My clit throbs between my thighs as I rock my hips as I think about licking his neck, his chest, the star tattoo on his navel.

"Why are you holding your breasts in your hands? Are you pretending that it's me?" he demands huskily. When I nod, he tells me, "Good. Then pinch them slowly, like you like it. And then go south and rub yourself for me."

"But I want to touch *you*," I say, his command sending prickles of excitement racing across my skin. "I want to run my tongue all over your chest and lick your nipples as I stroke my hands down your biceps and rub up your quads and abs. . . ."

His eyes twinkle with mischief and he shakes his head. "No, Brooke," he chides me. "Don't talk sexy to me if you're not going to do what I tell you first."

"I'll go south if you go south too," I dare him, my pulse beating frantically in my throat while the heat he's kindling inside me starts to slowly, surely, burn me.

He doesn't hesitate and moves. My body tightens, and a cataclysm of arousal seizes me as I watch his forearm flex and his arm disappear beneath his waist. I can perfectly picture his big hand stroking over himself, and my pussy suddenly weeps.

"Remy, I want to kiss you there," I choke, need clogging my throat, "and then I want to eat you all up, and afterward, I want to get all sticky and feel all loved and beautiful because of you."

His voice gentles as I watch his arm move slightly. "Brooke, whether I'm there or not, you *are* loved and you *are* beautiful."

"Remy," I say, going south too with my fingers because I'd promised him. When I find myself slick and tender and swollen, I inhale sharply. "I need you. Call me on the phone."

"What do you mean, little firecracker?"

"Call me on the phone."

We hang up in Skype and I answer my phone on the first ring, and his voice sounds closer. So close it spills into me, sexier than sex itself, deep and dark with lust, and I can hear his breath in my ear, and a passionate fluttering arises everywhere inside me.

"I need you, Remy," I explode. "I just need all of you—your heat, your mouth, your voice, you." I close my eyes and slide my finger over the outer folds of my sex, stroking myself like he strokes me.

"God, tell me how much you need me," he says, and his breathing sounds faster and a little rougher.

And suddenly his voice is just so close that in my head—he's with me, his lips near my ear, his husky timbre sending a weak quivering to my thighs, and I whisper to him, "So much it's torture to see you, to hear your voice."

His voice is raspy. "Baby, I need you around me, clutching the fuck out of me."

"I'm dying to see you."

"In three weeks we're fighting in Seattle, and I'm coming to you. And I'm going to strip you to your skin and reacquaint my whole body with yours. Every part of it."

"I hate that you can't be in me," I admit thickly, my eyes fluttering shut as my body loses itself in the sound of his voice and a flush of heat spreads throughout my skin.

He's breathing roughly. "Doesn't matter. When I'm there, I'll be all over you."

He's taken over my mind. I'm transported to our hotel room. To him. I'm there, in my head, with him. I imagine it all, remember it all. The way his thumb tweaks my nipples. How it rubs little circles of pleasure into my clit. How his tongue laves my areolas. Rubs against my tongue. Traces the seam of my lips. How it licks my nape. The back of my ear. The shell of my ear. Dipping into the crevice.

"Please," I gasp as I start thrashing, clutching the phone against my ear with my shoulder as I use one hand to cup my breast, the other to rub myself.

His voice makes me imagine his face as it tightens with need and pleasure, and it only yanks me further into this whirlwind of pleasure as I hear him growl, "Brooke, I've got my cock in my hand and I'm pushing it inside you, and I swear I can fucking smell you. Tell me what you're doing. . . ."

"I'm taking you. In me. I'm biting your neck and . . . Remy, *Remy* . . ."

I never knew I could come like this, but the instant I hear that low, drawn-out, sexy groan he sometimes releases when he's starting to come, I lose it. Because I've never seen anyone come like he does. Tremors wrack my body, and I thrash in place while I struggle to remain clutching my phone, because I refuse to miss a single breath of him, a single sound he makes.

We pant afterward, sated, but as I lie there trying to recover, an utter loneliness creeps over me, suddenly overwhelming me. I can't cuddle my lion, or kiss his lips good night, or feel his skin hot and hard on mine. I look down at my hand, wet with my own juices, and instead of feeling connected to him, for the first time, I'm more aware than ever that we're apart. "I miss you," I whisper sadly.

He's quiet for a moment, then softly, tenderly: "I want to punch things all fucking day. There's an ache in my chest I want to rip out of me, but it's so fucking deep, I could tear my heart out and it would still be there."

"Remy . . ."

"This is the last time I live without you. I'm half mad already and halfway into the fucking grave. I don't like this. Every single monster in my head tells me you'll run and I won't be close enough to catch you. Every instinct in me screams at me to go get you. Every bone in my body tells me you are MINE—not a part of me, but my brain understands why the hell I sent you away from me. The rest of me can't take it. You can't convince the rest of me being away from you is right."

"Remington Tate, I swear to you—I swear—that when I'm able to get up from this stupid bed and run again, you're always, always, going to be the one thing I'll run straight to."

ELEVEN

SISTERS AND FRIENDS

Those first few nights when I first slept with Remy, I used to lie and cuddle at his side, not knowing what he was doing on his iPad. Until one day I shook aside my sleepiness and decided to investigate.

"What are you doing?" I said then, straightening up to take a peek.

He sets the Apple aside and drags me onto his lap, then he adjusts me between his thighs and grabs back his iPad, whispering in my ear as he shows me the screen, "Kicking the computer's ass."

"What is it?"

"Chess."

I lean back against him with his hard arms stretched at my sides. "Are you winning? Of course you are," I answer myself.

I stare at the screen, at the white and black pieces, and he explains each piece and how it moves, the pawns being the most basic ones. We continue the game, and what I am enjoying is watching his brain work as he moves his pieces, and hearing his breath in my ear. And how every once in a while, he nibbles my earlobe and sets a kiss on me.

He tells me to pick which piece to move when he's up next. I decide to go for the big guns.

He laughs softly. "You don't want to move our queen."

"Why not? She seems like the most versatile and powerful piece."

He taps the queen and puts her back in her place. "The queen stays by the king." He kisses my temple.

"Why?" I counter.

"To protect him."

"From what?" I turn and stare into his laughing blue eyes, and he sets his iPad aside and cups my face, smiling, like I should know why the queen protects the king.

Then he kisses me, and just to play chess with him feels like I've learned something new about him. That I also love. Just like the rest.

God. He's a living, breathing treasure, and he's letting me discover him, and all I want is to get lost in the complex divine darkness and light in him.

Now, he's miles and miles away, flying to Chicago, but I've found that if I log in at night, I can play chess with him and let him beat the hell out of me. And I can write little comments on the screen, like, *I'm going to get you now!*

He only answers with a move that eats up one of my pawns.

And I make a stupid move and go, You're dead meat! Both your king and queen! But I'm gonna make your king watch while I kill his woman!

He types, Nobody touches my woman.

I go, But you?

Now you're getting the idea.

And I laugh, and then he calls me, and we forget the game, and I get lost in his voice and in the things he says to me.

By week two, I've visited my gynecologist, and I'm able to hear the baby's heartbeat. Melanie records the event on her phone and sends it to me, so I send it to Remy, and he answers with a ?

I dial his number and hear his rough voice. He always sounds a little impatient, like he'd rather do anything than talk on a damned phone, answering with a gruff "yeah." I tell him, "That's the baby's heartbeat."

We both fall quiet for a moment. Then he says, "Let me hang up so I can listen. I'll call you in five."

I laugh and then wait impatiently. . . .

By week two and a half, Nora has been stopping by less and less. She's somehow angry at me about something, or maybe I'm angry at her? I'm not sure. But even Melanie wonders what's up with her, and I sometimes wonder if she's grumpy because of Pete, for she keeps asking me about the fights, about our schedules, and about the Underground.

By this time, I've played most of Remy's songs. My favorites are Nickelback's "Far Away" and 3 Doors Down's "Here Without You"—which I listen to over and over at night.

Melanie is now on a first-name basis with the florist. I get red roses every day. Every day. She gets a call from Riley in the morning and in the evening, requesting a full report for Remington. If I liked the flowers? If I'm doing all right? I've been sending a text every day—okay, actually more than one—and Remy always answers me after training.

I've watched hundreds of movies and Internet shopped till I dropped, and I've been seeing my parents. Things may be tense with them, but it gets better every time they come for a visit. At least they now seem accepting of, and almost excited about, the baby.

By the third week, I have read the entire *What to Expect When You're Expecting* pregnancy bible and I've learned that the heartburn I'm feeling is normal. The weepiness? The anger? The mood swings? Normal. In the online forums, we90r64mama and 4uwtforever call it "pregnant-mama drama." I have laughed my head off with their anecdotes of feeling possessive of their baby daddies and doing a thousand and one crazy things like checking their receipts and their credit cards, and spying.

I really think I've been doing all right with the pregnant-mama drama, PMD, until the start of the fourth week, when the bed rest starts driving me up the wall. I'm trying to keep my mind busy, if not myself, but I miss running, I miss the sun, I miss the fights, and I miss *him*.

At midnight, I had insomnia—normal!—and texted him a long, detailed message that it had been raining in Seattle and I found a song I want to play him. Has he ever heard "Between the Raindrops" by Lifehouse? Oh, and has he gone running? I miss running—it's so frustrating to stare at these four walls. . . .

Then I told him I planned to get permission from my gynecologist so I could come and see him fight when he comes to Seattle next week. The only answer I got to all my questions was the one he texted:

No Underground for you yet, LF. Stay home.

Of all the things I imagined him saying, I never, ever imagined Remington would say this. And thus, the PMD began when all my sister's words came back to haunt me, about him being a sex god of the Underground . . . and suddenly the PMD worsened as I imagined whores pleasuring him while he was all alone without me. Who's giving him all the sex this primal male needs? It seems that all my pregnancy hormones are hard at work, not only helping me hold this baby, but hard at work driving me crazy in my head.

I forced myself to text: Why? Why don't you want me at the Underground?

He didn't answer, and all my fears raged even more fiercely, as I truly wondered: Why?

Don't you want to see me?

He answered: Just stay the fuck home and wait for me.
So he wasn't anxious to see me then at all?

You want me home? So all your fans can scream at you and
see you and not ME? Fuck you!

I added the red, fuming emoticon after that so he'd know he'd pissed me off, then I tossed the phone aside and stewed in my own juices until I wanted to explode. Stay home? Home is where *he* is. Motherfucker.

This morning my roses doubled in amount.

When Riley talked to Melanie this morning, he told her to tell me that Remington hoped I liked my flowers, and that he wants me to send the link of the song I told him about yesterday by text.

Ha.

I'm sorry, but I don't feel like sending him shit.

Our baby is doing well, and I'm so excited the cream seems to be working. The spotting has stopped completely, but the hormones in me? They are raging. I am *dying*. To see him. I've defended him, me, and our baby to my parents daily, telling them that I have not been discarded or used, that he's brought me here to be supported and taken care of, but to hear him say that he doesn't want me at the Underground sucks *balls*.

All the misery I've been trying to keep at bay is coming at me from all sides now that I'm angry at him and don't want to have *reason* to be angry at him, but, god, I can't help it. Being on bed rest, you have nothing to do but let your head come up with a thousand and one stories about what is going on *out there*—in the world, without you—and none of these stories are pleasant.

"Stop sending reports, Melanie," I say glumly that afternoon.

"Why? Riley asks, and Remington asked me to send daily reports before he left that day. He wants to know how you're doing."

"Stop giving detailed reports, period."

She seems to be completely unable to keep the laughter from her voice. "Hey, you want them too! Your eyes bug out of your head when I'm listening to the other end of the line like you want supersonic ears to hear. I've heard you call Pete and ask how he is."

I sigh and rub my temples. "I just worry about him."

I've called Pete to ask if everything was okay and he said yes. Like a true guy, he was not very talkative on the phone except to say that they're there if I need anything, and that Remington is training nonstop. I asked if he was speedy, and he said they were all focused on keeping that under control, and to relax, that he was trying very hard to stay blue.

What did that mean?

Pete called me a trigger once, and the thought that Remy might want to avoid me to stay blue eats me up like acid.

Mel stares at my forlorn face and shakes her head with a grin, as if she can't believe I've been reduced to this. "You're getting wrinkles as we speak; cut the frown already," she lightly says as she brings a bowl of homemade organic popcorn for us to eat while we watch yet another movie. "Sweetie, the Underground comes through here in a week—you should be beaming!"

"I won't even be able to *go*. Remington doesn't fucking want me there."

Taking a deep breath, I try to calm down as I wonder what would BBP—Brooke Before Pregnancy—do?

"Because he's coming to see you after the fight. Riley told me your man plans to sleep here with you during their three-night stay."

I cover my face. "That makes me feel even worse. Why is he arriving just in time to fight and not before, to see me?"

Melanie shrugs.

"What if Nora is right and he doesn't want me anymore?" I continue.

She squeals with laughter now. "Okay, first of all, Nora is a cheese-head with little holes in her head, and she's been lost all these days when she promised me she'd be coming to take care of you and is Lord-knows-where instead. She's up on cloud nine somewhere, and you're somewhere else—because these are definitely hormones talking here."

"I can't believe he doesn't *want me* there. I think someone else stole his phone and texted me. Maybe a stupid whore."

"Brooke, he's clearly protecting you and the baby." Melanie rolls her eyes at me as she searches my Apple TV for something to rent.

The monsters in my head prevail over her words. Baby is doing better. If my doctor gives me the green light, why wouldn't he want me there? Does he not even miss me?

"I just don't understand," I grumble, grabbing one of the same stupid magazines I've read a thousand times and tossing it against the wall.

Melanie drops the remote and comes to stroke my hair. "Like they say, men are from Mars. Some of the ones I've dated are even from YourAnus—the assholes. And *you*, my darling, are very pregnant here. You've been stressed about losing the baby, stressed about missing your guy, stressed about your mama and papa not being so supportive, and Nora isn't any help at all. You've been stuck with me, a *nutcase*, in these same four walls, for three weeks, without even feeling the sunlight. Chicken, this is why everyone who ever appeared on Big Brother went crazy, and at least they had a pool."

I shove her playfully and laugh.

But hours later, I'm staring at my living room wall, replaying all the scenarios of Remington not wanting me. Remington seeing someone else in the stands he likes. Remington realizing a baby—as it has proven so far—is a little more trouble than a man like him would want. I am torturing myself, and my mind has gained such momentum I can't even stop it.

"You're distant. Where are you? With Remy?"

"He must be fighting right now."

Right now, hundreds of people get to see him. Hundreds of women are screaming his name, lusting after him. Right now those blue eyes will have to look at something or someone else when they scan the audience and I'm not there. And even when he'll be here, in my city, he doesn't want me there and I don't even know what to do.

"Don't they stream it live on some Underworld site? Come here, I'll bet they do!" She tugs me to my room, opens my laptop, and starts Googling. My insides jump as I wonder if they do. She squeals when she finds a link and clicks on the volume. "He's there. Come here! Well, it's not him—do you think he already went?"

I scan the comments. They mention him, but the commentators seem to be asking when he'll be coming on. My heart squeezes with wanting to be there, and then Mel snatches up my hand when the announcer uses his most suspenseful voice: "I'm hearing a name out in the crowd. It keeps coming up. Can you all hear it too?" He covers one ear, and the crowd screams, in unison:

"RIPTIDE!"

My butterflies burst alive in my stomach when he goes, "That's right! That is RIGHT, ladies and gentlemen! Now welcome, unde-feated this season with a perfect score, the bad boy wonder, the one and the only, Remington Tate, Riiiiiiptide!!!"

My stomach flutters as he comes out, and the public roars in the background as the camera focuses on the ring. And then he climbs up into that ring, agile and aerodynamic, like he does. He jerks off his RIPTIDE satin robe—and the screams from the women almost break my laptop's speakers. Far away, I see a sign that reads FOREVER RIPTIDE'S in the air.

Fascinated, Mel and I watch him make his turn. He's smiling, drinking in the attention. Then I see him stop where he always does and automatically look at my empty seat, and then his smile falters. He pauses for a moment, then cracks his neck and goes back to Riley and turns away from the crowd.

"Aww. I think he misses you too. He never goes to his corner like that." Melanie sighs. "Brooke? Brooke?"

I'm crying into a pillow.

"Brookey, what's wrong?"

"I don't know."

"Brooke, what's wrong? Is something wrong?"

I squeeze the couch pillow tighter and then wipe my eyes.

"Ugh! It's rained more inches in my apartment than it has in the whole of Seattle," I groan. Then I stand and get away. I go to the kitchen, get a napkin, and am patting my tears when I hear the scream from the public as a big *thunk!* is heard. I rush back over and peer into the screen, and a man is splattered on the canvas, facedown, Remington standing before him, feet braced apart, chest heaving, arms at his side. Like a conquering god of war. Who I desire with every aching molecule of my body. Who can have any woman in the world and might not just want me anymore, and I cannot fathom the way my heart will break if I'm to live the rest of my life without him.

"Riptide! Ladies and gentlemen! Your victor, undefeated this season, leading the championship in the number one spot! RRRR-RIP-TIIIIIDE!"

My heart swells in my chest, and it throbs, and I grab the computer and turn it to me, see his arm is raised as he catches his breath. He's not smiling tonight. He's somber and panting, staring at a spot in the crowd as if he's lost in his thoughts.

"I love you so much . . . I don't know what I'm going to do, but I'm going to make you love me this hard too," I whisper, caressing his face on the screen.

"You're going to be a daddy, Rem!" Melanie squeals. "Your baby momma loves you so much!"

Remington turns his head to the ringmaster, and, with a nod, the announcer calls up someone else. My stomach tangles when I realize he's going to keep fighting.

Melanie answers the phone and I forget to tell her not to.

"Riley! What . . . oh, she's fine. Really? Well no, actually, she's also not doing good either." I close my eyes and look at my phone as they start talking about how badly we're doing. "Yes, yes, I told her he's coming over. Right after the fight? All right, she'll be happy."

She hangs up. "Remington just finished the fight and he wanted to know if you were all right, and Riley wanted to know how you're doing since Remington isn't doing so well. He wants you to know they'll be in town soon."

The frustration of being bedridden is enormous, but this added frustration of wanting to see him just boils me over. I can't stand thinking that he will be here in Seattle fighting and that I won't watch him fight.

Suddenly I grab my cordless telephone and start dialing.

"What are you doing? Who are you calling?" Mel asks.

"Dr. Trudy please? Brooke Dumas," I say, then cover the speaker. "Melanie, I don't care if he doesn't want to see me. *I* want to see him and I'm GOING to see him, period."

"What the hell are you talking about?"

"You need to get me into the Underground."

❤ ❤ ❤

"I'VE ALWAYS WANTED to dress like an old chick since I saw *Mrs. Doubtfire*," Melanie says as she pulls out the wigs we ordered off the Internet.

"Mel, I won't get out of that wheelchair—tell me again nothing will go wrong?"

"Dude, you cajoled permission from your doctor. It will be fine. Remy won't even know you went. We're young, Brooke! Hello? YOLO. You only live once." She huffs resolutely and goes to try on her floral "old chickie" dress.

"But I told the doctor I was visiting my boyfriend at *his* place," I remind her.

"That IS his place. The ring is Riptide's lair. Plus, don't underestimate the power of happiness. People heal better when they're in their loved ones' arms. The baby will love it, won't you, you adorable little baby?" she coos stupidly down at my stomach.

Biting back a laugh, I shove her away, but she's right, I'm pretty sure the baby will love it. Already I feel invigorated, and I don't really think the baby has been having fun with me in my current sorry state. I am in love with a complicated man, and he makes me feel complicated feelings. I have run it over in my head a thousand times, and I don't give a rat's ass if he doesn't want me there. I am going to go see my man. Period.

"What do you think?" I ask Melanie as I adjust my shoulder-length blond wig.

"Awesome. You look cheapish. Now let me paint you." She smears a makeup cake on me while the prospect of seeing him makes my heart wham excitedly into my rib cage. "Mel, my pores are drowning."

"Tut-tut! Hush! Now me."

I eye myself in the mirror as she does her own face. "Okay, I look like a prostitute. They're going to ask us how much we charge."

"You ding-dong, we have to make you not look like you."

"But you still look hotter! You're a hot grandma—why can't I be?"

"Because I'm the one who can still walk, and you're the one in the chair." She pushes me closer to the mirror and we look at ourselves in our floral dresses. Mel added a little cashmere sweater to hers and a flower to her gray-and-white wig, while my blond wig has an Alice-in-Wonderland black headband holding the hair in place.

I look completely unlike me, and if I added the big glasses we got, I would look even doubly less like me, but they're so big and disturbing to wear, I tuck them into my dress pocket as we head out to the elevator. "I don't want to distract him, all right? Remy can't see that I'm there. He might get angry. I don't even know what he'll do—he's too unpredictable. And we've never really fought without breaking up before, Mel."

"My darling chicken, judging by the roses he's sent, he wants to make up. And don't you worry! I will have you back here in an instant, and in the meantime we're getting you out of this GOD-DAMNED ROOM! Woo-hoo!"

❤ ❤ ❤

THIRTY MINUTES LATER we discover that the Underground is not a handicap-friendly place. We learned this when Mel tried to get me out of the cab, then into the chair, then into the nightclub, down the elevator, and into the Underground. She's huffing and puffing and telling me she doesn't look all that cool anymore, "thanks to you, pregnant chick."

I'd be laughing over how ridiculous she looks trying to get people to let us pass, but as we enter the crowded arena, it feels a little bit like coming home, and the mingled feelings of happiness and frustration over not being invited collide in me in a complicated little combo.

This is where I met him. Where I lost my heart in one breath. Where he fucked my name. Where he kissed my lips. Where he took the ring by storm, before he took me.

After about a thousand "excuse me, sorry, coming through" notices, Melanie finally draws me up to our seats. I had to buy tickets with my own card and I splurged, so I got us front-row seats, although not exactly center. They're good, and I'll be able to devour every inch of my Riptide from up close. He's not anxious to talk to me? Not anxious to see me? I'm dying for a mere glimpse.

"Remember to look the part of an older woman, Mel," I whisper as the first fighters of the evening start pounding each other's faces in.

"That woman keeps following us," Melanie says worriedly and points behind us, but I can't even turn. "She's like a she-male. A little scary."

I scan the area for Pete and see him, and right next to him, in the seat I usually occupy, is my sister Nora, grinning and flirting with him.

"Wow, Nora got Pete to get her a ticket?" Melanie says.

I don't know why, but seeing someone, anyone, even my sister, in my seat, sparks a thousand snakes of jealousy awake in me, and I am angry all over again. Not angry. Furious all over again over Remington telling me I couldn't come here. *Bastard.*

Suddenly the ring is vacated and I think I see Riley starting to walk over to take his place near the corner of the ring, and my pulse skyrockets.

"The last time he came to this arena, he gave us a record knockout and chased after one of our very own. . . ." The voice through the speakers flares, and the women scream and my heart just heats as I remember the way he came after me. "You know who I'm talking about. The MAN you are HERE to SEE! Say hello to the one, the only, Remington Tate, youuuuuuur Riiiptiiiiide!!!!!!"

Melanie holds her breath, then murmurs, "Ohmifuckinggod, I see him."

My pulse has shot up to the ceiling as I strain to see a flash of red, trotting toward the ring, but I can't see anything from this stupid chair. "I can't see him!" And god, I hate that everyone can see him but me.

"Dude, he's coming to the ring! Some chicks are coming over, but he's pushing through. He's a god, Brooke. Oh my god . . ."

And then I see him at last, and my heart literally stops and my stomach immediately constricts with emotion. *I love him I hate him I love him.*

He comes into my line of vision, a flash of red, and swings up into the ring, so lithe and muscled, so sleek and agile. The lights shine down on him as he gets rid of his red robe, and suddenly he's there. So masculine and raw. Every woman's fantasy and my *real.*

I will never forget the way he looks in his boxing attire, every muscle of his ripped torso hard and cut, tanned and glistening. I will never forget the way he smiles for his crowd. I. Am. *Dying.* He looks amazing. Perfect. Radiating male strength and vitality. Like he's been on a fucking beach and I've been in hell. It even feels like all the lights above rush down to kiss his suntanned skin. His rock-hard arms spread out, muscles taut as he starts slowly turning around. The arena almost trembles under my wheels—the screams are deafening.

"Fuck them over, Riptide!" people scream behind me.

"And then fuck me!"

His dimples flash for them, his eyes glint for them. He looks so blatantly happy I want to hit him. In fact, I want to go up there and crush his mouth with mine *while* I hit him.

"Brooke, I feel like such a bad friend that I lust over your man, but please tell me you understand!" Melanie says anxiously.

I groan in disgust at myself. I have been abandoned, and here I am, chasing after him like some groupie. Lusting after him because he is mine.

MINE.

"And now, laaaadies and gentlemen, we welcome the Mother of All Monsters, Hector Hex, Herculeeeeeees!" the announcer cries, and Melanie mutters, "Hooooly shit."

The moment the Mother of Monsters takes the ring, I swear I almost see the floor caving in with his weight. I've never seen this one before, but he looks even bigger than Butcher, and the knot in my stomach tightens tenfold. The new fighter looks like some sort of Paul Bunyan—enormous giant.

"What galaxy did that piece of meat come from?" Melanie asks, as perturbed as I am.

Remy taps boxing gloves with him, then he draws back and flexes his arm muscles, and I watch the tattoos between his shoulder and biceps ripple. And all my body ripples in remembrance of how his feels.

Ping.

They go center. My heart hammers inside me as the Mother of All Monsters slams Remington's ribs, and Remington comes back with a triple punch that is so fast and so powerful, it knocks the guy back three steps.

"Brooke, ohmigod!" Melanie says. "OH. MY. GOD!"

The giant comes back with a swing that strikes Remy straight in the gut. I hear the sound of the punch and wince, but suddenly I hear the sounds of the way Remington hits back. Fast and hard. *PAM PAM POOM!* The giant falls on his ass. Remington circles the ring as he waits for him to get up, sinuous, graceful, my powerful blue-eyed lion.

All my body remembers the way that lion moves over me. In me. The way his hips push with perfect precision. The way his hands coast all over me. Squeeze me. Tease me. The way his tongue rasps against me, tastes me, licks me.

The monster slowly gets up and shakes his head, as if he's confused, and before he can get in another punch, Remington hooks him with his right and knocks him back down—*splat* on his back.

Melanie jumps and screams.

"*YES!! YES! REMY, YOU'RE THE KING OF THE FUCKING JUNGLE!*" she screams. And he turns with that smile, and I freeze when he spots us. He's smiling indulgently at us, his fans, facing in our direction, when suddenly his stance changes—and his body seems to reengage. His dimples are still in place, but his eyes narrow just slightly as he surveys us, like a predator in hunting mode.

The bottom drops out of my world.

"I think he recognized your voice, you idiot!" I hiss under my breath, tugging Mel's skirt so that she sits back down.

But he's not looking at Mel. Oh, no. Remy is staring at me. Feet braced apart, his chest heaves as he suddenly lasers in on me. Me and *only* me.

His blue eyes bore into me, curious and questioning, and I am suddenly excruciatingly aware of everything I am wearing. The kohl around my eyes, the ridiculous red lipstick, the plastered-on makeup . . . I pray, quietly and fervently, that it's enough to shield me from him.

I expel a breath when his eyes slide to my right, to Melanie, and she adjusts her wig and breathes, "Shit on a fucking stick."

And if I thought I was free and clear, I completely, completely, underestimated him.

He looks at me again, and then, slowly, he shakes his head.

My heart clenches so hard I think my chest will have some permanent interior damage.

He drags a hand through his hair and restlessly paces around for a moment; then he lifts his head again, and when his eyes sear into me and he shakes his head again, this time with a sudden flash of his beautiful dimples, I think I come.

Electricity courses through me as his eyes darken with heat, his lips curl sensually, full of that male knowledge of his that I, contrary to what any of his fans say, *I* am his number one fan.

He knows exactly who I am. I can see chastising amusement in his eyes and can almost hear him say . . .

You little shit, I know who you are.

I see you.

I fucking see you!

I want to rip off this stupid costume, and just run up to him and climb him like a tree. Grab that hard jaw in my hands and kiss his mouth and drown him with my kisses and all the love I have for him that's been drowning me for weeks.

He curls his fingers at his sides when another fighter is announced, and as he takes the ring, Remy keeps looking at me, clenching and unclenching his fists, and the heat in his gaze, I can feel it burn in every part of my being, down to my toes.

The bell rings, and Remington winks at me, a wink that makes the crowd roar.

Melanie squeaks and squeezes my hand. "Tell me again how much he doesn't want you, you dopehead!" She points at herself. "This girl right here is horny on your fucking behalf! Ohmigod! He's completely doing you in his head!"

I almost moan when the fight begins.

Remington looks invigorated. He punches the new fighter repeatedly, jabbing, hooking, ducking, and he turns to me in between punches, just to see that I'm looking.

I am.

I see him.

I feel him.

I want him.

I fucking love him more than anything or anyone in this world.

The man doesn't stand a chance against him, and I watch in utter and complete fascination.

All these weeks, with all these hormones, missing him like crazy, wanting him like crazy, loving him like crazy . . . He's as close as I've ever had him in weeks, and I am dying for him so badly, I'm gripping my chair so tight my knuckles are white. I want him inside me like I want my next breath. Right now it's all I can think of—all I can think of is that he is mine, and I am his, that I am not letting him go, that I will *make him want me again* if he ever stops wanting me, and that there will never be a moment of my life when I will let go.

With every win, his name is called, his arm is raised, the crowd roars, and those blue eyes find me in my ridiculous outfit and his jaw tightens and his body tenses, as if he can't stand to see me without touching me. My entire body responds and I tremble in my seat with the way he looks at me. I may look awful, but he still wants me. Lust burns in his eyes, and the promise that he'll take me dances inside those irises. My heart throbs. I remember him.

I remember his skin, his calluses brushing over me. His breath. I see his body up on display, glistening with sweat, every cut and ripped inch perfect, and I can almost taste it, feel it slide against mine.

All night I am a mass of happiness, excitement, nerves, and quaking, overwhelming need.

"Mel, I don't want him to come see me in this costume," I tell her, for the first time regretting my clothing choices. I look ugly, whorish, unclean, and ridiculous, and this is not how I wanted Remy to see me tonight.

"All right, let's get you home and make him come to you," she mutters. She starts pushing me, and suddenly I hear the voice bursting through the speakers. "KNOCKOUT! Yes, ladies and gentlemen! Our victor this evening, once again, I give you, Riptide! *Riiiptiiiiiiide!!!!!!!!*"

His name echoes around me as the public chants, *"Riptide! Riptide!"*

"Of course you'd do the exact opposite of what I asked you to," a guttural, insanely deep and sexy voice whispers behind me; then I see a muscular torso move in front of me, and I'm lifted into a pair of deliciously sweaty arms.

Remington turns to Melanie instead of to me, and I hear him tell her, almost growl, "I'm taking care of this fireball. Riley can give you a ride home."

His scent spins around me and completely disarms me. I want to hit his chest and tell him to let me go, because I'm still a little angry, but my fingers have linked at the back of his strong neck in my fear of falling, and I'm motionless in his hold—absorbing the feel of his arms around me. Good. Scary good. His bulging biceps pressing into my sides, his thick forearms glistening with a sheen of perspiration, like the rest of him. The rest of beautiful, infuriating, complicated him.

"Have fun, Brooke," Melanie says with a twinkle in her eye as she comes to pat my shoulder, whispering in my ear, "Dude, in my life, I've never seen that glimmer in a man's eyes before; he's going to fuck you *so* bad."

In the locker rooms, Riley greets me with a beyond-thrilled grin on his face. "Hey, Brooke! Since Rem's got you tight, I assume you *are* Brooke?" he says as he hands Remington a small duffel bag.

Remy nods and whispers something to him, then he carries me outside and summons a cab and, instead of taking me home, gruffly tells the driver the name of a hotel two blocks away. He's dehydrated, and he unzips his duffel, takes out a smartwater and starts gulping it down as he uses his free arm to haul me onto his lap.

His grip tightens around my waist when I try to move from my spot, and my heart hammers crazily in my chest when he tucks the water back into his bag. He ducks his head, and takes the deepest, longest inhale of me he's ever taken. Lust spirals through me. I'm still a little bit angry, but between my thighs, my clit pulses to the point of pain. He grabs my face, turns me, and nips my earlobe, breathing heavily, completely aroused under my butt as if he wants me. As if he *desperately* wants me.

"God," he rasps into my ear, his arms clenching around me as he fucks his tongue into my ear. A tremor of need races up my body and makes me bite back a moan. I'm torn between hitting and kissing him because he's killing me. My panties are drenched, my breasts hurt, my heart hurts, every part of me hurts as he dips his tongue into my ear, outside the shell, behind it, with that same desperation I feel.

When we arrive at the hotel, I'm stewing in my own anger and at the same time simmering with lust because of the way Remington has worked himself into a crazy arousal in the back of the taxi. Rubbing his hands on me, licking and nipping me. Scenting me like he's starving for air.

He picks up a key from the front desk and then we're riding up in the elevator, and I say, "Put me down," in a thick, alien voice.

"I will soon," he murmurs back at me, his eyes flaming with heat as he looks down at me.

Even with those blue eyes taking me in in the most unsexy dress in the universe, in the worst makeup possible, with awful hookerish red lipstick, the primal lust in his gaze sprints through me like little lightning bolts of pleasure.

I feel like a simmering volcano, my blood stewing in my veins from an overpowering mix of anger and arousal. But the arousal, I hate how it's quickly winning as his scent keeps reaching my lungs. My tongue hurts in my mouth. I want to lick his throat and take that sexy mouth with mine and make him show me he still wants and loves me.

My heart whacks fiercely into my ribs as he slips the key into the slot and carries me inside, heading to the end of the hall, where the master bedroom usually is.

He sets me down on the foot of the bed.

"I don't know if I should kiss you or hit you." My voice quivers with emotion.

Then I feel reenergized and smack my fist into his hard pectoral and push at his chest so he goes away. I grab his beautiful face and crush his sexy mouth to mine. His taste shudders through me like a gunshot of ecstasy until I yank angrily away and hit his wall-like chest again.

"Your songs made me cry! I missed your voice, your hands! I'm a pining stupid pregnant fool for you, and you want me to stay like some fifth-century good little wife, waiting for you while you're out there wetting every woman's fucking panties. I *won't* do it. I *refuse* to be that girl—do you hear me?"

"Yeah, I hear you." He leans over and slides his fingers to cup the back of my head, then his husky, desire-thickened voice dances over my skin. "Now come here and kiss me again. . . ." He draws me closer and I hit his chest more weakly, moaning in protest.

"Did you touch someone?" I cry, trying to twist free.

He tightens his hold on my nape and fastens his hungry gaze on my lips. "No."

"Then why didn't you want to see me? I don't understand you!"

His eyes flash in frustration. "You don't have to understand me—just love the hell out of me. Can you do that? Can you?" His thumb drags with sensual roughness across my lower lip. "*Do* you?"

I can't reply. While he stares at my mouth with a deliciously carnivorous stare, I'm drinking in the shadowed jaw, the blue eyes, the spiky hair, his high cheekbones and square jaw, the dark slashes of his eyebrows, every beautiful inch of his face, so achingly close that every organ inside my body starts to throb. I hear myself whisper, "Do you still love me?"

"You've got to be kidding me," he says.

I moan as his fingers caress the back of my neck, the touch scrambling my brain. He intoxicates me with his nearness, makes me drunk with the smell of his sweat, his soap, him. Every time he's near, he heightens my senses, and I'm so emotional, all these hours missing him, all these strange hormones, my voice trembles when I speak. "Do you still love me, like before?"

"I'm fucking insane about you!" he cries in disbelief.

I close my eyes and moan softly, clinging fiercely to the words.

"I told you I loved you with every petal of every rose," he tells me in a low, husky whisper. Then he scrapes the pad of his thumb over my mouth again, more roughly this time, with more need, as his voice, velvet-edged and strong, sends a ripple of heat through me.

"At the institute one of my female doctors got a rose. She told me it was from her husband, because he loved her and he was away. Isn't that what you send when you're not there to tell someone you fucking love them? Brooke, I've never done this before, but it fucking hurts to look at you through a fucking screen. It hurts to text. It hurts like no fucking punch hurts."

He spreads his fingers open at the back of my neck as if he needs to touch as much of me as possible, his eyes glowing to such a fierce degree, it only makes my heart thud harder.

"Didn't you hear the songs!? They were all for you, Brooke. Didn't you know I thought of you? Missed the hell out of you? If I haven't showed you I love you, then tell me in what ways I'm fucking this up!"

"I wanted you to want me at the fight! Like you always do. You've always wanted me there before. Why didn't you? Why didn't you come see me before?"

"God, I *want* you there like I want nothing! Do you think I enjoy a second of this hell? If I'd come seen you before the fight, you think I'd have the will to leave you? How can you think this is easy for me, Brooke? How?"

The vivid frustration in his eyes cuts me so deep I drop my head, because, no, I don't think it's easy for him at all.

"You think you need me, little firecracker?" The gruff question travels all the way through me, and I have to press my thighs together to stop the tremor in me. "Baby, the way you need me can only barely cover half of the way I need you." The unexpected sadness in his voice yanks my gaze back to his.

"My game is half of what it used to be. I can't concentrate. I can't sleep. I can't get in the game. I'm like a robot out there. I feel a hole right here—right fucking here." He places his fist over his chest. "I'm trying to protect *my* girl. *Three* doctors, *three*, said she had to be in bed for the first *three* months, with no travel. I can't see her, I can't make love to her—I am *trying* to do the right thing when my gut screams that SHE belongs with ME." He narrows his eyes, exhaling roughly through his nose. "Every second that you and I breathe, you belong with *me*."

"Remy, I'm sorry. This is driving me crazy too." I cover my face and try breathing through my constricted throat, but he grabs my wrists and forces my arms to my sides, seizing my gaze with his own, his eyes vividly blue.

"I love you so much." He engulfs my face in both big, beautiful callused hands. "So fucking much, Brooke, I still don't know what to do with myself," he says, and kisses the bridge of my nose with a low, shuddering breath. "I miss everything about you, from the way you smile to the way you look at me to the way the bed smells when you're with me. I love you like I love nothing in my life, nothing. It eats me up inside like a disease to want to come get you and bring you back with me."

I start trembling at the end of the bed, all my emotions, all my raging hormones, all my cells, all my being, buzzing at his words. My entire body throbs with love, lust, and the physical agony of being denied my Remy fix for weeks. Shaking, I reach out and lovingly stroke three fingers down the hard line of his jaw. "This," I say, the word breaking from my lips, "is what I see in my bedroom. This face. This face is all I see, all I see, Remy."

"Damn you, take this shit off and let me look at my Brooke."

He grabs my wig and tosses it aside, then he holds my gaze as our smiles fade. The air between us pulses and leaps like our need is a living, breathing thing between us. "Why would anyone want to cover this hair?" Quietly, he eases the net off the top of my head, and the low rustling sound is all that is audible in the room.

Slow, deliciously expert fingers delve into my bun and work to loosen my hair, and the contact of his fingertips against my scalp sends frissons down my spine.

By the time he frees the mahogany strands so they fall on my shoulders, my thighs have dissolved into a puddle along with the rest of me. A thin sheen of sweat coats his thick throat, and his pecs glisten, too. His torso is so tight and so solid it seems as impenetrable as a steel wall, as if nothing can ever hurt him. His arm muscles bulge as he strokes his hands down my hair, and I'm as unraveled as my bun.

When I speak, my voice is as husky as I've ever heard it. "I was supposed to be an old groupie."

"My," he says, in a whisper that is so much deeper and rougher than mine.

"What?"

"My sweet . . . disobedient . . . favorite little groupie."

Being called *his* again . . .

A sound escapes me, and he hears me. Bolts of heat race to my sex as he edges one hand under my dress. Vividly tender blue eyes watch me as his fingers brush up higher inside my thigh, and my heart gallops full speed.

He looks at my mouth, and oh god, I'm flooded with need. He ducks first to taste my mouth, parting it, lipstick and all while, under my dress, his finger slides over the fabric of my panties. His tongue slides over mine, and as he lays me back on the bed, I shiver as I open my mouth and moan softly.

It feels right, right, *so right*. . . .

He teases the edge at the crotch of my panties; then he eases it aside and his finger directly caresses me. A thunderstorm of desire rages in me as I softly kiss him. He tastes like him, and also of my stupid lipstick, and I'm dying as he guides me open with his finger and then here comes his tongue. Hot and moist, going around mine, then coaxing me to follow him and drink from his mouth as he slowly eases that middle finger inside me.

My body arches to his.

He whispers, into my mouth, "If you can come to my fight, you can come in my arms."

My breathing goes as he drags his finger inside my channel. I feel me squeeze around him, my body greedy to have anything of his inside me. He adds his thumb to tease my clitoris, and when he edges back to watch my face as he plays with the wettest, hottest part of my body, his mouth is smeared with my lipstick, his jaw is tight with desire, his eyes brilliant blue, his beautiful face staring down at me, and god, I swear he looks as sexy as if some other woman kissed him. I'm jealous of myself and of my lipstick as I thrash and toss my head. "Remington . . ."

He groans and gives me another kiss, this one fast and hard, with a nip of his teeth, before he draws back and withdraws his finger.

Without any hurry at all, he tugs open each and every one of the buttons of my floral dress. Every cell in my body is frenzied as I sit up and help him undo the bottom ones while he undoes the top.

"Quickly, oh, god, touch me," I gasp.

"Shh," he croons as he parts the dress right through the middle, easing the fabric aside so he can take me in my white cotton underwear. My nipples poke out through the fabric of my bra, and my panties are damp, and I didn't think it was even possible for his eyes to get any darker or hungrier than they previously were.

"God, I could eat you."

Before I know it, he finds the center clasp of my bra with his thumbs, and as he shoves it aside and rubs his fingers around my areolas, he nibbles his way along my mouth, bottom lip, top lip, until he ducks his head and takes one nipple in his mouth.

Oooh, I hear. And it's me. Making all these noises. Undulating against him.

He rubs the tip of his tongue over the point of my nipple and ripples of pleasure shoot through me. He slides his hand back into my panties, and I drive my fingers into his hair. He seems so hungry, and I'm so thirsty, the instant his middle finger eases into me, I'm so swollen, so wet, so desperate, feeling his mouth sucking on my breast like he's starved for me, I start coming.

My fingers clutch his hair in a fist, and I make an *oooooohing* sound as my head falls back as my muscles start contracting and releasing, contracting and releasing, and he moves his finger slowly, dragging out the pleasure for me, as he sucks my breast even harder, unleashing torrent after torrent of pleasure in me.

"Oh god," I cry, and I rear up to cling to him and turn my face into his neck, where I run my tongue over his delicious taut skin, drinking him desperately. "Oh god, I'm dying for you to make me yours. To feel you. *You.* Inside me."

He watches me as I catch my breath, the possessive gleam in his eyes galvanizing me. "I'm not done with you," he tenderly tells me, making me lick up his wet finger. "I'm going to fuck your mouth with mine, your pussy with my fingers, with my tongue, with any part of me I can. And you're going to kiss my cock like there's no tomorrow."

"I want to kiss your cock now."

"Not now." He steps away and strips off his boxing attire until he's all tanned skin, muscles, tattoos, and . . . My eyes bulge as I watch him take his huge, beautiful erection into the shower and run the tub. He comes to get me, and my eyes burn at the sight of his beautiful standing cock, so close to the star tattoo above it.

I want to kiss that part of him like I want to kiss the rest of him. No. I don't just want to kiss. I want to lick. Suck. Savor. And claim him, mine, forever and ever.

Before I can grab him and play with him like he played with me, he takes my arm, pulls me to my feet, and then walks me to the huge Jacuzzi tub. Round and bone-colored, it sits in the middle of the room, and as he closes the knobs, I brace myself on one of his arms and dip my feet into the water, then I wait for him to follow me. He steps in behind me and lowers us into the warm water, turning on the Jacuzzi motors as we settle deep.

My eyes drift shut as he envelops me in his arms and immediately starts licking my neck. "Remy . . ." I breathe.

His teeth graze the back of my neck and then he rasps, into my ear, "Nothing in this world tastes as good as you, your skin, your tongue, nothing is as sweet and juicy as your pussy." He lifts me suddenly from the water and turns me around, but he remains seated in the tub and his face is level with my sex. He spreads his hands on my thighs to part my legs wider and buries his head between my legs, kissing my pussy for a whole minute, stroking my clit with his tongue, then shoving his tongue into my channel. I can feel his growl vibrate all the way through me, and when he's done tasting to his pleasure, he turns me back around and lowers me back with him.

"You get even wetter *after* you come," he tells me in my ear, his voice thick as syrup, then he quietly starts soaping my hair. "And these . . . are bigger and heavier."

He runs soapy hands over my breasts, and all my blood seems to be pumping south to my clit, and to the tips of my nipples. "Yes," I barely manage. "They're so sensitive, they're always puckered."

"They want to be sucked," he breathes against the back of my ear, and the way he rolls that in his tongue, as though he's already tasting my puckered nipples, makes my clit throb.

I can feel his erection on my back, and it's so freaking hard, it pulses against my skin, and my tongue is restless in my mouth because I need to wrap it around the head of his cock so badly. I take some soap and scrub my face, trying to get rid of all this makeup.

"There," I say, turning and quickly lathering his hair.

He watches me with a smirk, like he knows the reason for my hurry. As I kneel and run shampoo over his hair and try to wash it off with a conch by the side of the tub, I straddle him so that the huge bulge of his erection—the huge delicious bulge—is right there, between my thighs, as I wash off his shampoo. He leans over and starts sucking the wet drops of water from my nipples. I cry out, and he grabs my ass and drags me harder against the bulge while his sucking motions make my toes curl.

"Does that hurt?" he rasps, tugging the tip of a nipple with his teeth.

"No, ooh, Remy, it feels so good."

He groans and rocks his hips to me as he repeats his sucking on my other breast.

"Shit, Brooke, I could come just sucking you, hearing you . . ."

"I could come being sucked . . . hearing you groan . . ."

He grabs one breast and sucks the other so hard, I whimper and start moving over his hips, and before I know it, I'm imagining lifting my hips, taking his cock in me, and riding him, and begging him to fill me, again and again. He halts me.

"I'm not coming in a tub. The only place I'm coming is on you," he rumbles.

"Take me to bed to fool around," I anxiously breathe, wrapping my arms around his neck.

By the time he carries me out of the tub and wraps me in a towel, bringing me to bed, I'm a quaking mass of red-hot need. What he says next makes me quake even harder.

"I want to tear you to pieces, I want you so much. I want to pinch, bite, and suck your nipples, all at once." He lays me on the bed and opens the towel over me, then he immediately starts licking me dry. Oh god, I can't breathe, think, I think I can't even live as he starts pinching my nipples while licking me elsewhere.

"Remington . . ."

He is mesmerizing. The atmosphere around me has changed until all we have is a bed, and me, and him. I swear I can feel the thunderbolts between our bodies. He swirls his tongue up my throat, and I almost break at the feel of his familiar, deliciously raspy calluses on my skin when he drags them down my curves. "I've seen you . . . in my head . . . every fucking hour of every day . . ." he murmurs.

He scents my neck and cups one breast again, and I shudder when he squeezes the flesh and licks my collarbone. My fingers run down his slick back, his every muscle delineated under my fingers, and oh my god, he is holding me. In his arms. He's wet, the air cold, but all he wants is to dry and lick me.

I grab his stubbly jaw in both my hands. "Remington Tate," I moan, crushing my mouth against his.

He takes my lips with even more force, sucking my tongue. "*Brooke fucking Dumas.*" Watching me with hot eyes, he tortures my nipples with his thumbs, and I slide my hand down his body and start caressing his hard length.

"Make me kiss you." Curling my fingers around the head of his erection, I suck greedily on his wet tongue. "Tell me to kiss you right here. If I can't have you between my legs, I want you in my mouth."

He groans and slides his hands up to my cheeks. "That's where I want to be. The way you use your little teeth. Run that tongue over me like you want to live on me. I want to see these lips rimming the base of my cock so bad, I won't even last when I do . . ."

"God, shut up." I dive and take his cock in my mouth. Completely. Every hot pulsing inch that I can take, I take it.

A low, pained sound rips up his chest and he's so hard and ready, I can immediately taste a few stray drops of semen. My lashes sweep upward as I meet his gaze, and he's looking at me with raw ecstasy, seeing my lips rim around his cock. Not the base . . . he's too big, long, thick. But my lips are firmly wrapped around him as my tongue rubs his head.

I splay my hands on his abs to brace myself, and his abdomen clenches when I use my fingers to caress the star tattoo at his navel. My sex burns with need and complete jealousy of what my mouth has the pleasure of being filled with right now.

Remy holds the back of my head as if enraptured, as my tongue slides over his thick length. I shudder under the carnal, primal look in his eyes. I seize the base with my fists and I start to suck with my mouth, moaning in approval when he shifts positions. He stands at the foot of the bed, and I stay on all fours on the mattress as he feeds me more of his length. He groans and pushes, his eyes drifting shut. I can taste him, salty and ready to come already. He's pulsing and so fiercely hard, my sex aches with jealousy.

My breasts dangle beneath me as I lick him on all fours, when suddenly he slides one hand all along my spine, fondling every dent and rise, until he slides his middle finger down the fissure of my ass cheeks, then he runs down and down and to the entry of my pussy, and he dips that long finger inside me.

Pleasure bolts through me. I moan and rock my hips to take his finger deeper, raising my eyes to see his face, his beautiful wild, lust-hardened face, as he watches me give him the best goddamn BJ of his life.

His chest is jerking. I can feel the tension roiling off him as he fights for control. But I want him lost and primal. He's being careful. He's holding back. Rocking his hips softly.

"Are you hungry for me?" he says, and I know what he's asking is if he's going to come in me? God, I swear I don't even want to stop to say yes.

I start stroking the base with both hands and ease back to say, "Starved for you. Ravenous for you. Please give it to me."

The guttural sound he makes only makes me wilder. He starts gently fucking two fingers into my pussy at the same time he spreads one hand over the back of my head and holds me in place as he pumps his cock into me, each time feeding me a little more until he hits the back of my throat, and eases back. But I want him lost, as lost as I am, and I start moving my head up and down on him, fast.

"Brooke!" he yells, pumping my same rhythm, his head falling back in an animal growl. Then he groans and jets inside me, three warm and salty streams spurting in my mouth, and I'm so undone and intoxicated with him, I come the second that I taste him and, simultaneously, feel him rub his fingers out of my pussy and up to circle my clit. Colors explode behind my eyelids, and as my body shudders, I whimper and cling to his cock with my hands, feverishly licking the tip, wanting every drop, every last drop. Even when I finish, I gasp for breath and hungrily lick the corner of my lips and look up.

"Brooke," he says, staring at me with fierce possession, looking somehow marveled, then he lifts me and covers my mouth with his as he pulls me close to him, engulfing me in his arms, his mouth burning hot on mine as he lays us back on the bed. Maybe my mouth tastes of him, but he doesn't care, he kisses me like there's nothing left of us but our mouths. And I feel like that's the only part of me I can even move.

He lies us down to spoon me and cups my pussy possessively, lightly fingering me. "I like when you're so hungry for me," he whispers into my ear as he caresses my abdomen.

"I'm pregnant with your baby. We've been apart and it's been torture. I've been having dreams and I wake up sweaty and needing you and I can't go back to sleep, my whole body hurts," I whisper-moan when he cups my pussy.

He nibbles the back of my ear softly and uses his hand to gently penetrate me. "I haven't been able to have a decent night's rest since you left. The bed is so empty I'm either having a cold shower, or at the gym," he murmurs as he tugs on my earlobe. "But I get hard just thinking about you, Brooke. Thinking I put a baby in you." He nibbles the back of my ear softly and sticks his finger in me. Shuddering with need, I feel the length of his cock behind my buttocks, and he rocks it slightly to me, our hips moving. More delicious pleasure shoots through me when I realize he's not done. He rolls me over to face him, wraps a leg around his hips. "Move with me," he roughly commands, and then he's moving against me, fucking me without fucking me, our bodies grinding and rubbing.

My chest fills with love as we kiss, then we watch each other. His blue eyes, spiky hair, those bulging muscles. My sex grips wantonly with each rocking motion of his hips that brings the entire length of his cock rubbing along my pussy lips, stroking my oversensitized clit. *I love you*, I want to say, but the only sounds I can make are breathy bubbly ones.

"Who do you love?" he tenderly growls.

"You."

"Who's your man?" He teases his tongue into my mouth, then drags his deliciously raspy jaw along mine with a groan. "Who's your man?"

I love the feel of his stubble against my cheeks so much, I frame his face and stroke my jaw against his raspy one again. "Remington Tate, my Riptide."

"Do you want me all over you?"

"Hmm, I want you all over me."

When I say hmm, it's supposed to mean I won't bathe just so I can smell of him and his groan tells me it's driving him crazy that I said that. But he drives me crazier with the way he calls his semen "him." I freaking love how he likes me to feel him on my skin, inside me, outside of me, in my mouth. *Hmm* . . .

"You asked for me, Brooke Dumas." He pins my arms up over my head and clamps his fingers around my wrists as he drags his cock along my pussy lips, stroking my clit just right. He watches me in the same mesmerized, love-struck, lust-struck way that I watch him, memorizing him like he seems to memorize me. My neck arches as he slows the rocking motion, keeping me on the brink of ecstasy for a couple of delicious minutes as our bodies grind. And here we are. The rustling sounds of flesh against flesh, the slapping noises of our bodies, my moans, his groans, all I am aware of.

I whisper his name when I come, and my eyes spring open in that minute where everything tenses before it explodes, and I see him over me, closing his eyes tight, his jaw ground as he spurts all over my abdomen and convulses with me, his fingers clenching my wrists. I want it to bruise, the way he holds me down as he's coming and I shudder, both of us groaning, long, drawn-out sounds of relief.

When we sag, he pulls me up to his side and gruffly murmurs, "I've waited for this for thirty-nine days."

"And five hours."

"And a little over thirty minutes." Smirking in satisfaction, because obviously, I've been impressed to silence, he drinks in my face. He runs his thumb briefly along my jawline. "I think about you. Constantly. Day. Night."

He uses his thumb to tip my face back and looks at me like he wants to eat me; then he bends down and does just that. He kisses me like I'm both precious and edible, treasuring and devouring me all at once. He slides his hand up and down my back. The feel of his calluses on my skin makes me shiver.

He looks at me, his hair a charming mess, standing up wet. "You're so fucking beautiful."

"I looked ridiculous."

He laughs softly, then tweaks my nose. "Ridiculously beautiful."

Fastening his gaze back on my face like he reveres the sight of me, he then bends and kisses my stomach and sets his head there.

"Are you mad I came to see you?" I ask, setting my hand on his hair.

"No." He licks my belly button. "I know what I've got, and you're a little handful of trouble, that's who you are."

"Me? You invented trouble. You were born and instead of 'it's a boy' the doctors said, 'Ahhh, it's trouble!'"

His chuckle is low and throaty, then it trails into silence and he looks at me, his eyes sober, almost tormented. "God, how I need you." He props his forehead on mine and drags in a coarse breath. "How I go crazy thinking of you. The whole flight on my way here I listened to the song you've played to tell me you love me." His hot mouth takes me again and we kiss feverishly, and he pulls back to bend over and kiss my stomach again. His breathing is rough. He can't stop breathing me in. Touching all my body. Reminding me he owns it.

For hours we can't stop kissing and murmuring and making each other feel good, until we lie back and settle and he spoons me. He nuzzles my neck for a brief moment and places a kiss on the hollow behind my ear. Then he caresses me for a while, and when he discovers there's still some semen remaining on my skin, he picks it up with two fingers and rubs it into my pussy.

I gasp.

"Shh," he says softly. "I need to be here. Right here." He rubs his fingers inside my channel, licking the back of my neck softly, and I shudder and start coming. He chuckles softly and rubs me more, his warmth inside me, and it's like having him thrust in me. My eyes burn as I keep trembling, and he pushes the heel of his palm into my sex to drive me higher.

When I'm done, I'm still like a junkie, thinking of having him inside me. "When you make love to me again, I want you to stay inside me. All night, swear to me, part of you will be inside me, just like you promised."

He turns my face at an angle he seems to want me at and cradles the back of my head as he sucks my tongue like he's starved for it. "I'm going to fuck you for every night I haven't fucked you and then I'm going to stay in you."

He exhales slowly as if the thought alone got him all worked up, and his breath is warm on my face as he waits for my consent.

When I nod, he smiles his lazy, heavy-lidded smile at me; I smile back.

I feel happy. Complete. Like the world is spinning in the right direction tonight.

He takes some extra time grooming and petting me, doing all his fun stuff with me that makes all the butterflies in my tummy have trouble letting me settle down. I'm so weak I only moan and whisper how good it feels, and he whispers how good I taste, and how good I feel.

When he's done bathing inches and inches of my shoulder, throat, and ear with his tongue, and done petting his hand down my side, he spoons me with his bigger, harder body and our legs entwine like pretzels, and I sigh as we fall asleep. In the middle of the night he sometimes shifts his nose until he buries it in my skin. I reach behind me and caress his hair groggily, turn in his arms so I can smell him, absorbing every sensation of being back in bed with the only man I've ever been in love with.

And it feels like home has finally come to me.

TWELVE

HERE WE GO

Two days later we're still in the same hotel room, and I wake up with the most delicious sense of well-being when I notice that he's watching me. He's propped up on one arm, his muscles bulging. His sexy black hair is fully standing and he wears the lazy, sensual smile of a man who's been satisfied to a near-coma, and he looks so sexy in bed I want to eat him with a spoon. I make a purring noise as I roll to my side to face him.

"I don't want to leave this bed," I whisper, sliding a fingertip along one of his Celtic tattoos.

He strokes a hand down my arm, and the feathery tenderness in the caress is almost unbearable. He kisses the hollow of my ear. "Who do you belong to?" he asks softly. Again, his eyes tell me I'm his.

"You."

Reaching out, he squeezes me so hard against him, I gasp. "That's right!"

An odd little laugh leaves me, and it kind of sounded like a giggle. "You will never stop asking me that, will you? Oh, I hate you! Did you hear that? You made me *giggle*."

Laughing, he rolls me underneath his big body, and I hit his chest with one fist.

"You fucking made me giggle, and you didn't even say anything funny!"

"I fucking loved it. Giggle again now."

"Never!" I laugh, and it sounds like a goddamn giggle.

I *hate* giggling, but the genuine delight in his dancing blue eyes fills me with so much happiness, my chest feels like a detonated grenade as he laughs, and I continue to freaking *giggle*.

When he's sober, he surveys my face, feature by feature, and as the air shifts between us, our smiles fade. His body is crushing mine. His pecs smashing my breasts. His weight trapping me. I love it so much, even when it hurts to take a full breath.

His eyes turn liquid with love as he leans over and presses his lips over mine for three delicious heartbeats. We use no tongues, only the pressure of soft, dry lips, so full of love I could almost levitate.

My hands roam up the muscular planes of his back. "When do you leave?" I breathe.

"As late as possible and still be on time for the next match."

My hurt and disappointment seem to show on my face, for he tightens his hold on me as he eases to his side and brings me with him.

"Are you happy here? Are you treated well?" He nuzzles my temple.

"Nobody treats me or understands me like you. Except Mel."

"And your parents?"

"They love me" is all I say. I'm about to say they may not be too thrilled about our circumstances right now, but then I look into this man's eyes and realize he doesn't have parents who support and care about him, and I realize how very lucky I am. "Did you feel unloved when your parents didn't come back?" I ask him.

"Not unloved. Misunderstood."

He speaks casually, like it's truly nothing to him but a bland fact. A fact that breaks my heart every time I think about it.

"Oh, Remy. I'm so sorry. I hate them for doing this to you."

He gets up and grabs his lounge pants and I know he's going to want to go eat—*of course.* "Why? I didn't hurt. Why are you sorry? I'm still going to be a good father." He winks at me. "It's because they were so shitty that *I* will be a good father."

His eyes are brilliant, and I want to cry as we both stare down at my abdomen. We are really happy about this baby even though we didn't plan it. Maybe we are young and stupid, young and in love, but we are just so hopeful about having a family together. About just being together.

A banging on the suite door makes me frown. He scowls too, then points a finger at me. "Stay." He goes to open the door and I bury my face in his pillow, loathing that today he leaves me again. I talked to my doctor and she insists that I not travel until the first trimester ends, so there are at least two and a half weeks to go.

When I hear voices, I grab his robe, wrap the sash around my waist, and walk outside. Remington spots me in his boxing robe, and he reacts like he always does: I almost feel him tackling me in his head and fucking me like we haven't been able to fuck since I got pregnant.

Pete looks like he hasn't slept in days.

Remington is still eye-fucking me, his lips curled in the pure male satisfaction he gets when I'm wearing his things.

He crooks a finger and slowly beckons me forward. My heart melts and I come over, aware of him watching me as he extends his hand.

I stretch out mine, and he seizes my fingers and brings me to his side, where I impulsively start to rub his bare muscles while he talks to Pete.

But I'm so engrossed, pushing into the hard muscle, that it takes me a couple of seconds to notice the silence. A silence so absolute, you could hear a pin drop in the room.

"What's going on?" I stop what I'm doing while my gaze ping-pongs between them.

Pete restlessly loosens the knot on his tie. "I've got some bad news."

A kernel of fear settles deep in my gut. "What bad news?"

He looks at the floor and drags his hand through his hair, and I become aware of Remy staring at my profile, his blue eyes watching me with such intensity, the little kernel of fear in my stomach turns to a full-fledged knot.

"It's Scorpion," Pete says.

One word and my heart is a jackhammer.

"What about Scorpion?" The creepy crawly sensation on my skin surfaces with a vengeance. I hate thinking about him. Talking about him. I hate his name.

But Remington is here. Safe. He's safe. Isn't he? His eyes are boring into me. They look . . . worried.

Shit.

I'm cold. Paralyzed. Frozen.

"Nora spent the night with him," Pete adds, his voice surreally cold, almost like a robot's.

His words bother me in such a deep, frightening way, it's a miracle that I seem to still have enough brain cells to register what he's telling me.

My sister.

"They spent all this time at a nearby hotel. She came out with him, another woman, and his three goons. On their way to the airport; apparently there's a ticket in her name."

"She's leaving with him?" I stumble backward, that's how hard the blow is. "She can't leave with him, that . . . that . . . that ungrateful little shit!"

"Firecracker . . ." Remington says, but I'm too wired up to listen.

"Ohmigod. She's a pea-headed, unthinking, inconsiderate little *fool*! I can't believe . . ."

I'm freaking out, while Remington is calm and thoughtful. Arms crossed until those tattoos on his arms seem stretched by his muscles to the limit, feet braced apart in battle-stance, eyes glimmering in concentration. How can he, the fighter, be thinking, when I want to hit something? He did everything for Nora, on behalf of me. Everything.

And Pete! Pete is in love with her.

My eyes burn with hot tears of frustration and my mind spins around, replaying every moment of these past weeks in my head, replaying my conversation when she opened up about Scorpion and I was too concerned about Remington and my baby to pay attention. I've been so wrapped up in my head. I missed the signs. But what signs? This can't be real!

I go grab my cell phone and power it on, searching all my applications for a message. I have only messages from Mel, Kyle, and Pandora, but none from Nora. I dial her cell phone while Pete paces around, and Remington quietly watches me, his arms crossed, his eyebrows pulled low over his eyes as though he's trying to figure it all out.

"I don't like this, Rem," Pete says as he restlessly circles around, shaking his head. He looks as disheveled as if he'd just had a tussle with a crocodile. "If Nora tells him anything about Brooke being pregnant, and here, on bed rest, she'll be as vulnerable here as she will be on tour—except you won't be here to protect her. He could hurt you man."

"I go to voice mail," I interrupt, almost to myself. Then I hang up, and dial again.

Nothing.

God, what is wrong with her? He's the sort of man who sent me a box full of scorpions! He has no scruples; wants nothing but to fuck Remington again. And he's going to use my sister again—does she not even realize this?

When I shove my phone into the pocket of my robe, I find Remy watching me with a fierce frown. I know he likes this even less than I do, and I know he's figuring the connection too.

Nora returning to Scorpion at this opportune moment can be no coincidence. Scorpion lured her somehow. He wants to use her again. And I'm not letting my guy get hurt for anything in the world. *Anything.*

"I want to go on tour with you," I blurt out. Suddenly I don't feel so safe. I'm pregnant, we're apart . . . Remington has that fierce protective gleam in his eyes. I don't know what he'll do, but my protective instincts for both him, our baby, and myself, rage full force in me. "I want to go on tour with you," I repeat.

"Come here," he says softly, stretching out his hand.

In three steps, I'm in his embrace. Not even bears hug this way. I feel enveloped by everything that he is as he whispers, "When can you come with me?" His hands are warm and steady as he tips my face back to his. "Brooke, when?" he softly insists.

"Eighteen days." An eon. A lifetime.

His eyes flash possessively and he nods deliberately. "I'm here. At ten a.m. on that eighteenth day. Okay?"

What can I even reply? He's leaving today, and everything is a fucking mess. My eyes sting a little, and I drop my face so he won't notice.

An angry growl tears out of him as he steps away from me. "FUUUUCK ME WITH THIS!" He grabs fistfuls of his hair and whirls around to Pete. "We back off the season. He'll let her go once he knows I'm not fighting anymore. And I'm sticking where I'm needed. Call it off until my daughter is born."

When I realize what he's doing, I grab him by the thick arms until he looks down at me.

"Remington Tate!" His jaw is set at a determined angle, and I'm overwhelmed with panic. "I *promise you* by all that I am and all that I feel for you, I won't let anything, anything, happen to me or this baby. Anything." I cup his face and run my thumb over the dark stubble of his jaw. "We're *not* going to hold you back. I couldn't live with myself. You. Go out there. And fight. And win. Trust me. I choose you. I love my sister, but I love you more. We will help her when we can, but not at your expense! Not anymore. I'm not going to choose her this time. I choose *you*."

He fists his hand in my loose hair and looks directly at me. "I'm not going to make you choose."

My eyes burn again.

He crushes my mouth in a hard kiss, then stares determinedly into my eyes with a look that blazes through me. "I'll save her as many times as she needs saving. For you."

The steely glint in his gaze swamps me with unease. "No," I moan. "*No*, we don't even know what's happening anymore."

He clutches me tight. "I'm going to need your mettle out, little firecracker. I need to know you're safe every second of the day. You don't go anywhere alone. Don't answer calls from any numbers but ours and Melanie's. Don't receive any packages. Don't believe anything you read or hear about me. No contact with your sister without my knowledge."

His eyes flicker over my face, as though he's making sure I'm all right and unhurt. He then stalks into our bedroom and I follow him as he grabs some clothes and tosses me one of his T-shirts. "I want to talk to them."

"What? Who?"

"Your parents." He comes and tips my head back, his jaw set at a determined angle. "I brought you here to be safe, guarded, taken care of. I want to talk to your parents. I want them to look me in the eye and give me their word they're taking care of you. I'm posting a guard at your door, one at the building elevators, and one inside your place—don't argue with me," he stops me before I can start.

I cover my face with an angry sound of frustration. "Why are we talking about me? I'm worried about *you*!" I cry, dropping my hands. "He wants to fuck you, Remington. I swear if anyone hurts you I'm going to hurt them back tenfold!"

He pats my rump. "I'm a big boy. Now let's go meet your parents."

"I couldn't survive what you did last time! It's her decision now."

"This won't be like last time."

❤ ❤ ❤

WE WAIT FOR my parents in my living room.

I've gone through everything in my head, wanting to protect them, wanting to protect Nora, but in the end, I just don't feel like lying for anyone or to anyone anymore. My parents deserve the truth, even if it hurts. I won't sit by and watch them judge and withhold any affection from Remington because they believe he will hurt me, when I, *I* was the one who hurt him with my false sense of heroism wanting to save my sister.

God, but what if she's unsavable?

What if she's so far in that she will never come out, and if she does, what if, like a true junkie, she falls back in, over and over again?

When my parents arrive, they hardly look at me—their eyes fly straight behind me and up to Remington's face.

My father bristles. "You're her boyfriend? You're the one who knocked her up, then dumped her on our doorstep?"

Remington walks around me, a tower looking down at my dad. "Yes, that's me." He puts his hand on my stomach, adding, "It *better* be me."

I expel a breath. "It's you. Now, let's all relax a bit."

"I'm not relaxed," Remy counters in that low voice of his as he eyes my father, then my mother. "She's been alone. If I'd wanted her to be alone, I wouldn't have brought her home."

"I am fine, Remington. Dad, ease back and sit down." I grab Remy's wrist and he lets me pull him back and draw him to the sitting area, my parents following. He sits down next to me and splays a hand on my stomach, quiet.

I drag in a breath and look at my parents.

"Mom and Dad, Nora fooled you. She wasn't traveling the world last season. She was going out with a man they call the Scorpion. She was not in Hawaii or Timbuktu; she was traveling with him, at the same time I was traveling with Remington. Scorpion is a fighter too."

My mother's hand flies to her mouth but doesn't quite manage to smother her distressed little gasp.

"The Scorpion fed Nora drugs and kept her enthralled with him. In order for her to be released, Remy gave away the championship. And I think she might need our help again this year."

My mother's eyes dart to my right and up, and my father doesn't bat an eyelash, for he's been staring at nothing but Remy the whole time. By the tension of all those muscles next to me, I know Remington is keeping his eyes on him too.

"Oh, Nora," my mother sighs drearily as she clutches her head.

"You took a dive for little Nora?" my dad suddenly asks him. My father is a coach—and he respects athletes. "Threw the match for her?"

Remy laughs softly and leans forward, propping his elbows on his knees. "No. I threw it for *Brooke*."

My dad immediately stands, and in that same instant Remy slowly, in that lionlike way of his, comes to his feet.

"Remington, I think you and I got off on the wrong foot." My father comes around the coffee table and extends his hand. His entire hostility has vanished. He looks a thousand pounds lighter now and even wears a little grin. "I'm Lucas Dumas."

Remy doesn't even look at the hand—he immediately takes it and shakes it, hard and firm like he is, his voice gruff with emotion. "I'm Remington."

THIRTEEN

THE WAIT IS OVER

She left me a message.

In my room the night Remington left, I discovered a note tucked under my pillow.

It's not what you think. I will be back after the season. I've got this. Please don't come after me!

What. The fuck?

Puzzlement doesn't even begin to describe my reaction to the note.

I can't stop reading it. It's as though I want to read something hidden between each of the scrawled letters, but there's nothing.

Mom and Dad have been coming over daily, going Nora this, Nora that. They're used to her being flighty and irresponsible, but on this occasion, they're very concerned about what we told them. My guess is that the only reason they aren't completely losing it is because, before Remington left, he asked them to make sure I'm well taken care of, and he'd make sure Nora came back home.

My parents beamed. And me?

I excused myself to the restroom. Where I sat for a little while, trying to breathe. I *still* can't breathe well, just thinking about anything, anything at all, that has to do with Scorpion . . . and Remy. I considered showing Mom and Dad the note, but how can I add to their worry when they essentially can't do anything about it? I just can't.

However, I did show the note to Melanie.

"What the fuck does this even mean?" Melanie demands when I show it to her the next day.

She looks at me in complete bewilderment. "I don't know."

"I'll tell you what it means. It means 'I'm a little shit, just like you've always known I am but refuse to believe it. I'll be back once I fuck up you and your boyfriend's life again. Don't try to stop me.' That," Melanie says angrily, "is what it means."

Yet again, I remember what she told me about Scorpion, and I wish I'd paid a bit more attention.

"If she went back to Scorpion, then Scorpion is what she deserves," Mel huffs.

Feeling as confused about the note as the first moment I read it, I sigh and address the other woman in the room. "Josephine, do you want something?" I offer my in-building bodyguard, the "she-male" Melanie had said had been following us previously at the fight. I hadn't even known Remington—the adorable possessive jerk—had already hired someone to protect me. And Josephine is actually a very sweet, but clearly big and dangerous, woman.

"No thanks, Miss Tate," she says in her rather gruff voice from the corner, where she's keeping one eye out the window and the other on a magazine.

Melanie brings her hand up to stifle a giggle. "Do you call Riptide 'Mister Tate'?" she asks her.

Josephine nods politely. "Of course, Miss Melanie."

"Brookey, I can't believe anyone would call your guy 'mister' in any way. 'Mister' is for dudes in suits. Do the other two female guards call him 'mister' too?"

Josephine nods, and Melanie continues giggling delightedly.

Kendra and Chantelle are my other two bodyguards, purposely female because Remy would *not* have a male around me, but they're always doing rounds outside my building or around the elevators. Remington left in an extremely restless state because of Scorpion and Nora—damn them.

Pete assured him, "They got her sister now. They don't need Brooke to fuck you anymore—they'll do it through Nora again."

"No. No, I won't let it!" I promised. But I have heard nothing, nothing, from Nora—nothing but this stupid note.

"The anger I feel is beyond words, Melanie, beyond description," I tell her as I tuck the note into my pocket again.

"Chicken, I'd be fucking fuming. She does not. Deserve. A hero. Like Remy to save her. PERIOD! She wants Scorpion? Scorpion is what she deserves!"

"Mel, just thinking about what he did last year because of us makes me sick. I won't let him hurt himself for me or for anything of mine. Anything. Not even for this baby!"

Melanie hugs me. "I know, just don't work yourself up for the baby."

"Mister Tate is a very lucky man," Josephine blurts out from her chair, nodding.

"Oh, Josephine, there should be a new word for love between these two," Melanie says, pushing her blond hair back and tapping a manicured nail to her lips as she narrows her eyes thoughtfully. "Josephine, we should give them a name like Bennifer and all those famous couples. Help me think of one now that you're into all those gossip magazines. How about 'Bremy'?"

"Why don't I invent 'Miley'? For you and Riley?" I shoot back.

Melanie grins and plops down closer to me. "I *do* like his friendly little visits. He came over every night, and we had a blast. But he's got a good thing going, Brooke. He's loyal to Remy in an incredible way. He'd never leave what he has for me, and I'd never leave my life for him." She sighs and drops her head back to stare at the ceiling. "So I guess we're friends."

"With benefits."

She smirks cheekily. "Yeah." Then she grabs my hand. "But I want what you have. I've fallen in love a hundred times in my life! But never like you. So I wonder if I really fell or just tripped, you know?"

Smiling, I cup the tiny bulge in my stomach and grab her hand with the other. "Here. Feel this. This is the little bubble I told you about . . ." And even Josephine comes over.

"Is that the baby moving?" Josephine asks.

I nod and take her hand and put it next to Melanie's. "I think he's already starting to learn how to hook. But don't tell Mister Tate yet." I tease her with the *Mr.* part. "I want him to feel it when I know it's the baby for sure."

❤ ❤ ❤

THE EIGHTEENTH DAY arrives tomorrow.

The eighteenth day arrives *tomorrow.*

I have not died. No tragedy occurred. Nora did not try to make contact and put me in an awful position. Remy did not go black. My penance has been lifted and I. Am. Going. HOME. To Remy. TOMORROW!

With my beautiful baby safe in my womb, exactly twelve weeks old today.

I feel a thousand and one tingles inside me as I pack my stuff. And there's quite a lot of stuff to pack. So, yes, ultimately, I was given a platinum credit card and was feeling a little sad missing my man. And with the devil called Melanie perched on my shoulder as we goofed around on the Internet, I caved in and bought a lot of baby things and a couple of pregnancy things for myself too. It seemed that the more I bought, the more I was telling the energies around me—this baby is *happening*.

So I have tiny, tiny red Converse tennis shoes, some tiny baby outfits, just in case, and a onesie outfit that says MY DADDY PACKS A GOOD PUNCH. I also pack my *What to Expect When You're Expecting* book. Which is not a book, as I told Melanie—it's the damn pregnancy bible. So all that is tucked in the baby's suitcase.

I'm getting all my exercise stuff back in a separate one, because I will finally be able to resume light running again and I swear right now, running equates in my mind to flying. I cannot wait! And along with my sports attire, I add some jeans with the ridiculous pregnancy waistband—it's even more ridiculous how anxious I am to need to wear those instead of my normal jeans—and I've also got some loose pregnancy tank tops.

My phone rings as I continue packing and I answer to hear Pete's voice. "He's excited to come get you," Pete tells me.

"Oh, Pete, I'm so ready," I say as I glance around my room, happy I won't be seeing it again for a while, then tuck my running shoes into the zippered shoe compartment on the side.

"But I mean *really* excited," Pete says, clearing his throat meaningfully.

I hear a yell in the background, and a toe-curlingly familiar voice saying, "'Cause I'm the motherfucking king!!"

I stop packing and straighten, my eyes widening. "Is that him?"

"Yeah! He's getting speedy."

"Get over here already! I'm dying to see him!"

"The fight ends late tonight. But before the sun comes up, we'll be flying your way."

"Those motherfuckers want a piece of Riptide, they're going to get fucking drowned!" I hear in the background.

Laughing in sheer joy, I instinctively wrap my arm around my tiny stomach. "Is he black then?"

"Not yet, but he's getting there. I think it's accumulated. We're surprised he lasted this long. Fair warning, though. See you soon."

"Pete, you watch out for him! No *women*, Pete."

"You're joking, right? They could tear their panties off right now and he wouldn't be looking anywhere but toward Seattle."

"Can I talk to him?" I ask, and my chest feels all this weird, excited tightness.

A moment passes, then his deep, guttural voice spills out through the receiver and flies straight to my heart. "Baby, I'm so pumped up, I'm ready to kick ass and come get you."

"I know you are!" I say laughingly.

"I'm gonna KO everything they bring out, just for you."

"And I'll be waiting for you early morning too!"

"All right, sit tight—I'm coming to get you. Wear a dress for me. No. Wear something nice and tight. Wear your hair down. Or pulled up, shit, that drives me crazy too."

"I'll pull it up so you can take it down yourself," I offer.

He drags in an audible breath, and then there's a long silence, as if he's imagining doing just that.

"Yeah," he finally murmurs, and I can hear the growing terseness in his voice.

"Yeah?" I don't sound any better, clutching the phone.

I can hear his breath calming down, and he sounds like he's getting all rough and tender, like he does with me. "Yeah, do that."

He melts me, and the flutters in me get newly recharged. I pack all day and then shower, soap up, try on a thousand things to wear, even a couple of dresses. I try my hair up and down and twisted, and then settle on a nice loose white linen dress and nude ballet flats with my hair up in the loose ponytail I frequently wear.

The next day, I don't think I've ever prettied up so much in my life, and I can hardly sit still in Melanie's convertible. Mel is one of those few who've decided that even if it rains more than two hundred days a year in Seattle, the other 165 are worth driving with the top down—and here we are, with the top down, on one of those pretty and sunny 165 days, waiting for the jet to land.

"I think I see it," I say, pointing at the blue sky.

"Brookey, you're so sweet like this. It's like all your walls have come down and you're a fifteen-year-old completely in over her head." Melanie is thoroughly amused, her green eyes twinkling, her sunglasses perched atop her head.

I can't even respond, because the jet's two back wheels are touching ground, and the plane is so white and beautiful, streaked with a blue and silver line across its center that goes all the way to its elegant tail, I can only watch it land. Excitement makes my pulse dance as I curl my fingers around the car door. "It feels like I haven't seen him in a year."

"I'm glad to know I was able to make your time go by fast," Mel says sarcastically, and then she squeaks and pulls me forward with a clink of her bracelets. "Hug your damn chauffeur—I brought you to the airport, didn't I?" As the plane taxis to the FBO hangar where we're parked, I turn and hug her so tight I almost hurt her. "I love you, Mel. Be good, and come see me soon?"

"I will, when I finish with my current projecto!" Then she nudges me and nods behind me. "There he is."

I turn. The plane is parked so close one of its wings is less than a dozen feet from Mel's car. As the stairs are being pulled down by one of the pilots, I anxiously yank the car door open when Melanie screams, "Your stuff, silly girl! Hey, don't forget your head is on you!"

I come get my bag first, and when I turn again, Remington is covering the door. A thousand and one bells clang excitedly inside me. I know I should go haul my suitcases out of Mel's trunk but when he swings down, taking three steps at a time, and hits the pavement, I run. It feels like now I can run—and I run straight into his open arms.

I squeak and he catches me, squeezes me, and swings me around, laughing with me. Then we look at each other, my breasts heaving against his hard wall of a chest, my toes still hovering inches from the ground as he holds me in his arms, and I see how the little blue flecks in his eyes catch the sunlight as he looks down at me like he wants to hug me, pet me, feed me, and fuck me, all at the same time.

"Take me home," I breathe, clinging to his neck as he lowers me to the ground.

"My pleasure," he rasps, engulfing half my face in one big hand. His forehead falls to rest on mine as he angles his lips to mine, and we hear Mel yell, "Remy, take care of her! She plays a tough little cookie, but her melted chocolate center is for you, you know!"

He laughs and goes to thank her. Riley hops off the plane and heads directly to Mel. "Hey, friend," he calls.

Melanie "hey friends" him back as Riley pats Remington's shoulder. "I'll get her suitcases."

I watch as Remington comes back to me, his body moving sinuously in his loose jeans and a gray T-shirt that is supposed to be loose but hugs all the right muscles in the right ways, and I'm not even breathing when he scoops me up in his arms and looks down at me with eyes that blaze two words: *You're mine.*

He carries me into the plane as if we're a bride and groom and the threshold of the plane is the door to our new home. Diane squeals and Coach and Pete start clapping when he sets me on my feet inside.

"Yay! There she is!" Pete says.

"Ooooh, Brooke, you look so beautiful pregnant!"

"Now at last my boy can keep his head in the game," Coach grumbles, almost groaning in relief. With a soft laugh, I reach out to hug them, noticing that Remington tightens his hold on my waist and has trouble releasing me so that I can.

Riley climbs the plane then. "Damn, that girl looks good all the time. And so do you, B! You shine like a star!"

I hear a low growl behind me, and I think Remington has had enough of me hugging everyone. Before Riley can take a step forward, Remy grabs me by the hips and takes me, half carrying me, toward our seat in the back, and I know he's extra possessive when he's black, so I just settle down and lift his hand to lovingly kiss all his bruised knuckles.

"All right, Rem. She's back, so no more throwing hotel stuff! We need you fully concentrated," Pete says, in full business mode as the plane begins to taxi.

"As soon as we check in, I need your ass at the gym. I'll be damned if I'll let you face that motherfucker unprepared as we head to the semifinals," Coach says.

"I'm always at my best—it's *my* fucking ring he's in," Remington answers, but he's only half listening, his expression fiercely protective as he watches me kiss each of his knuckles.

"Thatta boy! That's what I like to hear," Coach says.

Remy turns his hand in mine so that his thumb can scrape my bottom lip. Liquid black-gray eyes rake over me, and the male appreciation in his gaze only confirms that this white linen dress was definitely the way to go. I'm three months pregnant, but I swear, just the way he looks at me now makes me feel like a virgin.

He reaches out, and I hold my breath in anticipation of his touch, of his hand, warm and strong, the calluses on my cheeks. I can't breathe as I feel the back of one lone finger curl and slide softly down my jaw. "Have you been thinking about me?"

"No," I tease.

He smiles indulgently and drags the back of that finger down to my chin, back up to my temple, and to trace the shell of my ear. "Someone else on your mind?"

Delirious with the sparks his touch ignites, I still manage to shrug mysteriously. He smiles indulgently again, like he knows there's no way I can think of anything but him—the center of the universe and the king of the world.

"You taking good care of my baby?" he asks roughly, and he blatantly lifts the skirt of my dress and slides his hand up and up, past my thighs and panties, so he can spread his fingers out on my bare abdomen. "Or have you been stealing out at night with a wig in old ladies' dresses?"

The team up in their seating area seem to have just asked him something, but he only makes sure the skirt of my dress is still covering the tops of my legs as he keeps his hand inside, and I can't even think, because the skin-to-skin contact has scrambled my brain. He smiles tenderly down at me as if he knows what he's doing to me. Then he slides his free hand under the fall of my hair and starts caressing me. An embarrassing purring sound leaves me, and I hear his answering chuckle as he watches me. Two months of abstinence. Of wanting and missing and longing. Now all my cells buzz awake. He's not even touching my breasts, which ache and feel heavier than ever. He's not even touching my sex, which is soaked and clutching with need, but oh god, I feel pleasure from the roots of my hair to the soles of my feet.

His hand holds steady over my abdomen, skin to skin, but his fingertips massage my scalp as he works toward my ponytail, and I feel the touch of his fingertips in every part of my body.

His chest expands on a deep breath as he ducks his head and touches his nose to my neck, and I notice he's breathing me in. Hot liquid need floods me and I almost whimper. Curling my fingers around the back of his muscled arms, under the sleeve of his soft

T-shirt, I breathe his name, and before I can finish it, he turns his head to mine and slides his tongue between the seam of my lips. *Oh*, please, *oh, oh.*

The moist lap of his tongue comes back again. Pleasure shudders through me as my lips part, while my famished body screams at him to give me more, give me everything I want and love and need right now, right now, *please, right now.*

He gives it to me, but slowly. He savors me, his hand opening on my nape, his thumb caressing the band of my ponytail . . . killing me softly. . . . I moan and rub his shoulders as he parts my lips wider and delves in to taste, deeper, wetter. We're moving so slow, it's like a dream. Then he starts fucking my mouth headily, heavily, savoring every centimeter he gains with his tongue, prolonging the length he withdraws before he once again comes forward to taste me. Heat spills through my body—he's driving me insane.

He undoes my ponytail and eases back to watch as my hair spills down to my shoulders, and his eyes, so black right now, devour me. He's manic and he's hungry, but he seems so happy—almost relieved—to see me, that I can see dozens of brilliant lights shining in his irises.

He slides his hand to the small of my back and pulls me close as he comes back in. His kiss roughens, and my head falls back to the seat from the force. Moaning, I move my mouth feverishly under his and don't realize I'm clinging until I feel his shirt fisted in my hands.

"I missed you," I gasp into his moving mouth, and he growls softly and licks down my neck. Every kiss is fire, back up my neck, to my ear.

"Tonight, after the fight," he tells me, his breath deep and slow, mine fast and labored.

He squeezes me as he stares down at me, surveying the dazed smile on my lips. "Your wish is my command."

"I command that you're mine this night again—you're mine forever."

He says it so seriously, I laugh, but he doesn't laugh. He doesn't even smile. He's looking at me as if waiting for me to say, once again, even if teasingly, that his wish is my command. I stroke his stubbly jaw. "What are you going to do to me tonight?"

He breathes in my ear, nibbling me softly. "Kiss you. Stroke and fondle you. Lick you. Pet you. Fuck and love you. Make you fall asleep with me in you." He moves his fingers, huge and strong and scarred, on my abdomen. "Don't you remember who put this in you?"

"Oh, I remember. It makes me hot to remember."

"And it makes me want to put a thousand of these in you. But why don't you look pregnant by me? Are you eating well?"

"Yes! Why?" I straighten as he withdraws his hand from under my dress. "You want me to blow up? You want everyone to know I'm pregnant?"

He leans back with his elbows on the back of the seat, the move delineating every muscle underneath his T-shirt as he smiles deliciously and nods.

"So everyone knows I'm taken and yours?" I insist.

He nods with an adorable smile that reaches all the way to his eyes.

"My butt is already huge and the girls are bigger too. It only makes sense that my stomach will follow."

"I happen to like the way the girls look in that dress. And your ass is fucking juicy."

"So why don't you count your blessings? I get big boobs, a big ass, and a flat tummy for a while."

His lids slip down over his eyes as he looks appreciatively at the girls, then a smile twists his mouth as he pulls me close. "Come here."

"You have a devil's glint in your eye."

His smile deepens into laughter. "Come here. I missed you."

"What are you planning, mister?"

He pats his lap. "I'll let you choose."

"Between?"

"Music."

"I like the sound of that."

"Kissing."

"You're making it tough."

"Petting."

"Now you're just being mean."

"Or all of the above."

Without warning, I jump up on him, and he laughs, instantly clutching me tight. "I got you now!"

"You had me when you looked at me," I quietly, smilingly admit, as if his huge ego really even needs another huge stroke from me. "By the time you winked, I was done for, *Mister* Remington Tate . . . sexy boyfriend, killer fighter, and father of my unborn child. You've definitely got me now."

FOURTEEN

PHILADELPHIA

He's very speedy, and he didn't like it when I talked to Pete and Riley on our way to the hotel. He didn't like it when I had to leave him to go pee in our room, and he paced in our bedroom waiting like some sort of impatient groom, slamming his lips to mine the second I came out and kissing me for just about half an hour until they came to get us for the fight. He didn't want to let go of me as he headed to the locker rooms, his hand tightening on my hips the deeper we walked into the Underground.

I told him that I couldn't wait to see him fight, and that I would be watching. He clamped his jaw and looked—proprietarily and thirsty as hell—at my lips. Then he nodded and patted my butt as he gave Pete strict instructions not to move a foot away from me during the fight.

Now Pete is attached to me like a Siamese twin.

He's the Man in Black and is now carrying a stun gun, pepper spray. You name it, Pete's got it. He even wears an intimidating frown today, like everyone should stay away.

"You take yourself way too seriously," I joke.

"What the man wants, he gets," he says with a chuckle.

A swarm of bugs awaken in my stomach as we head to our seats, first row to the right side of the ring. And it feels like a lifetime since I watched a fight. Excitement mingles with nervousness, and unfortunately the heartburn that seems to have remained after all my first-trimester nausea promises to come back with a vengeance.

"Remington bought the full box so you don't have people bumping close," Pete explains to me as we reach our seats, and I notice that the two seats to our sides and the two behind are empty.

Pete nods to someone across the ring, and I follow his gaze to see big ol' Josephine standing there, keeping an eye on us. "Where did Jo come from?" I ask, happily smiling at her and pleased when she smiles primly back at me. She stands, somehow, like an army man, and she manages to act very polite and discreet while at the same time looking incredibly intimidating.

"She had stuff to take care of and flew commercial to catch up with us. She'll be rooming with Diane and will be on your tail whenever Remington is not by your side."

I would have probably protested if I didn't like her so much, and if I hadn't heard how happy she was to have landed a job that clients usually hired men to do. So I keep smiling at her as Pete and I settle down and start watching the first matches.

"*Where's Remy?*"

"*Bring out Remy!*"

The crowd yells as the ring is vacated for the fourth time, and by the time the chant starts, there's only one name audible in the entire arena. "Rem-ing-ton, Rem-ing-ton, Rem-ing-ton!"

"The organizers loooove making the public have to ask for him," Pete says with a chuckle.

And finally, the speakers flare. "That's right, ladies and gentlemen! Bitches and manwhores! Girls and fucking boys! You want him? You got him! Say hello tonight to yourrrrrr one, yourrrrrr only, Remington Tate, RRRRIIIIIPTIDE!!"

My Riptide! my mind excitedly screams. *My* Riptide. *My my my.* Mine tonight, mine always.

All across the room, the people stand on every side of the ring. Some frame their hands around their mouths and yell, while others are jumping and waving posters with his name on them.

"Remy, I'd die for you, Remy!!" a voice behind me screams.

Joy bubbles in my veins as he comes trotting out.

His perfect strong posture and relaxed shoulders, his RIPTIDE robe covering the hardest muscles in the world, makes my nipples peak and all my body throb with need. As the lights from above focus on him, I greedily take in his dimpled face, but my gaze snags on the red lipstick marks on his jaw. And on his mouth.

I blink in confusion.

He grabs the ropes and swings inside, landing stealthily as a cat who already owns the squared space of that coveted ring, and then the robe comes off and Remington is on complete glorious display. I see him, but I'm still confused as to what I see on his boyish face; those marks, red and blotched all over his beautiful tan, until the truth starts sinking and sinking and sinking inside me, and each one of those kisses feel a little bit like a whiplash.

A thousand and one insecurities I didn't even know I had rear up inside me.

I imagine manicured hands touching his skin . . . lips on his lips . . . his growls for somebody else . . . his calluses rasping against somebody else's skin. . . .

A burn starts up in my eyes as Pete quietly tells me, "Brooke, it comes with the life. He doesn't ask for the groupies—he just wants to fight. It's no big deal."

"If I can just get the rest of my body, other than my brain, to understand that," I say miserably, and it feels that a black cloud of pain has dropped over me like a cloak on all my light.

A couple of seats to my right, a woman pulls on her hair and screams, *"Riptiiiiiiiiide! I want to drag you to my room and fuck you till I can't walk!"*

Lord, I want to hit that bitch so bad.

And there he is, beautiful and magnificent Remington Riptide Tate.

He does his turn, and I feel such pressure in my chest, I curl my hands around my baby and stare at the small little swell it now makes. I never regretted being pregnant, but now I feel so pregnant and so stupid.

I breathe, slow and deep, while all my insecurities gnaw on my insides. We're going to have a family together. I will be a mother . . . but he will *still* be a fighter, surrounded by young, pretty groupies who will do anything to have him.

Brooke Before Pregnancy would probably feel nobody could ever take him away from her.

But Pregnant Brooke feels a little bit at a disadvantage. Because maybe it hurts a little that he hasn't asked me to marry him. Maybe he doesn't even want to?

Why would he even bother, when I'm his already?

"Brooke, he's looking at you," Pete murmurs excitedly.

Still feeling more unsteady than I'd like, I drag in a deep breath and continue staring at my lap, at the stupid linen dress I wore when I prettied up for *him* this morning.

"Brooke, he's staring blatantly at you," Pete says, now in alarm.

The crowd quiets.

The silence becomes oppressive, as if Riptide has stopped smiling and now everyone knows something's going on.

I can feel *his* eyes boring into the top of my head. And I know that when I look up, all I will see is that red. Lipstick. On his beautiful face. Like the lipstick I smeared him with once, but that belongs to someone else today. Maybe one of the fucking whores he fucked when I was gone. *God.*

"Brooke, Jesus, what the hell?" Pete elbows me. "Do you want him to fuck up tonight?"

I shake my head and force myself to look at him.

He's staring at me with a look of complete wildness and anxiety. His legs are braced apart, his jaw tight and his stance defensive, and I can tell he senses there's something wrong with me, because his hands are fists at his sides and he looks ready to jump and come get me.

I hold his gaze proudly, because I don't even want him to know how hurt I am, but when he smiles at me, I just can't smile back.

His smile fades.

His eyes flash with hurt as he curls his fingers into his hands and the wildness in his expression almost claws into me, but I feel equally wild, and this time, I just can't appease him I am so fucking hurt, and angry, and jealous, and pregnant.

Vaguely, I remember there were times when I sat on these sidelines, wishing that magnificent raw beast up there were mine. And this moment I sit here, pregnant with his baby, hurting because some woman, or women, kissed and touched what I feel is mine, and suddenly I want what I had before. I want to be just a girl, just wanting a job. Simple. Simple goals and a simple life. But no. I can't have that now. Because I am more in love with Remington Tate than I ever thought possible. And he is as elusive as a falling star, one that nobody will ever really catch, and if you catch him, he will only burn right through you.

Like he burns into me right now, right in the center of my chest, my love for him *corroding* me.

Unable to look into his dark eyes any longer, I force my gaze away to watch his opponent take the ring, and my eyes slide over but quickly return, to the tattoo of a dark, elegant curled *B* on Remington's right bicep.

My heart stutters in disbelief. Staring at the inky design in confusion, I realize that yes, it's right there, on his right bicep: a perfect, beautiful *B*.

It does something crazy to me. My poor panties suddenly feel soaked, and I start to throb.

Remington turns to his opponent, and I see his lips curl cockily when he spares a look at the fighter he goes up against, someone young and jumpy, clearly too eager to get started.

They tap gloves, and Remington looks at me. Then, without smiling, he meaningfully flexes his bicep with the *B* and kisses it so that I see. A furious, hot little ripple runs down my sex, and I clench my legs together.

His smile flashes, as if he knows he makes me wet and I can't help myself.

The bell rings.

"When did he get that tattoo?" I ask under my breath. I can't stop staring at the mark.

"Right after we left Seattle," Pete tells me.

Remington goes toe-to-toe with the "eager young buck" as Pete called him, and immediately slams him; then he backs out and feints, making the new fighter come after him. The buck swings and fails, and Remington comes back with a powerful one-two punch that launches the man back like a cannon blast. The guy bounces on the ropes, and then falls facedown on the mat.

"Ooooooooooo!" the public says.

"Ouch, that must've hurt," says Pete, but he's grinning while behind me, someone yells, "*That's what you get when you go up against Riptide, sucker!*"

No matter what's going through my head, watching Remington fight is such a thrilling experience that, inside me, all my muscles brace as if I were the one fighting.

The other guy gets up, and Remington hits him again, his punches precise and powerful, his body moving sinuously, the sexy black *B* on his bicep rippling as that muscle hardens in action. I'm a mess of emotions as the fight progresses, and a drop of perspiration slides between my breasts.

My body temperature seems higher with the pregnancy, but watching my baby's father up there—a master of complete disaster, with that tattoo screaming to the world that he is mine, but at the same time kissed by some other bitches—makes me possessive and angry. I feel like a volcano.

After Remington knocks the young buck down permanently for the night, fighter after fighter is brought out to challenge him. He rams them so hard they bounce on the ropes, drop on their sides, face-forward, or onto their knees, all of them shaking their heads in consternation like their brains are shuddering inside them.

He's unstoppable.

Pete laughs at my side. "It never ceases to amaze me how much that man likes to SHOW THE FUCK OFF WHEN YOU WATCH HIM!"

I shake my head in disbelief, and Pete nods somberly. "Seriously. The difference in his blood work when he's exposed to you—the way you alter his chemistry and bring out all his testosterone, bring his fighter's instincts to life—it's incredible. Did you know men's testosterone rises when they see a new attractive female? His doesn't. It just goes through the roof when he sees you—*his* female."

Pete's words kill me. Remington always seems to want to prove to me that he is the strongest male in the world and the one who will protect me—and oh, yes, do I believe him.

He takes on a fourth fighter and then a fifth, his body a bulldozer of sex and strength as he pounds them down, one after the other, those dark eyes checking me out—in my seat—making sure I'm watching him. Every look he sends my way, I ache a little more inside me, get a little more angry and embarrassingly horny, until my sex is so swollen and my hands so tightly curled on my lap, I don't know what I want to do most: fuck him or slap him.

A sixth and a seventh fighter are brought out, and Remington is still not tired. He's blocking, punching, attacking, and defending.

"*RIP, RIP, RIP, RIP, RIP!*" the public chants to him, and Pete joins them, pumping his hands in the air, chanting the same word as the thousand people here, as the ringmaster grabs Remington's thick wrist and raises his arm in victory.

"Our winner! Once again, ladies and gentlemen, I give you Remington Tate, youuuuur Riptiiiide!!"

Those dark eyes search for me in the stands. The second they find me, my pulse pounds fiercely in my body, my heart fluttering like a winged thing in my chest as he stares at me and smiles. A shiver runs through me at the sight of those dimples, the white smile, the dark, scruffy jaw—and that fucking red lipstick.

When I can't seem to make myself smile back, his eyebrows draw low over his eyes, and he grabs the rope and climbs down from the ring.

"*Riptide, Riptide, Riptide!*" I hear the excited people start chanting.

Forcing myself to hold his steely dark gaze, I stand on shaky legs, watching him come over. He gives me his hand, and I look at all that fucking lipstick on his face, and then at his hand, and I grab it. My jaw tightens as he hauls me down the rows.

"Keys," he barks at Riley, and Riley hops down from the corner of the ring and trots to walk next to us.

"I'll drive you guys."

Into the back rooms we go, and Remington stops at the lockers to grab his duffel, never letting go of my hand. I can't stop looking at the lipstick on his damn, sexy, infuriating mouth, and at the *B* tattoo on his sexy, hard bicep. Conflicting sensations spiral in me so fast, I don't even know what to do with them except grit my teeth. Releasing my hand for the barest second, Remington pulls on a white T-shirt and jumps into a pair of black sweatpants, then he grabs my hand, rams his fingers through mine, and leads me outside. He shoves me into the back of the Navigator, and once we settle in our seats and Riley starts the car, he grabs my face in one hand, his eyes glowing with the same hunger they've glowed with all day. Or maybe even more. He bends to kiss me and I twist my face around.

"Don't," I say.

He forces my head back around and murmurs in a low, desperate voice, "I want you to look at me when I fight. I've been waiting what feels like forever to have you look at me." He crushes my mouth with his, and lightning streaks through me as his lips press to mine. The need inside me is so great, it takes all my willpower to force my mouth shut under his as I twist free with a moan.

"Don't kiss me!" I hiss.

He seizes my face in one open hand and turns me around, and he takes my mouth again, forcing my lips to part so he can thrust his tongue in me with a groan. I moan as his tongue touches mine, fighting weakly as I squirm between him and the seat and I push at his shoulders, twisting my head away.

"Let go!" I moan.

"God, I need you like I need to breathe. . . ." He slides his callused palm under my dress, stroking his long fingers up my thigh as he presses a path of hungry, wet kisses up my throat. "Why are you playing games with me? Hmm? I need to be inside you right now. . . ."

"Did you tell that to your groupies?" Panting and angry as his hand advances up my thigh, I push at his granite chest and make a frustrated sound when he doesn't budge. "Tell that to the one who kissed your chin, your temple, your jaw, and your fucking mouth!"

He edges back with a confused scowl.

"You've got lipstick all over your face, Remington!" I say, straightening my dress.

With a low, exasperated noise, he drags the back of his forearm across his lips, then looks down at it and narrows his eyes when he sees the red streak on his skin. He clamps his jaw shut and falls back in his seat, dropping his head back with a groan. He rakes his hands through his hair and stares angrily at the ceiling, breathing through his nose. I try sliding to the other end of the seat, but his hand shoots out and clamps around my wrist.

"Don't," he rasps, like he's in pain.

I swallow a lump of anger in my throat as he slides his hand from my wrist to my hand and links our fingers. The entire ride, I am acutely aware of his palm against mine, his thick, long fingers laced through mine, holding me tight while my chest feels like bursting and imploding, all at the same time.

We get to our hotel and Riley cautiously checks on us via the rearview mirror. "I'll pick up the rest of the team now," he says.

"Thanks," Remington flatly says as he helps me down from the car. Then, with his hand still holding mine, he walks me across the lobby to the elevators.

We hop on, and his scruffy jaw is still all streaked in red. Even with those streaks, his face is every woman's fantasy. His hair rumpled and black, those sweatpants riding low on his hips while that T-shirt clings to his eight-pack and broad shoulders and bulging biceps. He's still the same sex symbol he's always been, while I feel more pregnant than ever, with the tiny bump of my stomach.

He pulls me into our room, the door slamming with its own weight behind us, and the instant he lets go of my hand he grabs me by the hips and lifts me up to set me down on the dining table.

"Don't do this to me." He nips my neck and slides his hand under my dress again, raising it up quickly to cup me over my panties this time. "Don't fucking do this to me now," he groans.

I start to shudder when he drags his mouth up to my jaw, nipping my lips as he rubs the tip of one finger over my panties. I hate the whimper that comes out of me, but he seems to like it, for he groans and heads straight for my mouth. I jerk my head away, my voice soft and pained. "I want to kiss *you*, not them!" I cry, weakly pushing at his big chest.

"It's me." He pulls his hand out of my dress, grabs the sides of my face in both hands, and kisses me, smearing me with someone else's lipstick as he covers my mouth and forcibly opens me. I push on his chest until I can't push anymore while his tongue overpowers mine and he curls his arms around my back as he leans me down on the table, his arms protecting me from the hard surface as he suckles on me with desperate hunger. "It's me," he rasps, rubbing a hand along the side of my body and to my breast.

I whimper needily and hate that I do. I'm so wet. I need him so much. He smells so fucking good. I'm going crazy, but when he covers my breast with one hand, I'm still so jealous and angry, I try to push his hand away. He makes a low, pained noise. "Brooke . . ." With a frustrated sound, he grabs the fabric of my dress in both fists and rips it open in one jerk. I gasp as he spreads the fabric aside to reveal me in my underwear, his dark head quickly diving so he can drag his tongue over my skin, from my belly button upward, as he parts the material even more and strokes his hands up my ribs.

Tremors run through me and I clutch the back of his head, torn between pulling him up to my mouth and pushing him away; instead, I pull him up by the hair. *"No,"* I groan, and he eases back and looks at me with those wild-animal eyes, and I know I shouldn't provoke him, I should calm him, but I am jealous out of my fucking mind. He has turned me into this. Loving and obsessing about him, wondering who he's been with. He might not even know himself—but *they* know, and they aren't me.

Seized by a new determination, I sit up and angrily grab his jaw and start scrubbing my palms and fingers furiously over the marks. When I can't remove much of them, I grab his white T-shirt and pull it up to wipe him. He stands there, breathing harder than he does when he fights, looking at me like he's begging me for something—for me—as he patiently lets me wipe him clean.

My fingers tremble. His eyes are brilliant in the shadows of the suite as I scrub, but I still can't get the lipstick off, and I can't stand it.

I lick my finger and then rub saliva on the lipstick marks, then pass his T-shirt over the damned spot.

He grows frustrated and shoves his fingers into his mouth, then starts rubbing the places I am, our fingers bumping as we scrape our saliva all over his jaw. I lift the T-shirt and scrape again, going breathless as it finally starts coming off.

I stop when there's nothing left, only his hard jaw, a little raw, my body on fire with need and my heart on fire with love and every inch of me burning with jealousy. And I grab his hair and lean over and set a kiss right there, where another kiss used to be, desperately trying to erase anything before. And I set another kiss there, and another where another mark used to be. He grasps my hips tight as I drag my lips along his jaw and head for his mouth, and I kiss it, fast and almost as if I don't want to, and ease back, sucking in a breath as I let go.

He raises a brow. "Done?" he asks in a haggard voice, and I don't think I'm breathing when I nod.

His chest expands as he grabs the stained T-shirt and lifts it in one single, fluid move, tossing it aside. "You and I are going to make love now. We don't have to wait a second . . . longer . . . to be together."

Shivers run through me, and my voice is raw with emotion. "I can't stand seeing their lipstick on you, Remington—I won't let them kiss you. And this isn't some pregnancy craziness talking or my insecurities! I told you a long time ago that I won't share. I won't share you."

"Shh, baby, I neither expect you to nor want you to." He eases my tattered dress off my shoulders, then lets it spread out beneath me on the table. He urges me down and then looks at me splayed for him, with my knees folded back. He touches me everywhere— my legs, my arms, between my breasts—as he leans over. "Coach was tying up my hands, I had my headphones on. I didn't see them coming until they were all over me. It won't happen again. I kiss no one. I kiss no one. But my little firecracker."

He ducks to my breasts and licks one nipple through my bra, sliding his thumb under the plain white cotton, easing the fabric down and hooking it beneath the rising swell. "I am going to lick these and I am going to suck these and I am going to do whatever I want with these."

My heart pounds hot blood through my veins as he lowers the fabric on the other side and licks the sensitive peak, sending bolts of pleasure everywhere in me. My breasts are bigger, thrust out, the nipples darker and puckered, and he cups them as if exploring new territories that delight him. The sound that rumbles up his chest causes me to make a small little sound of my own as I squirm need-ily. His eyes lift to mine when he hears that sound, and he grabs my hips and drags me to the edge of the table, my butt flying off the very edge, and he jerks loose his sweatpants. Suddenly I feel how hard he is, his heavy erection brushing against my soaked entry as he leans over to lave and lick my breasts again, his hardness nestling into the apex of my legs.

"Sensitive?" He presses one nipple in with his thumb, then the other, his hands rough but gentle. I arch and mew softly. I want a bruise, I want to ache, I want to ache in my skin and my muscles like I ache inside with love for him.

"Yes," I gasp and there's a lump in my throat and tears of need in my eyes.

He takes my lips in a voracious kiss, then ducks his head and groans into my neck, "Brooke." He caresses between my legs and pushes his thumb into my body as he turns his head and strokes my tongue with his own. My insides tremble when he draws back to observe how debauched I look as he thumbs me.

I see the raw need in his face as he watches; then he lifts his hand and licks his glistening wet thumb. Oh god, I see him—primal and male, still with that boyish charm and that disheveled crazy black hair, and I squirm and moan because I want him, I want him, I WANT HIM.

"You're restless, what do you want?" The ragged need in his voice makes me tremble as I say, "I want to lick you like you lick me," and he nods and bends over and gives me his tongue first; then he cups the back of my head and presses me to his neck.

Wet and burning hot, his skin is silk under my twirling tongue. I shiver as I go up and grab his hair and suck his top lip into my mouth. He tastes like he does, and he tastes like he wants me. We kiss intensely, and my breathing hitches even more. He tears my bra as I bite his lower lip, and he's breathing deeply when he pulls down my panties and draws back to see me fully naked now. His eyes trace me, devour me. He sees my breasts just thrusting out, bare, and they're fuller, and I know he desires them. He cups one, like he's knowing me for the first time. *This* is what he did to my body. *This* is what happens to my body after him.

He touches my other breast, then he immediately cups them both and fondles them and starts playing with them, watching what he does with brilliant dark eyes.

His lip is bleeding from my bite in the place it always opens, and his chest is slick with sweat. I protest. "I bit you," I say.

"Just put your lips on it."

"Remy—"

"Put your tongue on it." He bends again and nudges my lips with his, and I softly lick him, the way an animal instinctively cleans a wound. I suck on that bleeding lip gently. He drags his nose over mine and then licks my lips open. I hug him and part my legs and circle them around his hips.

Need races through me as he grabs my ass and lifts me in the air. I lift my bottom to help him, and I'm so drunk with desire my vision blurs as he carries me a couple of steps to the sofa.

He kisses my neck as he lowers me, then he circles his thumb between my thighs exactly where I'm wet and I mew softly. "You ready for me?" His voice rasps over my ear as he strokes my wet folds with his fingers. "Get ready for me."

He pushes his long finger inside me to make me wetter, but I'm so drenched, it slides in easily. I contract and almost can't keep from coming as he rubs inside my depths.

He slides his lips down my body and bends his dark head, his tongue running over my clit, lapping lightly as he holds me open by the thighs. I grip the back of his head, watching him do this to me. Then he kneels at the end of the sofa, grabs my hips, and drags me down a couple more inches—and he starts pressing in. Full. Hot. Harder than anything I've ever touched. I arch my body and gasp as he guides every inch of himself inside me, while my eyes lock on to his and his lock on to mine. He cups my face and drags his thumb down my bottom lip, pulling it roughly and lovingly as he keeps easing inside, until he's fully seated in the deepest part of me.

I whimper as he rocks his hips.

He leans over and kisses my ear. "You miss me."

I turn and kiss his mouth, gasping as I tilt my hips. "I feel like I've never been this wet and swollen."

"I've never been this hard." He pulls out and then eases back in, slowly and pleasurably. I feel him part me, open me, take me, fill me, then leave me. . . . I whimper and am about to beg him to come back in when he does . . . he comes in . . . rocking back in . . . the muscles of his arms, his Celtic tattoos and his *B*, rippling as he moves. The third time, he pins my arms up above my head and thrusts harder, the move jerking my breasts.

I scream and he muffles it with his mouth. I breathe deep, inhaling his scent.

"I love you . . ." I choke.

He stops in me, breathing hard. A low, guttural sound tears deep in his throat as he turns and starts licking my ear. Then he slides his arms around me as though to protect me as he picks up a rhythm that is fast, determined, raw, and primal.

I'm almost crying as I tilt my hips and turn my head to his ear, gasping as he savors my neck, squeezes my breasts, fucks me hard and fast. "Oh god . . . Remington . . . Remington . . ."

He sets his forehead on mine as his hips continue expertly rocking into me; then he brings his thumb up and starts to caress my clit while his cock drags, hard and pulsing, inside me. I loosen and shatter, shuddering uncontrollably as he takes my mouth with his deliciously hot kiss. Love, lust, need course through me as I come and thrash beneath him.

"All right?" he asks, slowing his motions as I continue to come.

"Yes!" Every inch of me screams for him. I arch up against him and undulate a little, wanting more, wanting *him*. He growls like he can't hold back and pulls out, then thrusts back in, driving forward harder, holding me with one arm around my waist as I arch and he holds me in place with one hand as he enters me. I moan, and say, "Remy."

His eyes are burning me as he drags a hand down the arch of my throat, between my breasts, then bends to lick me again. "Mine," he whispers softly, reminding me.

"Yours, yours," I say as my orgasm builds in me.

He presses his nose to my ear, growling as he comes, hot in me, his big body tensing over me, a guttural animal noise wrenching from his lips before he rasps again, "Mine."

After he comes and holds me for a minute, he lifts me up in his arms, still inside me, and I tuck my nose into his neck. He carries me around the kitchen and grabs two green apples in one hand, then gives one to me as he carries us to the master bedroom.

I bite into it with a crunch as we settle down under the covers, and he bites into his own with a bigger crunch. We kiss a little, and he tastes like juicy, lemony apple. He finishes his first, then licks the juice from the corners of my lips, and I offer up my apple to him because I suspect he's still hungry. He takes a big bite, smiling down at me when I turn it around and bite from where he did.

His legs move restlessly under the sheet, and I know my speedy Remy won't sleep tonight, but if he wants to make love to me all night, he can. I hope he will. I shift to keep him still inside me as we both eat my apple and bite it on the opposite side at the same time. We laugh in unison, and I tell him, "Right now our baby is the size of a plum."

"A plum?" He opens his mouth so I give him more apple, and I move my fingers to shape the size of a plum with my free hand.

"A plum," I repeat.

"So little," he says tenderly, sliding one big hand to the small curve of my stomach.

"So little," I breathe, curling into his big warm body with a sigh, listening to him finish my apple and letting him lick all the juicy drops that fall on my skin.

FIFTEEN

HOW TO TAKE DOWN A TREE

Remington is absolutely in love with my four-month-pregnant belly. I'm starting to really show and it excites him. No, it *more* than excites him. I'm excited too—I freaking *love* my pregnant belly! I feel amazing. No more nausea. And I do somehow seem to "glow," but I think it has to do with the way Remy makes love to me as well as with the baby he put in me.

He measures my bump every morning with his hands when I'm standing studying myself in the full-length hotel mirror. Whatever he's doing (out of the shower, brushing his teeth), he comes up to me to survey me as well, his gaze glimmering with pride as he cups me and measures me. His voice is gruff this morning. We just woke up and he's naked, behind me, his lean, large body perfectly visible in the mirror behind mine as he ducks his dark head to nuzzle me. "You think you're eating enough?" he whispers in my ear, right before he presses me back to him and brushes his lips to the hollow at the base of my throat.

"I'm not going to start eating like you!" I accuse as I turn in his arms and link my fingers at the back of his neck, grinning up at him like the love-struck fool he's made me. Playfully, I poke his dimples. "We've established you have issues. You just want everyone to know I'm pregnant and taken."

He lifts me off my feet so our mouths are aligned and he plants a big kiss on my lips, squeezing me. "That's right!"

Today at the gym he wants to show me how to throw him—or, more especially, anyone threatening me—down. Now that I've been walking, then trotting a little, with full doctor approval, I feel like a million bucks. But what most makes me feel good is the way Remington looks at me. Hot-ass proprietary, *this is my woman, this is my kid.* I read that it's completely normal to be hot and bothered when you're pregnant, but I really can't smell him without burning with the need to tear his clothes off and jump his sexy bones. Which I've been doing at least twice a day, to his complete male delight.

He hasn't been black in the two months since I got here, but he's been plotting something with Pete and Riley. The fact that the three of them are so secretive about it worries me. I think it has to do with Nora, but when I told him, "Remy, Nora sent me this note. She doesn't want us to do anything about it and I might just wait until the final to talk to her," he just chuckled and said, "Leave it to me now, all right?"

But it's not all right.

I'm scared shitless.

This morning, he had a strange reunion with Pete and Riley in our living room. He looked at me and quietly asked me, "Can I talk to the guys alone for a moment?" Since then, I've gotten all worried about their plans.

And that's the only part about being pregnant I don't like. I despise being treated like an imbecilic, weakling, delicate little flower.

No, sir. And today I will prove it at the gym when I, in fact, succeed in throwing Remington Tate—pregnant belly notwithstanding.

I watch him do full sit-ups, his breaths fast and even, in and out, in and out. I watch him do three rounds of jump rope and three rounds of shadowboxing—swing, punch, swing, punch, guard, duck . . . his chest sweaty male perfection, the intensity with which he works out getting me all worked up. Coach yells at him from the sidelines, and Riley times his speed and makes notes on a clipboard.

By the time Remington is soaked and beckons me forward in the ring, I'm worked up to a lather of complete and total lust.

"Ready?"

Nodding, I climb into the ring with him.

I've got one of my catsuits on, one with a zipper right in the middle. His eyes suck me up in it and I swear they heat everywhere they touch. He pulls his gaze back to my eyes. "Ready?" his voice is gruffer.

"You have no idea how ready I am. I'm going to kick your ass and it's going to feel amazing."

"Kick my shin first, and then my ass—" He pulls me closer, his breath hot and warm on my ear as he whispers, "The key to throwing me is to take me off balance. If I or anyone heavier than you is balanced, you won't ever knock them down."

"Okay," I say as he sets me aside, because the one thrown off balance with his nearness is *me*.

"You kick my shin, I rock off balance, then you sweep your leg out like you did last time and kick the weakest part of my heel—watch how you do it now! So rock me, then knock me down."

Nervous butterflies take flight inside me, and I groan and roll my eyes. "I feel like I'm going to get hurt again. You're still a tree, Remington."

"With a fucked-up shin." He waves me over, his lips curled in amusement, his dimples sexy and playful. "Come on. Keep your balance and throw me off mine."

I look into his playful, glinting blue eyes while all my heart feels is about a ton of love, sitting right on me. "Hurting you goes against my every instinct," I say dramatically, as if I truly believe I could nick him.

"You won't hurt me one bit," he says, laughing.

Then I seize him by the jaw and kiss him square on the lips before I draw away and stretch my legs. "All right, my pride says this must be done. What if you were Scorpion?"

He scowls. "You throw him, baby, and I mean now. Come on, rock my world, my little firecracker."

I do. I kick his shin, putting all my weight into it until he says "ouch"; then I swing my leg so fast, I catch the back of his leg and feel him topple the instant I connect. But he's still Remington Tate, and he naturally seems to stabilize. He plants himself back up, taking me off balance when he does. I squeak as I start falling, and he instantly grabs me and throws himself on his back, breaking my fall.

He chuckles as we straighten.

"You let me win," I accuse, narrow-eyed.

He shakes his head. "No, you did that on your own," he assures me.

"You're a big, incredibly fit liar," I say, shoving him.

He chuckles and sits up straighter with me on his lap, brushing my ponytail to the back of my head. "It wasn't that hard, was it?" he asks me, stroking my cheek.

"No," I breathe, then say softly so only he can hear in his ear, "but *you* are."

He looks at my mouth, and I shift on top of him. He ducks his head and smells me, and I feel tingles rush all over my skin when his nose connects with the back of my neck.

"Do you like sparring with me?" I ask silkily as I prop my arms on his shoulders, getting all excited and worked up because of his massive erection under me.

"Hmm," he says as he lifts his hand and seizes the back of my neck. "I like it when we spar like this. . . ." He kisses me softly and pushes his tongue into my mouth, and I feel electricity rushing from his tongue to my whole body. He's wet from his workout and tastes hot and thirsty, and I feel even hotter and thirstier as I clutch his chest, his muscles slick and hard as I straddle him.

He fists my ponytail in his hand, holding me in place as he lifts his head slightly and gruffly says, "Riley . . ."

"Yeah, I'll tell Coach." Riley can't conceal the laughter in his voice as he brings over some towels and drinks before he crosses toward the exit.

"Remington . . ." I chide.

His lips curl deliciously at the corners as he fingers the zipper of my catsuit and Riley yells over to Coach, "Hey, Coach, we gotta hit it so the guy can have his way with Brooke!" They disappear through the gym doors, and as they lock shut, Remington works his lips heatedly up my neck. "It's not possible for anything to be this beautiful," he murmurs to me as he slides his open hand sensually along the curve of my spine.

"So this is where we get to the kissing part, because it's near impossible to get me out of this," I whisper.

"It's coming off," he says, licking me. He kisses my mouth and holds my neck while he kisses me. Then he uses his free hand to lower the zipper of my catsuit. I squirm and moan because we've never tried this with me wearing something this complicated.

"It can come off, but not easily."

"Let's just make some room for me," he murmurs hotly into my jaw as he reaches down to the apex of my legs and peels off a bit of fabric from each thigh; then he yanks and tears my catsuit open at the seam. I feel air steal through the opening and to the burning center of my being. He reaches a hand inside the tear and says, "Hang on to my neck," as he maneuvers to tear and pull off the panties I'm wearing. He yanks them off and extracts them through the tear, his eyes twinkling, and a rush of arousal sweeps me like a storm.

"Oh please." Bringing his head back to mine, I take his delicious lips, my hips rocking desperately over him.

He lifts me for a second then shoves his sweatpants off and brings me back down with one hand on my hip, that lone hand strong enough to ease me down and impale me on him. Big. Hot. Hard. *Mine*. I moan and lick his neck, lost as my walls stretch to take him. He grabs my head and takes my mouth harder. He's moving, loving, lifting, and lowering me with one hand, the other on the back of my neck, holding and cupping me as he kisses me, his mouth strong and commanding, opening and tasting, retreating, teasing.

I come fast and hard, and his arms tighten like vises as my contractions ripple through him. I hear him growl softly as he lets me milk him. Then he lifts me up and carries me across the ring, resting me on the ropes. One of his arms protects me, and he hasn't for one second pulled out from inside me. He starts moving again. I moan softly. I feel like I'm floating, suspended in the air by a thread and his arm, the only connection in my body to his arm and his cock in me. My ponytail falls behind me, my throat arches, and he's there to devour it. I mew as he moves and sink my fingers into his bulging arms, feeling his biceps flex and contract with his body as he pumps me.

We don't speak. We don't need to speak with words; we speak like this. I lift my head and bite and lick him and gasp as I hear his breath, his muscles flexing and moving as he moves in me until I come again. He never, ever comes before me—he waits, primes me, watches me. His eyes darken as he watches me come now; then his jaw works and his body hardens as he sinks deep and holds himself there, and that's where he explodes, when he's all the way in, and I'm coming around him, hugging him within me, rippling and grasping him.

Instead of sagging this time, we tighten our hold around each other when we're done. "Stay in me," I plead to him. I'm catching my breath, my nails gouging his shoulders.

He pulls me closer and sinks his head between my breasts and breathes hard, like my skin is his air, then he lightly bites the top of my breast.

"I want to live in you," he tells me in his gruff, tender voice that makes me melt, and he clutches me tighter and licks and laves his bite, his jaw rasping my skin. "God, I want to die in you."

My bones feel liquid in my body, but even relaxed, I feel that pull of all his tornado energy working on mine. "You're so possessive, I know you'll take me with you."

"No, I'd never hurt you."

I laugh softly. "It won't be your choice. You'll take me with you because *I* will go where you go. You're going to be the end of me, Remington Tate, but that's the way I want to go."

His face twists with pain as he drags the backs of his knuckles along my jaw. "No, Brooke. I will protect you even from me."

We stare at each other for a moment, and the determination in his eyes to protect me only reassures me that, whatever happens, my life will always be intertwined with his, come good or bad. I will walk by his side, run, fight, cling, and chase his dreams, which have now become mine. "Like you said, I'll love you if it kills us," I whisper as I stroke his face. "We all die. I'd rather die loving the hell out of you."

"Baby, I'm the one who'll love the hell out of you," he says thickly, squeezing me, making me laugh in complete and total happiness. "Remy . . . where are we going to have the baby?"

He straightens up and lifts me in his arms, with my legs still locked around his hips as we cross the ring. "Wherever you want to have it. It'll be off season. I can take you anywhere you like."

"I was thinking I could keep my apartment. At first, I wasn't going to renew. But it might be smart to have somewhere to touch base. And I have a spare bedroom I used to do yoga in and could turn into a nursery. Melanie's all for decorating it. . . ."

He sits us down on the stool at the corner of the ring, where a basket of towels and drinks awaits us. He grabs a towel and eases me onto his lap as he slowly starts cleaning me up, his profile calm and relaxed. "I'll ask Pete to renew your lease for another year while we look for something else," he tells me. "You can use the card I gave you to charge anything you'd like."

I wind an arm around his neck and poke a hidden dimple. "So I'm to be your kept girlfriend and employee? Officially?"

He grabs the back of my head, angles my face up almost to the ceiling, and licks a path from under my chin right up to my mouth, where he roughly engulfs my mouth with his. "Officially, you're Mine."

❤ ❤ ❤

"WILL WE GO through the usual route for vaccinations, or will we find a doctor who works with us a different schedule? There's so much evidence vaccines could be the cause of autism," I tell Remington one night.

I'm eating tons of vegetables. I've read that different-color vegetables provide different antioxidants. Green veggies provide different ones than purple and orange ones, so I'm eating a rainbow every morning, noon, and evening. The best for Remington's baby.

Also, pineapple is the fruit of the moment. It is all I want to eat. As soon as we reach every location, Remington orders Diane to bring all the organic pineapples she can find. I blend them with bananas to make smoothies. I eat them with cayenne pepper. Diane sautés them for me with little bits of turkey. I am a pineapple freak and Remington is amused like hell because of it.

"I'd say it's a girl," Diane told me yesterday, "because you're craving sweets. But you look too good. When you have a girl—at least, when I had my girls, I looked like shit."

"Why?"

"Girls steal your beauty. And your man's love." Her lips curl as she studies my stomach with narrowed, curious eyes. "But I wouldn't trade my girls for anything. Have you done the string thing with a ring?"

"No," I say and she explains how you wrap a string around a ring and hold it over your belly and watch it do either circles for a boy or lines for a girl. It sounded silly, but, of course, now I lie naked in bed and hold the ring I borrowed from Diane over my tummy. Remington is playing chess on his iPad, the backs of our heads pressing as he does his thing and I do mine. We're going to Austin in a few weeks, and I know it's starting to make him restless, because he's not getting a lot of sleep.

I really marvel at the way he uses chess to center himself. All those nights he would be restless before and grab his iPad, resting it on me, I had no idea he played chess.

Now, I tie the ring onto a thread as he tells me, "We'll get a doctor we like and have him work with us on our vaccination schedule," and I nod as I finally hang the ring over my stomach and watch it move. "Is it a circle or a line?" I ask.

He stops playing and sets the iPad aside, turning to watch. I think it's a boy because I'm carrying low and sleep on my left side, and my hair is full-bodied and shiny, but I'm not sure how true those old wives' tales are.

"It's doing both," I answer myself of the damn ring, laughing. "What failure!" I squeak when he grabs me by the underarms and drags me to him.

"What do you want it to be?" he asks, spreading out over me and brushing a loose tendril behind my ear.

"Anything. I'm just so curious to know."

"You can know," he tells me, kissing the tip of my nose. "I'll take you to a doctor so you can know, but I don't want to know."

"Why don't you?" I slide my arms around his and stare into his blue eyes. "Are you afraid of loving it too much, too hard, before you even meet it?"

"Whatever they say, it won't be real until we hold it." He drops to his back and pulls me to his side; then he cups the back of my head and sets my face against his neck in my special crook, and I close my eyes and lightly lick him like he's taught me he likes. He is so big, he loves so hard, he fights so hard. I'm giving him what he has never, ever had and never even probably knew he wanted. He's afraid to hope. . . .

The next day, I hang around the sidelines, watching him pound the heavy bag. Hit. Hit. Hit. I'm doing some yoga stretches when I feel a definite bump coming from inside me. I stop breathing. I feel it again and I go utterly still, and it comes once more. It's not a bubble. I feel as if something inside me is punching me, just like Daddy is punching the heavy bag.

My heart leaps and I leap just as hard to my feet.

"Remington. Remy! Remington fucking Tate!"

He swings around and stops the swinging bag with one hand.

"Feel this!" I take his glove off with shaky hands and toss it aside and put his hand on my stomach, my heart racing. *Come on, little baby. . . .*

Remington frowns in puzzlement. It kicks.

He narrows his eyes and presses his big hand closer, his eyes flicking up to mine. "Is that . . . ?"

I nod.

All of a sudden, he flashes me a white, arresting smile, his dimples as deep as I've ever seen them, his eyes bluer than the sea in Tahiti as he ducks his head as if ready to talk to the baby. "Tell her to do it again," he whispers.

"She pays no attention to me." My lips tip up in a smile as I nudge him playfully. "And it's a he. Because my hair is shiny and I'm carrying low, I think. And he's got quite a punch. Maybe if you ask him nicely, he'll show you more of his moves."

"Kick for Papa and let's move it!" Coach yells from the other side of the heavy bag.

Remy smirks at me and Riley comes over, all lazy surfer-boy swagger.

"He moved? Jesus, I have to feel this," he reaches out.

"Don't touch," Remington growls, slapping his hand aside.

"Dude, she's like a sister—"

"Hands off, Riley," he warns, shoving him aside with one arm.

Riley releases a great peal of laughter, while Remington grabs me closer with one hand and keeps the other spread on my abdomen, our gazes holding as we wait like two dodos for the baby to move.

When the baby kicks again, and he bursts out laughing, I'm so full of love, I hug him. "Is that real enough for you?" I breathe, a smile dancing on my lips as I tip my head up at him, my nostrils catching the delicious scent of his soap and sweat clinging to his skin.

"That felt fucking surreal," he whispers, his eyes alive with joy, and, as if it were a contest for speed, he kisses my forehead, my nose, my cheeks, and my chin; then he grabs me by the waist and flings me in the air, a squeak of alarm leaving me as he catches me.

"Remington Tate, you're the only man who flings his pregnant girlfriend in the air like that!"

"She's a little firecracker and she loves it!" He flings me up again.

That night, for the first time, we play baby his first song. Remy puts his headphones on my stomach and plays Creed's "With Arms Wide Open."

The song tells the baby how he'll show him the world and receive him "with arms wide open," and I swear I can feel the baby's comfort while his sexy, beautiful father stretches out beside me and starts kissing me.

"Has she got my hook?" he asks thickly, between those soft, drugging kisses as we hear the music trail into my tummy.

"He has definitely got your hook, because of course it's all about you," I softly tease, cupping his jaw.

He laughs. "All about me?"

"All of it. Everything. My whole life," I say with a dramatic flair that makes it obvious I'm exaggerating, but his smile is so dazzling and huge, his big lion's ego so grand in the room, I pat his jaw and laugh, and for some reason, I just have to say it again, if only to keep looking at that big wide grin on his face. "Yes, Remy, it's really all about you."

SIXTEEN

AUSTIN AWAITS

"So it's all over the headlines that Riptide's girlfriend is pregnant," Pete says as we fly to Austin.

Now Josephine flies with us too, and today she sits with Pete, Riley, and Remington in one of the living room sections, while Coach is on the bench, and Diane and I occupy one of the other living room sections. Remy and the men seem to be discussing my security for the two Austin fights. Apparently, we're approaching semifinals, so Scorpion will now be fighting on the same evenings as Remington.

A part of me is anxious to see if we'll bump into Nora at the fights, while another part of me dreads the outcome of such an encounter.

Remy is in a gruff, overprotective bad mood. The fact that his fucked-up parents live in Austin and that he sold the house where we usually stay undoubtedly annoys him. Pete rented another house to keep us away from the media, but Remington is not appeased. I know he doesn't like the thought of me being in the same state as Scorpion, much less the same zip code.

While I show Diane the pictures Melanie sent me of color schemes for the baby's room, I hear Remington's voice, low, as if he doesn't want me to hear, but authoritative. "Anyone approaches her or so much as looks wrongly at her, you take care of it *immediately*."

Out of the corner of my eye, I see how Pete nods somberly and smoothes a hand down his black tie. "Don't worry, Rem, I'll protect her as if she were mine."

"She's not yours, dipshit. She's MINE."

"Mister Tate," Josephine interjects, "I'll be on standby making sure she's not in any way threatened or inconvenienced."

"I really love this blue-and-green scheme," Diane tells me, disconnecting me from the conversation on the other side of the plane.

Turning back to the images, I sadly tell her, "I wish that ring thing had worked. Remington doesn't want to know, and I don't want to find out from a doctor and spoil it accidentally for him."

"Hey!" Riley yells from the other section. "What are you guys going to call it?"

Remington's shoulders are hunched as he leans over and studies something Pete is showing him on his phone, and I don't think he's even listening to me, but I still say, "If it's a boy, I haven't been able to think of anything. But I have the perfect name if it's a girl."

"Oh, yeah, what?" Riley asks, leaning back on his arms, curious.

"Iris," I say softly. Remington instantly turns to look at me, and the intimacy of his gaze bores and burns through me like a wave of lust and love crashing through me.

"I like Iris," he says gruffly, nodding approvingly.

It takes Pete a lot more effort to get Remy to concentrate again on whatever Pete was showing on his phone, for Remington keeps looking at me across the plane. I can't concentrate on what Diane says either, for I keep looking back at him.

It just feels wrong to have all these seats between us, my iPod tucked in my bag, and my guy so far away.

He leans as far back in his seat as possible, and across the plane aisle, he stretches his arm and opens his large hand. I link my fingers through his, and then it feels right again. He keeps checking out his man stuff, and I keep talking with Diane about baby stuff, his hand holding mine across the aisle.

❤ ❤ ❤

AS PETE AND I settle down in the Austin Underground, I have the misfortune of spotting two of Scorpion's goons watching us from across the ring. I blink in surprise and immediately scan the crowd for Nora.

I can't find her anywhere, and when my attention drifts back to the goons, I find that their attention is still on us.

One of the guys has a shaven head, and the other proudly wears a scorpion tattoo on his cheekbone, just like his boss used to before Remington carved it out the day he went for Nora.

Nora . . .

The thought of her fraternizing with Scorpion and his minions makes me wretched, and the thought unfortunately also comes with the sensation of a thousand legs crawling on my skin. I'm torn between the multiple urges: to vomit, to run away, and to march over to these thugs and demand they tell me where my sister is. I feel like a compass gone crazy and I don't know what to do, where to point, or how to react, so I instead sit here and keep watching them—feeling very much like a little baby doe, even if Pete sits beside me, armed to the teeth with little gadgets.

When the two men slowly rise and start working their way around the ring, the realization that they're heading straight for us makes my lungs constrict. My heart kicks fiercely into my rib cage while my rioting insides fall completely still in dread.

Tense in his plastic chair, Pete whispers, "They're probably going to watch Scorpion fight later—or they're scouting Remington.

Check how he's fighting, if there's any visible injury. Please, for the love of god, don't do anything, and *ignore them*."

I watch the pair stop before us with a sinking in the pit of my stomach. "Don't move, Brooke," Pete warns under his breath.

Fiercely aware of the now nearly six-month-old baby in my round little stomach, I force my eyes down to the cement floor while my blood vessels dilate inside me. My legs shake as I curl my hands protectively around our baby, whose heart we've already heard and who I want as far, far away from these men as possible.

But these are two of the jerks who tried to provoke Remington into fighting at a club last season, and pretending I don't see them when I can actually smell their stench goes against all my instincts to kick their insteps and smash their nuts in.

"Hello, Remy's bitch. Want to give us a little kiss?" one of them sneers.

Rage and impotence well inside me as the rows of seats start filling up around us, and I force myself to keep my eyes on their feet and hope they'll go away, or that Pete will finally grow some bigger balls and do something.

"I suggest you two get lost," Pete says calmly.

"We're not talking to you, skinny, we're talking to the whore. She don't remember her pussy got as wet and sopping as a seal when the boss made her kiss him? Right at this very moment your little sister is getting fucked well and hard by the boss, right in front of all his other girls."

My head snaps back up as my body flushes in humiliation. Shaking in my seat, I clench my teeth and fist my hands at my sides as I wish for a couple of bottles to crack across their skulls. "Go back to the hole you crawled out from and tell your asshole boss that Riptide is gonna *bury* him this year!" I grit out.

"Brooke," Pete grabs my elbow in warning while the two assholes laugh.

"You want us to tell him you said that? Remy's newest whore?" The bald one spits on the ground, a centimeter from my feet. "*Do* you—bitch?"

"I'm warning you guys to leave," Pete repeats, rising to his feet and reaching into his jacket.

I'm full force defense mode, and my blood is pumping as I flip out my middle finger at them. "By all means. Tell him to fuck off and that he'll soon regret not leaving my sister alone."

Suddenly, Josephine grabs the guys by the backs of their shirts, her voice deceptively calm as she asks, "Looking for a real woman, gentlemen?"

Pete pulls me up from my seat and drags me down the row while my heart pumps with such violence, I can barely breathe.

"What was that about?" Pete spins me around, his eyes aflame in indignation. "A little bit of pepper spray in my pocket make you feel all freaking feisty?"

"Pete, you're a daffodil. Why didn't you use it? They were breathing down our necks!"

"Brooke, a little subtlety, please! You can't provoke these dudes! If they come back when Remington is fighting and he sees they're within two feet of you, he'll leave the ring and be disqualified, and that's the last shit we need. . . ." He trails off, drags in a deep breath, and scowls at me. "What did he tell you to do just now in the locker room? Huh?"

I remember Remington's request clearly, and instantly my voice drops. "To sit tight in my seat."

"Well then! He might like that you're a little firecracker, but I don't want you going off on my watch, and I certainly don't want to get burned."

"Pete, Remy wouldn't like me to sit with my head bent while those two bozos called me names. I am *certain* he wouldn't expect me to do nothing."

"He does not expect you to do nothing—which is why he appointed *me* to try to keep things under control."

"If he were *you*, he would've done something, and if I weren't pregnant, so would *I*!"

"I'm not fucking Riptide, Brooke. Look at me!" Pete signals at himself in his black jacket and tie. "I admit I'm not pregnant myself, and I could've used one of these little toys I have on me on them, but that would raise all kinds of red flags so that when Rem came out, he'd notice something was up around you and drop the fight. It's not always about attacking. Sheesh."

"Pete, I'm sorry, I get it. Let's go sit—I'm just glad they're gone," I say, and we both exhale as we head back to our seats and settle down to watch, but my hands still shake with the adrenaline pumping through my veins.

The room is swarmed with people by the time the first fight is announced through the speakers.

"Welcome, welcome, ladies and gentlemen . . ." I hear.

The noise and excitement surround us as we watch fighters come and go. Seeing all that blood again, hearing the crushing sounds of bone against bone, begins to make me anxious.

Remy . . . oh god. Just thinking about how he could bump into Scorpion in the locker rooms spikes my nervousness to the roof.

I'm breathing in and out when Pete tells me, "You know what, Brooke? He told me he didn't want anyone looking at you, so you're right—he would've wanted me to take them as far away from you as possible, immediately. But I can't take it so literal, dude. I'm trying to keep things calm around here. Please understand I have to be the cool head here."

"I understand, Pete, but you," I exaggeratedly say, "are like a loaded gun without a trigger."

"We're in direct negotiations with Scorpion, Brooke," he tells me then, under his breath. "The last thing I want is to aggravate the situation, or it'll only cost Remington more."

"*What?*" My eyes widen. "Do you know anything about Nora?"

"Only that this time Remington is taking care of things—and

you're to be left completely out." He purses his lips meaningfully and nods, and I can't even argue, for just then Remington is called out, his name exploding through the speakers and around the crowd.

"Yes, sir, bring out Riptide for these people!" the announcer yells, and the crowd roars, "*RIPTIDE!*"

My heart skips a beat, my awareness immediately shifting to focus on the one flash of red approaching the ring.

This fight night is so meaningful. Not only because we heard that Scorpion was disqualified for using brass knuckles at a fight the night before and because Remington is in first place point-wise by a lot of points, but because I know that Austin is the place where he was born—where he, in his head, believes he was rejected. But not by this crowd. Oh, no. Never by this crowd.

The arena reverberates with bloodthirsty screams as Remy hops into the ring, bringing all the color to that blank and boring space.

"If he goes through tonight with no loss, then we'll be leaving Scorpion way behind. All good news," Pete tells me.

I nod in excitement, my eyes focused on nothing else but Remy now.

Riley and Coach take their places at the corner while Remington removes his RIPTIDE robe and hands it over.

While his opponent is called up, Remy raises his arms and grins to his public, then he points at me—and the people roar. "*Brooke, Brooke, Brooke,*" they begin chanting.

He laughs, and I'm red-cheeked with the sudden knowledge that everyone here knows about me now. His adoring fans all know I'm Riptide's pregnant girlfriend, so what the hell. I wave like a dope and send him a kiss, and I love the way he grabs it and slams it to his mouth. I think that's what the people were asking for when they chanted *Brooke*, because the instant his arm swings out to grab my kiss in the air and slam it down, the crowd goes wild, and we laugh in unison.

A new fighter gets into the ring, lacking any of the fanfare of Remy's entrance, and the fight begins.

Remington is especially playful with the younger fighters. They seem to expect him to be powerful, but not so fast, and I can see it drives them insane. He feints a lot, gives them a little play, and then he finishes them off without mercy—to the delight of his crowd.

Tonight he goes through twelve fighters and ends up soaked and slightly bruised on his left side. When we head back to the rental house, he starts drilling Pete as soon as he hits the large living room that separates into long halls, each leading to a separate room. "Everything okay on the sidelines?"

"Uh, sorta."

"Any scouts around?"

"Two. The same as usual."

"They look at Brooke?"

"Uh . . ."

He swings around, his eyebrows furrowing. "They fucking look at Brooke?"

Pete looks at me, then at him. "They came over to talk. Brooke flipped them the finger. I told them to go, Josephine came over. I pulled Brooke aside."

Remy looks at me, and now his brows are raised high. "You flipped them the finger?"

I bristle. "Would you rather I'd kicked them in the nuts?"

His disbelief shifts to Pete. Ever so slowly, he drags a hand through his hair in frustration, down to the back of his neck, then he shakes his head and grabs my nape as he steers me toward our hall. "We'll discuss it in our room," he grumbles at me.

"Good night, guys," Pete says.

Remington stops and swings around. "No sign of Brooke's sister?"

"None," Pete says, and the emotion in his face almost breaks me. He and Remington engage in some silent form of man-to-man communication, and then that's it, and we head in different directions.

As soon as Remy ferrets us into our bedroom, I'm pressed back against the door and I find his nose buried in my cleavage as he smells me again.

My pussy clenches as he growls, "Why'd you flip off those assholes?" He jerks his head back and gives me the full force of his blue-eyed stare. "What did they say to you?"

"They were just in our faces, and I hate to say this, but Pete's like a loaded gun without a trigger."

"Is he now?"

"It was actually a good thing that he could keep his cool tonight, because I couldn't. I'm crazed just thinking Nora is out there with those men. What are you going to do?"

He shakes his head and heads for the shower. "You're to stay out of it."

I start after him. "Won't you at least tell me?"

He opens the shower stall door, and levels his most somber stare to date on me. "For us, Brooke," he sternly whispers, stroking his hand all along the curve of my abdomen. "For the three of us. I'll have your promise you'll stay out of it. And if you break your promise to me, so help me god . . ."

"No! So help me god, if *you* put yourself in danger because of her . . . because of me . . . I'm going to . . ."

"What?" He cocks an amused brow, then pats my ass with a smirk. "I like it when you punch me, and I like you angry too."

"But I'll be very fucking mad—like you've never seen me!" I glare menacingly at his chest as he starts stripping his boxing gear. "Don't, Remy." Reaching out before he enters the shower, I grab his jaw and force him to look at me. "Promise me."

Amusement twinkles in his gaze as he runs the back of one finger down my temple. "What am I going to do with you, firecracker?"

"Promise me," I urge.

"I promise you," he tells me, "that your sister will be back with you very soon, and I'm crushing that insect this year." He chucks my chin and goes into the shower, and I can't explain the relief I feel. He's never lied to me. His words aren't so bountiful, but they carry such weight. He is winning this year, and whatever he's negotiating, Nora will be free soon. Marginally relieved, I go pull out my oils. It takes him exactly four minutes to soap up, wash his hair, and step out with a towel around his waist while he uses another to dry his chest.

"Get over here and let me rub you down," I tell him, and as he follows me to the bench that we usually find at the foot of most of our hotel beds, he pulls me into his arms and kisses the hollow of my ear.

"Who do you belong to?" he asks softly.

Melting.

"Some lucky guy." I urge him down to sit, fighting the urge to kiss every inch of him just yet.

"Tell me his name," he commands as he drops down so that I can rub his muscles. He watches me kneel before him and set all my materials nearby, and he wears a devastatingly sexy tilt to his lips that is frankly irresistible.

"Why? Do you like the way his name sounds in my voice?" I ask as I unscrew the lid of my arnica oil.

"I fucking love it. Tell me his name now." Hot blue eyes watch me as I pour the oil into my palms and rub my hands together to warm the liquid before sliding it slickly along his chest and shoulders.

"But . . . he's . . . complicated," I whisper, curling my fingers around his collarbone and throat. "I know him very well, and yet . . ." I pause and rub the arnica oil all down the solid length of one muscled arm. "And at the same time, he's always still a mystery." Sliding back up his arm and to stroke the oil across his trapezoids, I whisper in his ear, "He goes by Riptide sometimes, but I call him Remy. And I'm crazy about him."

His chest rumbles with a chuckle, and I see the little stars of delight dancing inside his eyes as he looks into my face and tweaks my nose. "You're good for my ego, Brooke my-pregnant-beauty Dumas."

"But don't let that ego get even bigger," I warn him, now rubbing the warm oil along his pecs as I drop my voice and tell him, "You're mine."

Smiling, I slide my fingers down his forearm, I stroke down to his palm, then I impulsively lift his hand and kiss his knuckles, looking into his blue eyes, which shine with tenderness as he watches me. "This is mine, too?" I ask uncertainly.

He lowers his voice to a playful rasp as he runs the back of a finger along my cheek. "Depends, little firecracker. Do you want it?"

"I want it."

"Then it's yours, baby girl."

Taking his other hand, I repeat what I did with the first one and kiss his knuckles. "And this one?"

"Do you want it?" He raises his eyebrows and happily jerks his head in the direction of the door. "All those ladies out there wanted it."

"But *I* want it," I protest.

He smiles indulgently and runs the back of a finger down my jaw again. "Then it's yours."

My voice thickens when I jerk down his towel so I can slick the oil into his calves and powerful thighs. I admire his sexy smile, those dimples and that rumpled hair. I ask, "What about you? All of you?" As I slick my oily hands up his eight-pack, I lift my head to search for his lips. He groans when I lick the seam of his mouth. Softly. I continue massaging his flesh as I start moving my lips over his. He's a fighting machine and he's mine, and my eyes briefly slide shut as I tend to him and breathe, "What about you, Remington? Are you mine?"

His thick rasp makes my nipples bead. "Do you want me?"

God. My adorable big man of a boy. A boy with the strength of a thousand men. Playful and possessive. I am dying from need and love as I whisper, "I want you," in his ear. "All of you. Black and blue and any other shade you come in."

Groaning, he draws my head down to his lips and kisses me, hard and deeply. "I'll answer that to you in bed." He grabs my hand as if ready for the bed part, but I laugh and pull back.

"Five more minutes!"

He shakes his head. "Two."

"Four."

"Three, now take it or I'll toss you up on the bed right over there, right this second."

"Done."

"Done, I toss you up on the bed?" he prods.

"Done, three more minutes!" I cry laughingly, speeding up my hands as I rub them along his hard pecs. My laugh fades when my thoughts drift back to the Scorpion's men. "She used to slip into my bed at night when she had nightmares. She had such a vivid imagination, she'd see things, good and bad, where there weren't any."

"What are you talking about?" he asks huskily.

"Nora," I say, unable to hide the sadness in my voice. "I just want you to know why I . . . I don't know. Why I've always protected her. She seemed to need me, and we fell into those roles. She's always needed protecting. But now I wonder if I don't let her solve her own problems, will she ever learn a lesson? I've always wanted to protect her but now nothing will ever make me risk the baby and you, not even her."

His expression is so gentle and understanding, a little knot of emotion winds in my chest. "Shh. Relax," he says, stroking a hand down my hair. "He's not getting the championship, or the prize, or your sister. He's not winning. I. Get. It all. Do you hear me? I get the gold, the championship, the sister's freedom . . . And I get to protect, and please, and love my girl."

SEVENTEEN

AUSTIN IS A WHIRL

A group of deer leap across the greenbelt area behind the sprawling gardens of the Austin rental home. I point at them and say, "Look!" but Remy just grunts; he's a little busy flipping a gigantic tractor tire over, again and again.

It's so hot here in Texas, sweat trickles down my neck and dips into my cleavage.

Squinting in the afternoon sun, I ask Remy and Coach if they want anything from inside, and Coach shakes his head, while Remy grunts and starts turning the tire in the opposite direction.

"We're almost done," Coach lets me know. I nod and raise two fingers—meaning it'll take me two minutes to go make my fifth trip into the house for lemonade.

Inside the house, I spot Riley at the edge of the living room, and he's so motionless I almost *don't* see him. His hands are jammed in his suit pockets, and he's staring at the front door with a huge frown. My body kicks straight into high-alert mode, and a cold little kernel settles deep inside my tummy.

"His parents," I say in disgust.

His *parents*. Two specimens of people who did not deserve a penis and ovaries, much less be permitted to reproduce something as magnificent as Remington! Raise him? Oh, no. Those assholes just grabbed their boy, checked him into a mental institute, and never came back.

Tight-lipped, Riley gives me an affirmative gesture. "Pete's handling it."

Curling my arms around my stomach by pure protective instinct, my gaze falls on the front door along with his. "Why do they keep bothering him? Do they want to make amends?"

"Brooke!" Riley almost chokes on my name, his laugh one of the most humorless, sad laughs I've ever heard anyone give. "They're assholes. We've gone through this dozens of times and they know Remington will make them go away with a damn check."

A potent anger overtakes me as I think of the way Remy gets restless every time we even get near his hometown. Last season, his parents looked him up again and found themselves on the receiving end of a check with his signature.

"They don't deserve anything from him. *Anything*," I whisper.

Before I know it, I'm charging across the living room.

"B! Just let Pete make them scat," Riley proposes to me.

But instead I swing the door open and there they are, on the porch, pretty as you please. The man . . . he's big as a mountain, beautifully aged. I swear it almost hurts to see the resemblance to Remy in him. Eyes the same electric-blue shade as Remy's instantly train on me, but the expression in these eyes is completely different. The life and vitality, the drive and strength I see in Remington's eyes are completely lacking in his father's.

And his mother? As she surveys me with a critical eye, I survey her back, and in that neat little homemaker dress, she looks small, calm, and sweet—which only makes the confusion I feel more overwhelming.

These are people I could smile at in an elevator, or passing by on the street. They seem good and caring, but how can they be? How can they have abandoned Remy and then have the gall to come knocking on his door, again and again, like it's their right to?

The mere thought of abandoning this little baby I hold inside me repulses me, and I still can't fathom why anyone would do that to their own son.

"You've left him alone his entire life. Why can't you leave him alone now?" I demand, glowering.

They have the gall to look genuinely horrified at either my appearance or my outburst—or, quite possibly, both.

"We want to talk to him," the woman says.

Because that's what she is, just a woman. I can never look at her and think of her as anyone's mother, especially Remy's.

"Look . . . we've heard about the baby," she adds. Her eyes drop to my stomach, and I feel Pete draw closer to me, as though he expects her to reach out and touch my stomach, and he, on behalf of Remington, plans to stop her. "This baby," the woman continues, pursing her lips into a thin line and gesturing at me, "could be just like him. Do you realize?"

"Yes," I say, thrusting my chin up. "I *hope* he is."

"Our son is in *no* condition to be a father!" the man thunders in a deep, booming voice that startles me. "He can hurt someone. He needs to be medicated and *contained*!"

"Ohmigod, you hypocrites! *You* want to talk about good parents?" I ask, so outraged my lungs can't even work right now. "Your *son* has grown into an honorable, noble man despite what he has to deal with, when *you're* the ones who abandoned your only child! You took his childhood and threw him away, and you want to come here to tell him how to live the rest of his life?"

"Our son is sick! We want him to be treated and to check in with the mental facility periodically to make sure he's calm and serene, like a normal person," the woman says.

"No! You're the ones who are! At least *he* knows what his problem is, but I think you both should figure out yours."

The door behind us swings open, and Riley steps out with the fiercest glare I've ever seen him wear.

"You missed out on an incredible human being," Riley says, and they look so shocked at his calm, threatening words, I think this is the first time he's stepped out to greet them too. "As his parents, you were supposed to lift him up and hold him up. We're not sorry for him, really, because he thrived. But we are sorry for *you*."

"We're his *family*," Remy's mother huffs.

"You *were* his family," Pete corrects as he steps closer to me. "He's ours now. And this is the last time we will ask you to leave. Next time we see you here unwelcomed, we'll get the authorities involved."

The man looks at me, and it feels so strange, eyes so much like Remy's glaring at me with such cold contempt instead of tender heat. "You have to have some silly head on you to let my son get you like that," he tells me, pointing at my stomach.

Suddenly I'm drawn back into a muscled wall. My breath tangles in my throat when a huge hand opens protectively over my midsection, and the sound of Remington's voice from over the top of my head sends all the little hairs in my arms standing.

"Come near her or anything of mine again, and I'll show you in a heartbeat how dangerous I am," he says in a dead flat tone, all the more predatory for its quietness.

The volatile energy emanating from his large frame makes my pulse accelerate in anticipation of his parents' reply. Neither of them seems capable of holding Remington's stare too long. Lips pursed tight, the man grabs his wife and drags her down the walkway toward the small car at the curb.

My limbs are shaking, most of my weight resting back against Remy when he clenches my hips and tightly murmurs, "Get in."

We go inside.

Remington grabs a water bottle from the kitchen and drinks it all down quickly. He's still in his workout gear, his muscles glistening. He shakes his wet hair then he drops down on one of the living room couches and sends the empty bottle spinning on the floor, angrily watching it twirl. His elbows rest on his knees, his broad shoulders hard and tense, and his dark head is bent as he stares at nothing but that spinning bottle. Round and round it goes.

"I don't think your parents like your choice of woman, Rem," Riley speaks first. He's trying to make light of what just happened, but nobody laughs. The tension in the air is so thick you'd have to hack at it with an axe.

Remington lifts his head and pins me down with violently tender blue eyes. "They ever come near you, I'm the first to know. Do you hear me, firecracker?"

The fierce protectiveness in his gaze makes an equally protective feeling wrap tightly around my gut. "They weren't looking for me, they were looking for *you*."

"I don't want them near you. I don't want them near our children," he angrily says. My heart wrings in my chest; did he say "children," in plural? I want to smile and hug him for this, but the look in his eyes is almost . . . raw with pain.

"Are you done?" I ask lightheartedly, signaling outside, to where he was working out.

He nods slowly, his face tight as he watches me head over to him.

He's brooding, his anger palpable in the air. He wears a strange expression, as if he's trying to pull himself together. He keeps clenching and unclenching his jaw. I hate that he had to come face-to-face with his parents, but time and again, he's proven that he'll do anything to protect me.

My head feels both bruised and swollen as I drop down at his side and take his arm, seizing his thick wrist and starting to work on it. "I can't believe two assholes like them created something as wonderful as you," I whisper softly.

Pete quietly goes into the kitchen and Riley heads out to the lawn to help Coach clean up.

Their footsteps fade, and everything around us feels muted as Remington looks at me. His voice carries that calm, deadly quiet it does when he's getting extremely busy battling something within himself. "They're right, little firecracker."

I feel like I've been struck with a baseball bat right in my chest.

Inhaling a slow breath, he looks at me fiercely. "Brooke, I wouldn't wish a father like me on Scorpion's offspring, much less my own kid."

No. Not a baseball bat. I think I've just been slammed into by a train. Pain streaks through me, and my hands fall from his arm. "Please don't say this. Please don't think anything other than that you'll be the best father."

He clamps his jaw, and I can tell he softens his voice for my sake. "It could be like *me*."

"How like you?" I fiercely counter, clutching my stomach. "Beautiful, inside and out? With more willpower than anyone I've ever known. Herculean, generous, kind—"

He looks so tormented, I seize his jaw and force him to look at me. "You're the best thing that's ever happened to me. You're human, Remy, and real, and I wouldn't have you any other way. We want this. We want a family together. We deserve it—just like anybody else."

He clamps his jaw and grits his teeth, "Little firecracker, wanting it doesn't mean it's right. I'm fucking worthless for anything but fighting."

"No, you're not. You're a great fighter, but that's not what makes you YOU. Remy, don't you see how inspiring you are? You're honest, driven, passionate, fierce, and tender. You protect and provide without any expectations. I've never heard you judge people, criticize. You live your own life by your own rules and do your best to protect those who surround you. You love even harder than you fight, and I've never seen anyone fight like you. Nobody taught you how to be like you—it's just you. Any shape you come in, you are the only father I would have ever wanted for my children, and the only man I will ever love. Let those two go. They biologically made you, but they. Did. Not. Make. You."

He absorbs my words, and as he thinks about them, I grab the back of his head and pull him down so I can kiss those beautiful lips, and stop them from saying any more hurtful things about himself.

His mouth, hard at first, softens under my pressure, until I feel the tension in him ease as he tongues me back and murmurs against my lips, "You're blinded because you're mine."

"No. I see you because I'm yours."

He eases back to search my expression, his gaze shining protectively on me, I *know* he will do anything to protect me and our baby.

"They don't agree with my choice. Are you all right with it?" he asks me.

God, I'm all right with anything he does, that's how much I trust, respect, and love him. I know he's asking about his choice to use natural means to control his illness. It probably takes him double the effort that it would take him to medicate; it takes discipline and an entire lifestyle devoted to his well-being, and, frankly, it's not like he's making a political stand out of the issue. It's his life and he's trying to live it, and I want to live mine with him. Everyone who has ever been sick or has ever been on medication long-term knows that when you fix one thing chemically in your body, you give something else up. Look at the list of side effects. There is *no* magic pill for health.

We are works in progress, and health is not a static place. It is a goal that is always moving and needs to be chased, daily, and forever. Remington will always fight this fight . . . and I will always fight it with him.

"I'm okay with your choice, Remy," I say to him, holding his gaze so he knows that I mean it.

The smile that appears on his face is oh so tender. "We're going to have a little someone who depends on us. You have to tell me if it's too much for you, Brooke."

"I'll let you know," I agree.

He takes my little hand in his big, callused one, and we both watch our hands as we interlace our fingers. "Then give me your word you'll tell me if I ever get out of hand and you'd like me to medicate, and I give you my word I'll do it the instant you ask me to."

"Remington, I give you my word," I say, squeezing his hand.

"And I give you mine." He tugs me closer and wraps me in his arms, and I slide right in, absorbing his strong, protective embrace as he spreads his fingers on my round stomach and ducks his head over my shoulder to look at the swell. "I will protect you until I die," he whispers against the back of my ear. "Nothing will ever hurt you two. If she's like me, I'm going to hold her up like they never did. I'm going to show her she can still thrive. It's still worth it."

I'm completely melted as I turn my head to bury my nose in his sweaty chest, not wanting to be anywhere else. "It's going to be a he. And he's got this. Like you do."

EIGHTEEN

BLACK

They triggered him. His parents. They've ignored him his whole life, and the times they come see him, all they do is hurt him. It didn't take but a couple of hours after their visit in Austin for Remy to go full-blown black.

I know it was thanks to them. Pete knows it. Riley knows it. Coach and Diane, they know it too.

The morning after their visit, he could barely get out of bed, and it's been like this for days now. Remy is down and out. It hurts to see him like this so much, I feel as if I'm getting kicked in the stomach, daily.

"He up yet?" Pete asks me from the living room today. The team is scattered across the couches as they watch me close the door of the master bedroom behind me. I shake my head in despair. Remy has sunken down so far, he is completely closed off like I have never, ever seen him.

He barely looks directly at me. He barely eats. He barely talks. He is in a bad, bad mood, but he seems to be fighting not to take it out on anyone, and therefore, he says nothing, absolutely nothing at all. All I can see of his inner struggle is those fists of his, curling and uncurling, curling and uncurling, as he fixes his gaze on a spot and keeps it there, for minutes and minutes and minutes, as if whatever he sees is inside him.

"Shit. It's a bad one," Pete says, dragging a hand down his face. He keeps calling it a "bad" one.

The faces of Diane, Lupe, Pete, and Riley look the way I feel: wretched.

"Did he at least take the glutamine capsules?" Coach asks me, his forehead furrowed all the way up to his bald head. "Otherwise he'll lose the muscle mass we've worked so hard to put on!"

"He took them."

He just took them from my hand, shoved them down with a gulp of water, and plopped back down on the bed.

He didn't even pull me to him like the times he's manic.

It's like he doesn't like himself . . . and he doesn't like *me*.

Quietly, and feeling as gray as if I have a thundercloud above me, I go and sit on a chair and stare down at my hands, and I feel everyone's eyes on me for a long, *awful* minute. They bore into the top of my head, like I'm supposed to know how to deal with this shit. I don't. I've spent two nights holding a big, heavy lion in my arms, crying quietly so he doesn't hear me. The rest of the days, I have spent rubbing his muscles, trying to bring Remington Tate back to me.

Remington just doesn't realize *he* is the one who holds us all together. Now we're all scrambling to hoist him up. We are so co-dependent, we are somehow *all* depressed with him. I know for a fact, after seeing everyone's faces for almost three days, none of us will smile until we see two dimples again.

"Does he say anything?" Pete breaks the silence. "Is he at least angry at those assholes? At something?"

I shake my head.

"That's the problem with Rem. He just takes it. Like a punch. And he keeps standing but he takes it. Sometimes I wish he'd just say what he feels, damn it!" Pete stands and begins pacing.

Riley shakes his head. "I respect that, Pete. When you open your mouth to say something, it makes it real. Whatever's running through his head, the fact that he doesn't voice it means he's fighting it. He's not letting it matter enough to spill it out."

I drop my hair as a curtain and blink back the moisture in my eyes, refusing to let them see how all this affects me. But it does. I was depressed once in my life. It's a big, black, dark hole. This was not some light depression where you're sad and have PMS. It's the overwhelming feeling that you want to die. And wanting to die is completely against all our survival instincts. Our normal instinct is to kill to protect our loved ones, to kill to survive. Just imagining that Remy is feeling all the same mess I felt when my life blew up around me pulls me so deep into the darkness that I worry about being able to get him out, rather than falling right in with him.

Whatever it is he's feeling, I need to remind myself he can't control the thoughts his mind is throwing at him. His mind is not *him*, even though right now it controls his reactions. I want to support, to be steady, understanding. Not emotional, needy, and like I will fall apart at any minute. And god, at six months pregnant, I am definitely emotional, needy, and falling a little apart without him.

"At least he's coming down to punch those bags. You don't know how deeply I admire him for that," Riley adds glumly.

"Do you think he'll pull through before the fight, Brooke?" Coach asks me. "By god, watching my boy get humiliated last season out there . . . This was his year. This was his *season*."

"I don't think he'll fight tonight," I admit.

"So we can say good-bye to a first place ranking," Pete swears.

"You can't let him fight like this, Pete! He could get hurt. He could *hurt* himself," I burst out; then I drag in a breath and try to calm down.

"It would have been better if he didn't remember," Pete says, with an infinite amount of bitterness in his voice.

"What do you mean?"

"It would be better if he didn't remember anything his parents ever did to him."

My protective instincts surge with a vengeance. "What did they do to him?"

There's something alarming about the way Pete hesitates, about the way his eyes slide across the group, and then settle back on me. My pulse flutters faster than normal by the time he finally speaks. "They committed him because he went black for the first time when he was ten, Brooke. But first, they thought he was possessed. They got all fanatic about it and had an exorcism performed on him."

When those last words filter into my troubled brain, I am so heartbroken and torn, my heart withers in my chest. I make a sound and cover my mouth.

Diane covers her face.

Curses fall from Riley's lips as he turns his head to the carpet.

Coach stares down at his hands.

The silence that stretches . . . it is taut with sorrow, with disbelief, and this agonizing frustration . . . of an ill little boy who was so misunderstood . . .

I think of "Iris"—the song he has played to me. The song where he wanted to be seen and understood, by me. When not even his own parents understood him.

Oh god.

"He was put in an exorcism circle in his own home," Pete says, driving the dagger deeper inside me. "His room was stripped of everything so he wouldn't hurt anyone, and he was roped to his bed. They went at it for days—we don't know exactly how many, but over a week—until a little neighbor who used to play with Rem came in looking for him, and those parents intervened. The 'holy man' was dismissed, and Remy was just committed instead."

There's not a sound in the room.

I've stopped breathing. I feel like I've stopped *living*.

"Unfortunately," Pete continues, "he remembers that manic episode, because at the institution, they did some experimental hypnosis to draw his memories out. See if some therapy would work. Not that it did. Worse is, his own body would have *protected* him from that hurtful memory if we hadn't fucked up with that damn hypnosis."

There's still not a sound.

But I can hear my heart beating inside me, so hard. Hard and ready, like those times when I could sprint like the wind. I can even hear the blood gushing through my veins, fast and furious. I am *ready* . . . and angry . . . and desperate to *fight* something. To fight *for* him. I remember him telling me he had a memory of his parents. How his mother crossed him at night. An indescribable pain cracks tiny little places inside me. Oh, Remy.

"So he remembers all of that?" I ask, while the middle of my body burns with impotent rage.

"I know he knows they're *wrong* . . . when he's blue. But when that black side comes, I know he thinks about it." Pete's frustration and despair is carved into every line of his face. "It's only natural to wonder why you weren't wanted."

"But he *is* wanted!" I cry.

"We know, B, calm down." Riley rises to his feet and comes over.

He hugs me to him, and I realize my hands are on my stomach, and the image of my Remington as a boy enduring such a thing because of something that was not his fault rocks in my head. Oh, how I wish I had his fucking evil parents in front of me now, and at the same time, I'm glad they aren't here, because I don't know what I would do or say to them. But I want to hurt them for hurting him! I want to hit and scream at them and run after them with a pitchfork. I clench my hands and ease away from Riley. He and Pete are like my brothers now, but Remy doesn't like them to touch me, and I don't like to do things that hurt him—even if he can't see. I want comfort, but the only comfort I want is from the man in the bed in the master bedroom.

Quietly, I head to the master. "I'll see you guys later—thanks for checking up on him."

"One of us will be around," Pete calls.

I don't want to make noise, so I wave from the door and shut it closed behind me, and my heart does all the crazy stuff it does when I see Remy. His big muscular form is on the bed, sprawled face-down, like a lion at rest. My playful boy, my protective man, my jealous boyfriend, my cocky fighter. My misunderstood little boy.

My eyes run down the length of him, his spiky hair dark against the pillow, his jaw beautiful and square. He's quiet and resting. Resting like he's wounded in some place my hands can't reach and my eyes can't see.

Reaching behind me, I turn the lock, then ease away and start stripping off my clothes. It's not for sexual reasons I want to be naked, but because I need to feel his skin on mine. He has never, ever slept a night with me with anything between us.

He likes feeling me, and I ache to feel him.

Climbing into bed, I spoon him from behind. "Look at you," I say, imitating what he says to me sometimes as I buzz my lips across the shell of his ear and slide my hand around his shoulder and to his chest, spreading my hand where his heart beats. He groans as I kiss the back of his ear.

"Look at you," I say lovingly in his ear. I lick the back of his ear softly, like he does to me, running my hands down the length of him, petting him like he pets me. "I love, adore, cherish, need, and want you like I never thought possible to love and adore and cherish and need and want another human being or anything in this world," I whisper. He growls softly as if in gratitude, and my eyes well up, because it's so unfair he has to deal with it. Why does anyone have to deal with something like this? Why does a beautiful person who doesn't want to harm anyone feel chemical impulses to hurt himself? To feel life is worthless? That he is worthless? To think he might rather die?

He doesn't need to tell me. I've been there. But I've been there only once. He is there so often, and no matter how many times he pulls himself back up, he will always know with certainty that in the future he will be dragged back down. He's such a fighter. Lovingly, I trace my tongue over the grooves of his abs, his muscled arms, his throat, at the seam of his lips.

He turns away. "What am I doing, Brooke?" he asks.

I stiffen at his blank tone of voice.

"Do I think I can be a father? That I could even be a husband to you?" He turns with a strange, pained noise and buries that sound in the pillow, his muscles bulging as he slides his arms under the pillow to hold it to his face.

"Remy," I say, forcing my voice to stop trembling and the pain inside me to shut. The fuck. Up. "I don't care what your mind is telling you, how it's making your body feel—you *know*. Remy. You know. You are good and noble and you deserve this. You want this." I slide my arm around his waist and press closer.

"I deserve to be put down. Like a dog."

The tears that had formed only moments ago slide out of my eyelids. "No, you don't, no, you don't."

He shifts away from me but I don't let him. I twine my arms around his shoulders and stop him from rolling farther away, and I run my fingers through his hair and caress his scalp. "I love you. I love you. I love you. I love you like a crazy fucking lunatic. If you're a mess, I want to be a mess with you. Just let me touch you—don't pull away," I whisper, sniffing. He groans and turns his face into the pillow again, and as I touch him, he almost winces. But I touch up his arm, trace the *B* on his bicep, the Celtic tattoos. The noises he makes, like a true lion, like a wounded lion, make me feel as desperate and fierce as a lioness trying to lure back the interest of her mate.

I've thought it difficult, sometimes, when he's manic, because he's such a ball of energy, and so difficult to control. But nothing is as hard as right now, when my fighter is down in the dark, when he doesn't want to do anything. When he feels he's not worth it.

Brushing my fingers up his jaw, I scratch my nails into his scalp in a way I know he likes, and he lets me, but he doesn't open his eyes, only makes those low, dark growling noises.

"Do you want to listen to music?" I ask him, and he doesn't say no, so I reach for his iPod and place an earbud in his ear and one in mine, and I play "I Choose You" by Sara Bareilles.

He listens to the song as I pet him, exactly like he has petted me, and I want him to feel exactly how his petting and licking make me feel. I want him to feel cherished, protected, understood, wanted, loved, and nurtured. So I try my best . . . and I know my hands are not as big as his . . . and I know my tongue is smaller on his nape . . . but I know he likes my touch and he likes my tongue on him. . . .

So "Iris" plays, about the world not understanding . . . and him wanting to be seen by me. . . .

So "I Choose You" plays about me choosing him . . . and how he is becoming mine and I am becoming his. . . .

And I whisper in his ear, "I will always choose you, Remy. From the first day I saw you, I loved what I saw and every day I love it more. And I love what I touch, the man I hold right here, right now." I press the mound of my stomach into the small of his back. I'm unquestionably pregnant now, and it's a tough maneuver to get the fit just right, but I really want to hold him as close as I can.

He suddenly rolls over. His arms wind around me like vises and then he rests his forehead between my breasts, holding on to me. He doesn't look at me, but I feel his need. I graze the top of his head with my lips and relax in his grip, so he knows I like being here.

Suddenly, he groans into my skin and his muscles ripple as he eases off me with visible effort and plops back down on the bed. "Go out, baby. Go somewhere else. I'm no good like this."

Something squeezes in me. I don't want him to feel coddled or pitied, so I plump my pillow like all is well and say, "I don't want to go anywhere. I'd rather be here with you."

He spares a look at me, and my heart moves just to feel those eyes on me. It beats even faster when he reaches out. He slides his fingers into my hair, his gaze never leaving me. His eyes have never been so bleak; he looks haunted, but in the black of his irises, I still see *him*. That fire that is him. That drive, that intensity, lurking in the background like a tiger. His hands coast down my spine, then drag around to my front and pass over my hard, sensitized nipples, then he rests his head on me and spreads his hand open on my stomach.

"You really want to be with me," he says gruffly. The hunter in him is still there. The lion. The raw instinct that is him. He pins me down with a questioning look that almost feels like a command. Yes, his eyes are dark and bleak, but those irises are still alive and hungry. Hungry for my affection, I realize. For me.

"Yes, Remy," I say, without a hint of doubt, either in my voice or in me. "I do want to be with you. And don't call me a masochist, because you're my everything. My adventure and my real, rolled into one sexy, jealous, beautiful package, and you make me ridiculously happy. Nora might have turned into a junkie, and now I realize I'm no different. I'm addicted to *you*. You're my crack, and you also happen to be the only dealer."

He closes his eyes and exhales.

"You might not want to be with you now, but *I* want to be with you," I tell him. "I left my entire life just to come be with you. Just you. And you *know* it wasn't a bad life." I stroke his hair. "I made my rent; I had good, caring parents, kick-ass friends, and could get a job in my new career. I left all that. I've left my dreams behind so I can come chase after yours—and after you. Like some stupid groupie." An amused little laugh leaves me.

He lugs his big, solid body up to a sitting position on the bed, tips my head back, and cuts off my laugh with his mouth. "You're no stupid groupie," he whispers into me, sucking up my reply before he adds, "You're my female, and you're too fucking good for me."

I shudder when he pulls me down and under him, and I moan and touch every bit of his skin that I can. "And you're my male and are too good and precious for anyone, but you're still *my*. Male. Mine."

He growls and rolls over onto me so his erection is between my legs, his tormented gaze clinging to mine for hope as he jerks one of my legs around his hips. Then he grabs me by the knee and does the same with the other.

"I love you," I say breathlessly. I thought I said it all the time, but I guess he needs me to say it right now, for the way his features go raw when he hears it makes my insides bubble with the need to say it again. Lifting my head, I repeat it with each kiss I place on his face. I decide to say it until he tires of it, and it takes a long, long time for him to finally take my mouth to quiet me.

At least sixty-four kisses.

He enters me on kiss thirteen. He moves in me, pushing deep each time I say "I love you," taking it with a thrust, like the only way he thinks I will love him is for him to take it forcibly from me. "I love you," I moan out on the next thrust, and he closes his eyes, and I feel him desperately sucking up my tenderness. I try holding my orgasm at bay as I hold on to his shoulders, saying "I love you, I love you," but he's hot, he's beautiful, he needs me, and I need him. He takes me to the peak even as I fight it, and I orgasm at "I love you" number sixty-two.

His eyes look even more ravenous by then, like all my *I love yous* only kindled more of his hunger. And when he starts coming in me, he watches me as if he's not sure he believes me yet, because he can't believe himself to be lovable. So when he can't help himself and crushes my mouth with his and shoves his tongue in, rough and hard, I grab him and kiss him back even harder.

He shudders in me, his muscles clenching. He grabs my hips to still me, but I rock them, coaxing him to come all the way in me. He moans softly and suckles my tongue, and I curl my legs tighter and lock them at the small of his back, my arms tight around him as he lets go, and when his muscles stop flexing and rippling, I still remain holding him, so he won't get rid of me. He spares me his weight when he sags, and I come with him, entangled, burying my face in his neck as he rolls to his side. He's still in me, and I don't want him to come out.

"Don't come out," I moan.

He comes out as he turns me around, then maneuvers himself back in and starts licking me, one hand splayed on my breast, the other over my stomach. I moan and think I want to cry with happiness, because my lion is back. At least he cares enough about something. About us.

Like the baby and I care about him too.

Later, he plays a song for me called "Hold Me Now" by Red, and I realize he's just asking me to hold him. I do, turning to him once he's stopped grooming me, urging him to set his face down on my chest until his big body seems curled like he's trying to fit himself to me, and even then, his hand is spread possessively over our baby.

❤ ❤ ❤

A WEEK PASSES.

Aside from the few hours Remington forces himself to go train, he stays in our room, and he doesn't seem to want me out of his sight. He doesn't talk to me much, but he keeps an arm around me like a vise, and he wants me to feed him and fuck him all the time. I try keeping him interested in life, so I tell him about little things I'm able to glimpse when I go out of the room to bring us food. I tell him that I caught Diane and Coach kissing the other day. I tell him that Melanie is hard at work finding patterns for our baby's room, and that Pete seems sad about Nora. He likes listening—I know he does.

The final approaches, and Remington hasn't yet made it to the fighting ring on any of the recent nights. He's dropped to second place after Scorpion. He could've fallen even more, but Scorpion lost a couple; he's fighting while on drugs, according to Pete, and he hasn't been as sharp as usual. To think that Nora is with that asshole worries me sick. She could be equally drugged and helpless, but the thought corrodes me in such a way I really can't think about that now. All I want is for Remington to successfully finish this season—this is his *dream*. Then . . . then we have to find a way to once again get Nora home safe, even though I know, in my gut, the men have been planning something, but it doesn't help my unease.

But now we're three days away from the big fight, and Remington is still completely dark. Today he went to train and didn't even look anyone in the eye. I know he feels things, bad things. I know he doesn't voice them because it would be losing, and he won't ever lose. *Except for when he lost for you,* a sad little voice tells me.

Everyone has grown extremely worried, and I feel especially concerned when Remy asks me to call Pete and Riley. They knock at the door of the master, and I cover Remy's naked body with the white bedsheet so that only his muscled back and arms are exposed, and lead them inside.

"They're here," I say.

Riley approaches first and kneels at the side of the bed. "Hey, Rem, how you doing?"

"Bad," he warns.

"What's up?" Pete says.

Silence.

"I want you to take me . . . to the damn hospital . . . and schedule me."

Riley's eyes flare wide, as do Pete's. The boys look at me for a moment, and Remington repeats exactly what he has just said. "I want you to take me . . . to the damn hospital . . . and schedule me *to get that procedure*," he adds.

Something in his words—in the way the men hesitate before answering—send a new rush of alarm skittering through me. "You want to do that again," Riley says

He nods against his pillow. "*Now*," he firmly stresses.

Riley turns helplessly to Pete, who after a moment grabs his phone. "First we need to see when it can be done. Let me call the hospital," he says and starts dialing, stalking out of the room.

"It'll perk you right up," Riley says as he shoots up to his feet and pats Remington's back with a solid *thunk*.

Remington grabs him by the tie and pulls him closer as he sits up. "Don't fucking patronize me. Just take me there and don't you dare let her see," he grits.

My eyebrows flick upward when I realize Remington thinks I left the room, and Riley's eyes shift momentarily my way, a signal to not to let on that I heard. But I'm not lying to Remington ever again, so I step forward.

"I want to be with you. If they medicate you or do anything else to you. I want to be there and I'm *going* to be there."

He straightens at the sound of my voice, but he first looks at Riley. "Riley . . ." he warns. Riley loosens his tie as Remy swings his head to look at me. "You stay here and I'll be back." He speaks gruffly but with obvious caring, using a complete different tone with me than the one he'd been using with the men.

"I don't think so," I stubbornly counter, because, seriously, I'm not budging on this. The three are acting as if I'm an incompetent, weak little rosebud!

Remy narrows his eyes and clamps his jaw at my stubbornness, and I lift both my eyebrows and cross my arms.

"*I* go where *you* go. Understand? Whatever it is, it's no big deal," I say.

He stays locked on my stare, a muscle working in the back of his jaw.

"It's no. Big. Deal!" I assure, bluffing with everything I've got.

But I'm not letting him out of my sight.

NINETEEN

BLACK VERSUS BLUE

Fully aware that I'm accompanying the guys almost by force, I wisely stay quiet during our ride to the hospital. Everyone seems to be on the same channel. Not a word is exchanged. Barely even a look. We all seem to expect Remy to say something, but his attention is firmly fixed on the passing city scenery, his profile hard in determination. I don't really think he's seeing anything; he's lost inside his head.

When we arrive, I feel the warmth of his body suddenly envelop me as he bends down and takes my lips briefly with his. His voice shivers through me as he tells me, "I'll be out soon."

"No! I want to go with you!" I call to his broad back as he disappears down the hall with a nurse while Pete goes to the desk to check him in. I begin suspecting it is, in fact, kind of a big deal when Riley starts talking to me like I'm a baby.

"It's so much better if you stayed here, Brooke," he practically croons.

I scowl. "Don't treat me like a flower, Riley. I want to be there for him. I *need* to be there for him."

Pete heads in the direction Remington disappeared, and I quickly jog to him. "Pete, can I go in with him?"

For a moment, there's a man-to-man communication going on between the guys, then Pete finally nods at Riley and tells me, "I'll come get you when he's prepped."

"Prepped?"

Pete disappears down the same hall Remington did.

"Riley?"

I'm completely confused here.

Riley sighs. "He's having a procedure to induce a brain seizure." And as he starts to explain, I listen as if I've just slid to the other side of a tunnel, and am getting farther and farther away by the second. A fire burns in my eyes and all I know now is that the hospital walls are white. So blank, and plain, and white. ". . . while his brain will receive an electric current . . ."

The heart is a hollow muscle, and it will beat billions of times during our life.

I've learned, in my short life, that you can't run if you tear a ligament, but your heart can be broken into a million pieces and you can *still* love with your whole being.

Your whole, miserable, insanely vulnerable fucking being . . .

I can feel my heart thumping hard as ever in my chest, *thump thump thump*. Even though I'm trying to act like it's NO BIG DEAL, my brain reels as I try to grasp what Riley has just explained to me. That Remington is about to commit himself to electroshocks. A fucking *electric* current is going to be sent through his scalp to his brain to give him a fucking *brain seizure.*

Now he's telling me that there could be some short-term memory loss, that he will be given short-acting anesthesia, that his blood oxygen levels and heart rate will be monitored, that other than the possible short- or long-term memory loss, there is no other known side effect. I swear that when I replay in my head the scene of Remington disappearing down the hall with the hospital staff, I hear a low, dull sound echoing in the cold, white walls—a low, dull sound coming from *me*.

"Oh, Riley." His name comes out in a low, wretched moan, and I cover my face as panic and fear rise in me like a tide, drowning me.

My pulse falters when Pete appears and signals to me. I run over and follow him, half dying and half as alive as I've ever been from sheer panic, into a room. I see machines, become hyperaware of the unsurpassable coldness of the hospital, and in the middle of the room, I see him. He's being strapped down with Velcro bands around his thick wrists.

His beautiful body spread out on the flat surface, he's covered in a hospital robe as he faces the ceiling.

Remy.

My beautiful, cocky, playful, blue-eyed boy and my serious, somber man who loves me like nobody in my life has ever loved me.

The urge to protect him from whatever is coming is so overpowering, I approach with slow but determined steps, one hand curled under my cantaloupe-size tummy where our baby is. My whole arm is shaking uncontrollably as I reach out for the large, tanned hand that is strapped down to the table. *Strapped.* To the table. And my voice cracks like glass as I lightly rub my fingers through his, trying to sound calm and rational while I really feel crazy enough to scream. "Remy, don't do this. Don't hurt yourself, please don't hurt yourself anymore."

He squeezes my fingers and flicks his eyes away from me. "Pete . . ."

Pete seizes my elbow and tugs me away, and I freak out when I realize Remington really doesn't want to see me here. He hasn't looked into my eyes. Why won't he look into my freaking eyes?

I turn to Pete as he pulls me out of the room, my voice a degree below hysterical, "Pete, please don't let him do this!"

Pete grabs my shoulders and hisses, low, so that we don't draw attention, "Brooke, this is a common procedure used on people with BP—this is how they pull people from suicide watch! Not everyone finds the right dose of medicine, and the doctors are aware of that. He'll be sedated through it."

"But it's just a fight, Pete," I argue miserably, pointing into the room. "It's just a stupid fight and this is him!"

"He'll pull through. He's done it before!"

"When?" I cry.

"When you were gone and we had to keep him from *slitting his fucking wrists because of you!*"

Ohmigod. My heart shatters so hard, I think I hear it, and it's not just my heart, but my entire body is breaking down on the inside, cracking under the grief of what Pete has just told me. The hurt is so great, I curve myself protectively around my stomach and I frantically try to remember to breathe, if not for me, for this baby. His baby.

"Brooke, this is the shit he's lived with his whole life. He's up, he's down, he's all over the place. His decisions might hurt but making them gets him through it. This is how he was formed—this is why he's who he is. He is strong because of this bullshit! You can be pitiful or you can be powerful, but you can't be both. He is powerful. You have *got* to be strong with him—he'll break if he knows this breaks you."

Even though my fears have completely gnawed away all my confidence and my stomach is about to turn over, I somehow manage to pull myself into some semblance of a person. I manage to straighten my spine and lift my head, and take a small, ragged breath, because I will do this for him. I will do it with him and I will prove to myself, and to him, that I am going to be strong enough to love *the hell out of him.*

I suck in another breath and wipe the corners of my eyes. "I want to be there."

Pete signals at the door and gives me an approving nod. "Be my guest."

My steps are quiet and almost hesitant as I go into the room. He's big and massive and strong, I know, even if my heart is a rag in my chest and all my blood seems to feel like ice inside me, I am going to prove to him that I am worthy of being his mate and the one who will stand when he can't. I don't know how I will prove this, because I am toppling, like a crushed building, as I walk inside. I look all right, but inside of me, in my very soul, I'm disintegrating, nerve by nerve, organ by organ.

He looks at me now—straight into my eyes, and I can see the worry in his dark eyes. Of course he's afraid I'll topple. He doesn't want to see that in my eyes. "Okay?" he asks me in a husky whisper.

I nod and reach for his hand. My reply should be, "More than okay." Right? But I just can't get any more words past my closed throat. So I rub his fingers with mine, and when he squeezes me, I remember our flight out of Seattle, this hand, the one I will not let go of, and I squeeze back as hard as I can and smile shakily down at him.

"That's my girl," he rasps, brushing his thumb over mine.

He's strapped and about to receive electroshocks and he asks me about *me*. Oh god, I love him so much, if he dies I want to die with him and this is no fucking joke. I blink back the tears and squeeze him harder.

"Can I hold his hand?" I ask one of the nurses.

"Sorry, you can't during the procedure," she tells me.

Remington cautiously watches me as I force myself to step back and they attach some electrodes to his forehead. A ball of fire is in my throat, in my heart, and in my stomach. I am not even breathing when a nurse asks him, "Are you ready?"

"Hit me," he answers, his eyes briefly flicking over me to check my reaction before he faces the ceiling again.

They start the IV flow to sedate him.

They begin asking him questions. "Full name?"

"Remington Tate."

My eyes well up.

"Date of birth?"

"April ten, nineteen eighty-eight."

"Place of birth?"

"Austin, Texas."

"Names of your parents."

"Dora Finlay and Garrison Tate."

I can barely take the fact that he is strapped, talking about his fucking parents, who made him black like this, his voice deep and strong, answering whatever they ask him.

Then she tells him, "Count from one to a hundred." And they put a mouthpiece on him.

He starts to count, and I count in my head with him. His eyes shut. Beautiful dark lashes against his strong cheekbones.

My protective instincts rage so loud I want to scream at them to stop, now that he can't see me and he can't keep me from stopping this. But I stand here, because he wants to do this. Because he is strong. Stronger than me. He will whip himself into shape just like life has beaten him to it.

Then the shock goes.

His big body seizes and tightens on the table.

My body tightens and begins to implode.

The machine makes a beeping noise.

His toes curl.

I didn't know if he'd be flailing, breaking things because he's so strong, but his body remains relatively still as he takes the shock in his brain. Oh my god.

Oh my god.

Oh my fucking god.

I am in love with Remington Tate and he has Bipolar 1, and it crashes down on me like an avalanche.

I don't think I've ever cried this way. Despite putting all my effort into not crying, the tears are literally exploding out of my eyes and my arms are shaking and my body so weak with grief, I edge back to lean against the wall and unsuccessfully try to suck back all my tears.

"Hey, Brooke, hey," says Pete, kneeling at my side, hugging me.

"It's so hard," I say, covering my face and trying to pull away from him because Remy wouldn't want it. Remy wouldn't like it. "Don't touch me, Pete, *oh god*, this is so fucking hard. *So fucking hard!*" He grabs me and shakes me a little, his voice comforting, his eyes showing pain.

"He's not suffering, Brooke. He just wants to get better. Brooke, he is NOT a victim. He makes his choices based on his circumstances. He'll worry about you. You need to condition yourself like he has—please, I beg you to be strong."

I nod, while all I can think of is Remy's beautiful brain, his beautiful body, my church, my sanctuary, enduring this.

"Brooke, it hurts me too. All right? It hurts me too. You can't let him see that. He's strong because as far as he's concerned, this is his reality; he deals with it—he's never had any different. He doesn't lament it. Don't let him see this breaks you or you're going to break him. You don't have to save him; just be with him while he saves himself."

Getting a grip on myself, I nod and wipe my tears as I try to piece myself together. I squeeze the tears out of my eyes as I try to stand and the nurses and doctor say it's all done.

Remy is still sedated, on the table, and they've removed his mouthpiece and somehow cleaned his air ducts. I grab his hand when they unstrap him, bring it to my lips, and kiss each of his knuckles, then wipe them dry of my tears with my lips.

The way Remy is taken care of . . .

Pete is such a good man, it breaks my heart that my sister must not have seen it.

"Pete, my sister really liked you—I don't know what happened," I whisper.

His eyebrows fly up to his hairline. "What? Brooke, I like her too—I still do. But I won't leave my brother for just anyone."

Nodding in silence, I study Remington's large hand. Every callus, every line in this palm . . . the rise of his knuckles, the length and shape of his beautiful fingers, the short stubs of his clean, square nails.

Quietly, I stroke the lines in Remy's palm and then lift my head and smile into Pete's kind brown eyes. "One day you'll find someone who makes you want to do anything for her. Pete, I'm going to take care of him. You're going to teach me to take perfect care of him."

He smiles and pats my shoulder. "Until then, neither of you is going to have to do this on your own." He puts a hand on Remington's shoulder, and I swear in heart and mind, even if not in blood, he truly *is* Remington's brother, and at this moment, how I wish my sister and I were as close, and as loyal, as this.

"Brooke, I did something I'm very ashamed of, and I think I owe you an apology," Pete blurts out. Seeing the despair in his eyes plants a cold little ice cube in the center of my belly.

"When you were gone, he got so bad. He was on suicide watch at the hospital, and they kept sedating him when he woke up, because he destroyed things and tried to go after you. They gave him antidepressants, and they didn't work, and with rapid cyclers like Rem it's not a good idea anyway. So we had to start him up on this." He signals to the table. "We did it for several weeks so he could be discharged. . . ."

He looks at me, and I don't think I'm even breathing. I'm just staring, waiting for more, confused and partly numb from the roller coaster of the day.

"After the first three treatments he got a little better, so he was discharged, and we came three times a week for ECT for a couple weeks. During that time, he was still black. We brought him fourteen women."

My heart cracks at the mention of them, and I feel myself erecting several mental blocks as I grip my stomach and my brain screams, *I don't want to know, I don't want to know, I don't want to know!*

"I make all these women sign paperwork that they won't talk, no pictures, that they'll use double protection. . . . They all came out half an hour later with the condom packets intact, confirming they couldn't get him to turn over or even raise his head from the bed. He told them all to leave. All of them."

I keep staring, and Pete rubs his face with his hands, and adds, "He didn't sleep with any of them, Brooke, no matter how hard we tried for him to. He was obsessed with your fucking letter, reading and reading it every moment he was awake. When he finally pushed through that depression and came into his blue eyes, he had no recollection of anything. Maybe because he was black, or maybe because of the electroshock's side effects. He had about twelve treatments. But we'd almost lost him, Brooke, you know? Riley and I were . . . we were pissed as hell with you too! So we told him he'd been having fun with all these women."

"Pete!" I gasp in complete and utter horror.

"I'm sorry! But we wanted him to remember how it used to be, before *you.* So that he would remember that there are hundreds of women out there, not just you." He shrugs and looks at me almost pleadingly. "But even when we tried to make him think he was doing fine without you, I guess his head is not what rules a man like

him. He heard all about the women, didn't comment on it, then
started packing and said we were flying to Seattle, and that we had
to arrange to get your sister back to take to you. So yeah. *I*—Riley
and I—*lied* to him," he says. "It's been killing me. Now, once he
knows the truth . . . he'll never trust us again!"

His voice breaks, and he turns away as Riley comes into the
room. Riley looks back and forth between us, sensing something's
up. Finally, Pete says, in a dreary, tired tone, "I told her, man."

Riley meets my disbelieving stare, his face crestfallen. "B," he
says.

That's all he says. A letter. The one letter that's tattooed to Remy's right bicep.

"You have to tell him," I say and I glance at one, and then the
other of them, not even able to bear the hurt I feel for Remington
right now. "You can't ever, *ever*, lie to him again. It's not fair to him!
I did that once too, and I understand you wanted to protect him as
well . . . but it's *confusing* to him. It's confusing to forget some of the
things you do. You can't—none of us, can ever—lie to him again.
Do you both hear me?"

Riley strokes a hand down his face and his voice wavers too.
"He's going to fire our fucking asses."

I look at them both, their expressions torn, and I shake my
head. "If you really believe that, then you don't know him at all."

❤ ❤ ❤

HE WAKES UP on the bed soon after the guys leave. His eyes are lazy,
but they settle on me and sharpen. They're not yet blue, but I see a
little life in those black pools, and I feel a little tingle inside me that
becomes a huge knot of emotion.

"Look at you." He speaks in a drug-thickened voice. I can hear
the obvious praise in his words, as if I look pretty fantastic, and

when I see a dimple peek out, the force of my emotions almost cripples me. He doesn't know he was a mess without me, but now I do. He doesn't know he was brought women to pleasure him and that he didn't want them. He doesn't know he is magnificent, perfect, beautiful, noble, good, and everything, everything, I have ever wanted.

And right now, it hurts like a bitch to know that his brothers, whom he takes care of and loves, also didn't know what to do and ended up lying to him.

"Look at *you*," I tenderly counter, immediately kneeling on the floor next to his bed and setting my cheek on his knuckles. I kiss every bruise on his hand once more.

"Hey, I've got this, I don't want you to worry," he says, stroking his free hand along the back of my head.

"I know." Ducking my head, I rub my face against the sheet so he maybe won't see the stray tears leaking from my eyes. I kiss his knuckles lovingly again. "I know you do."

Even with the anesthesia's thickening effect, his voice still has the same effect on me it always has. "Get up here. What are you doing down there?" he murmurs gruffly as he tugs me up. I know they gave him muscle relaxants, but even so, before I know it, he pulls me over him and stretches me like we sleep at night when he's in my bed. My round stomach gets in the way, but it's not enormous, so I tilt to the side and smell his neck and bury my face in his chest as we adjust.

"Your nurses will kick me out if they see this," I say.

He grabs my ass and adjusts me a little better. "I won't let them. You're my medicine."

I close my eyes and he smells like him. His arms are his. Everything is normal, except I'm wearing clothes and he's in a hospital robe, and we're not in a hotel room. He is still him, wearing my heart on his sleeve. Everything I want, right here, in my arms.

I slide my hand to his jaw and kiss any part of his face I can as I clutch him a little desperately. "Remy, you're my king." I hug him hard. "There's no chess game for me without you."

He shifts and works the control under the bed so that we sit up slightly. He adjusts me on his lap, his lips on my ear. "You're the queen who will protect me," he says in amusement, and when I nod because I can't speak, he strokes my hair as he looks into my face, and I know—even if he doesn't tell me—that my eyes are swollen and that he can tell I've been crying. I feel his lips press into my eyelids, first one, then the other, as he fists a hand in my hair and roughly pleads, "Stay strong, my little firecracker. Stay strong with me."

I nod. "I'll try, because you inspire me."

"We got you what you wanted, Rem," Riley says from the door. I'm so comfortable in his arms I don't even turn to greet him. And then I feel something smooth against my cheek. I open my eyes and see Remy holding out a rose to me. Him. In the hospital. Giving me a rose with those dark but twinkling eyes with the blue flecks.

"Remy," I say, a confused, puzzled laugh leaving me.

"I'd give you a whole fucking garden if I could." He tips my chin back and holds me in that stare. "For being here, right now, with me."

"Oh, god." I duck my head into his chest because I can't take it, my fingers curling into his hospital robe. "I will be here every time you need to do this. I will be here, I *promise you*."

As we're checking out of the hospital, I get a text from Melanie.

How are things in Happily Ever After? Other than happy?

I smile as we get back into our rented Escalade as if this were just another Monday, and Remington climbs into the car with me and puts his arm on the back of my seat, like he always does. I've been through hell, and I'm back in heaven, and suddenly I know that's the way my life will be: after the dark, I will always, always find my light—which is him.

I type back, Perfect

"The last time the shocks helped us pull him out of suicidal thoughts, but we had to do three a week, and we just don't have time for that now. We can't give him any more muscle relaxants, so we'll have to hope this was enough of a reset," Pete tells us all.

"I'm fucking fine," Remington growls. We all seem to search his gaze, and it's Riley who gathers up his courage to speak.

"Rem, Pete and I would like to have words with you about something," he says, looking briefly at me and using a voice that practically begs me to coax Remy into reason. "Pete's got an update on Brooke's sister, and we just want to tell you something. Tomorrow morning before you hit the gym?"

"I heard," he says simply, surprising everyone in the car. "I'm still thinking about what to do with you bozos."

"Shit, Rem," Riley says, aghast. "I'm about to go change my fucking pants, just be reasonable."

Pete looks really upset. "Rem, I swear to god I wouldn't ever have lied about anything else— it seemed harmless; it seemed it would only help your state of mind."

"My state of mind isn't helped knowing I can't trust you dip-shits," he growls, and they both go quiet and continue looking sick as he adds, "You're my brothers, but SHE IS MINE. If she'd left me because of your lie, I'd kill you right now. I'd goddamn kill you both."

"We'd bring her back to you, Remington," Pete promises. "I swear, if we'd known the level of your . . . I swear we'd bring her back to you."

"Rem, we were trying to help you survive. Like we always do. We thought it was over, dude. We thought we were helping. But then Brooke came back and we realized how wrong—shit, how wrong we were. We don't even know how to correct the record without looking like idiots to you."

Remy is thoughtful for a long time, and the three of them exchange strange, brother-like bonding gazes. Then Remington nods and slides his arm around my waist, pulling me to him, and when he nuzzles my pulse point with a soft growl and curves his hand over the roundness of my stomach, all the tension eases from my shoulders. I melt into his arms.

A thousand fuzzy things flutter inside me when I hear him inhale again, longer and deeper this time, like he needs my scent to calm down and find his center. I duck and kiss the top of his dark head, running my hands through his hair. I swear I can't stop kissing him. I kiss his jaw, his temple, reach for his hand, kiss the backs of his fingers.

When we get back to the suite, Diane serves dinner, her face all aglow at seeing him at the table, and when Remy looks at me across the table and pats his lap, I almost run to it. When he lifts his fork to me, I feel like a stupid starved bird that's being fed for the first time in a century.

When he asks me, "More?" quietly, intently watching my mouth as he lifts his fork, I nod and bite it all off and then, before I even munch, I press my lips to his, because I can't express the relief I feel after this procedure, seeing that he's all right. And actually a little better.

He lazily hits the bed, his body still relaxed with the remains of the anesthesia and the muscle relaxants they gave him, the mattress squeaking as he falls on it, all muscular and loose. "Come here," he calls without even lifting his head or looking to see where I am.

We just brushed our teeth and I'm picking up the clothes that he left littered around, then I add mine to a neat pile in the corner chair and slide naked under the covers with him. Our skins touch. Every sensation is heightened to me. I am grateful for his touch.

For hearing his voice. For every single moment I have right now with him. I now see how precious it is. Every song he plays me, when that brilliant mind is all right and blazing with light and thoughts. Precious, even, when he's in the dark, quietly fighting it and clinging to *me*.

His arm curls around my waist, and his fingers curl at my hip bone as he drags me over to spoon me. My anxiety over having watched him go through what he just did still rushes through me, and I can't help but press extra hard to his body. I hear him rumble out a chuckle in amusement.

To hear his soft, sexy laugh . . .

Oh god.

"It's not funny," I say tearfully as I face him. "It's not fucking funny."

"Yes, it is," he whispers with one adorable dimple, his voice deep and textured as he rubs the pad of his thumb down my nose. "Nobody's ever worried about me before."

"Yes, they do, Remy. Everyone who you love, loves you too. Pete, Riley, Coach, and Diane. They're just better at hiding it from you."

He looks at me thoughtfully, then he spreads his hand on my stomach as his lips scrape, soft and tender, over mine. "I've done this before. I've got this, little firecracker." Those dark eyes watching me, he rubs his thumb over my forehead now. "Don't get that little face for me, all right?" He crushes me to him and squeezes his eyes shut, groaning as if it feels good to him to hold me. "I want to make you happy. I want to make you fucking happy, I never want to make you sad."

"Okay," I say, still a little emotional, pressing my lips to his jaw.

"Okay?" he says, turning his head and pressing his lips to mine.

Sliding my arm around my stomach, I lace my fingers through his as I nod. "More than okay."

Running my free hand over his hair, I curl one of my legs around his hips and rain a thousand and one kisses on his face, making him chuckle. I laugh softly with him, a smile curling my lips with every kiss I continue to press on him, but I don't stop.

Now I know that he is really mine. These fingers have been mine from the moment they touched me. This face. These lips. His huge, kind, protective, possessive, and forgiving heart. He's been mine since I've been his, and knowing this makes me feel like I'm being pieced apart, then put back together new and whole and happy.

"I want to sleep with you in me," I plead, dragging my open mouth along his jaw, my fingers suddenly almost clawing the skin of his shoulder as I breathe in his warm skin and try to get closer with my swollen tummy in between.

He slips his hand between us and starts preparing me with his fingers as he turns his head to slowly, leisurely take my mouth, his tongue slowing me down, licking into me with lazy pleasure. "Are you ready?" he murmurs heatedly.

"Fill me . . ." is all I can say, and a breathless sound bubbles up my throat as he grabs me by the waist and sinks me down on his length, filling me up so I am so full and so penetrated by him, I can hardly talk, or breathe, or think of anything but that Remy is inside me, pulsing and hot, his mouth taking me, slowly, quietly, reassuring me he's got this. And he's got me.

❤ ❤ ❤

HE'S STILL BLACK the day of the fight, and the atmosphere in the presidential suite is thick with tension as we wait for him to get ready.

Pete, Riley, and Coach hover by the master bedroom door, while I'm being eaten alive by my own sick worry, because I seriously don't know if he should fight like this.

"Mention that motherfucker's name!" Coach hisses to Pete. I think he wants to provoke Remington's turbulent energy into action, but Pete shakes his head.

"We won't use anger. He's full of self-hatred when he's low," Pete whispers.

But what I've personally most felt is his inner struggle. He's been inside himself, fighting. He doesn't release a word of self-loathing, but I sense that he thinks the words, he feels them in his soul. The electroshock helped, but he's still *low*. It breaks me that he needs to fight like this.

"Try warming up those muscles, Brooke," Pete suggests.

Coming over to where Remy is tying up his boots in silence, I slip my hands up and down his back and loosen up any muscle that I can, awakening them with slow, deliberate hard presses of my fingers.

"All right, Rem, let's get pumped up. I know you like this one," Pete says as he sets Remy's iPod on my speakers.

"Uprising" by Muse bursts through the room at high volume. The rebellious beat of the music seems to reach Remington's ears, and his muscles start engaging under my fingers, like he can't help but respond.

My heart quivers a little. Is he coming into himself?

He's been so busy fighting inside himself, I just wonder if he has enough fight left for Scorpion.

He jerks on his other boot while I rub his hard muscles and try to transmit every ounce of good and healing energy I have to him. I warm each muscle, one by one, moving up his back, paying extra attention to his rotator cuffs. When I can't stop myself from bending down to his dark head to ask him how he feels, he swings around and grabs the back of my head, holding it as he locks his mouth to mine and plunders me.

When he pulls back, my mouth burns from the wet heat of his, and his eyes simmer with a dark and fierce desperation. He stares at me like I'm the only hope in the world, the look in his eyes so wild and fierce, he lights the hope inside me that maybe he'll fight. Maybe he wants it bad enough to push through this. I *know* how badly he wants this win, and I *know* how completely he loathes it when his black side fucks with him.

"Remington, dude, this is what you've been waiting for." Pete seizes his shoulders and draws his attention to him with a reassuring squeeze. "Everything you've ever wanted is within reach. Everything. You have plans after the championship, I know you do. Winning will make them happen. Brooke, the baby . . ."

At those words, I see him pinch his eyes shut for a quiet moment, then he drags in a long, slow breath. Pete bends to whisper something in his ear, and Remington nods and gruffly tells him, "Thanks." When he opens his eyes again, he gets up, and the synapses in my brain seem to fire up in excitement.

Draped in his fighting gear already, his ripped, tan body looks every inch the prime-time fighting machine he has built himself to be. When he says, "Come here, Brooke," I'm so insanely nervous about this fight, I almost stumble forward as I go. He takes me in his arms and hugs me tight, placing a warm kiss on the back of my ear. "I need you in my peripherals, at the very least. At all times. At all times."

Suddenly, my insides shudder with the knowledge that he *will* be fighting, and come hell or heaven, I *will* be watching him. "I won't move from my seat!" I promise.

He zeroes his attention on me for a second longer, then he kisses the back of my ear once more and pats my bum. That's all he does. Then he starts jumping in place, twisting his arms up and around himself, and the entire atmosphere shifts dramatically as the team starts breathing again.

"Where's Jo?" he gruffly asks Pete.

A tingle begins in my middle as I realize he truly *is* coming back.

"She's already scouting the area," Pete says, and there's a quiver of excitement in his voice as he probably realizes the same.

"Neither you or Jo is to take your eyes off Brooke, do you hear me?" he commands as he cracks his neck to one side, then the other.

"We got you, buddy!" Pete assures him.

"All right, are we ready here?" Coach swings the duffel containing Remy's clean clothes, Gatorades, and extra headphones over his shoulder.

"Ready," Remington answers as he retrieves his iPod from the speakers. The music dies instantly, and we all watch him grab his headphones from the nightstand and latch them onto the silver iPod.

"Hell yeah, that's my boy!" Coach yells out.

Riley woots. "That's the MAN!"

"Who's kicking ass?" Coach pounds Remy's back as they head for the door.

"I am." I hear Remington's low growl.

Coach pounds his back with an even harder *thud*. "What name will they all be screaming tonight?"

"Mine."

"Say it!"

"Riptide."

"That's not how the motherfuckers say it!"

Remington slams a fist to his chest and yells, "RIPTIDE!!"

"THAT'S RIGHT!" Coach yells back.

They knock knuckles, and then Coach leads him out of the room and to the elevators, the rest of us following behind. "Do you have enough for this fight, boy?"

"I got it."

Coach nods, then prods, "What will we do if he doesn't submit, boy? You already know what to do?"

"I know what to do."

As I listen to that last calm statement, my blood pools in my feet, and it feels like every other part of me trembles as I break out in a million goose bumps and then some. A part of me wants to be brave and watch this fight, but I don't remember ever feeling so lacking in courage in my life.

With a sudden frown, Remington shoves a thick finger into Coach's chest. "Whatever happens, you don't throw in the towel. Do you hear me? We NEVER, EVER submit."

The tension in the air rises dramatically, and a couple of gazes are exchanged. When there's no immediate reply from Coach, Remington pushes him back a step. "Coach. You do not throw in the towel. We don't submit. *Period.*"

Coach's eyes flick briefly in my direction—briefly, yes, but not briefly enough for me to miss the hesitation in his gaze before he nods. Exhaling beside me, Pete takes my hand when we hear a *ting*.

"Let's go," he murmurs.

We board the elevator, but I'm so freaking nervous, my fiercely pounding heart is going to break a couple of my ribs by the time we get to the Underground. Remington quietly fiddles with his iPod, his black headphones in one hand. He's trying to get into the zone. With all the love I have for him in my heart, I watch him duck his head, place his headphones on, and play his music.

"Why'd you promise?" Riley confronts Coach while Remy listens to his music, his tone accusatory. "If things get butt ugly, we're not letting him die out there today!"

"His eyes are coming blue! If someone's going to die tonight, it isn't our boy!" Coach contests.

All right, this is all *crazy* talk! My stomach is coiled like a poised venomous rattlesnake, and I just can't take standing here like a mute for a second longer. "Pete, what are they talking about? I'm starting to freak the hell out here."

"There have been rumors about this being the match of the decade," he answers under his breath. "They're both stubborn as heck, and one needs to submit for the win, Brooke. It could get bad. Like you said . . . *more* than shit happening."

A little flash of last season's final plays in my head, unbidden and unwanted. I remember Remy's fallen body on the bloodied canvas floor. The crowd screaming his name. And then the silence when they realized their Riptide—fierce, passionate, beautiful Riptide—was down.

While all my insides twist and tangle like pretzels at the memory, we start shuffling out of the elevator, but Remington grabs my hand and holds me back. He whispers in my ear, "In my peripherals."

His eyes bore into me, and I pray, pray, pray that he doesn't see the fear in my eyes, but he pulls his headphones down to his neck, and I hear the music streaming between us. Crazy and fast.

"In your seat at all times, Brooke," he tells me, and he slides his hands into my hair and slams his mouth to mine, stealing a taste of me while giving me a taste of him that leaves me drugged and dazed. He sets his forehead on mine, his gaze incandescent as he looks at me. "I adore you with every breath I take—in every ounce of me, I adore you." With another fast and hard kiss, he slaps my ass. "Watch me *break* him!"

As we ride to the Underground, he keeps an arm stretched on the back of my seat while he listens to his music. The rest of the car is dead quiet. I can taste the violence in the air as he walks away into the locker rooms, and I want to shout a thousand "I love yous," but he's with his iPod now, getting into his zone.

"Pete, is he really ready for this?" I whisper uncertainly.

"I sure hope so, Brooke. I'd hate for this episode to take another one of his dreams. Come on," he says as we jostle through the crowd toward our seats.

At least two thousand people fill the arena tonight. The Underground has been teasing its public the entire season, and now they're bloodthirsty to watch Scorpion versus Riptide. Faces are streaked with red, simulating blood. Bright red *R*s adorn women's cheeks and the top rises of some of their breasts.

I see red, Riptide's red, streaked across the seats and way in the back, with the standing crowd, where there's also a little bit of black too. Scorpion black.

Settling down in my seat next to Pete, I notice that Remington has once again secured two more empty seats to our sides, and it seems like we wait for a lifetime. Staring at the emptiness of the center ring only seems to makes the crowd scream louder as they wait for Remington and Scorpion to fill the 23 x 23' square space they see.

"Riiiptiiiiide!" a group of friends scream in unison across the ring from me.

Behind me, a chant begins: *"Bring them out! OUT! OUT! OUT!"*

The speakers crackle as if the microphone has been turned on, and an announcer appears up onstage. I almost leap out of my skin.

"Ladies and gentlemen, hello!" People roar their greeting before the announcer continues. "Well, here we are this evening with you all! Are you people ready? Are you all READY for a fight unlike any other? *Unlike ANY OTHER, people!* Ringmaster?"

The ringmaster by the corner of the ring turns all his attention to the announcer.

"Sir, we won't need your services tonight," the announcer gallantly says, adding a dramatic bow that causes a thundering roar to blast around the arena as the crowd stands and screams its approval.

"That's right!" the announcer yells in a booming voice back at the crowd. "Tonight, there are NO rules, NO ringmaster. Anything goes. ANYTHING GOES, PEOPLE! No knockouts—this is a fight of submission. Submit!"

"Or die!!" people excitedly yell.

"Ladies and gentlemen! Yes! It's a submission fight here tonight in the Underground! Now, let's call your worst nightmare into the ring! The man your daughters cry about. The man you want to run from. The man you *certainly* don't want to be up in the ring with. Our defending champion, Benny, the Blaaaack, Scorpionnnnnn!"

I'm hyperventilating. I don't know how I thought I would cope sitting here, watching this match of the fucking decade, because every organ inside me is shivering from nerves and I think I'm going to vomit my heart out. Anything goes. *No* referee. Just like they thought it would happen, it *will*, and I don't even know for sure what state of mind Remington is fighting in.

"Pete, I'm going to puke," I choke out, sucking in deep breaths as my stomach tightens in a hard, sudden contraction.

In the distance, a figure with a black robe flapping behind him approaches the ring, and the nausea rises full force as I see him.

Scorpion.

With his giant middle finger sticking in the air, I decide he's even worse than my Voldemort, because this guy is actually *alive*.

"*Such* an asshole," Pete says in disgust.

The last time I had the displeasure of watching Scorpion come out to fight, Remington threw the fight to rescue Nora from that disgusting specimen of a man. And Nora, where is she now? What is Scorpion doing to her? Remington told me to trust him, and I *do*, but my fear is so great as I look into the face of that disgusting nightmare, every ounce of reason in me has fled. It's impossible to silence the frantic screaming in my mind, telling me that Remington is going to get hurt tonight. He's going to get hurt and once again, *you can't stop it! You can't do anything about it!*

Suddenly, I spot Nora across the stands, and an awful anger and hurt sweep through me as she carefully avoids my gaze.

Scorpion jumps up to the ring, and as his team removes his robe, the extra-large black scorpion he seems to have recently tattooed all across his back greets the crowd as he turns around to let everyone see it. The guy is still uglier than someone's asshole, and I feel a perverse pleasure seeing that scar on his terrible face courtesy of Remy.

"The good news is, he's still disgusting," Pete says.

"Pete, I can't believe my sister would be clear and free of him and then go *back* to that. It makes me sick." I steal another glance at Nora across the ring, and her betrayal cuts me like a knife.

"It's not what you think, Brooke," Pete tells me, then nods at the ring. "Your guy's got it. Just wait and see."

"What do you mean?" I ask in bewilderment, but if Pete answers, I don't hear.

Scorpion just turned in Nora's direction, and she looks up at him with a somber expression that doesn't really strike me as the look of a love-struck young woman. Then he jerks around to look at me, only to lift his middle finger in the air. Straight at me.

"Oh boy, Brooke, for the love of—"

I lift both my middle fingers in reply, and the beast smiles his yellow smile at me.

Pete gasps and groans as if in digestive pain. "All right, if Remington knows he just flipped you off and you just flipped him . . ."

"Booooo!" people instantly yell, and he shows them the bird too, along with his yellow smile, and as if that isn't gross enough, he also grabs his groin and squeezes. *"BOOOOO!!"* the crowd yells.

God, I can't understand why my sister would be with such a specimen! She used to be so romantic. She used to want a prince. And she goes with Scorpion?

"And challenging our champion tonight, we all know his name! We are *all* waiting to see if he's gonna bring it to this ring tonight. So . . . is he? Get rrrready to welcome the one and only Remingtooooooon Tate, yourrr Riiiiiptide!!"

It's impossible to quell the lightning bolt that runs through me on hearing his name. It had been noisy when Scorpion came out. But the way people start yelling for Remington makes my throat close with emotion and my heart jerk inside my chest.

"Rem-ing-ton! Rem-ing-ton!"

The chant tears through the crowd. The color red takes over the entire arena. Then I see the one spot of red that I'm dying to see as his shouted name surrounds me as completely as his color does. *"Remyyyyy, kill him, Remyyyy!"* *"Go, Rrrrrriptide!"*

My body functions heighten in every way. My lungs, my heart, my adrenals, my eyes, every part of me *strains* for him. The instant he comes trotting into the arena, I'm spun in a whirlwind of nervousness, fear, and excitement. I'm torn between the urge to usher him to safety and the want to cheer him on like the rest of his fans do, to let him know that I know if anyone owns that ring, it's *him*.

With one easy leap, he takes the ring and immediately lets Riley pull his robe from his shoulders. I swear I hear a collective sigh from the women close to me.

"Remyyyyyyyy! Kill him, Remy!!" one shouts.

And then, the amazing happens.

He starts with his signature cocky turn. All his muscles are glorious, tan, and hard, and I hear a woman scream nearby that his body should be immortalized, it is so masculine and perfect. Then he looks at me. Blue eyes shining. The bluest of the blue. His dimples flash, and I realize with a shuddering in my heart that this is what Coach meant about his blue coming back. His eyes are *blue*. Clear, beautiful, brilliant blue. Those eyes and dimples talk directly to the butterflies in my stomach, and I explode with them.

A frenzy of emotion shoots through me, and suddenly I know, with every fiber in my being, he's got this. He does. He is Remington Tate. He's a man who falls and gets up again and again. He pushes, plows, plunders, goes on. He's. Got. This. I remember who he is. Where his drive comes from, some unnamable source that nobody in this world possesses. He is unconquerable and unbeatable—and he is going to crush Scorpion, just like he's wanted to.

The bell rings, and my guy doesn't waste time. He goes straight out to center ring, and while Scorpion seems to think they will jump around a bit, Remington jabs him three times, quickly enough to make the ugly animal stumble back.

Bubbles of excitement pop inside me. I cup my mouth and my screams instantly join the others. "Remy!!"

"Brooke?" Pete forces me down to my seat, but I'm so excited, I can't stay down long. I feel him, Remington, in the weight in my belly; I feel him alive inside me and his energy within me.

The fight begins full force.

Remy slams his knuckles into Scorpion's jaw, the punch jolting him. My chest can barely contain all the emotions inside me as my lungs labor for air. God, I've been waiting to see this happen for what feels like a thousand years, and I can barely stand it. The crowd has been waiting just as long to see this, and they're yelling at the tops of their lungs. And so am I!

"Go, REMY!!!"

"Kill him, Remy!"

"Remington, I fucking love you! Ohmigod, I love you!" I scream.

"Brooke!" Pete says direly, and signals to my stomach. "All that jumping can't be good."

"It's good, Pete. It's so good!" The baby is shifting, and I'm getting some tolerable contractions, but I've felt them occasionally—I read the body starts practicing up to three months before delivery. I think baby feels my adrenaline. Or he knows Daddy is fighting. He squirms every time after a contraction, and I think there's just too much action for him to relax now. How can we relax watching this? *Ohmigod!*

"I don't know what it is about Remington and that ring," Pete says. "But he just gets in it and whatever he's living, he performs. Riley says it's muscle memory, but I'm not too sure."

"It's *Remy*, Pete," I tell him excitedly, and I grab and hug him.

Remington slams perfectly again, guarding, bouncing, and hitting, while Scorpion hasn't landed a single punch. Not a single one.

A chant spreads through the crowd: *"Kill him, RIP! Kill him, RIP! Kill him, RIP!"*

Pete told me that all the coaching in the world can't turn a fighter into a strong hitter; you're either a fierce puncher or you aren't. He'd said that speed, you might work on, but not on making your hand heavy, and now I can see the difference in punching power.

Now I can see why Scorpion had to cheat to win the championship last season.

Between rounds, Remy bounces with energy, while Scorpion sits on his stool with his head lowered to the ground, his team working on smearing Vaseline or something on his cuts.

The bell dings again.

Remington comes off the ropes and jabs, but this time Scorpion jabs back, fast and accurately, disrupting his rhythm.

They go into a clinch. Remington jerks free and hooks with his right. Scorpion covers and comes back with a powerful punch that lands square in Remington's rib cage.

The breath is knocked out of him, but Remy isn't rocked. No. My tree isn't rocked. Instead he starts punching those punches in bunches, his face concentrated and fierce, and Scorpion's head starts swinging, blood pouring out of both his nostrils and from a cut near one of his eyes.

Scorpion hits back, his fist connecting with Remington's jaw, causing blood to spill out of his mouth. Another contraction seizes me, and this time I'm having trouble remembering to breathe. The fight is intense, both thrilling and excruciatingly painful to watch.

The whirlwind of punching continues. Bouncing, chasing, they keep hitting each other. The difference in punching power is apparent. Remington is faster and stronger, and Scorpion seems to be the punching bag of choice today. He's rocked, and he's almost flattened out, but he won't fall and keeps swinging out and landing punches right back at Remy. He grabs Remington by the neck and tries to throw him to the ground, and when he can't, he lifts his knee and jams it into his stomach.

"Whaaat! That's not fair!" I cry.

"Remington is a boxer; he never uses his legs except to stand, but anything goes here, Brooke. If Scorpion wants to bite . . ."

Fear peeks back inside me, and another contraction grips me, hard enough to make me bite back a moan of pain and sit down for a moment.

With an angry growl, Remington shoves Scorpion back and starts bulldozing him. Punch after punch. *Wham! Wham! Wham!*

I've seen him kill his speed bag, and his heavy bag, but I have never, ever seen him kill another man like this. Scorpion covers his head and ducks, and Remington charges, ramming into his gut, one, two, three times. Scorpion bounces back on the ropes and falls to his knees.

He spits on the ground and gets up with an effort, while Remington eases back as he catches his breath, his eyebrows low over his eyes, his eyes glimmering like a predator's.

Scorpion charges forward and gets a lucky straight punch to Remy's jaw, then he lands another hard punch to his right rib cage. Remy rocks backward.

I see the yellow grin on Scorpion's face when he aims a third punch straight into Remy's temple and Remington bounces back on the ropes with a sound that is so distressing to hear, I jerk in my seat with a raw cry of pain.

He straightens with a shuddering breath that expands his broad chest, and my heart feels butchered. The pain I feel every time he takes a punch makes my contractions feel breezy! I inwardly wince as he approaches Scorpion again, now bleeding as freely as his opponent.

They go back at it once more, and I hear all those noises of their punches, *pow pow pow!*

My nerves abrade on the inside as the rounds drag on. One after the other. Neither submits. Neither falls. Squirming anxiously in my seat, I feel a pop, and then a slick sound reaches me—and I look down in horror to see that there's water trickling under my skirt, down my bare legs. "No," I say.

Feeling myself go white in sheer panic, I glance up at Remington and then at Pete, and he's so engrossed in the fight, I mentally close my eyes and tell baby—*please, please, not until your dad is ready.*

I'm only six and a half months. Seven, at most. I can't go into labor now!

Remington charges with one fist flying out, his arm swinging repeatedly. He's so fast, I can barely see his movements, can mostly only hear the sounds of repeated bone crushing bone.

There's no question. My labor has started. Contractions. Everything I read in the book is happening. My water just *broke*. Thank god it's not flooding, but it's trickling down my leg, leaking out of me. I drag in a deep breath as the pain takes hold. The contractions before my water broke were *nothing* compared to the pain I feel now as my abdomen seizes and squeezes. But Remington is fighting up there, and I'm not going anywhere until he's ready to leave.

Ohmigod, I hadn't even had time to be scared of the labor until now!

I'm so busy trying to remember how to take the slow, relaxing breaths that I read about that I don't notice Nora has left her seat and has charged over to me.

"Are you all right, Brooke?" she asks worriedly.

Shit. She noticed. "Fine," I gasp, as my contraction eases.

"Brooke, Benny won't submit. He'd rather die," she adds in a shaky voice, tears shining in her eyes. "You don't want Remy to kill him, Brooke—the things it will do to his mind! And Benny is not all monster, he's *not.*"

"Nora." Pete reaches out for her hand and draws her over to him. "It's taken care of, Nora. Scorpion won't be hurting you again." Looking into her eyes, he lifts his hand and touches her face, and Nora's breath catches at the touch. A palpable sizzle stretches between them, and Pete gentles his voice as he continues, "We've negotiated. We're getting it."

"What?" I ask in puzzlement. "What's going on?"

Pete stands to give Nora his seat and then takes the empty seat to my other side. "Pete, what's going on?" I demand.

"Pete!" Nora cries. She shakes her head wildly, and Pete hesitates.

"PETE!" I demand furiously. "I swear I can't take this bullshit right now!"

Pete pulls on his tie for a moment then ducks his head to my ear and rushes out, "Scorpion is out for Remington's blood. He doesn't think Remington can make him submit or that he has it in him to kill him—he made Remington agree that any championship match would be by submission. If our guy wins, he gets the championship but, most important to him, the . . . *video* of Nora."

Nora makes a pained little noise and buries her face in her hands, and I'm just so stunned, my brain almost squeals as it tries to process. Nora was being blackmailed with a video of her? And Remy . . . agreed to this?

"He wanted to do it," Pete tells me immediately.

"God, Nora," I say. The thought of that madman using my sister to make Remington have to make the soul-killing choice to, what, *kill* the Scorpion made me fear for us all. If the bastard couldn't beat Remy, he was determined to turn him into a *killer*?

And make him go black forever . . .

I focus all my attention on my sister when another contraction takes hold, and Nora slowly slides her hand over my stomach. "Is it the baby?"

Sucking in a breath and leaning over to her so Pete doesn't hear, I nod. "Yes."

"What do I do, Brooke?"

"Just hold my hand while I watch my guy *take this*."

As if he's listening to me, Remington continues terminating Scorpion up there. My nerves are in shreds. Scorpion's nearly black blood is splattered across the canvas floor, and although he's stumbling, he refuses to fall.

Panting for breath but unstoppable, Remington grabs him by the neck and jerks him around to face the empty space where Nora's chair sits empty. His lips move as he mumbles something into Scorpion's ear, and right when Scorpion lets out a sneering laugh, a loud crack fills the arena.

"*AAAAAA!*" the public gasps as Scorpion's elbow breaks and his arm dangles limply from the middle down.

My stomach knots as the fight gets even more vicious and Remy corners Scorpion on the pole and slams his head from side to side, attacking him like he would his speed ball. Scorpion struggles and rams a knee into Remy's gut.

"Brooke," Nora sniffles, "they're going to kill each other!"

A burning ball of fear gathers in my throat as we both watch the fight in mounting dread. They're still hard at it. Scorpion has thrown out a couple of kicks, and they're back at center. Remy is caked with blood, both Scorpion's and his own, and although Scorpion can barely stand straight, he angrily charges with his shoulders, trying to butt Remington with his head.

"One of them has to stop *now*!" Nora whispers under her breath.

"It has to be Scorpion," I say.

And then, Remington delivers a rapid, strong one-two punch that instantly drops Scorpion to his knees. A bellow of excitement erupts among the crowd, and Remy wipes the back of his arm across his brow and seeks me out among the spectators.

When he finds me, he doesn't take his eyes off mine as he grabs Scorpion by the hair and yanks him up to his feet as he shows him Nora next to me.

He whispers something to Scorpion, and in answer, Scorpion spits red blood on the ground.

Remy shoves him away and takes position again, raising up his guard in a way that clearly says, *All right, asshole, then we'll just keep fighting and see who wears out first.*

So they fight again. Remington swings out and punches with that same unnatural force that his crowd loves, and they immediately scream in approval as we watch all his muscles tighten and clench as he works them. Scorpion lasts two jabs and a hook—then he falls *splat* on his face.

The public is roused and excited, and a familiar chant rises up in a crescendo: *"REM-ING-TON! REM-ING-TON!"*

"Rip! Seal the deal, Rip!!!!!!!!" a young man shouts from a corner of the first row.

Silence descends as Remington approaches Scorpion's motionless body, and I don't think I'm even breathing. My heart is doing all sorts of movements in my chest while I hear Nora start sobbing quietly next to me.

Scorpion crawls on the ground. Remington's gaze is trained fixedly on me, his broad, glistening chest expanding on each haggard breath, and I know my forehead is scrunched in pain, but please, please, I don't want him to realize anything is wrong.

"Go, Remy!!!!!" I scream, but I can't stand, so I have to scream it from my seat. He turns and slams Scorpion back down when he tries to get up.

The people howl their approval.

Remy grabs Scorpion's healthy arm and cracks all the fingers of his hand in one move; then he breaks his wrist.

Scorpion's eyes bug out. He starts squirming as Remington

slides his hands up to his unbroken elbow. Remington starts twisting it at an awkward angle, and a painful contraction rips across my
body, making me swallow back a pained moan.

Scorpion thrashes beneath him and starts sputtering. Suddenly,
there's a loud yell, and a black towel falls into the ring, right next to
Scorpion's writhing body.

Remington clamps his jaw when he spots it, and the public boos
when they realize Scorpion's team has submitted for him. Disappointment flashes across Remy's face, and it takes him a couple of
seconds before he finally, finally, releases his opponent. Scorpion
spits a ton of blood from his mouth and looks up at him, panting.

Remington starts to walk away but, hearing Scorpion mutter
something under his breath, he turns and slams down his fist and
knocks the miserable insect unconscious.

"RIPTIIIIIIIIIIIIIIIIIIIIIIIIDE!" I hear the announcer scream.

Remy looks at me, his expression as fierce as the pain inside me.
A storm of testosterone whirls around him, and I can see his emotions seething in his blue, angry eyes, silently screaming, "Do not
fuck with me or what's mine ever again!"

He comes to the edge of the ring and I shake my head no, not
to come. I want to see him up there with his arm raised, taking his
damn title, hearing his name on the announcer's lips, hearing that
same name tearing through the speakers.

The announcer grabs his arm and yanks it up in the air before
Remington can reach the ropes, and happiness swamps me and
mingles with my pain as I hear . . .

As I hear what I was supposed to hear that final fight a season
before . . .

"The winner of this season's Underground championship, I
give you, REMINGTON TATE, RIIIPTIDE!!! *Riiiiiiiiptide!!* Riptide . . . where are you going?"

My eyes sting and he becomes a beautiful blur.

I'm sobbing because I know he's just jumped down from the ring and is coming to get me. I know he knows something is wrong—he always knows. I don't need to tell him. Pete sits by my side, oblivious to it. But my sister knew. And Remy, he knows. I feel his arms, sweaty and bloodied, as he kneels before me.

"Brooke, oh, baby, she's coming, isn't she?" When I nod, he says, panting and with blazing blue eyes as he wipes my tears, "I got you, all right? You got me, baby; now I got you. Come here." He scoops me up, and I cry into his damp throat and wind my arms around him as he starts carrying me to the exit.

"He's not . . . supposed . . . to come yet. . . . It's too soon. . . . What if he won't make it . . . ?"

All my emotions had been corked up and bottled, and now they're flooding me. We were supposed to do this after, after this fight. After we had the room ready. After we went to Seattle.

The crowd mobs us and the fans reach out to stroke his damp, tan, muscular chest as he makes a path for us, ignoring every yell, every call, everything but me.

"RIPTIDE, YOU ROCK! RRIIIIPPPPTIIIDE!"

A song begins blaring—absolutely *blaring*—through the speakers, and I don't recognize the singer or the tone, when a voice joins in.

"At the request of our victor, who has a very special question to ask . . ." I hear the announcer say as Remington bulldozes us through the crowd, with my head pressed to his chest. I hear his heart beating. His breath. Every part of him, I feel it.

He keeps going through the throng of people, and even through my pain, I notice fans have white roses in their hands as we walk past them, and some are tossing them at us from the stands. Then I hear the song's lyrics go on, until two words hit me like a shot of adrenaline racing through my bloodstream: *Marry me.* . . .

"Wh-what?" I gasp.

He doesn't answer.

He's snapping instructions to Pete to pull the car around as we finally exit the Underground, and when we get into the car, Nora climbs up in front with Pete.

Remington takes my face in his hands and looks at me, his voice thick with emotion and dehydration, his face swollen and bloodied and killing me because I can't do anything about it.

"The song was supposed to ask you to marry me, but you'll have to settle on me doing the asking," he whispers, his eyes glowing blue and powerful in the dark. "Mind. Body. Soul. All of you for me. All of you mine."

He squeezes my face between hands that are damp and callused and bleeding.

"Marry me, Brooke Dumas."

TWENTY

WHEN THE TIME COMES

I said *yes!*

And I've been replaying his proposal in my head, over and over, while I stop thinking about these painful contractions. They're getting closer and closer—less than a minute passes in between each. The urge to push is acute as I lie waiting in the hospital bed, but I'm not supposed to push yet.

Remy tucks a loose hair behind my ear with a pained expression. "Brooke . . ." is all he's been able to say, almost like an apology as he looks down at me.

It hurts me to look at him. His face is streaked with blood and his jaw is slightly swollen. I want to touch and tend and mend it, but every time I try to reach out and do something about it, he stops me and sets a kiss on my palm instead.

"We need ice for your face," I protest.

"Who cares about my fucking face," he counters.

And then I moan when another contraction grips me and he growls like he feels it.

He clamps his jaw as he struggles to keep it together. When the nurse checks me at seven centimeters, she asks if I want to walk to get up to ten? I don't want to, but I nod. Remington visibly shudders as he tries for control, and he helps me up from the bed. I clutch his forearm for support as we start walking out of the room, begging him, "Stay with me. Stay with me, okay?"

"Okay, Brooke," he murmurs automatically.

We link our hands together, and his reassuring squeeze fills me with courage as we walk down the hospital hall.

He wraps his free arm around my waist as a fresh wave of contractions shakes me. "Distract me," I plead.

"Did you like the fight?" he asks in my ear.

His blue eyes dance in delight, his lips stretched crookedly due to the swollen part of his jaw, and I painfully burst out laughing between contractions—because of course, of course, Remy would like to know.

"It kicked ass like you did, but now your baby is kicking the shit out of *me*."

He helps me back to the room. Soon I'm in a haze of pain and all I want is to push, push, push.

By the time the doctor tells me I can push, I'm already exhausted.

Wrapping his strong arms around my shoulders from behind me, Remington buries his nose in my neck, as if my scent calms him. His scent calms *me*, and I try not to yell for his sake, because I want him with me, and I know he would never want to forget a moment like this. Chewing hard on my lip, I push and squeeze his hand while I swallow back my groans. Pushing harder against the pain, I push another time, harder and longer. I'd never wondered why it was called "labor" but now I know. After several more breath-stealing efforts, the baby finally slips out, and I groan tiredly as the pressure in my body eases, dropping my head back onto the table.

The doctor catches it, and through a gaze misted with relief, I see something wet, slick, and pink.

"It's a boy," we hear, and then the baby's first cry tears into the room. His lungs may not be fully developed, but that soft little wail still makes my heart overflow with joy.

"A boy," I gasp.

"A boy," Remington gruffly repeats, and my chest floods as I hear the acceptance and contentment in the word. Remy doesn't need to tell me, but I know that now, our son is real to him. Our son is real to *both* of us.

I smile quietly to myself while my eyes brim with tears. The doctor mumbles to the nurses as they cut the cord. "Breathing on his own. No complications. He's still preterm—we still need to incubate."

"We want to see . . ." I cry breathlessly. My arms are so weak that I can barely lift them, and I don't even know why, since they hardly did anything while I pushed.

The tiny baby lets out another howl as they clean him, and then at last they bring him over to us. I don't think Remington is breathing, while my own breath rushes out of my throat as I hold this tiny bit of life for the first time.

The doctor starts fixing me up while the nurse waits to take the baby to the NICU, but Remington has bent his dark head to mine. We nuzzle each other over the baby's bald little head.

"I love him, Remy," I whisper as I angle my head up, eager to feel his warm breath on my face, his lips on mine. "I love you so much. Thank you for this baby."

"Brooke," he tersely rasps as he engulfs us in his arms. I know that deep down Remy doesn't believe he deserves this. Nobody taught him that he did, so I squeeze his big shoulders to me as tight as I can with one of my weak, trembling, tired arms while I hold the baby with the other.

"If he's like me, we will support him," he whispers worriedly in my ear. "If he's like me . . . we'll be there for him."

"Yes, Remy. We will teach him music. And exercise. And how to take care of this little body. It will be strong and astound him and maybe frustrate him sometimes too. We will teach him to love it. And himself. We will teach him love."

He wipes his eyes with the backs of his hands. "Yeah." And he sets a kiss on my forehead. "Yeah, we'll teach him all that."

"Come hug us again," I plead when he steps back as if I and this baby making the little chipmunk crying noises couldn't possibly be his.

He moves back in and we melt in his embrace. He has the best hugs, and we fit perfectly right in. I feel him wipe a tear from the top of my head again, and it makes me start crying softly too. He is so strong. I never thought this small moment would do him in. I hold our baby in one arm because I need to hold Remington in the other. "Come here," I encourage, holding out one arm. Then he drops his head and nuzzles me and I don't know if my face is wetter than his. "I am so in love with you," I whisper to him. "You deserve this and more. While you fight out there, I will fight for you to come home to *this*."

He growls an exasperated sound and wipes his eyes again, like he hates crying. Then he grabs my face and kisses the back of my ear, his voice thicker than I've ever heard it. "I fucking love you to pieces. To pieces. Thank you for this baby. Thank you for loving me. I can't wait to make you my wife."

❤ ❤ ❤

I'M IN A private room by the time I get to see Nora again. She comes in looking flushed and happy, followed by Pete, who looks almost as flushed as she does. Maybe even more so. While Pete slaps Remington's back and congratulates the new dad, Nora makes a beeline straight for me.

"Brooke, I saw him! I saw him through the window! He's the tiniest baby there is!"

"I know, Nora, he's so very little!" My voice quivers with emotion as I talk about him. "He's not supposed to even be here yet, but the doctors are amazed by how well he's developed for his age."

She settles down at the corner of my bed and reaches for my hand, her eyes sparkling with happiness. We hold stares for a moment, and though I don't want to wipe that smile from her face, I have to ask the question nagging at the back of my mind.

"Nora, what were you doing with Scorpion?" I wince as I try to sit up straighter, then I reach under the bed and adjust my position a little better. "Why didn't you tell us he was blackmailing you so that we could help?"

A flush spreads from her chin up to her forehead, and she buries her face in her hands again. "It's just so embarrassing."

Remington signals from the door that he's going out with Pete, and I lock gazes with my big lion, his hair disheveled, in the sweatpants and hoodie he just changed into, and I realize we have a *baby together*, and my chest swells so powerfully, I feel like I'm going to float like a cloud.

He whispers softly, his gaze shining with a mate's pride, "We'll be outside."

"I'm sorry I caused you so much trouble," Nora tells him.

He holds the door open and shakes his head, with one dimple peeking out. "No trouble at all."

When the door shuts behind him, all I can hear is my sister's soft sobs in the room, and my own voice as I reach out to pat the back of her head and gently ask her, "Did he hurt you?"

She grabs a tissue from inside her small purse and pats the corners of her eyes. "No. He was a mess. He said he missed me. He wanted me back and would do anything to keep me. It's probably why he was fighting so fucking bad," she says. "I'm *glad* he lost. I just hate that it still hurts me."

"Oh, Nora."

"When you came home, I couldn't even think straight. You're so . . . protected. Having his baby! He's so in love with you. While I was in *hell*! Benny said he would spread the video around if I didn't come back. He wanted to hurt you again. He wanted to have a way to make Remington lose. I didn't want to be with him, but I was afraid he would blackmail you guys with that video about me! So I did. He offered me . . . drugs. . . . I wanted them. I really did, but I knew if I took them I'd never come home. My plan was to stay with him"—she pats her cheeks as her tears keep streaming, even though her voice is steady and strong—"until the season ended, and then he wouldn't need me to hurt you two anymore. I figured I'd find a way to get the video back and run away from him."

"Nora . . ." I open my arms, and she leans over and rests her head on my shoulder. "We need to move forward now," I whisper. The words come out almost like a plea, because I have a baby now. A baby. He will need me, like my partner does, and I need Nora to be strong on her own. Remy has protected her for me, but I appoint it as my duty to protect my son and my guy just as fiercely—and this includes from my own family.

She curls out her pinky, like we used to pinky promise when we were young. Laughing, we hook them together. "Just don't tell Mom and Dad. They're desperate to see their grandchild and are flying over as we speak," she tells me.

"Nobody has to know about the video. But they must have been thrilled to hear your voice on the phone."

With new, curious excitement, she signals at the door. "So what are you guys going to call the little thing?"

I grin at her, ear to ear, and whisper, "I have no idea, so I hope the dad does."

♥ ♥ ♥

HIS NAME IS Racer.

Racer Tate Dumas.

Because he was racing to the finish line, before we even set up camp.

The nurses say he's a big boy, for a preemie, even though Remy and I think he's so tiny.

God, he is perfection. Ten tiny fingers. Ten tiny toes. Pink little mouth. Little button nose.

He's needed the incubator for four weeks now, but apparently he's almost ready to go home. He doesn't need a tube to be fed anymore, and he now weighs eight healthy pounds, which impresses everyone who can't believe he was a preemie. Then, of course, they see the father and understand why this preemie is kind of big and healthy.

Remington spends the day training for next season while I hang around the hospital, determined to feed him my own breast milk so he'll get all the nutrients and immune system benefits he needs. I'd also read about a "kangaroo method" where the nurses set the baby against the mother's bare skin to strengthen and mature all of his systems. I love reading about all the scientific evidence of what skin-to-skin contact can do.

So once a day, the nurses bring Racer out to me, where I open my shirt and feel our naked little baby on my bare skin. Sometimes Remy is here, and he spreads out behind me, so he's my kangaroo, and then I'm the baby's kangaroo—as the method is called. But no. Remy doesn't feel like a kangaroo behind me; he's too primal for that. He nuzzles my collarbone and peers down at our baby while I feel him on my skin, and it's exactly today, as we are doing this, when Racer finally opens his eyes to look up at us. And they are blue, an achingly familiar pristine blue, and I fall in love for the second time in my life.

❤ ❤ ❤

WE'VE BEEN DISCHARGED from the hospital, and the three of us are in Seattle, playing house at last.

Today is the fortieth day after labor, and tonight Remington and I will finally be able to have sex. Except he's determined that the first time he takes me again . . . I be completely his. So, at noon, we're off to city hall.

God, I am. Dying. To have my way with my baby's sexy daddy.

"He's asleep," I whisper, from the chair in the living room where I sat to feed Racer this morning.

Remington is still in his pajama bottoms and bare-chested, and he comes over with such a proud, protective gleam in his eye, I die at the look on his face.

"Come smell him," I whisper with a big, besotted smile.

He comes and takes a big whiff from the top of Racer's head.

"He smells good, right?" I say.

"As good as you," Remington gruffly whispers, and as I smell the baby, he scents *me*.

We laugh, and he slides his hands under my body to scoop me up and tells me, "Hang on to him."

I do. He lifts me up while I hold the baby and carries us to the bed. "Diane is so excited about him—they all are. Is she here yet?" I ask.

"She's on her way," he says.

I nod eagerly.

Our iPod speakers are playing "Kiss Me" by Ed Sheeran. The song seems familiar somehow, but the familiarity of it really hits me as I set Racer down on the small cradle on my side of the bed, and Remington wraps me in his arms and starts kissing me. I want to do the girl thing and complain about my stomach. It's still not completely flat, but he likes it, he kisses it. I want to complain with all these hormones in me, but I feel precious, treasured, and so lucky, I don't even have words to say how much I wish this for the people I love. I know what it means to Remington to have a family now. He never lamented not having one. But now that he has one, I know he sees the difference. I know he *sees* what he was missing. Now he has a family to take care of, and one that takes care of him.

The knock on the door breaks us apart, and when Remy opens it, Diane steps in, beaming as she sees me in Remington's red robe and him in his pajama bottoms. "I thought you two would be ready already!"

He kisses me roughly and excitedly, his eyes burning with a sheen of fire. "Go get ready. I can't *wait*. To make you Mine."

"I'm *yours* already!"

He scrubs his thumb down my lip. "I'll be making you Mine your whole life."

Running into the bathroom where I'd set my clothes out, I slip into them with fast, eager hands.

I can't really leave Racer for more than a couple of hours, and our appointment is at twelve, so I didn't want to torture myself with complicated attire. So I choose a plain but pretty white skirt and lacy white top to wear. Remington told me he'll give me a big church wedding later, that he just can't wait to make me his. I told him I don't care about that, I just want the *man*!

The butterflies he gives me flutter full force as I pull my hair back in a bun that looks careless but pretty; then I try to perk up my face a little bit by pinching my cheeks so that nobody can tell Racer wakes me up so often at night.

When I walk out, my guy is already in the living room. Every single hormone in my body threatens to crash in on me and give me the weepy baby blues when I look at Remy in his black suit. Tall and broad-shouldered, he's perfectly sculpted, his spiky hair all mussed as always, his blue eyes twinkling with love and excitement, and his dimples . . . he is all man, all boy, and all mine.

Before I know I'm crying, he comes over and he wipes my tears with his thumbs, laughing softly at me for being so emotional. Then he licks the corners of my eyes, sweeps me off my feet, and carries me out of our apartment.

The entire gang crowds city hall, everyone except Diane and our precious Racer, who we're not supposed to expose too much until he gets stronger.

There's Melanie, Riley, Coach Lupe. Coach even holds up a five-by-eight picture of a smiling Diane, telling us, "She wanted to be in both places at once, so I offered to bring her picture while she takes care of the future champion!"

My parents laugh by his side. My mother has tears in her eyes, and my father is beaming with pride. Pete and Nora stand by them, holding hands, since they're trying to make a relationship work now that we will be in Seattle for a couple of months during the off-season. And Jo. She's here, too, with that pert little grin and that army stance.

The excitement I feel bubbles in my chest and burns inside me as Remington and I walk up to where we will sign, my hand linked to his—to this tanned, callused, huge hand that I will never let go of.

And then we're officially signing, getting married. He takes my hand in both of his, his blue eyes twinkling and liquid and entirely proprietary as he slips a ring on my finger.

The ring is platinum. "The white diamond is you," he says in a terse whisper, lifting my hand up to my line of vision. And to the right of the central white diamond is a blue diamond, and to its left, a black diamond.

"You're the other two," I say, and the depth of my feelings nearly choke me as I frame his hard jaw between my small hands and kiss the hell out of him. "I love you."

Then I take his big hand and slip the platinum band I got him, engraved smoothly on the inside, TO MY REAL, YOUR BROOKE DUMAS.

"MR. and MRS. RIPTIDE!!!" the gang calls when we're done.

We laugh and Remington lifts me up from the ground, flings me up in the air and catches me. "Now you're Mine," he claims happily then squeezes me close and his laugh turns into a smoldering gaze. Running his eyes admiringly over my face, he holds the back of my neck, leans down, and gives me the softest, gentlest, most lingering kiss he's ever given me in his life.

"We got you a gift, Brooke." Pete and Riley hold out a box as they come over. "It's from the team, including our new member, Jo." I wave at Jo at the end of the aisle and then tear open the gift.

A flash of red appears, and I pull out a shiny red robe identical to Remy's boxing robe. But this one reads RIPTIDE'S GIRL.

Smiling delightedly, I hug them, but not for long, because I hear a growl and am pulled into bigger, stronger, more possessive arms.

Forty days of pent-up sexual desire ride with us on the way home. Primitive sexual energy swirls between us like a growing tornado, feeding on our emotions. On our happiness, our love. Our need. When we enter our apartment, Racer is sound asleep in his cradle, which Diane seems to have pulled out to the living room. She sets down a magazine when we come in and, with a happy squeal, embraces Remington so tight, he chuckles in surprise. Then she wraps her warm arms around me.

"I hope you both know I will treat this baby like a grandson," she tells us.

"Diane," I say with emotion, completely moved by her words, "thank you."

Remington smiles at her, his dimples all gorgeous, and Diane hugs him one last time before she leaves. Remy pulls off his black tie and tosses it aside. Flicking open the top button of his snowy white shirt, he pulls me into his arms and takes my mouth, mating his tongue to mine as he lifts me to a sleek wood console by the entry.

"I need to kiss"—he slides his hands all over my curves—"my beautiful wife."

Shudders of happiness and love course through all my body as I slide my hands into his spiky hair and devour his lips as fiercely as he does mine. Racer wakes up, on the clock, with a sudden wail, and we both tear free and turn to the noise. Before I can push off the console, Remington sets me down and kisses the back of my ear, his voice terse: "Feed him so you can feed me next."

"I have a good idea of what you want, so okay."

"Okay?" he calls as he ambles into the kitchen, and I lift Racer from his cradle.

"More than okay!" I shout. "Bring the cradle when you come to the bedroom."

Quickly, I sit at the edge of the bed and I jerk my top off, pull my bra down, and press our protesting little baby up to my breast, checking the clock to alternate between breasts.

Soon, Remy sets the cradle down on my side of the bed and starts pacing.

My lion is restless.

A supercharged sexual current floats between us—it has been charging for forty days. In my mind, I have fucked Remington a thousand ways, and I know he's been eye-fucking me every day.

While I feed Racer, Remington watches intently. He finishes one peach and two apples, and he is now pacing again, watching me feed our son as he flicks open the buttons of his jacket, then of his entire shirt. His eyes are hungry. *I* am so hungry. I've never yearned like this. We're used to quick fixes in this life, but there's no quick way of fixing your body after childbirth, and we had to wait no matter what. But god, Racer is such a good baby. He eats and sleeps. I feel like he knows that Daddy is special. And he tries to make it easy on me. I guess if he doesn't, we'll just get help. We have options. Choices. We own ourselves, our lives, and we and the people around us are happy with them.

"You done yet?" he asks roughly, pacing to come see as he untucks his shirt from his slacks. He's so possessive. Every day, every night, he pulls me close and tells me I'm his. But he doesn't realize every time he says that, he's also saying he's mine. You can't really own something that doesn't own you right back, not even a car.

While I feed our son, we listen to music and play each other songs, and play songs for Racer. Now Remy's shirt drapes to his sides, revealing his eight-pack, and he comes and puts his hand on the breast Racer isn't already occupying. He holds my neck and leans down and kisses me.

Desire rushes through my veins, and by the time Racer stops suckling and dozes off, Remington edges back and looks at me, his lids weighted, my lips throbbing from his kiss.

"Do you remember asking about family you didn't miss because you never had one?" I whisper, reaching out and curling my fingers on his jaw, loving that his lips look swollen from our kiss too. "You don't miss it because you *do* have one. You built one, Remington. You went straight to being the head of one. And you know what? Your family isn't with you because of destiny or blood or because they have no choice. They're with you because they love you. And chose you." I gaze into his blue eyes. "*I* choose you."

Still keeping Racer to my breast, I reach behind me and pull out a folded envelope that I tucked into my nightstand behind me. "I wrote you a letter."

Lips curling cockily, he reaches out for it, but I hold it back with a smile of mischief. "I'll trade it with you, in exchange for my old letter."

"No," he says, tweaking my nose.

I laugh. "You greedy man! Yes!" I insist.

"What does it say?" he asks, his eyebrows raising in a dare.

"You'll get to see if you give me my old one, which I wrote when I was young and scared, and you get this new one, which I wrote now when I am . . . when I am *yours.*"

His eyes blaze at my last words. When he pulls the old letter out of his nightstand, I quickly take it away, so that he never has to remember that I left him, because now I will never leave. "You can read this new one any time," I tell him as I stand and head for the cradle, and his eyes flash. He nods as he places it on the nightstand.

Instead of reading it, he watches me set Racer down, and as he waits for me to settle him on his side, he goes to the iPod already sitting on our speakers. When we drove back from city hall, I told him I felt like playing him "From This Moment" by Shania Twain and Bryan White, and all of a sudden, the song is filling our bedroom.

My heart trembles as I turn around to look at him, my hands empty, empty of *him.* He curls his fingers at his sides and drags in a deep breath, his gaze blazing with blue-hot yearning, and in a fraction of a second, we both snap into movement on the opposite sides of the bed. I start to frantically strip off my skirt and he jerks off his shirt, our eyes watching what the other does.

I'm naked before he is, and I climb into bed and crawl across it, reaching out to undo his pants. In one jerk, he grabs the back of my head and crushes my mouth like he hasn't kissed me in his whole life. Sparks race throughout my body as our mouths feast and we both make starved groaning sounds. Eagerly I push his dark slacks down his hips, and the buckle hits the floor. He kicks them aside and lowers me to the bed, and not for a moment does his mouth leave mine. My hands slide up his hard muscles, his smooth skin, as I feel all his calluses rasping over me and every part of my body awakens for him.

"I want you, I love you like nothing in my fucking life, *nothing,*" he passionately rasps, brushing my hair back, and I shudder as our lips lock again and we roll on the bed. He pulls my arms up and laces our fingers together as I lock my legs around him. He eases inside me, and I gasp and mew and lick into his mouth as I feel his length, his width, his pulsing hardness advancing in me. Groaning in pleasure, he licks me back, penetrating with slow, delicious control even though I feel the vibrant tension in his body above mine.

"You okay?" he rasps, heatedly kissing my neck, opening his fingers on mine and linking them together tighter as his lips rub and dance over mine.

"More than okay," I breathe. Arching my spine, I part my mouth as his tongue delves and takes mine, our hips rocking, our mouths moving fast while our bodies move slow and lingeringly as we make love to each other for the first time as husband and wife.

"I love you," I whisper like a chant as he fills me, over and over, and he repeats it back to me every time he pushes inside, squeezing my hands. "I love you too."

He leaves me all sticky, on the inside, and on the outside, and when we're spent and tired, he growls and pulls me close and slides his finger down my thigh, then he slowly and lovingly pushes his semen back in with his fingers as he spoons me. Using his nose, he brushes my hair back, nuzzling my neck as he does all his lionlike things, grooming and licking and loving me, whispering that I am his. And I close my eyes as he clutches my stomach, like we sometimes forget Racer isn't there anymore, and I clutch his hand over mine and nod when he murmurs in my ear, *"Mine."*

At night, Racer doesn't cry out to eat, and I wake up startled and concerned, only to find Racer soundly sleeping in his father's arms. Remington holds him like he holds me, firmly but gently. Racer makes little chipmunk noises as he breathes, his hair dark as Daddy's, but his skin pink and soft, whereas Daddy is big and hard, and suddenly, I am quietly crying from the happiness I feel.

The heart is a hollow muscle, and it will beat billions of times during our life. About the size of a fist, it has four chambers, two atria, and two ventricles. I use it like I use my soul, and my body, and my bones, my fibers, my nerves, to love with every particle and molecule in me. It pumps life into me so I can give this love freely to this one man, and to this little boy he gave me.

I'm in love and I will be forever changed by this love, by this man, and our new little family.

I used to dream of medals and championships, and now I dream of a blue-eyed boy who will grow into a man, and of my blue-eyed fighter who one day changed my life when he put his lips on mine.

TO HIM

Dear Remington,

I was a post-college girl when I came to see you fight, and you have turned me into a woman. You have made me a wife. And you have made me a mother. And you have made me, and every day make me, the happiest woman alive. I am going to spend the rest of my life loving you. And our children. And running with you, eating with you, letting you scoop me up, throw me in the air, and lick me up. I will be your friend, your lover, your nurse, your exercise buddy, your love, your wife, and the lioness who fights by your side. I will always, always be your number one fan. Thank you, Remington, my love, for inspiring me every day with your gentleness and your drive. Thank you for being the father I couldn't even have conjured for my children. Thank you for giving me a little fighter. I want you to know I will be very happily working with you so we can also soon welcome our Iris.

I love you, and am in love with you, forever and always, now, and every second in between. Black and blue, every inch of you, magnificent you, is mine. And I'm going to treasure and cherish you, always.

Your Brooke

ACKNOWLEDGMENTS

I am so excited to be releasing *MINE* and the wonderful Real series through Gallery Books!

I'm eternally grateful to my wonderful agent Amy Tannenbaum and the Jane Rotrosen Agency for their support and encouragement; to my amazing new editor Adam Wilson, who is the best I could have ever hoped for; and to the talented people at Gallery Books who are making it all happen, including the best copy editors and publicists ever! Thank you Jennifer, Lauren, Kristin, Jules . . . for loving this series like I do.

And, thanks to the lovely Enn Bocci, for joining the team and helping us spread the REAL love all around! To Sarah Hansen for yet another kick-ass cover. And of course . . .

Thank you to my beautiful husband, my beautiful children, and my beautiful parents; you make my life beautiful all year-round.

To the loveliest daughter in the world, for reading before everyone else did and giving a thousand thumbs-up.

To my author friends who read this first, among them Monica Murphy, Joanna Wylde, Kim Karr, Jen Fredrick, Wylie Snow, and

L. M. Augustine. Writing is a lonely business and you get so much more done when you have understanding friends who can push you through a little hump.

To Kati Brown, you deserve special thanks and love from me. Your input on this book was golden. Thank you, Kati!

To Stacey Suarez, the best fitness expert and dearest friend, an expert on all things athletic and nutritional.

To my dear and talented Marilyn M, and Erinn G., and to my fabulous assistants, old and new; Anna, Ellie, and Lori and Gel. Thanks for giving me more writing hours.

Also, a huge special thanks to all you amazing bloggers who've been incredible supporters of Remy from the start. How can I even thank you, except with sharing more of him with you? Thank you so much to each and every one of you, and please forgive me the lack of space to name each and every one of you who've e-mailed, read, reviewed, and been completely wonderful! You are unREAL!

Neda, I have no words for your friendship, support, and overall wonderfulness with the amazing blog tours you helped plan, and my love goes to all those who participated too. Jenna, your video rocks! Thank you all!

To the amazing Dana, Erin, and Kelly, and the lovely "Scaries" who are actually angels in disguise. Hugs to Dominique, Stacy, Jen, and Kerry.

To all of my readers, who have waited, patiently, for this story; thank you for loving my characters like I do!

And lastly, but very especially, to everyone who has suffered or suffers from any form of mental illness, and to anyone whose loved ones suffer from mental illness: I do believe there is light in the dark, and I hope you find yours.

XOXO!